ENDURANCE

ENDURANCE

TIM GRIFFITHS

First published in 2015

Allen & Unwin
83 Alexander Street
Crows Nest NSW 2065
Australia
Phone: (61 2) 8425 0100
Email: info@allenandunwin.com
Web: www.allenandunwin.com

Cataloguing-in-Publication details are available
from the National Library of Australia
www.trove.nla.gov.au

ISBN 978 1 76011 154 0

Set in 11.5/16 pt Sabon by Midland Typesetters, Australia
Printed and bound in Australia by Griffin Press

10 9 8 7 6 5 4 3 2 1

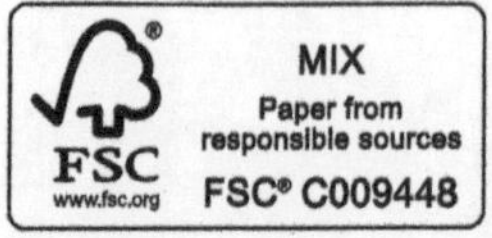

The paper in this book is FSC® certified.
FSC® promotes environmentally responsible,
socially beneficial and economically viable
management of the world's forests.

To Jenny

Prelude

I awake in darkness to the sound of canvas flapping. Fresh squalls come across the spit and the drumming on the roof intensifies as snow and sleet beat down on our makeshift home. My bedding is damp, my feet are lying in water and my ribs ache from the shingle floor, but I do not want to move just yet. There are twenty-two of us survivors trying desperately to be warm and keep breathing under this upturned lifeboat. My wretched companions are greedy for their miserable lives. With nostrils clogged by soot from burning seal and penguin blubber, and despite their numerous afflictions, they produce a cacophony of wheezing, snuffling and snorting. They are worse when they are awake.

It is the better part of a year since we abandoned ship and it is four months we have been marooned on this piece of rock, but our sojourn must now be coming to an end. Our stores are virtually gone and there are but a dozen cartridges left for the rifle. In another month there will not be even a trace of our existence. The ocean will see to that. My photographs and cinefilm will never be found. Our story will be unknown to the world. We will be unknown.

I am disturbed by a body shuffling past me, I don't know who. Nothing is said. There is no light under the lifeboat. I will have to move soon but better to wait till I can see.

There is a conflict coming in our little group. Some will want to go and some are incapable of going. There will be unpleasantness. I will not stay. We are crammed in here like sardines and the more crowded it is the more alone I feel.

To perish like this without any record does not seem much of an adventure. Fame is so elusive and to get anywhere I have had perforce to throw in my lot with others. There is still time to pray to God but I am untrained and not good at this. Yet I admire our creator's wild beauty that entraps us here.

Each day on this rock passes much like the other. It is mostly impossible to stay outside in the bitter cold for any length of time. I have plenty of time to wonder how I came to be here. There is nothing I could or would change. I do wonder if Pa is watching. Does he know where I am? I am determined to stay calm and not be overborne by circumstance like those around me.

If only my photographs could be rescued, then people could see and believe what has happened to us.

Part I

1

Glebe and Lithgow, 1898–1910

Pa was forty-eight years and five foot six. I was thirteen and already five foot ten. The look on his face I won't forget. And his slurred speech ringing in my ear, 'You rude ungrateful bastard!'

We were both in shock.

'Hit your own father, would you?' he growled, and came at me again.

My punch was instinctive, though there was plenty of anger there too. He'd been drinking, and this time when I connected he stumbled and fell badly. He'd tried to throw me to the ground. He'd done it before only this time he was struggling, and now he was down. There was blood on his face and he was nursing his arm and swearing at me. 'Get the bloody hell out of my house!' He stayed on the floor. Ma was screaming at me for what I'd done. Little Eddie and Doris were in tears.

I grabbed shoes and a coat from the boys' room. Before I reached the front gate my dear mater seized my arm. 'Stay away, Jamie!' she said. James was my first name. 'Send me a letter with where you are,' she said. And I knew she meant it 'cause she gave me Pa's cap and five shillings. 'Stay away,' she said again, and ran back inside.

I've never told this to anyone before, not anyone. I didn't like to dwell on it. Fact is I was always treated as the trouble-maker. So I just cropped it from the story of my childhood. Even now people ask how a boy from Glebe came to live by himself in Lithgow at such a tender age. Of course I give a good story. I tell them I was expelled from school for playing truant once too often and had to leave home to find work.

It could easily have been the truth. There was certainly no way the teachers at Glebe Public School could control me. There were too many of us street urchins. I pretty much did what I wanted, came and went as I pleased. They passed a law to stop truancy, but we were doing them a favour by staying away. If all the pupils turned up at the same time, they wouldn't have had enough desks for us. At school I learned to play the fool and act the goat. I didn't mind getting into trouble. 'Grow up, Hurley,' my teacher would say. I guess I never did. I was always playing tricks at school and for some reason I never stopped.

There was another school, a newer one, nearby at Forest Lodge. That's where the toffs went. They were scared of us Glebe Public boys. We'd give them a beating as soon as look at them. Douglas Mawson went there but I didn't know him then.

The school didn't miss me but I thought my ma would. I was angry she had said that to me, to stay away. Like they couldn't handle me and didn't want me at home. It made me fierce to run away as far and as long as I could. I wanted her to suffer. I know Ma regretted it. Years afterwards, when I had my first big chance to go with Mawson, she tried to make up for it and almost caused a disaster—but more of that later.

I ran straight down Bridge Road to the docks at Pyrmont. I knew what to do. I had watched other fellows do the same, though they were older. I bought a loaf of bread and wandered down to the railway yards alongside Darling Harbour. The railway crews had finished work and as darkness descended with no one around it was more than a little creepy. It was cold, too, though I didn't seem to feel it then; I had conceived an epic plan which would save me from both a severe beating at home and the boredom of school. I'd never had the guts before to jump a freight train. But now I had a good reason. Consequences just didn't come to mind.

I picked out a goods wagon near the end of a long freight train. As soon as it creaked forwards I walked alongside then, seizing the moment, I jumped up on the wagon and squeezed under its tarpaulin cover.

In my grand plan it was warm under the goods wagon tarpaulin. But within an hour my body was shivering. I hadn't factored in that it was midwinter. A few more hours and the train started climbing on its way up the Blue Mountains. At times the train slowed to a halt. Then with a loud clanking of wagons it would take up its weight, jerking my head back and forth and keeping me awake.

As the train climbed the temperature dropped. It dropped way below what I'd experienced. I guessed it was below freezing. I was sitting on wrought iron, which sucked the warmth out of me. Later in life I would get quite used to being cold. In those extreme conditions I found being able to tough it out depended on whether things were looking up or if things were grim. Thinking back now to that journey I don't remember feeling anything at the time, just a naive sense that somehow I could escape, that there would be a way.

Hours later the train was running downhill into the town of Lithgow. I stepped off just before it reached the siding but my legs were numb and I fell heavily. I was exhausted and could barely stand so stiff were my limbs. It was still dark as I walked into the town of which I knew nothing except men went there for factory work.

Running away had seemed a grand idea but the reality was that I was petrified and totally knackered, and remorse was creeping in.

I saw light from the side entrance to a bakery. The pungent aroma of fresh baked bread turned my stomach inside out. The baker took one look at me standing in the doorway and, without a word, broke a steaming loaf in two and gave me one of the halves. I dug my fingers inside the crust and pulled out a handful of scalding hot, doughy bread which tasted better than anything I could imagine. He told me to sit inside near his oven till the shop opened. I sat down and promptly passed out.

When I woke it was light. The baker told me which way to head for the ironworks. I doubt I remembered to thank him. In the weak sunlight my sense of wellbeing returned. It was still a grand adventure. Although there was no one I could tell.

Within the hour I was having my first job interview.

'Name?'

'Frank Hurley, sir.' I had decided to use my middle name to thwart any enquiries.

'Age?'

'Sixteen, sir.'

'You wouldn't be putting up your age to get more money, would you?'

'No, no sir.' I was glad I had Pa's cap; it made me feel older, 'And I'm happy to do anything on account of me having no experience.'

He gave me a long look, and said, 'Alright then, Frank Hurley, eh?' You can start tomorrow as a fitter's assistant. Be here at eight.'

'Thank you, sir . . . and sir, my wages—would they be a pound?'

'What, a week? You've got no idea, sonny. You'll find out soon enough.'

'Thank you, sir.'

'And you don't have lodgings, do you, son? Try here.' He scribbled an address on a scrap of paper. 'Tell them you're at Sandford's and you'll have some pay next week.'

I did as he suggested and soon enough I had my lodgings, sleeping on the floor in a room with two other ironworks boys. They were older. When they returned to the boarding house that evening they filled my head with names of machines I'd never heard of and warned me who to steer clear of. They told me the only reason Sandford's was hiring was because the other fitters' assistants had fallen into vats of molten steel and burned to ashes. I didn't sleep much that night.

I was scared by the stories from my fellow lodgers of what the next day held. Lying awake I couldn't quite believe the turn my life had taken. I had often dreamed of running away, but I always expected I would be sent back home. I was surprised at my success and the distance I had travelled. Ma would be expecting me to be staying at one of my haunts around Glebe. She'd be thinking I'd turn up the next day like a bad penny. Little did she know I was on the other side of the Blue Mountains and had a big person's job. I was full of self-pity, half wishing I might wake up at home. Then again, there was no telling if I'd broken Pa's arm and what he would do to me. I just didn't know how long away I could last.

The following day I entered a world like no other. Sandford Ironworks was some miles outside Lithgow in the middle of a broad valley. Along the upper edges of the valley were rocky cliff sentinels, so steep they looked impossible to climb. I could see Sandford's in the distance as I walked the stretch of dirt and puddles that was the main road. There were huge warehouses and high chimney stacks in what once had been farmland. Smoke and steam clouds billowed above it all, carrying the stale smell of coal fires and, worst of all, the foul odour of sulphur. There were stockpiles of coal and iron ore with rail trucks, wagons, vats, pipes and hoses cluttering the dirt yards outside the factories. It was a bleak manmade scene on a damp and freezing morning.

I walked through the ironworks gates wearing the same clothes I had worn out the front door of my home in Glebe. In a detached corrugated iron office I gave my Lithgow address and signed my name with a flourish, the one thing I had practised at school. I was issued with gloves and goggles and told to report at the entrance to the main furnace room.

My dear mater had often questioned me about what I would do after leaving school. I'd had no clue. How could I? I only knew what I didn't want to do: I didn't want to do what my pa did. He'd learned a trade as a typesetter with Fairfax and Sons, then with the Government Printers. Now he was head of the union, the Printing Trades Federation, I would usually be in bed by the time he came home from the pub. Ma said it was the only place the union could get their members together for a meeting. She was always making excuses for him. When he was home we had to tiptoe around him; Ma said he had a lot of worries and I had to stop being so noisy. A lot of time too he'd be away in the country for meetings. Anyhow all he did now was meetings, talking and drinking with people and carrying on. He didn't think much of my skylarking and when he was under the weather he'd tell me I wouldn't amount to much. I could not see any way of reconciling with my pa. His temper was matched by my stubbornness. Of course at that age you assume your parents will always be there. I little thought this might not be the case.

After my first day as a fitter's assistant at the Sandford Ironworks I knew I had found what I wanted to do. It was glorious. I got to see inside the whole ironworks and all the furnaces. The main steel furnace made all sorts of useful things. Molten metal was poured into moulds for spikes, points and crossings for the railways across all of New South Wales. There was a rolling plant from which workers with giant tongs pulled out great lengths of extruded red-hot iron. And there was a new blast furnace which was like looking into hell itself. Steel poured out white-hot. There were large steaming vats that galvanised the iron. Winches and cranes could raise and suspend massive pieces of iron and equipment that a man could never lift. There were all sorts of engines, flywheels and lathes that drilled and cut and welded.

My large clumsy hands, which had let me down at rugger and cricket, seemed to revel in operating tools, fixing equipment and doing the routine factory jobs doled out to me. The more things I mastered the more I was asked to do. I prided myself on not leaving till my jobs were finished. I learned the importance of caring for my tools and equipment and getting the best out of them.

After the idleness of schooldays and playing truant around Glebe, hiding from both teachers and police, my days at Sandford's were full and exhausting. My curiosity about steel-making had me reading all the manuals and books I could find. I drove the bosses up the wall with my questions. But if there were big jobs on, they always asked for me. One of the foremen took me under his wing. He was known to everyone at Sandford's as Big Bill. He was one of the best. Bill would say, 'Near enough is not good enough.' Pretty soon I was working with Big Bill on most of his jobs.

That first week I came home from work, ate the dinner cooked by my landlady and fell asleep straight after. I didn't write home. On the Sunday I started writing to Ma but something made me stop. I wanted her and Pa to stew. They didn't want me at home and here I was with a job and lodgings all successful like. They would be worried like hell.

There was a lot that I wanted to remember, though, and tell someone about each day, so with my first pay I bought a leather-bound 1898 diary with lined pages, half price it was. That night, I started writing down everything that had happened to me. The diary was better company than the other lodgers who, being older, would disappear after dinner. They didn't ask me to come with them and that didn't worry me.

By my third week, however, I started feeling things were not the way they should be. I cried at night for no reason at all and it must have showed at work. It was Big Bill who told me I was suffering from homesickness. When he heard I hadn't written home he gave me a talking-to. He said the police would be after me and that I would be a 'missing person'. Being a 'missing person' did not seem like a good start to a career and I didn't want the police knocking on my land-lady's door, so that night I wrote a short letter to Ma, told her I was alright and was working and gave her the address of my lodgings. That was all. I really wanted to hear first from her.

Four days later, when I got home from the ironworks, my landlady handed me my first-ever letter. I took it straight to my room. It was from my mother.

> Dear Jamie,
>
> Your pa and I have been worried sick about you. I prayed to God you were safe. Your pa is sorry for what happened and we are both sad you are so far away.

Ma asked me to write to her about my work and lodgings. She didn't ask when I might be coming home. I lay awake a long time that night, well after the other lodgers had come in.

Big Bill was pleased when I told him I'd heard from my ma. He asked me if I'd like to come with him on the weekend to a place called Kanangra Walls. I couldn't say yes quick enough. Weekends were the worst for me, as I had little to do if I wasn't working.

Bill lived with his missus just the other side of Lithgow. On weekends he did a lot of walking and climbing, which she couldn't do on account of she was expecting. Early on the Saturday morning I met Bill at the Lithgow railway station and as paying customers (my first time) took a train to a little village called Hartley. Here Bill found an open coach which took sightseers to Jenolan Caves. After travelling several miles through undulating sheep and cow pastures, the coach made its way through thick scrub and emerged near the edge of a cliff.

'You'll need to prepare yourself for what's up ahead,' said Bill as the road became deeply rutted and strewn with loose rocks and boulders. 'This old road was hacked out of the sandstone by convicts in chains only sixty years ago. The redcoats whipped them without mercy. Look, you can still see the crushed convict bones used in making the road.' He pointed to numerous white pebbles scattered through the red dirt (I later learned these were quartz). 'The convicts dropped dead from exhaustion. Many of 'em took their freedom by stepping off the edge of the road and falling to their death way below.' I could see Bill watching the look on my face.

The road narrowed till I could have sworn it was less than the width of the dray in which we were perched. I was seated on the far left-hand side and found myself looking straight down a sheer precipice. At times the wheel below me passed within several inches of the road's edge. I figured I would have no chance if the edge crumbled. I braced myself to climb over Bill's head to safety, if need be. And yet the driver seemed to consider there was little point in going cautiously to his death. He had those horses trotting along at a fair pace, clearly trusting to their sense of self-preservation. Until then

I'd considered myself pretty daring for hanging off the back of the steam tram that went down Broadway to Central Station. Jenolan Caves may have been only a day or so from Glebe, but for me it was as good as a lifetime.

After alighting alive from the coach I was very happy to follow Bill on foot along a path through the bush. I'd agreed to help carry some of Bill's equipment, which turned out to be quite heavy. Bill bought, sold and repaired used cameras as another string to his bow. We had two cameras with us and a solid wooden tripod almost as tall as me. We carried woollen blankets rolled up like a swagman's and a billy with tea and sugar along with salted meat and potatoes for an evening meal.

Bill impressed me with his ease in the bush. But what captivated me most of all was a small camera called a box brownie which Bill let me hold. I had never in my life held a camera before. That Saturday afternoon standing on the top of Kanangra Walls a thousand feet above the valley below, I held Bill's box brownie camera to my chest and, looking down into its small peephole, I saw in the aperture a mirror image of the broadest and most spectacular valley I had ever looked upon. To the east was a series of ridges on which the sun was now retreating. The most prominent ridge, Bill said, was Katoomba, some thirty miles away. Between this ridge and our vertical cliff wall we looked out on a canopy of gum trees. The bush below was completely still and silent, but Bill told me it was full of wildlife: wallabies, goannas, echidnas and, if you knew how to find them, koalas and platypus.

Once the sun dropped I shivered in an icy wind.

'That cold air is coming straight off the Snowy Mountains in the far south-west,' said Bill. I looked in the direction he was pointing, hoping for a glimpse of snow-capped mountains, which I'd only ever seen in storybooks. But I couldn't see anything, so I knew the mountains he was talking about must be a long way away. Despite the cold in Lithgow, the only thing I'd seen approaching snow was a heavy frost around my lodgings.

'I'd like to see those Snowy Mountains one day, Bill,' I said.

'Well if you go by steam train and coach it will take you almost a week to get there. I've never been, and being a father soon I'm not likely to either.'

'Ah well, maybe there is no snow,' I said. 'Like the Blue Mountains aren't blue. Might just be a lot of talk.'

'Oh, they get snow alright . . .' Bill said as he started heading back along the track, with me hard on his heels, 'some winters it snows here in the Blue Mountains, so I reckon the peaks in the Snowies really cop it then.'

'Tell you what, Bill, I'm saving my wages. I'll buy my own box brownie and get a picture of some snow for you.'

We dropped down below the ridge. I followed Bill along a series of rock overhangs. We came to a cave that was dry and had the look of being lived in. The sandstone ceiling was blackened by cooking fires. Bill dropped his pack and asked me to gather wood. I was none too happy about our campsite. I was scared of snakes. Only half a mile from my home in Glebe there were plenty of blacks and browns along Blackwattle Creek. Bill laughed and told me what I already knew, that they'd be hibernating. Just in case, I brought plenty of wood to keep the fire going all night.

Bill made tea in the billy and cooked up a meal which was plain but welcome. 'Hunger makes the best sauce,' said Bill. As we ate, he told me stories of his travels.

'My father was with the railways. We was always on the move. Every year or so we'd pack up the trunk and move to another railway town. Then my brother and I worked as jackeroos. We were droving as far north as those Queensland rivers will let you. Now my brother's heading off to Africa to fight the Boers. Taking his horse with him. But I can't go, can I, being married and all. But just imagine the photographs I could take in Africa.' I could hear the regret in his voice.

I didn't say anything to Bill, but I did start to think that maybe one day I too could travel to faraway places, not just spend my life in Lithgow or Sydney.

That night we camped rough, wrapped in blankets on the dirt, I slept better than I had for a long time.

The following weekend Bill invited me home to watch him develop his pictures in a shed he called his darkroom.

'Pictures can be on glass plates with chemicals or on rolls of photographic paper,' he explained. I stood back as he swirled the film in solution in an old laundry tub under the dim light cast by a red lamp. 'The picture is already stored on the paper. You're looking at a chemical reaction.' Then out of the blackness I saw an image take shape, an image of myself, a small figure in a landscape of towering cliffs and dark shadowy trees. I had been captured. It all seems so matter of fact today but at that time I thought Bill must have some kind of magical powers. I felt I had been initiated into one of the secrets of the universe and of mankind and our memories of things past. I was as impressionable as the photographic paper.

I determined I would buy a camera. If Bill could master this magic, then I could too. I could see it was a portal to many things and was excited by the idea I could go off travelling to all sorts of places and at the same time create a record of my exploits to show Ma. It was a fad for many but for me I could not learn enough about the mystery of photography. In truth I had no idea where this might lead. But I could see immediately it was more exciting than all the modern machinery at Sandford's.

Cameras became an obsession for me. I learned all I could from Bill. I bought my own camera and improvised a darkroom at my lodgings. The camera became my companion on numerous day-long excursions. Bill increasingly had other things to keep him busy, so I was usually by myself. I found I preferred the freedom of setting my own pace and finding the exact spots I wanted, at the time of day I wanted. My homesickness was overtaken by a love of photography, of discovering an image that filled the lens and capturing it perfectly, without any loss of sharpness. I would then develop that picture in the darkroom and transform it into my composition. I was still alone, but with my camera it didn't seem so bad.

My letters home became more civil. I apologised to Pa. He had no broken bones and was all mended. He wrote saying he forgave me and that he was proud to hear I was doing so well at Sandford's.

It was a full eighteen months before I was reunited with Ma and Pa. Sandford's won a contract to repair the engines of a cargo ship in Sydney. They sent an engineer and a work party, including myself, to stay on board the ship in the Sydney docks while the work was carried out. I was but a mile from home. After a day or so, and without any prior warning, I knocked on the front door. There were hugs and tears from Ma, until I had to pull away. I didn't ask to stay and that night I returned to my berth on board ship.

At the shipyard I discovered yet another world, quite unlike Sandford's. I worked alongside the ship's engineers and boiler room men. They were a different breed. If they had families, they rarely saw them, but their stories of exotic ports raised my wanderlust to another level.

I would not return to Lithgow. At the end of our ship repair contract I gave notice to Sandford's and signed on with the shipping company, which was anxious to get the vessel back on its routes of trade. That evening I went home to Glebe and announced I was going to sea. I hadn't expected the furore this unleashed. In hindsight I should have slipped away quietly. I wasn't good at anticipating these things.

'Jamie, you 'ave no idea the dreadful lives these sailors lead!' My mother's voice still had the faint accent from her French parents, who had been vignerons in the Hunter Valley. 'The sinful places they frequent, the diseases they 'ave. You have never been good at understanding people. They cannot read or write. Would you want to be like them? At least finish a trade. The ship's officers have certificates. You could be a marine engineer and not just riffraff.'

'But it's a chance to travel. Why should I stay home? There's nothing for me here!'

'Am I nothing? Jamie, you should be ashamed. You don't even have normal feelings for your own mother!'

My father's contribution took my legs away. 'Jamie, whilst you're on board that ship, it won't be leaving port.' He was a Trades Hall bigwig now and I knew it was no idle threat.

Pa was as good as his word. The ship sailed without me. Instead I found myself unemployed and living back in our already strained household in Glebe.

I took solace in Sydney's photographic shops, studios and photoengravers. Here I discovered opportunities to learn which Lithgow had been unable to provide. I spent hours at Harrington's camera shop in George Street, and became friends with Henri Mallard, a camera salesman who worked there. He organised a job for me behind the counter. It didn't last; I wasn't born to serve people like that. I left before I was asked to leave. But Henri and I stayed in touch through our interest in photography. On weekends we journeyed by train to the coastal fringes of the city and explored the dramatic sea cliffs and rock platforms.

On a scorching-hot New Year's Day, 1901, Henri made me don a borrowed suit and dragged me with our cameras on a packed tram out to Centennial Park. Huge crowds were gathered and brass bands played popular songs in the shade of newly erected pavilions. Though they were of little interest to me, there were dignitaries whom Henri wanted to photograph. Queen Victoria had appointed a new governor-general, Lord Hopetoun, who had come out from England to represent not just New South Wales but all the colonial states. His job that day was to declare the Commonwealth of Australia as the newest country in the British Empire and swear in Australia's first-ever prime minister. When I asked Henri what that meant he replied, 'More taxation and more politicians.' Despite our suits and impressive cameras, Henri and I were turned away from the rotunda where the formalities were to take place, and had to be content with panorama shots of the crowd.

Meanwhile, things were a bit fiery at home. Pa arranged interviews for me to obtain an apprenticeship as an electrical fitter and instrument maker with the Telegraph Department. I was fascinated by the practical science of the department's work, but it didn't hold my interest the way photography did. I often disappeared at lunchtime or after work to visit Harrington's. As a result I may have taken my day job too lightly and been too cocky for a young apprentice. One morning I was called into a meeting and, to my shock, was told my lack of dedication was unacceptable and my services no longer required. Harder still was the unhappy argument which followed with my father. 'A jack of all trades,' he said. 'That's all you'll ever be!'

But a jack of all trades can be well placed to seize an opportunity. At that time every shop in Sydney was selling photographic postcards. I could see that the photographs I was taking were the very type that sold best: crashing waves, spectacular sunsets, sailing ships and dramatic headlands. Before long I found lucrative employment with another former Harrington's colleague, Henry Cave, producing postcards which sold like hot cakes out of his workshop not far from

Circular Quay. I didn't need to deal with customers. During the day I captured images to outsell all others and in the evening I worked on the negatives. We produced and printed thousands of cards for sale.

I had the knack and the daring to get the shots that others couldn't. There was no such thing as a telephoto lens; you had to get the camera close to the action. I ruined a good many cameras trying to capture waves crashing at the Gap, but I managed to save some of the best shots. And with my tripod on the railway tracks at Brooklyn I held my nerve as speeding steam trains hurtled around the sandstone cuttings. I then had to take off in great haste before I was beaten up by irate train drivers. My little brother Eddie often came with me and helped me run with all the camera gear.

Learning from others, I became a wizard in the darkroom. Taking the photograph was only half the job. What a shot lacked could easily be added. I imbued a sense of drama by turning to good use the negatives of pictures I had taken of sunrises, sunsets, black storm clouds, southerly busters building up over Sydney and massive banks of white cumulus clouds. By composite printing I could add these to any subject, sometimes combining several negatives to get everything needed for the perfect picture. Cumulus clouds were my favourite. There were very few landscape pictures that could not be enlivened by the addition of cumulus clouds. They were a natural adornment to a landscape panorama.

One of my favourite subjects was the South Head lighthouse. My experimental night-time shots did not do justice to its powerful electric rotating beam. Eventually I camped for the night with my camera in a fixed position and obtained multiple exposures of the light shining in all directions. Using composite printing, I was able to create a photograph showing the lighthouse beaming to all points of the compass. This postcard sold over twenty thousand copies.

There was a gleam in my father's eyes now that I found myself at the cutting edge in the printing trade. He knew all the major publishers and we talked excitedly about business and people he knew who could help. Every week there was a new illustrated magazine on the newsstands craving spectacular front-page photographs—the kind of photographs I could supply.

I was working sixteen hours a day, seven days a week, and making a name for myself with articles in photographic journals, so Henry Cave really couldn't say no to making me a partner when I asked, but he insisted on charging five hundred quid to buy in. That put a stopper on me. I was nineteen with no savings, and the banks were not as excited as I was. That's when Pa made his proposal. It wasn't my idea. He sold up the lease on the family home without telling me. Said he was thinking of doing it anyway. The family no longer needed all that space, he said. We left our house in Derwent Street and moved to a smaller place in Lodge Street. Pa came up with the money and that was the start of Cave & Hurley, which did well for several years.

That was how I first learned that Pa had not been a union leader all his life. Often after he'd knocked off from work he would come in of an evening and help me with sorting out orders and updating the bookwork. One night over a whisky he told me that before he was married and tied down with family he had been an entrepreneur with a small printing business in the Hunter Valley. He'd been successful and hired more and more staff. Then one day his bookkeeper didn't show up for work, just disappeared, the financial records and journals gone with him.

'He stole from you?'

'He blew it all on the gee gees and cards. I had no idea. You just can't trust people Jamie.'

'You had to start again?'

'Start again?' He studied the glass in his hand. 'In country towns you can't just start again. There was barely enough cash to pay wages. I could have kept going—I didn't need much to live on—but it was the debt, Jamie. Debt is an insidious bastard. It had crept up on me. Well one day the bank stopped my cheques. You should have seen the looks I got in town when that happened. Then my suppliers wouldn't give me stock unless I paid 'em cash. My business came to a grinding halt. I was lucky to leave town with the shirt on my back. I arrived in Sydney penniless and was damned lucky to get a job at the Government Printers. Before long my workmates elected me as their rep and then a delegate to Trades Hall.'

'Did you ever want to do something different?'

'Oh, by then I'd met your ma; fell for her accent, I did. Her folks were French vignerons who had nothing more than dirt and vines and their daughter. Next thing you know we are married and she is expecting your oldest brother. I never had another chance to make money. But Jamie, play your cards right and this is your chance to rise up.'

In the postcard trade at that time business opportunities seemed to just keep coming. I hardly had time to scratch myself. But there was a lot of competition out there and you had to be quick to see where the market was heading. Henry Cave was often reluctant to branch out in new directions. He had a young family and was coming in late and going home early. We argued, and eventually things between us were so tense we couldn't stand being in the shop together. Pa thought we'd manage better ourselves and decided to buy Henry out.

'Get rid of him,' he said. 'He's taking the money and credit for your photographs.'

Pa persuaded the bank to give us a loan.

It wasn't long before I realised this was a mistake. The debts were bigger than Henry had let on and by then I was paying wages for twelve girls who were hand-colouring postcards in the shop premises which I was leasing. Paying the bills was pretty tight. Pa helped out with some of the more pressing accounts.

Pa by then was a frequent visitor to the shop. We hadn't had a row for a long time. He was better than me at juggling our accounts week to week and chasing up payments due. He said I ruffled people's feathers and didn't know how to keep the bank manager happy. It was easier to leave that to him. He must have been worried about losing the family money. He wouldn't pay himself a wage. We worked shoulder to shoulder, but in all too brief a time things came unstuck.

One lunchtime Pa and I had been going through the accounts. Some of our suppliers were writing very stern letters. There were threats of bankruptcy. It made me jumpy when I could see Pa getting anxious. It was a boiling-hot day just weeks before Christmas 1907. That time of year there was always a lot happening at the union and Pa had to head back for some important meetings. He left the shop and caught a tram up George Street back to Trades Hall. But he never reached his office. When the tram pulled up at King Street he fell unconscious off his seat. His heart had given way and he was dead. I heard the passengers complained they were made to hop off and catch another tram.

No one came to the shop to tell me so I only found out when I arrived home that night.

Ma was a wreck. She collapsed on the lounge and there was nothing I could do to help. 'He wasn't old, he wasn't old,' she sobbed.

I worked the next day and didn't shut the shop until the day of the funeral. My brothers and sisters gave me a hard time over that. They didn't know things were that tight I couldn't afford to close.

Pa's wake was marred by arguments with my siblings which left me feeling very isolated. I was bereft in my heart, and in my head I knew I was facing financial ruin. Losing Pa was the end of the cash flow for the business. Within months I had laid off most of the staff.

Things got worse. By 1910 the postcard market collapsed. My customers were mostly small retail outlets and one by one they closed down, leaving me unpaid. The big outlets for postcards, John Sands and Swains, survived by undercutting the market and they wouldn't deal with me. I owed Harrington's more than I could repay.

Having this experience at only twenty-five certainly had a lifelong effect on me. Afterwards, if people thought I was too mercenary or driven by a desire to line my pockets, I wasn't apologetic. I enjoyed being paid for the work I did, even if I loved doing it. I had an abiding fear of debt.

Greater than these misfortunes was that my brothers and sisters no longer talked to me. Pa's estate was in the red. Their inheritance was gone and it looked like Ma would have to move again. Dreams so quickly turned into nightmares.

Part II

2

With Mawson, 1911

It was just before closing when my friend Henri Mallard burst in the shop door.

'Frank, you're going to be famous! You're going to thank me for this—if you survive, that is!'

'Henri, I don't need more risky photographs. I need to sell what I have.'

'No, listen: there's an Australian expedition going to Antarctica. Douglas Mawson is in charge. If you bothered to read the paper you'd know about it. Anyway, they need a photographer. They've asked me, but of course I can't go.'

'Why not?'

'Why not? Too bloody dangerous! And too bloody cold. But you're used to the cold. You never even heat the shop. Anyhow, I said you would be my first pick. You have to write to Mawson.'

I shrugged. 'I know nothing about it. And I'm stuck here.'

'What is there to know? It's a scientific expedition to set up bases and explore the place.'

'Your boss at Harrington's wouldn't let me go—I owe 'em too much money,' I said, though I was starting to feel torn by the idea.

'Frank, think about it. If Mawson picks you, Harrington's have to let you go.'

I did think about it, all night—and the more I thought about it, the more the idea filled my head. Mawson was famous. He was an Australian hero. He'd been to Antarctica with Shackleton. To travel to an uncharted continent and be the first to capture photographs of an unknown landscape would be an epic adventure.

By the next day, the idea of disappearing into the Antarctic had begun to seem the solution to all my woes. It would be an escape from creditors and the damned postcard business. Creditors would have a lot of trouble serving court papers in the Antarctic. If the expedition was successful, my reputation would be made. And if I failed to return from the frozen south, well then nothing else mattered.

I fancied I had some prospects of being appointed, but I also knew there would be better credentialed and more experienced contenders. How could I get the jump on them? Now that the idea had taken a hold on me I did not like the idea of leaving things to chance or, worse still, of missing out. Henri told me that while the expedition had wealthy backers, it was short of funds and Mawson was still out on the public-speaking circuit raising money. I knew all about money being tight.

In September 1911 I penned a letter direct to Dr Douglas Mawson and offered what I hoped would be my trump card: I would provide my services 'absolutely free'. My board and lodging would be met by the expedition. I knew if I had the good fortune to reach Antarctica and return alive that my photographs would command a high price.

My letter secured an interview with Dr Mawson, but only just; he agreed to meet me at Central Station in Sydney for ten minutes before he boarded the train back to Adelaide. Plainly he did not consider me a serious prospect. So I bought a return ticket to Moss Vale, two hours along the route; this, I reasoned, would give me the time I needed.

At Central Station I was able to pick out Mawson from his picture in the newspapers. A tall and fit-looking gentleman, he was lugging two suitcases along the platform. He was dressed more smartly than I had thought necessary for myself, and looked quite formal in a three-piece suit and necktie with a very white starched winged collar. We shook hands and I grabbed one of his bags and led him to his compartment. I'd hoped to impress him with my initiative in arranging to share his carriage for a couple of hours. Instead he looked tired and was a little curt when he interrupted my spiel to ask, 'Can you cook?'

'Cook? Yes, yes, I can cook. No one's died yet!' Dr Mawson didn't even smile. 'And a lot of the time over an open campfire.'

'Won't be open campfires where we are going.'

That was stupid of me.

'Have you ever been outside Australia?' Mawson wanted to know.

'Well, no, but I've toured the coastline doing landscape and ocean photography. I've taken pictures in some bitterly cold and exposed places.'

'Have you ever travelled at sea?'

'I've lived and worked on a ship for months at a time,' I replied, which was true, if misleading. 'And I can turn my hand to most things.'

'What about cinematography?'

'I don't see any problems there. I'm up with the latest technical equipment.'

'But it's not even mentioned in your letter. The public expect moving pictures, you know.'

'I'm sure I can do it.'

'Well it's essential. The expedition funders expect me to recoup their monies. I'll be publishing a book with photographic plates in colour as well as black and white. There'll be the usual lecture tours, but with moving pictures and lantern slides. Gone are the days when people are satisfied with sketches and watercolours.'

'Of course,' I replied. 'The public want the latest in everything. That's what sells. That's the business I'm in.'

'And what line of business was your father in?'

'A printer. He was a printer.' I knew not to mention he was a union man.

'And where were you educated?'

I stumbled over this question until Mawson saved me by pointing out we had both grown up in Glebe. He then described the hardships of working on the ice, but these concerned me not a bit. As I departed at Moss Vale his parting words were, 'I'll let you know.'

Three days later I received a telegram: YOU ARE ACCEPTED STOP MAWSON.

My excitement knew no bounds. Not only was I accepted, but at Mawson's request and at his cost I was to immediately attend the film company Gaumont & Co for training in use of the cinematograph—of which, in truth, I had little idea.

Then out of the blue came a letter from Mawson:

> I am not at this time able to confirm your appointment. I am concerned with your health and have doubts as to whether you will be sufficiently fit for the demanding work of the expedition.

I was aghast. What could have happened to change his mind about me? Was someone out to deliberately foil my escape? But who? My creditors? Why would someone oppose me just when I had a chance of success—why did people always get in the way of my achieving something?

I wrote back to Mawson, querying his sudden change of heart. He replied, enquiring if there was a chance I or anyone

I was close to had shown any sign of consumption. In my reply I assured Mawson someone was badmouthing me. At twenty-six I had never in my life visited a doctor; I offered to undergo a full medical examination.

This I did. The medical tests came up all clear. I sent the results to Mawson, and waited impatiently.

Finally in late October I received a letter from Dr Mawson offering me a formal contract, but which stipulated the expedition would own copyright in all my photographic work. Instead, I was to receive a salary of three hundred pounds—though as far as I could tell, no money would be received by me for at least a year and a half after the return of the expedition. I was in no position to argue and quickly agreed. I was left stewing as to who had slandered me to my new boss; it was not until I was to join Shackleton that the truth was revealed.

Within four weeks I was required to assemble in Sydney all the cameras, lenses, filters, glass plates, developing trays, film, chemicals and incidentals to provide the photographic services required for more than a year. At the same time I finalised my business affairs. I leaned heavily on the goodwill engendered by my appointment to the Australian Antarctic Expedition to stave off bankruptcy. Henri persuaded Harrington's to write off my debt. I assigned my lease on the shop in lieu of monies owed. Other creditors came to the party on the promise of publicity and 'guaranteed' orders for materials by the expedition.

My mother greeted the news of my appointment and imminent departure with unsurprising gloominess.

'Don't you know, Jamie, 'alf the people who go to those places do not return, and for their poor family it's years not knowing if they're dead or alive.'

I heard nothing from the rest of the family, none of whom came to farewell me at the crowded dock in Sydney in late November.

The expedition vessel *Aurora* had been chartered out of London and was being fitted and stocked in Hobart. I was one of several AAE members travelling together from Sydney to Hobart to join the ship. There were an awful lot of doctors, professors and academic boffins at the farewell in Sydney. These were colleagues of the other expedition members appointed by Mawson. It dawned on me that, though they were mostly close to my own age, they were all university men, with degrees in various sciences; geology, biology, meteorology and so on. They were going to be my companions at close quarters. How would they regard someone who had not even finished school? It was only when assembled for the newspaper photographers that these gentlemen even acknowledged me. Two—Archie (Dad) McLean and Les Whetter—were medical doctors. Johnnie Hunter and Charles Harrisson were biologists and one young fellow, Charles Laseron, said he was a taxidermist, which I confess had me stumped. Three gents were wireless operators; they seemed friendly enough.

I was standing off to one side when a young fellow approached me.

'Hello, Les Blake's my name. You must be Hurley, the photographer.'

'Yes, official photographer.'

'I'm new, I've come down from Brisbane . . . I'm the ca-ca-cartographer . . . well, a geologist, really.'

I found myself stuck for words and enormously self-conscious. What had I got myself into? I had no more knowledge of the Antarctic than one could read in the newspaper. I was nervous an official would drag me away as an imposter. But no one did.

In Hobart I had my second meeting with Dr Mawson. He was cheery enough as I went through the stock of camera gear which

I had to bring on board *Aurora*. He made plain the importance of my role to the financial success of the expedition: whatever we achieved, there had to be pictures. I came away strongly encouraged. More daunting for me was being introduced to the other expedition members. There were thirty-one of us selected by Mawson. Unlike most of the expeditioners, I also took the trouble to learn the names of *Aurora*'s twenty-four man crew.

One of the oldest on the expedition was *Aurora* herself. Built in 1876, most of her life had been spent in Newfoundland as part of a sealing fleet. At one hundred and sixty-five feet, she didn't look big enough for the people milling around and boxes of cargo stacked alongside. From bow to stern she was a floating time machine. She had a dark hull of solid oak, but large steel plates had been bolted onto the bow for cutting into ice. She had three masts. The foremast was of the old-fashioned square-rigged style with wooden cross spars. The main mast and mizzenmast, however, had been schooner-rigged with low-slung booms for triangular sails, ideal for going into the wind. Finally, and most importantly for navigating in ice, she had a single-boiler steam engine. Its chimney stack protruded unattractively near the stern.

Dr Mawson called all expedition members on board. He introduced Captain Davis, a pale thin bearded fellow in naval uniform who was in charge of *Aurora*. He quickly became known as 'Gloomy' for his complete lack of humour. Next the Doctor introduced Frank Wild, who had previously explored Antarctica with Scott and Shackleton. Wild had a small but solid build and exuded competence. Mawson then made the first of his many speeches to us.

'In my hand I have a cable bearing the good wishes of His Majesty George V. Our expedition has the blessing and support of each state and even the present federal Labor government.' There was a titter of laughter. 'It is the first of its kind by the

Commonwealth of Australia. Its success depends on each of you fulfilling the responsibilities for which you were selected.'

Mawson continued with more pointed remarks.

'We can expect adverse conditions. Your diligence and preparation are not just required but are matters of life and death. And let me remind you that, whatever your special skill, you are all expected to provide labour for the expedition. There is no room on board for servants.'

It was soon apparent that Mawson had in mind the immediate labour required for the hundreds of boxes of goods and equipment on the dock to be opened, catalogued and shipped on board. Each of Mawson's Antarctic bases was to be independent of the other and able to subsist for eighteen months. Every item had to be coded and packed for each separate base. I gathered Antarctic weather wasn't conducive to a leisurely unpack and there would be no time to search for missing 'doll's eyes, toothpicks and left-handed hammers'.

My thoughts began to lift from personal concerns to broader anxieties like how to start a cooking fire when living on ice; could a fellow answer the call of nature without risk of frostbite; if we would have guns to ward off polar bears. I was smart enough to keep these anxieties to myself. I wondered if Mawson would do an Amundsen and suddenly announce we were actually going to the South Pole! Would we come across Captain Scott's British expedition or the plucky Norwegians? The newspapers were waiting anxiously to learn which of these expeditions would first reach the pole.

With men like Scott, Shackleton and Mawson, the British dominated the field of Antarctic exploration. Our expedition was made up mostly by men from Australia. Each day I grew more excited to be part of this pioneering discovery of the last unknown continent. If successful, it would be one of the first-ever achievements by our new nation, just ten years old. There was a sense we all shared that each of us had been selected on merit and for our youth. Each person contributed a special skill. It made me determined I would excel. I may not have had a university education, but I was a daredevil with a camera and would prove it to the world. But then doubts would come flooding in. The disconcerting fact was that I had never before touched snow let alone taken a photograph in alpine conditions. How did one photograph snow? Would there be enough light and what would happen when the sun disappeared for months at a time? I dared not ask these questions of Mawson, and hoped they would not be asked of me before I knew the answer.

I made sure I was conspicuous among those who put their back into lugging the heaviest loads on board. Some of the fellows looked to have spent little time doing manual labour. Here was something I could do alongside the best of them. Mawson, too, even though he was the boss, got stuck into the lifting and carrying. We worked from first light sometimes till eleven in the evening. No union rules here. Pa would not have approved. I noted that despite *Aurora* being completely crammed, Mawson had brought on board an extensive library from geological science to books of verse by Tennyson and Coleridge. In Lithgow I had become an avid reader of Robert Louis Stevenson, Jules Verne, Poe and Dickens. I determined I would work my way through Mawson's collection of volumes.

On the few occasions we were given leave to stretch our legs in Hobart, we were instantly recognised by the general populace. Mention of *Aurora* resulted in us being regarded as celebrities. I found myself swept along in a wave of excitement with my new colleagues. Before I knew it, Azzi Webb—our Kiwi magnetician—and I were entertaining three young ladies over fresh strawberries and cream in the parlour of a fruit shop. This was a marvel in itself, considering I was usually painfully shy around women.

In serious tones Azzi feigned great knowledge of Antarctica, but had trouble explaining his own name.

'It's a nickname. It's short for Azimuth.'

'Is that from the Old Testament?'

'No, no, it's meteorological!'

'Meet who?' they laughed.

I insisted it was just his Kiwi drawl until he became quite tetchy. He was such a serious fellow, younger than me, but together we were full of stories that produced gales of laughter among our new friends.

But we had few occasions for leisure, in between packing and loading. It was not long before every available inch inside the ship was full. I could not see how we would fit the very large objects, including prefabricated huts and an aeroplane which, having crashed, was without wings and was to be used as a tractor. Eventually these were hoisted on board and lashed to the deck along with water casks and tins of petrol and kerosene. Captain Davis then announced we would depart with the tide the following afternoon.

•

Saturday, 2 December 1911. We are given a heroes' send-off. We are not heroes, though, save for Dr Mawson. Mostly we are unknowns who dream of achieving great things for ourselves, our country and for the British Empire.

There is a brass band and 'God Save the King' is played more than once. The lord mayor of Hobart, dignitaries and politicians are in attendance, as are reporters and press photographers. The telegram of good wishes from King George V is read aloud. The crowd yells loud 'hurrahs' as the men toss their straw boaters and the women wave their lace handkerchiefs.

Before embarking I had put to Captain Davis my ideas for filming on board *Aurora*. The cinematograph on its tripod weighs over ninety pounds. Most cameramen are content to stand the camera in a stationary position and wind the film through. However, since working at the Sandford Ironworks I delight in the use of pulleys, winches and flywheels to achieve novel effects. Captain Davis with some reservation has agreed I am allowed anywhere in the rigging that I can climb. So as the crowd swells and *Aurora* separates from the dock I am forty feet in the air, perched on a yardarm off the foremast. I have used the pulleys and halyards on the mast to winch the cinematograph up alongside me and have then strapped it securely to the yardarm to hold its weight and with just enough movement that I can tilt and pivot at the same time. With my legs wrapped around the yardarm I wind the crank handle, two turns a second. I am happy as a lark. It does not trouble me that, because of my camera's distance, I miss out on the handshakes, hugs and kisses that Les Blake, Azzi and the other boys receive.

•

Before leaving the Derwent River we pull into the quarantine station and pick up forty Greenland huskies. The dogs are quite striking in their appearance, solid with wild wolf-like faces. They do not bark, but howl and nip at their leashes as they are brought on board to their newly built kennels on the main deck.

Looking after the dogs on their 'round the world' trip were two of the few non-Australians on the expedition: Belgrave Ninnis, a young lieutenant in the British Army, and Dr Xavier Mertz, a Swiss lawyer and skiing champion. Mawson greets Ninnis and Mertz warmly. Ninnis is tall and lanky with a boyish face, big ears and a ready smile. Mertz is short and very dapper with a neat moustache and speaks the most amazing 'Ingleesh'. We soon find ourselves mimicking him, which he accepts with good humour. Les Blake, Azzi and I watch them bring the dogs on board one by one.

Les remarks, 'I heard these chaps just missed out on selection with Scott's expedition.'

'Lucky for them they have a second chance with us,' says Azzi.

'But why did the dogs have to stay in quarantine with them?' I joke, surprising myself with my new-found confidence.

Within days of leaving Hobart the weather deteriorates and the crew reef sails before they are ripped asunder. The overloaded *Aurora* rolls and dips like billy-o. It is as if we are imprisoned on a carnival carousel with no brake. Waves come over the deck and cause havoc with the dogs and cargo. The foredeck is several feet underwater as she plunges through wave after wave. The dogs are terrified but their howling is drowned out by the storm. Their poop washes everywhere. One by one most of the expedition team fall ill with seasickness. They lie helpless in their bunks. I have been wondering how I will fare. I keep busy and am spared.

After a week we run down the western edge of a dramatic landfall, Macquarie Island, on which the bleak weather permits not a single tree. To escape the worst of the breeze we tuck into Caroline Cove, a narrow inlet on its south-west corner, Captain Davis sends in a boat to determine the cove's suitability. Les, Azzi and I are among the few expedition members well enough to go ashore. We plot our way through a narrow channel which opens up into a spectacular inlet surrounded by steep tussock-grass hillsides.

We have entered a zoo without walls. The sea around our boat is alive with scores of penguins leaping and diving. There are thousands more in rookeries along the edges of the cove. Seabirds disturbed by our arrival are squawking and swirling in front of us, trying to lift themselves back up the hillside. We cross a sandy shoal into deeper water and observe that most of the large rocks along the cove are home to large cumbersome-looking sea elephants drying and sunning themselves. As we scrape the shingle Les and I leap overboard and drag the boat through a large troop of royal penguin spectators. They have inquisitive eyes, bright orange chests and earmuffs and are most reluctant to vacate their spots. They stand around me chattering in a language I do not understand and peck at my legs as if to say, 'Do you mind!' I am more threatened by the sea elephants, which exceed twenty feet in length. They shake their heads at us, then smoothly drop into the water and disappear.

I am in a photographer's paradise. While the others labour at establishing a small stores depot I am at liberty to capture whatever images I can. The boat goes back to *Aurora* and I request they bring more photographic plates and the cinematograph on their return. In the meantime I explore the hinterland.

A lively stream leads me up several hundred feet between the hills above the cove. As I ascend, the ground opens out, there is a babble of commotion and I find myself the centre of attention of some thousands of birds. I have stumbled onto a major rookery of terns, boobies, shearwaters and many others I don't recognise. They are in the middle of nesting and their eggs are strewn across the tussocky ground. The birds squawk their protests and I am deafened as I reverse my path back down the hill. I spy colourful Maori hens and the nests of giant petrels whose young have hatched into grotesque fluffy toys. Along the shore large flocks of royal penguins are begrudgingly prepared to put up with my company. The boat returns and I find a convenient spot to set up the tripod.

After only a few exposures I am accosted by one of the sailors and told that I am to return to *Aurora* at once. Mawson and Davis have decided the cove is unsuitable for a permanent anchorage and we are to search for a more protected shelter.

I am stunned. This is a remarkable opportunity to obtain unique photographs and footage; I have never seen photographs of these creatures in the wild taken on anything like the modern equipment I have, and there is no telling if such an opportunity will present itself again. Reluctantly I do as am I bid, inwardly fuming.

By evening we have sailed to the north-eastern tip of the island, but are unable to go ashore due to the strong surf. In the morning the surf is still too big and we again wait at anchor. Shortly, a solitary figure emerges above a dune behind the beach. He disappears and then there are several figures excitedly waving. Using flags they semaphore that their sealing ship, *Clyde*, has been wrecked. The figures endeavour to launch a lifeboat but all their attempts are rebuffed by the surf and their boat overturned. In response to their further messages, *Aurora* ups anchor and rounds the sand spit to its western side, Hasselborough Bay. There we find a suitable spot to land. Mawson and Davis decide this is the ideal site for our proposed Macquarie Island base.

Hasselborough Bay has nothing of the wildlife which abounds on the southern tip of the island. One of the shipwrecked sealers, a fellow named Hutchinson, confirms my suspicion that the north of the island has been the most regularly inhabited by man and, as a result, its seal and penguin populations have been completely decimated. He tells me it is a rugged twenty miles to Caroline Cove and would be much quicker by boat than overland. It is unlikely *Aurora* will return to Caroline Cove and, in any case, it is the photographs from a walking tour that I am after. Hutchinson appreciates my interest and offers to guide me if I can provide supplies.

I present my plan to Mawson, but he is occupied with unloading and setting up a wireless transmission station to link with our Antarctic bases.

When he doesn't respond I press further.

'Look, you know the crew rushed me into the boat to leave Caroline Cove. Well, I think I've left the main lens for the cinematograph on the rocks where I set up. I can't find it anywhere. It's essential for the moving pictures you want.'

Within a few hours Hutchinson and I are on our way south. We are accompanied by the biologist Charles Harrisson, whom Mawson has asked to look for any useful specimens. I am ecstatic, despite being weighed down with a huge load of supplies, cameras and tripod.

The best walking is along a central plateau, but it is criss-crossed with lakes and watercourses and we lose our bearings as thick fog constantly rolls over the top of us. There is nothing for it but to find our way back down to the shoreline and climb a series of rocky headlands separated by shingle beaches. By evening we are done in and there is a cold steady drizzle. The only flat ground with anything approaching shelter is already occupied by elephant seals. We chase them off but they leave their stench. We are not prepared to go any further. Pulling blankets under our oilskin jackets, we spend a damp and uncomfortable night.

At the end of another day of hard going we stand looking down on a beach crowded with royal penguins and the ribbed carcass of their giant predator, a wrecked sealing ship, its hull dismasted and smashed open by the waves. I have secured the photographs I wanted of the Caroline Cove seal and bird colonies. Harrisson, in the meantime, has collected a large number of king penguin eggs and other specimens.

We head back to the north-east and in darkness drop down a ravine that leads to Lusitania Bay on the east coast. Hutchinson leads us to a sealers' hut in which we soon have a fire going. The hut is grimy and foul-smelling, but it is dry. As the fire dies down the hut comes alive with rats, which Harrisson explains arrived from the shipwrecks and now infest the island. My blanket is like the King's highway to the rats, but eventually I sleep.

In the morning I look outside and see we are surrounded by king penguins, standing around nonchalantly in pairs. Many shelter from the wind behind a huge cast-iron tank, not much smaller than the hut we have slept in.

'Harrisson, wake up, we've got guests,' I say. 'There's thousands of penguins outside and they want back those eggs you pinched.'

'Not thousands,' said Hutchinson. 'Not anymore. When Joe Hatch built this hut there were over a hundred thousand kingies, just on this beach alone. You see that old steam digester there?'

He pointed to a barrel-shaped pressure cooker.

'Hatch had it specially made in New Zealand. He put the digester smack bang in the middle of the colony. Well, you've seen how curious penguins are. They watched his blokes toil away. Then the men cranked up the boiler and Hatch and his crew pulled out their clubs and started working their way through the birds. Knocked 'em all on the head. Hardest bit was tossing them into the boiler. Less than a thousand here now. Hardly worth bothering with.'

Harrisson and I went quiet and looked at each other.

'Of course,' said Hutchinson, 'that was after the sealers killed every fur seal on the island. Not a single one left now. Only reason there are still elephant seals is they were on beaches sealers couldn't get in and out of.'

'That's a lot of dead penguins and fur seals just to get oil,' Harrisson observes.

Hutchinson shrugged. 'Man's got to live. It was good money then, especially with the big colonies here—but those big numbers have all gone now so Joe Hatch is gone. They wiped out the seals in five years. After that the digestors on the island processed up to 200,000 penguins a year. Plenty of work then. But I won't be coming back here again. No sirree. This is my farewell. Can't tell you how pleased I was to see you lot. Thought I'd never get off the place. Other sealers will be back, though, most likely finish off these penguins this summer . . . If you're a nature lover, you're in the wrong place. Wait till you walk up the north end of this bay. You'll see carcasses of hundreds of sea elephants. Actually you'll smell 'em first 'cause we don't bother with their hide or the meat. We just want their blubber for the oil.'

We have another long day of it up the eastern side of the island. Harrisson's collecting box is full and as we climb yet another headland I observe him discard items. Presumably their scientific value is less than the exertion required. Not too long before dusk he spies a magnificent albatross perched on the hillside a little below us and about thirty yards away. The biologist is awestruck.

'Its wingspan would have to be at least ten feet. I should have brought a gun.'

'I could get him with a rock,' I say, thinking of my days with the gangs around Glebe. 'Or I could try with this.' And before I know it I have taken a tin of corned beef from my swag and pitched it furiously at the majestic bird. The albatross is knocked flat and does not get up. Harrisson has his prize. I am immediately aghast at what I have just done. I sense the others are too, though they say nothing.

No thought has been given to how we can carry back the dead bird. It's a two-day walk to *Aurora*. Nor does Harrisson have equipment to skin it, which would reduce the burden. We are on the verge of leaving it behind when Hutchinson volunteers to carry the whole albatross across his shoulders.

Next morning, with Coleridge's 'Rime of the Ancient Mariner' ringing in my ears, my right foot becomes wedged between two rocks and I fall forwards, twisting my ankle. Shortly afterwards, no doubt due to fatigue from the rugged terrain, Harrisson twists his knee.

Nevertheless Harrisson's pace is more than I can maintain. Hutchinson stays with me while the biologist goes on ahead to

Aurora to fetch help. The next morning good old Mertz and Ninnis set out to find us. The look in their eyes says we are quite a sight, grimy and battered by the elements, me using my tripod for a crutch and Hutchinson with a giant albatross spread across his shoulders. On my back I carry my glass plate prizes, though it will be a few days before I can see how my shots have turned out.

I rest up in the hut erected for our Macquarie Island base party. Boxes of stores have been unloaded, along with generators and electrical plant for the wireless station. Large wooden masts have been brought ashore to be erected at the top of a prominent hill. Mawson hopes to use Macquarie Island as a relay station and maintain wireless contact from Antarctica with Hobart and the outside world. Our most experienced expeditioner, Frank Wild, has adapted a flying fox used by the sealers. Using heavy rocks from the top of the hill as a descending counterweight, Wild and his work party haul up the masts and other equipment from the beach. This presents an immediate opportunity for my enthusiasm to film from moving objects. To the amusement of Mawson and ribbing from all as being the one who shot the albatross, and despite my crook ankle, I take the opportunity for a return trip on the flying fox. With one hand cranking the cine camera, I hang on desperately with the other to avoid further mishap.

On Christmas Eve, I farewell Les Blake and others of the Macquarie Island party. *Aurora* raises anchor and a strong northerly fills her sails and drives us south. The island is soon lost from sight, our last contact with the known world. Smooth brown petrels remain our constant companions, skimming above the swell. Between *Aurora* and the horizon whales sporadically breach and spout.

Christmas Day is celebrated at sea with claret and cigars in the mess room and numerous toasts. Frank Wild raises his glass: 'To our wives and sweethearts . . .' and then all voices reply in unison, 'And may they never meet!' I join in loudly though I have neither wife nor sweetheart. The others are so confident. Do they all have a wife or lady friend?

Aurora is entering the seas directly below Australia and New Zealand where no living person has ever ventured.

Mawson explains, 'The French explorer Dumont d'Urville and the American Wilkes passed this way in the 1840s. Their ships sailed right past each other without so much as a bonjour. D'Urville believed he saw land under the iceshelf and he gave it the name Terre Adelie to honour his wife.'

'I never met a woman called Terry,' I say and Mawson gives me a look.

We know *Aurora* will eventually run into the southern icecap. It remains unknown if we will find land and, if we do, whether it will be connected to Victoria Land, the landmass further east under the icecap from where Scott and Amundsen set out several months ago in their race to the pole. Will we sail into walls of ice or, if we see land, will it be an archipelago or an island continent like Australia?

In the meantime I have shown Mawson the glass plate images of wildlife from Macquarie Island and he is well pleased. I feel a sense of relief that I have started on my work. I have opened the first chapter on all that may lie ahead. I was never good at waiting.

Gloomy Davis tells each of us it is the worst time for collisions with icebergs on account of summer having unleashed a disintegrating icepack into our path. After five days south from Macquarie Island there is a rush on deck as the cry goes out, 'Ice on the starboard bow!' We pass close by a small berg with intricate caverns and streaks of blue and green light. Soon there are bergs all around us and Captain Davis regularly changes course to avoid them. One berg we pass is almost a mile long. Its sheer walls are higher than the masts on *Aurora*. The berg breathes with the swell. Across the water comes a rhythmic boom as waves rush in and out of its icy fissures and caverns. It is a beautiful but lonely sound.

For me the icebergs represent a new challenge: to capture their purity and grandeur in a landscape where there is little to indicate their true dimensions to the human eye. I experiment with foregrounds through *Aurora*'s rigging but the scenes are overcrowded. I have more success strapping the cinematograph facedown below the bowsprit. As I wind the film through the camera, the steel bow of *Aurora* cuts through the floe, splitting and rolling the ice port and starboard.

The floe continues to increase and through blustery winds and fog emerges not land but a wall of ice a hundred feet high which bookends Aurora. We turn starboard and retreat, heading west at the same time. We look for every opportunity to push southwards. Days go by. New Year's Day 1912 comes and goes. We keep sailing westwards, looking for any sight of land. We are knocking on the edge of the unknown world: 'Here, there be dragons.'

On 8 January *Aurora* rounds an ice wall and there before us is a broad stretch of water dotted with islands and a rocky promontory in the distance. As we draw closer the promontory turns out to be a series of islands in front of a low rocky shore which Mawson names Mackellar Islets and Commonwealth Bay respectively. We head for this piece of exposed land fringed by ice. The whaleboat is lowered and I push myself forwards, holding my camera. Mawson gives me the nod and with Frank Wild, our astonomer Bob Bage and a few others we are rowing past islets and bergs to the shore. Some of the islets are just bare rock crowded with seals and penguins. Other more exposed islets have the appearance of collapsed puddings covered with thick white icing from layers of sea spray.

Once past the islands we row into a fine inlet. One hundred yards wide and four hundred yards long, the inlet is sheltered but not deep enough for *Aurora*. From the whaleboat we look down through crystal-clear water to rocks covered in bright green seagrasses. Excited penguins dive beneath our boat in the freezing waters. Nearer shore the depth reduces until I am looking down about forty feet, then twenty, then ten, to stones and trailing seagrasses.

The keel of the boat scrapes on rocks. Mawson at the bow steps ashore. There is an unholy ruckus behind him as we jostle to be first to follow. On the icy rock my feet go from under me and I am suddenly the centre of attention as I land on my backside. 'Well, Hurley,' says Mawson, 'you are the first human to sit on Terre Adelie!'

3

Terre Adelie, 1912

We landed without ceremony, certainly in my case, and took stock of what we could see. We walked southwards across the rock and ice, slightly apart, like actors walking to the edge of a stage and peering into the void. Unused to solid ground my legs stumbled on its uneven surface, which seemed to sway beneath me. There was no breeze and without the sound of wind in the rigging and waves buffeting the hull there was an eeriness to the silence. I could hear the rustle of my Burberry outer garments and the sound of my breath as it formed clouds of vapour.

There were no inhabitants of this shore, no spear or gunfire resisted our arrival. There were no human defenders, no skulls and crossbones or dragons to warn us off. Our binoculars revealed no hidden pairs of eyes peering from the dark shadows of the gloomy landscape. No people lived in this place. There had been no humans ever to visit this part of the Antarctic continent for thousands of miles in either direction. This place, the very base of planet Earth, was repellent to humankind. It was an arid desert. There was no water to drink and virtually nothing to eat in the long winter. Apart from penguins and seals, there were few summer visitors. In winter even the sun stayed away and darkness prevailed. Virtually the whole of this land of ancient rocks lay hidden deep below mountains and chasms of ice.

The Antarctic mountain ranges were much higher than the Australian Alps but permanently under ice. Glacial freezing swelled in the winter and pushed ice northwards off high plateaus, gouging and churning to the sea with the brute force of glaciers. The sea froze, then in summer broke up and launched gigantic bergs across the oceans. I learned from Mawson these glaciers carried rocks and stones he hoped would unlock secrets from the frozen heart of the continent. Like all geologists he was after fossils, impressions of the animate on the inanimate. He must be an optimist, I thought, to come to this place.

Having seen nothing of the Antarctic continent but ice cliffs I felt huge relief to come ashore on solid rocky ground. One could live and build a house on rock. I did not see how habitation could be made on ice. Mawson named this place Cape Denison.

Despite the desolation that greeted us we knew that somewhere on the far extremes of this icy wasteland there were two parties of Europeans, if they were still alive, desperate for fame and glory, fighting the blizzard to be first to reach the southernmost axis of the planet. Much later we learned Amundsen had reached the South Pole some three weeks earlier and was on his way back to his ship, *Fram*. Scott was still a week away from reaching the pole and the bitter realisation there was no reward for second in such a race.

Cape Denison offered us a bare toehold on the edge of the continent. The rock that formed the cape, said Mawson, was ancient gneiss, folded and gnarled by pressure from the ice plate. Denuded of ice and snow, the cape extended for half a mile in each direction. A series of large boulders just south of the cape appeared to hold back a collar of plate ice and glacial moraine. To the east and west the plate ice ran down to the sea. In both directions ice rose from the sea in steep cliffs up to one hundred and fifty feet high. Mawson messaged *Aurora* that we would make this our winter base. There were of course no alternatives and no more time. The whaleboat returned for the first load of equipment and supplies.

It was only as the first boatload was coming ashore that Antarctica signalled its opposition to our landing. From the stillness above the ridge a wind sprang up and was soon whipping our faces with drift ice at a vicious forty miles an hour. It picked up and doubled its velocity to reach gusts of eighty miles an hour, which knocked us to the ground. Other than Mawson, Wild and Davis, none of us had experienced anything like this. The gale was completely disabling and brought unloading to a halt. Once we were all in the whaleboat we cast off and were blown back to *Aurora*, which was struggling to stand off the cape in foaming seas. This was almost a premature end to the expedition. We were badly knocked about as we came alongside, but got aboard safely. Captain Davis made for nearby ice cliffs to shelter from the wind.

We dropped anchor to ride out what we believed was a freak storm. Two days passed before the Antarctic blizzard gave pause and we made a second attempt at unloading. Countless trips in an overloaded whaleboat saw only one case tumble into the bay. Over six days, interrupted by fierce storms, boxes of foodstuffs and supplies for a two-year stay were stacked on the ice, along with panels for the construction of two huts, twenty tonnes of coal briquettes and hundreds of large benzene tins with which we erected an impromptu shelter, but only for non-smokers.

'See you next year, Hurley.' Frank Wild and Charles Harrisson both shook my hand in farewell. They were leaving. Wild was in charge of setting up the AAE western base. More than that, our only link to civilisation, the *Aurora* under

Captain Davis, was departing with Wild's party to search for a suitable landing site before the seas froze.

I was disappointed to see Wild go, as he was more approachable than Mawson. I would miss his practical down-to-earth manner.

Davis, we found out much later, steamed to the west for a month without sight of any suitable landing place. Running low on coal, he decided to return to Hobart for the winter. Frank Wild, however, would not admit defeat and instructed Davis to drop him and his party on the iceshelf. He and his men used a flying fox to lift some thirty-six tonnes of supplies to the very top of the cliff, where they made camp an unknown distance from land and without any natural shelter from the blizzard. There they stayed for over a year.

Back at Cape Denison the eighteen of us stood on the ice, wondering if we had seen our last of *Aurora*. It was nine o'clock in the evening, and still light as we pitched camp. For some lads it was their first time in a tent.

No one slept too well that night, and by 5 a.m. we had started the desperate race to erect living quarters. Nothing was straightforward in those temperatures. Many jobs could only be done by the temporary removal of mitts and gloves, and soon we had our first experiences with frostbite. Metal tools were impossible to hold. Putting nails or drill bits between your lips was a mistake only made once. Goggles fogged up, but unprotected eyes watered continuously and caused snow blindness. Sweat froze, but cement for hut foundations refused to set. Pre-cut timber for walls and joists no longer fitted, having been warped by constant drenching with seawater on board ship. Moisture of any kind quickly froze and filled drill and bolt holes rock hard so redrilling was required. Steel drill tips became brittle from extreme cold and shattered under pressure. The permafrost ground was so hard dynamite was needed to blast foundation stump holes, but once in position dynamite sticks would freeze inside a minute, unnerving us as to whether unexploded charges were still 'live'.

For two weeks we worked eighteen-hour days, often to midnight, to erect a hut. I was in my element. I took no photographs and instead moved boulders to build foundations, bolted floor joists and assembled wall frames. As walls went up some shelter was gained, but using hammer and nails on the windward side was a misery and could only be endured for limited periods. I found I was one of the most skilled members of the party at joinery, metalwork and electrical work. Despite multiple university degrees and doctorates, most of my colleagues were bungling amateurs with a hammer or saw. But I joked they knew other important things, which I didn't, like the names of rocks. Dr Mertz was one of the most enthusiastic as he nailed up the ceiling from the inside using four-inch nails, until interrupted by the cries of Bickerton, our engineer, who had been sitting on the roof.

Having assumed responsibility for assembling the main stove, I took Mawson to one side. 'Doc, the stove fittings are not in any of the boxes. Did they come ashore?'

He looked at me very sternly. 'Hurley, they have to be if we are to get through the winter.'

I returned to my search, but a few hours later reported again to Mawson the parts were nowhere to be found.

'I can tell you, Hurley, the stove fittings for this hut are not on *Aurora*!'

Then it occurred to me. I said, 'I know where they are. They're in the box that slid off the whaleboat.'

'Are you sure?'

'Doc, I've checked everything here. That must be where they are. Azzi and I both saw the box go overboard.'

At low tide Mawson and Azzi pushed off in the boat and prodded the kelp with oars for almost an hour. A shout from

Azzi confirmed they could see the box, but despite hooks and ropes it could not be raised. I was gobsmacked when Mawson stood up, dropped his trousers and ripped off his jumper and undershirt. I was sorry my camera was not handy. There was a splash as Mawson dropped into the bay. Azzi looked most agitated. Mawson's legs gripped and lifted the box which Azzi hauled on board, followed by Mawson, who flew up over the side and dressed in world-record time.

Mawson was shivering noisily in a sleeping bag in his tent when I informed him the box had been opened and contained tins of strawberry jam. It was one of the few occasions I heard him swear.

The fittings were eventually located and I soon had the stove operating as the hut went up around it. Shortly before completion, however, the learned bacteriologist Dr McLean was blown off the roof while working in gale-force winds. He grabbed at the chimney as he slid past, causing the recently installed internal stovepipe to oscillate wildly. Inside the hut the stove and flue began shaking violently. Ninnis bravely grabbed and held the hot stovepipe until it came away in his arms and he was blackened in a cloud of soot. McLean landed harmlessly in snowdrift.

By the end of January the hut was complete. Mawson instructed me to ready my camera and we all gathered outside. The Union Jack was hoisted and the Australian flag alongside. 'I hereby take possession of this land,' said Mawson, raising his voice above the roar of the wind, 'on behalf of the king and the British Empire!' At my insistence the men removed their thick woollen helmets for the occasion. I yelled, 'Will you lot stop bloody shivering and stand still!' I allowed an exposure of less than half a second and captured the moment on a glass plate. Quickly the men gave three cheers then scrambled back inside before their ears froze. 'King George won't be coming here too soon,' I said to Azzi.

In the morning we woke to find stockpiles of fine drift snow had blown in during the night and buried a number of sleepers. There was a lot of plugging of gaps and cracks to be done to seal the hut from the blizzard. Our hut was twenty-four feet square. Three sides each had three sets of double bunks and Mawson had his own smallish room. The cooking area occupied most of the fourth side and in the middle of the room was a long trestle table for meals which between times served for all manner of scientific work, research and entertainment.

In the north-western corner of the hut a small room was constructed five feet by five feet. This was my darkroom. I built a series of narrow shelves along one wall to store my chemicals. On my left I installed a workbench with a slight downwards slope, like a desk. This was for brushing and cutting and touching up negatives and plates. In the right-hand corner was a small sink for developing. Once inside and with the door shut I had my own private space where I could be alone and undisturbed under the dull red glow of my developing lamp. There was only room for one person standing or perched on a stool. I could move neither forwards nor backwards, but could turn around and work freely for hours at a time. Working as I did in darkness, its small confines were of little account. In the winter, when there was no sun and when outside activities were limited if not impossible, it was my universe where I lived and worked. It was my darkroom in the hut under the snow in the dark world.

Immediately on the leeward side of our hut was constructed a workroom which had initially been intended for a separate eastern base. Our sleeping quarters had a door through to the workroom from which one could exit to an enclosed verandah which had the latrine at one end and a door to outside at the other.

I felt great relief on completion of the hut. For all the ferocity of the winds, we could now survive for a year with the rations we had and the abundance of seal and penguin meat in the summer months. However, in the event of any catastrophe we could not reach civilisation for at least one whole year. No boat could reach us until the summer thaw. Only Gloomy Davis and his crew knew our location. Only Gloomy would be able to find us. No one spoke about this. We had to trust he would make it back to Hobart and return safely the following year. He was such a prickly navy man, which I surmised came with the burden of knowing we relied on him for our lives.

I was unused to the society generated from the eighteen of us being thrust together so closely in the hut. We mostly called each other by surnames or nicknames. My nickname was Hoyle. I was allocated a bunk adjoining my darkroom. Mawson, of course, had his room. There was then a peculiar pecking order, not unlike the Dewey System, by which the scientists arranged themselves on upper and lower bunks around the walls of the hut: biologist, geologist, meteorologist and so on. Living outside the hut we had nineteen dogs. They were great company for all of us and in due course we had sledging teams and our own personal favourites.

My friend Azzi was in charge of magnetic observations. His work had to be done hundreds of yards away from our living quarters so as to avoid distortions caused by metal machinery and equipment. Setting and reading magnetographs could take Azzi up to an hour or more. Together we built two tiny huts. Both had standing room only for two men. They looked like privies, a 'his' and a 'hers' in the snow. Walking back with Azzi from the magnetograph huts one day, the dogs commenced a wild howling. They were chained on the northern side of the hut. We saw them straining at their leads to escape a huge monster advancing on them. At that distance we could not tell what it was or where it had come from. We ran to the hut calling at the top of our voices but none inside could hear. One dog alone was straining at his leash in the face of the monster and keeping it temporarily at bay, even though it was at least ten times his size. As we drew closer we could see the dog was Johnson, one of the smallest of the pack but with the biggest heart, and the monster which towered above him was a huge sea elephant bull.

Bob Bage emerged from the hut with a rifle and the sea elephant was quickly killed. He measured eighteen feet long and weighed two tonne. Laseron needed help to skin the creature before the carcass froze. A block and tackle was required to lift off the meat and blubber, which was then cut up by Ninnis and Mertz and stored for the dogs. The skeleton and skin went to the biologists. That night, Johnson received an extra serving for his bravery.

One thing the dogs did not like was incessant wind. None of us, including Mawson, had any experience of a wind of such constantly high velocity. It blew for days at a time above a hundred miles an hour and gusting at times well above this. The anemometer recorded gusts up to two hundred miles an hour. The blizzard always came from the south, sweeping over the top of the polar plateau and roaring down the slope to the water's edge on Commonwealth Bay. It screamed as it discovered our wood and iron hut perched precariously above the shoreline, and it ripped frantically at our roof and chimney. It howled in the wire stays that braced the chimney against its ferocity, and rattled and shook the hut's walls. Its shrieking drowned out voices in the open air and made hard work of normal conversation inside the hut. It stole from us any object lying loose on the ground. Gloves and mitts were such frequent casualties that mitts had to be strapped to our jackets.

If we went out in a blizzard without crampons attached to our boots the wind would slide and drag us into the bay. We learned the art of leaning on the wind as we walked. For short distances it was easier to crawl.

I became determined to somehow capture the blizzard on film. I devised all manner of shields to protect the cameras from the drift of snow and ice which penetrated everything and froze the mechanism and my fingers. I modified and enlarged the camera switches so they could be shifted and adjusted while wearing gloves.

Filming by myself with a tripod in the blizzard proved impossible. I enlisted Azzi's help to carry the cinematograph, heavy at the best of times, into the shelter of a small overhang. As we trudged over an icy hillock we were struck by a powerful gust and both of us lifted off the ground. I sought to wrap myself around the cinematograph as we were dropped to the ground several yards away and were then rolled backwards across the ice. Azzi and I scrambled back to the hut, having suffered only minor injuries. The camera, though, was out of action for a week.

A few days stuck inside the hut gave me cabin fever. I was champing at the bit to explore over the ridge line to the south and so was disappointed at the end of February when Mawson picked Madigan and Bage, two of the scientists, to accompany him on a sledging trip. Mawson did, however, agree that Mertz, Bickerton and I could assist in the start of the journey, which was all uphill into the wind.

We set out late afternoon when the wind dropped slightly. We wore harnesses from which we ran leads to the sledge. The snowdrift blew hard and cold and low to the ground so that we could not see our own feet.

Dragging a sledge on ice was a new experience for all except Mawson and our technique varied considerably.

I learned to stamp my feet until my crampons gripped the ice then lean forwards using my weight to gain ground. This in turn depended on the hardness of the surface. The ice was interspersed with fissures and ridges. The fissures or crevasses were filled with soft snow and difficult to see. The ridges were like rock walls to the sledge runners. Being our first attempt there was a lot of waiting around to get started and pausing for fiddly adjustments. However, after only several minutes of sledging I was sweating profusely inside my Burberry. Before we could reach the top and look across the plateau, Mawson sent our support party back to the hut, then he, Bage and Madigan continued over the top of the ridge. It was a taste of what was to come and enough to realise that sledging was going to be perilous.

The following day Mawson's party was literally blown down the hill in close to white-out conditions. They had endured a cold night, their gear was torn and they returned without the sledge. Madigan's hood was almost completely full of snowdrift, which the warmth of his face and breathing had melted into an ice visor through which he could barely see. His face was badly frostbitten and he had to be restrained from pulling off a hard white section of his cheek which he assumed was a piece of ice.

Several days later, at the end of the evening meal, Mawson called everyone back to the table. We squeezed together all anxious to hear what the Doctor had to say.

'As it is almost March, there will be no more attempts to sledge up onto the plateau until after winter. I have heard talk that our program of sledging trips can't be achieved. But it is far from certain the wind strengths on the plateau will be as severe as we have experienced. These winds are katabatic. They are cold air currents dropping several thousand feet from the centre of the Antarctic continent, increasing in velocity as they hit the coast. In any case, we will use the winter to strengthen our tents and equipment.'

From March onwards the weather worsened; the strength and duration of the blizzards increased. The wind was regularly over eighty miles an hour. The snow blew down from the plateau and encased our winter quarters. We felt safe in the hut, but a number of men questioned how we could possibly travel any distance or expect a tent to stay intact in the blizzard.

One March morning, after a fierce storm, Mertz came running into the hut and without removing his Burberry jacket announced to all at the breakfast table, 'Der bot iss gone! Der bot iss gone!'

'The whaleboat?' said Mawson, standing up from the table.

'Ja, der valebot.'

I grabbed my outdoor clothing and with Mawson and others followed Mertz down to the edge of the bay—but there was nothing to see. There was not even a trace of the whaleboat, which had been securely tied up in the lee of a small ice cliff, where it should have been sheltered from the clutches of the blizzard. Even the mooring lines, which were of enormous breaking strain, had gone. It was some time before we worked out that the boat and its moorings and a large section of the ice cliff to which it had been anchored had all been dislodged by the wind. The whaleboat, attached to its own iceberg, was now well on its way to Tasmania. Unspoken, though loud and clear in my mind, was the thought that if Davis did not return, the whaleboat had represented our only means of escape—and none of us knew whether Davis had made it back to advise others of our whereabouts.

The wind played games with us. There were times when it mysteriously called a truce in its barrage on our settlement. And yet looking up to the polar plateau we could still observe its force blasting off the ridge in a continuous stream of drift ice. If the wind stopped in the middle of the night, we were wakened by the eerie silence. If it was daytime, we would rush outside to attend to the numerous jobs that required doing. Often enough, as soon as we ventured out to take advantage of the calm, with a mighty whoosh the wind would sweep down the icy slope. At other times it would eddy outside the hut and form whirlwinds or willy-willies which would pick up everything in their path and disappear out to sea.

There was one battle with the blizzard Dr Mawson was anxious to win. Having gone to great lengths to set up a wireless station on Macquarie Island, he was intent on erecting a mast to send and receive signals from Commonwealth Bay. No one had ever used wireless on the Antarctic continent. The mast was strong Oregon timber and needed to be erected in stages and braced with cables at each stage. It was eventually raised to ninety feet. But it incurred the wrath of the blizzard, which destroyed the structure before any transmission was received. It was not until early 1913 a mast was again erected. In the meantime, and throughout the darkness of winter, we remained cut off from the outside world.

If we had one of those scarce autumn days when I could venture outside with a camera, then that evening I would be up late in my darkroom checking results. It was a constant battle to achieve a standard that satisfied me. The ever-present drift of snow permeated all my attempts at camera shields and lens covers, and consequently moisture and ice on the lens spoiled many shots. Frequently there was not enough light and the subject matter would be a moving blur or, worse, a dark smudge. Then all too suddenly the clouds would break and the sun, always low to the horizon, would flood the camera lens with reflected light.

The blizzard remained determined to end our existence. It was unrelenting in its malevolence. I was constantly retreating before its might to the shelter of the hut to clean and repair cameras and lenses made useless by the snowdrift and the freezing-cold temperatures. But I never gave up trying to capture its ferocity. With Azzi's help I made a shelter beneath a small rock overhang and a fixed anchor point to steady the camera. I took multiple exposures and in the evening examined the results. I had captured grainy spotted spectres of Azzi leaning forwards unnaturally and in the background the dark outline of the hut. But it said nothing of the chilling howl or unseen force that suspended gravity, or the thousands of ice crystals that brought frostbite and blindness. I did have one promising image of getting ice for the hut's drinking water with silhouetted figures nicely in focus on their hands and knees, and another of Azzi leaning forwards into the gale with a large pick. In the darkroom I brushed up the swirling drift on the photographs to convey the force of the blizzard and the hellish desolation of the place. Soon the picture told a vivid story of man against nature. I knew it was a picture newspapers would buy. I put it aside to show Mawson in the morning.

By April the blizzard gave up its attempts to blow our hut off the continent and instead sought to smother our encampment with snow. Before long the hut was completely buried to the level of the chimney. Curiously, it was easier to maintain the warmth of the hut in winter, but shovelling to maintain ventilation became an everyday chore.

Mawson devised a roster of duties to manage the domestic life of the hut. I was relieved to see this included all the scientists, as I felt sure some had thought they would be excluded from mundane jobs. We each took turns for one week as cook, one week as mess man, and one week as nightwatchman.

I enjoyed each of these positions, but especially my times as cook. I soon realised I had considerably more experience at cooking than most of the scientists. Cooking for eighteen colleagues involved substantial anxiety for the likes of Azzi, Ninnis and Percy Correll, a mechanic who at just nineteen was the youngest among us. They were easily intimidated by the usual criticism, no matter how good-humoured. It was the job of mess man, or cook's assistant, that was the least popular, as the mess man was the slave of the cook and responsible for all cleaning and dirty work. It was a great leveller for anyone getting a little uppity and there were a few of these emerging in our small, remote colony.

Hannam, Hunter, Laseron and I were the most confident and flamboyant in our cooking. We founded the Society of Unconventional Cooks, distinguishing ourselves from those slavish disciples of Mrs Beeton. There were others who became known as Crook Cooks. The stove was, of course, the focal point in our winter quarters around which all else revolved. It was the source of heat and life through the long dark winter that followed. The stove kept the hut at a temperature just above freezing point, which Mawson directed as ideal for maintaining an active work environment. And of course with eighteen men in a small space and washing at best a weekly and more commonly a monthly activity, the hut had the pungency of stale wet socks. This was best dealt with by keeping things frozen.

I enjoyed my stints as nightwatchman. The night watch was really the only time I had the hut to myself. It was ideal for writing up my diary, cleaning and maintaining cameras and lenses, or working in the darkroom. I did my best work in the quiet of the evening. Mawson ran a strict regime of lights-out for all. The night watch called 'Rise and shine' at eight o'clock in the morning. Sleep patterns, said Mawson, were an important tool in fighting melancholy. 'Hurley to bed, Hurley to rise . . .' was a rare glimpse of his sense of humour.

Hut life offered little or no privacy other than by the curtain of garments strung on lines to dry above the stove. With little natural light, vigilance was required, and on more than one occasion, without a word to anyone, I fished a sock or glove out of the evening meal. The hut was of course crowded with equipment and specimens in various stages of drying. In between meals the trestle table was everyone's work desk. The bunks in the daytime were for resting and letter writing, though, of course, there was no postman.

The bunks and sleeping arrangements were cramped and the men were not quiet sleepers. They slept fitfully, tossing and turning, appearing to wake and and even calling out. Some fellows were not at all discreet in pleasuring themselves under their blankets. Were it not for the blizzard outside the cacophony would have been intolerable, and only when the wind stopped and the snoring orchestra swelled to crescendo did they wake, protest at their neighbour and then roll over and fall asleep again.

I was relieved at how most of the men accepted me, even though I was not a 'varsity chum'. I befriended Azzi Webb, whom others complained was young and cocky. I heard the same said about me, and maybe that's why we got on. Ninnis, despite his very proper upbringing and posh accent, was always eager to join in, as was Mertz. Young Percy Correll was a jack of all trades, a bit like me. Bickerton was the handsome dashing adventurer type. Bage, Laseron, McLean, Close, Hunter, Hodgeman, Stillwell and Murphy were always cheerful and laughed at my jokes, or at least laughed at me. Hannam was curt, perhaps because of the failure of his wireless, and only Madigan and Whetter ignored me altogether.

At times it was hard to keep up with all the banter around the table which had become the centre for all activities. I imagined this banter was part of university life. Controversial topics could be fiercely debated over several days. I quickly learned not to pipe up with any idle opinion. The simplest remarks were liable to be ruthlessly attacked and debunked. 'Should women smoke?' had the hut split for days into rival camps. 'Do women prefer university men?' I thought was one-sided balderdash, especially in the absence of women. I stayed out of the debate 'Can a gentleman vote Labor?' lest someone ask my father's occupation.

Women were a frequent subject of interest. The hut contained experts on most subjects, but we had no expert on the opposite sex. None of us had, as Bage joked, a 'trouble and strife'. Those whose bunks featured a portrait of a young woman were closely questioned for all details of interest until tempers started to fray. Madigan's girl, Wynne, was very fine looking and the pick of the crop. Hunter's portrait of his girl only emerged on special occasions.

'She gave me her picture to bring away but I don't expect she thinks about me,' he said. 'I hope *Aurora* brings a letter from her.'

'That's tricky, old chap,' offered Azzi. 'My girl's keen as mustard, writes a good letter too.'

'What about you, Hoyle?' asked Bob Bage. 'Who's waiting for you?'

As my romantic prospects were non-existent, I opted for humour. 'Didn't you see them all at the dock?'

'Come on, confide in us, your secrets won't leave this room,' urged Bage. 'Tell us about those girls in Hobart.'

'Oh, those girls. Well they ate my strawberries and cream and still wouldn't give their address.'

'More information, Hoyle.' The others were now banging on the table. There was no escape.

'Alright then. Well, if you must know, I've had many affairs of the heart. But the trouble with all my love affairs is that the objects of my affection know nothing about it. My love is of the unrequited kind.'

'Tell us who!'

'The first girl I was keen on I met at school. I didn't know any better and told her straight out I liked her. She just shrieked, "Oh no, not you. You've got gollywog hair!"'

This caused much laughter. 'Since then, well, I've had more rejections than hot dinners. Before I left Sydney I spoke to a girl who didn't mind my barbed-wire hair, but as soon as she found out I was going with Mawson that was an end to it. "What, that madman?" she said "He's off his rocker!"'

When we first arrived at Commonwealth Bay, the nights were dark only for an hour or so when the sun dropped briefly below the horizon. But by April it was dark even at breakfast time. One morning I woke early to find the hut unusually cold. The fire had gone out and there was no sign of Percy Correll, the night watch. I checked the logbook and saw his last entry had been made not long after midnight. I threw coals and some fuel on to start the fire, quickly dressed in outdoor gear and crampons, and alerted Mawson as I left.

Outside the hut it was forty degrees below freezing. The air was solid snowdrift and the wind was gale-strength. In these conditions we usually followed rope and wire leads to find our way. It was only the gale that conveyed any sense of direction. Calling out was of little use and I decided to return and get help. Then, only a few yards in front of me, I saw what looked like a boulder in a small hollow. I slid alongside and found it was Correll, facedown in the snow on his knees as if praying. He let out a cry as I bumped into him.

'Percy!' I yelled, but he could not speak. Nor could he stand up. I lifted him over my shoulder and stumbled back what was no more than twenty yards to the drop down to the hut entrance.

Once inside we put him in a sleeping bag in front of the stove. That evening he explained, 'I had gone out to the coal stack and was coming back with a full armload when a gust knocked me down. I rolled several times before I finally anchored myself. I was fine, but after walking back into the wind the hut was not where I expected. I backtracked and tried again but found nothing I recognised. I tried twice more. I couldn't find anything to get a bearing on. I thought I'd wait till the visibility improved.'

We all knew it had been a close shave.

Winter dragged on. We yearned for sunlight but we knew also we would then have to leave the relative safety of the hut. I worked my way along the bookshelves. I was determined to participate in the evening pastime of reading aloud favourite pieces. Each of the men could recite a favourite poem. I became a specialist in performing Coleridge's 'Rime of the Ancient Mariner' with dramatic gesticulations.

The ice was here, the ice was there,
The ice was all around . . .

Mawson frequently read in a schoolmasterly tone from his well-thumbed copy of Marcus Aurelius's *Meditations*.

Frank Bickerton could do a fine version of Henley's 'Captain of my Soul':

Out of the night that covers me,
Black as the pit from pole to pole,
I thank whatever gods may be
For my unconquerable soul.

Kipling was popular with everyone, and Bob Bage was regularly called upon to give his version of 'Gunga Din', which never ceased to impress me:

'E carried me away
To where a dooli lay,
An' a bullet come an' drilled the beggar clean.
'E put me safe inside,
An' just before he died:
'I 'ope you liked your drink' sez Gunga Din.

And with a strong emotional finish:

Tho I've belted you and flayed you
By the living Gawd that made you,
You're a better man than I am Gunga Din!

But the all up favourite was the young adventurer poet Robert Service, who had left Scotland to travel to the Yukon and the Arctic.

From the Pole unto the Tropics is there trail ye have not dared
And because you hold death lightly so by death shall you be spared.

Mawson and Bage, though, preferred Browning and said Service was a mere rhymer.

However the work I read most was the *Encyclopaedia Britannica*, usually with the *Oxford Dictionary* alongside. I was assiduous in making up for my lack of formal schooling. Every day I learned new words and tried them out in my diary.

With the onset of winter the water in Commonwealth Bay commenced to freeze. Standing on the edge I could see water turn into blocks of ice in the midst of the kelp. The kelp was then stretched to breaking point as the ice floated upwards, sometimes breaking free and taking a small forest with it.

Smaller crystals of ice were constantly freezing and drifting to the surface. This ice was then immediately blown northwards. If the wind paused, these crystals would cling together and form a serrated crust on the sea. If the wind held off for a few hours, the crust would become thick and strong enough to bear the weight of a man.

After a still day, virtually the whole bay had frozen. The temperature was some sixty degrees below freezing point. The iceshelf presented a spectacular promenade around the base of the frozen white cliffs, which were unapproachable for much of the year. I lugged my camera and tripod out onto the ice, which readily took the combined weight. I walked over a mile, following the edge of the sea cliffs to the north-east. The crystal walls rose some two hundred feet above me, often in a sheer vertical rise.

I had set out alone, driven by the novelty of the opportunity. The isolated location gave rise to that sense of one's insignificance. I looked up at the unclimbed precipices and drew my breath nervously, wondering how best to capture the sense of awe they created in me. In the absence of the blizzard my breathing and the crunch of my boots on the ice were the only sounds I could hear.

It was first a groan then a slow grinding crack which loosened the plate of ice on which I stood. In slow motion my legs descended, the tripod wobbled and the heavy camera fell away from me, but without breaking through the ice. My outstretched arms arrested my descent through the ice plate. Apart from shock from the cold, I could feel a strong westwards current dragging me under the ice. Instinctively I kicked and launched my torso out of the water and up onto the ice. As I put weight on my elbows the ice gently continued to crack and I was swimming again. My legs were being swept sidewards under the ice and I tried lifting myself more frantically, but the ice, once fractured, would not hold my weight. As all feeling in my legs drained away, the stupid futility of my predicament began to overwhelm me. I had pursued my own company once too often and there was no one to assist, let alone observe my demise. Fighting against rising panic, I pushed the camera forwards using a leg of the tripod and dragged myself towards a lump of berg that was wedged in the plate ice. The iceberg had solid handholds; grabbing them I dragged my frozen body out of the sea.

I lay prostrate only momentarily, as I knew I would die of exposure if I did not make it back to shelter quickly. I moved as carefully as I could back across the plate ice. Even as I did, snowdrift commenced swirling wildly off the cliff tops, the wind picking up and the sky darkening. The blizzard whipped along the shoreline of the bay, fracturing small ice formations, and here and there the ice plate broke and wind waves formed in the newly opened stretches of water. Within minutes the scudding wind and the turbulence of the waves broke up the entire mile or so of plate ice that I had walked across. The ice was driven northwards and the whole of Commonwealth Bay became a tumult of whitecaps.

My heart raced as I pushed myself homewards through the freezing chill of the blizzard. My saturated clothes gave no protection and were heavy as lead. The wind leached away any body warmth I had left. My legs chafed badly in trousers as solid as stovepipes. I fell down the entrance to the hut and delivered the badly knocked-about camera to a stunned-looking Ninnis. With my remaining energy, and cheered on by my amused colleagues, I stripped in front of the stove. It was some time before I could control my jaw so as to speak.

Midwinter, and the sun appeared less and less, until it stayed away altogether, though a few hours of twilight each day reminded us of its existence. I yearned to be outside using the cameras but it was gloomy at best and opportunities were few. I was confident I knew the kind of pictures that would sell well. My images would not just be for scientists but for the general public. Winter, however, meant staying in the hut, waiting for the weather to improve. Tempers frayed. On Midwinter's Day Azzi, in a fit of pique with Mawson, walked out of my carefully planned flashlight portrait of our whole group and could not be persuaded to return.

We were kept busy with preparations for spring and Mawson's plans for multiple sledging expeditions. Our tents were restitched and reinforced, sledging harnesses adjusted and crampons fashioned and fitted. The biologists and geologists were busy poring over and labelling specimens spread across the trestle table. I stumped them all for a short time with a curious piece of moraine I found. 'Volcanic pumice,' they confidently opined until I eventually disclosed it was a discarded attempt at fruit loaf the dogs had dug up.

I remained in awe of Mawson and sought to impress him with my enthusiasm for the expedition. I fervently hoped that once winter was over there would be ample opportunities for camera and cinematograph. I had no idea what scientific advances could be made, but I knew my photographs would be unique.

It was during the winter that I realised not everyone was as enamoured with Mawson as I was. I had naively assumed that the other expedition members, being handpicked by Mawson, well-educated and from similar backgrounds, would be entirely harmonious and stick together like glue. I was surprised when I first heard criticisms of Mawson's leadership. Mawson did not pursue popularity and things had not been going well. Instead of three Antarctic bases we only had one, maybe two if Wild had found a landfall. We had failed to get beyond five miles from our hut and no inland depots had been established. Hunter could do no marine dredging due to the loss of our boat, our aeroplane had no wings and the blizzard prevented any testing of its use as a tractor. Wireless transmission had proven impossible and was a most depressing failure. The blizzard also prevented geographic work and it was plain to all that sledging trips would be perilous. Madigan and Azzi openly questioned Mawson's geological fieldwork. It was Madigan who first described Mawson as 'Dux Ipse', which Azzi explained meant 'the leader himself'. Mawson was an authoritarian. He behaved like a schoolmaster and Dux Ipse, or DI, became his nickname. I never used it. I knew that life for him was a serious business. He was able to take conflict in his stride. He was damn keen the expedition be a success and so was I.

Every Sunday morning Mawson gave a religious service. He called everyone to the table and, once we were seated, he would stand and ask God to bless the work of the expedition. Then he read aloud the Gospel from his prayer book and sometimes Bage or Madigan did a scripture reading. Not being overly familiar with the Common Book of Prayer I always took a back seat. Prayers were followed by the singing of hymns, which we all joined in. A small pedal organ had been shipped on *Aurora* but it sounded dreadful. Bickerton tinkered with it till all its pipes were in working order. He now accompanied the hymns, growing louder as his confidence grew. 'Nearer My God to Thee' was a favourite. I imagined I was the only Catholic among the expeditioners. In Mawson's circles a Catholic upbringing was a liability and I kept it to myself. Much to Ma's disappointment I had stopped going to church after running away from home.

And it was in the darkness of winter, and despite our weekly religious services, that I witnessed fracturing in the naive picture I had of our small community. By that time many days passed in mundane repetitive activities and mood swings created a tetchiness from which not even Mawson was exempt. During one of my weeks rostered as cook, I experienced a lot of trouble with Whetter. As a medical doctor he was luckily not in demand. Instead, Mawson had given him the daily task of cutting and retrieving blocks of ice to maintain our water supply. This was a constant and laborious job and Whetter resented it greatly. After initially appearing not to hear my requests for ice, he said, 'I've already brought in the ice for today, Hurley. You'll have to organise yourself better tomorrow.' He continued reading as he lay on his bunk. He had a superior air about him and I knew enough not to take him on. Mawson, however, had also sought his assistance digging out snowdrift from the entrance.

'Why on earth have you come on this expedition if you have no intention of helping?' Mawson's raised voice froze all activity and conversations throughout the hut.

'Well I certainly didn't come to do labouring and cleaning all day!' Whetter retorted.

'What on earth did you expect? You're a blasted fool if you believed others were going to do all the jobs for you.'

'We'll see who's a blasted fool!'

There was a long silence and then Mawson dropped his voice and the conflict moved into Mawson's tiny room, and we were all able to listen without having to feel embarrassed.

Any vanities or personal failings were dealt with mercilessly by our hut society.

'Championship, championship!' was the sarcastic cry in vogue with the university set, and was soon adopted by all who witnessed any act of human folly. Bob Bage left a frozen tin of red kidney beans on the stove to thaw and forgot about it. The tin exploded, spraying red kidney beans through the hut, the bunks, the clothes drying and all who were nearby. This was followed by cries of 'Championship!' The red kidney bean stains could still be seen on the roof and walls the following year.

Though, for my part, I did not fancy being the object of ridicule and kept my gaffes to myself, I was always keen however to lighten the mood. A dead penguin in Hunter's bed was a good start. For the gamblers among us I converted a cinefilm winder into a roulette wheel and ran a chocolate bank. Together, Hunter, Bage and I devised all sorts of pranks and tricks to stir things up. This developed into the Society for Prevention of the Blues, with its crowning achievement being a midwinter operetta. I put to good use tricks and practical jokes I had seen Big Bill perform at Sandford's in Lithgow. On one occasion when tensions developed across the work table I attached thin acetylene tubing from my mouth through my beard. After lighting my pipe I broke the sombre mood by appearing to blow smoke out my ears. I was quite happy being the centre of attention if it was comical. When I'd had enough company I would retreat to the darkroom.

When the blizzard was at its most turbulent, the aurora was most dramatic and Azzi's magnetograph most erratic. Late one evening, Azzi came in from the magnetograph hut. 'It's a clear night outside for the lights.'

Mertz jumped up. 'I vill come.'

He and I quickly grabbed our Burberry jackets and mitts, and stood in the lee of the hut, unable to converse due to the din of the wind off the roof. The three of us peered up into the northern sky. Low in the sky to the north-east was a flat yellow glow. It pulsed softly then unfurled upwards a shimmering green, flickering in the darkness and transforming like flames to shades of red and purple, fading then glowing then fading into a blackness in which the southern constellations of stars reappeared. The aurora was a mystery. I could not register the colours of its emanations on a glass plate. It was a creature of the Antarctic night that defied photography.

Without warning the blizzard eased, then stopped altogether. The drift swirled upwards then settled. We stumbled away from the hut and looked back to see the dark line of the Antarctic plateau. Azzi and Mertz went inside to warm up but, driven by restlessness, I strode down to the edge of the bay and along the western shore. It was bitter. I had reindeer-fur boots, finneskos, on my feet without crampons and it was a rare pleasure to walk without being belted by the wind. I pushed on up the rise till I had a fine view across the plate ice and the ocean beyond. My finneskos squeaked as I stepped through snow.

At the edge of the cliff I stopped. I heard the muffled sound of footsteps behind me and turned, but saw no one there. To the north, above the distant glimmer of sea and beyond, the ice plate was darkness, though somewhere beneath that darkness was home. I revelled in this small interval of solitude. My body would soon be shaking with cold and I knew I must return to the society of the hut, but the overwhelming silence held me in a trance and my legs refused to turn about.

From where I stood I could make out the faintest sound of bells as small icicles snapped off and rolled down the ice slope to the frozen sea, tinkling as they bounced from top to bottom. A memory stirred within and I uttered Tennyson's '*Break, break, break, on thy cold gray stones, O sea*'. There were no stones visible here. '*I would that my tongue could utter the thoughts that arise in me.*' I thought of a tram in George Street and a middle-aged man in a suit slumping forwards from his seat. I thought of my mother having to move out of our family home. Since departing on the expedition I had barely spared a thought for family. I felt both shame and sadness welling up, and regret that I, of all people, did not have a single photograph of my own parents.

'Hurley, you've no crampons on, and the wind will be back up in a matter of minutes, man!' It was Mawson, calling through the still night air. 'What were you thinking?'

I turned away from the scene, my face deep within the hood of my jacket.

4

South Magnetic Pole, 1912

The four of us huddled together around the table in the hut, our faces only a few feet apart so we could hear each other above the roar of the blizzard.

'Azzi,' said Mawson, 'I want you to leave everything to Bob apart from magnetic readings. This is your opportunity to get the first set of truly accurate readings all the way to the South Magnetic Pole. But Bob will be in command. It will be his decision that determines how fast you go, how far you go and which way you go.'

I was pleased to be sledging with Bob and Azzi. Bob Bage was an Australian army lieutenant with an engineering degree and skilled in astronomy. I assumed he was older than me, but this was due more to his neatly trimmed beard, balding pate and pipe. Whatever the scrape, he was always calm. Our objective was the South Magnetic Pole, which Azzi informed me was not as distant as the South Geographic Pole, but was constantly moving. Not only that, so close to the pole compasses ceased to be reliable. Mawson had arranged other parties to map the coastline both east and west of Commonwealth Bay. Mawson, Ninnis and Mertz were doing the longest trip; using dogs to pull the sledges, they were heading east to join up on the map with the areas explored by Scott and Shackleton.

Azzi looked up. 'What if, once we are up on the plateau, magnetic south turns out to be an entirely different direction to its current bearing? What if there is no reliable heading?'

Mawson nodded. 'If the compass needle starts taking you in circles, it will be Bob's call as to whether you follow a bearing or simply head geographic south. I'm afraid it's going to be a massive dash to get as far as you can.'

Mawson then turned to me. 'Frank, your priority is to help Azzi get the best readings he can up there without losing your hands to frostbite. Take photographs when you can, but no cine camera. Eight hundred pounds is already too much weight on the sledge.'

And so, on 10 November 1912, Bage, Azzi and I left the hut and made our way the five miles to Aladdin's Cave, which had been dug out in the spring as a supply depot and emergency accommodation. It was no more than a vertical shaft leading into our manmade cavern with room for four to sleep. Mawson, Ninnis and Mertz were at Aladdin's Cave that day. They had two sledges and dog teams, and were making their final adjustments. They expected to travel the greatest distance but we would be going the furthest south. We were both due to return in twelve weeks.

We loaded some extra supplies onto our sledge and attached a mileage wheel at the back. Bob was anxious to keep moving. Mawson decided his party would stay overnight in Aladdin's Cave. There was a high level of excitement and nerves. I took photographs of our two groups, then we said our farewells.

I joked with Mertz as we removed mitts to shake hands, 'If you bump into Captain Scott or the Norwegians make sure you get their autographs.'

'Ya, I can say hello to Captain Scott. He vud be surprised to see Ninn and I here with the Australians.'

'We're not as famous but we'll do alright. Though I reckon our journey would be faster if we had you and your dog team.'

'Ya, you like zee dogs. The Doctor is not so keen. He is telling me Norwegians eat their dogs. I would like to bring them home. Vee vill see. God speed you.'

•

Starting at Aladdin's Cave saves us having to pull a full sledge up the steep slope from the hut. However, it is still uphill from Aladdin's and this is our first crack at man-hauling an eight-hundred-pound sledge. Half this weight is food, though, so we can look forward to the load gradually lightening. Mawson has calculated the amount of food our bodies require to pull the sledge four hundred miles in adverse conditions.

That first few hundred yards from Aladdin's is daunting. None of us say it, but pulling that load is backbreaking. The harness has shoulder straps as well as a belt and it is the shoulders that take most of the load. It's hard to believe we could possibly make anything like the distances required. Over winter there has been no opportunity to train. We are out of condition and our technique and coordination are poor. It is a case of putting our heads down and pulling together as best we can. We have a support team waiting for us at Eleven Mile, which is the furthest food depot we established in spring. John Hunter, Herbert Murphy and Joe Laseron should be there, and I am determined to reach them that evening, if only to have help the next day.

The harness pinches and rubs as I shift my weight. Several times I drop down through soft snow to my waist. On one occasion I look up to see Bage and Azzi have likewise dropped through a snow-filled crevasse. The weight of the sledge starts to drag the three of us backwards through the snow until Azzi forces the brake lever into the snowdrift so we can find our feet.

Any loss of momentum is energy-sapping, so we avoid stopping. Even so, it is almost midnight when we finally come upon Eleven Mile camp. The three-man support crew there have a meal ready and help to set up our tent. We collapse inside and do not emerge for twelve hours, feeling very stiff and sore.

As soon as we start the following day it commences snowing and the wind starts to rise as conditions decline. We are so unaccustomed to dealing with the load and coping with the fierce drift in our faces that we have only covered three miles when Bob wisely calls a stop for the day. The wind by then is seventy miles an hour. We have no idea what it could get up to on the plateau, but we know setting up camp in these conditions is not easy. As soon as we secure the sledge I grab the pick and break off several large blocks of ice. We need these to prevent the tent blowing away. Bob pulls out the tent which, due to the difficulty of assembling in windy conditions, already has internal bamboo poles fitted into its apex.

With Bob holding the tent flat on the ground pointing windwards and with the entrance topside, Azzi crawls under and into the tent and lifts and spreads the poles, pushing into the wind as the leeward side drops down behind him. Bob rolls his whole weight onto the bottom windward edge, from which extends a large flap for this purpose. I then move across the blocks of ice to take Bob's place holding down the tent and then shovel snow to bed down the windward side and around all edges. Bob and I pass gear from the sledge to Azzi inside the tent, including a canvas floor, our cooker, a ration bag and our reindeer-skin sleeping bags.

The tent has a yard-long tunnel entranceway which Bob and I shove ourselves through and tie up behind us. Once inside the tent and out of the claws of the blizzard, my exertion stops and as my body slows, my sweat cools, and I start to shiver. I get my Burberry trousers off and wriggle into my frozen sleeping bag, keeping my arms out so I can start the primus and make dinner. It's a long time before I feel any sensation of warmth from the sleeping bag. We don't speak because it is impossible to hear anything over the frightful racket the tent is making. The tent legs have not been stretched far enough apart and the japara fabric is vibrating and cracking in the gale. Pushing out the leeward legs from the inside is only a slight improvement and none of us are keen to go outside and fix it properly.

Azzi shoves snow into our Nansen cooker. The ice protrudes above the pan like a snow covered mountain. It quickly melts down and Azzi empties in the pemmican dried beef pre-mixed with pure fat and then ground Plasmon biscuits. As soon as this is steaming hot I pour it into three mugs. This is our 'hoosh', which we will have for dinner and breakfast every day. It is remarkable how we come to crave this porridge-like mixture. I refill the cooker with ice. By the time Bob and Azzi have finished their hoosh, the water is steaming again. This time I pour in our special mix of cocoa, sugar and glaxo milk powder.

The wind does not abate and I do not sleep well. The tent cracks like a whip above my head and my nerves feel every gust. I am anxious as to whether the japara will hold up till morning.

The next day, conditions prevent us from sledging. I don't get out of my sleeping bag, but I do start up a new diary for the sledging trip.

On 13 November the wind drops noticeably. We eat hoosh and bread. I find my pants but they are like flattened stove-pipes. A crowbar would help to open them and get my legs through. I have been lying on my woollen helmet and it is crushed flat, as are my mitts and gloves. I have forgotten to put these in my sleeping bag and they have frozen solid. I shove them under my jumper next to my undershirt to soften them up, and in the meantime get my boots and crampons ready and all my other loose items. There's only enough room for two of us to sit up and get dressed at the same time, so Azzi stays in his bag watching Bob and me twist and turn and bump into each other.

Yesterday, during the blizzard, Bob and I lifted a section of tent floor and dug a small hole for urinating. I need to open my bowels so I rush to get outside and do my business before the wind picks up. I walk downwind and take a shovel with me. Wedged in ice, the shovel gives me something to hold to avoid being blown backwards off my haunches. In blizzard conditions it is only possible to defecate if a companion supports and holds a groundsheet around you to stop you freezing. There is no water so hand-cleaning requires vigorous rubbing in the snow, and quickly to avoid frostbite. I have learned to shake out the few inches of snowdrift which accumulate in my undershorts before I pull them up.

As soon as I have finished my business I am keen to pack the sledge and go. 'Come on, pass out the cooking bag,' I call to Bob and Azzi, and in rhyming slang, 'Let's hit the frog and toad.' I find I am the most impatient; Bob especially seems to take forever getting ready. The cooker and the floor come out and are packed away, sleeping bags are shoved in canvas covers. Azzi stays inside holding down the tent as I clear off the snow blocks and Bob and I collapse the tent into the wind and get it on the sledge.

We are moving quickly now, yet it takes an inordinate time before we are ready to start pulling the sledge. We soon learn the three of us need to be ready at the same time; standing around in the cold waiting for one of us to adjust a harness strap or gaiter is deadly. Bob releases the brake and we lean forwards with weight in our shoulders, but the sledge does not shift. It is frozen in like a cake decoration. I grab the pick and smash away the ice along the runners. Even then the sledge does not move, so deep is the snow.

'One ... two ... three ... *pull*!' Bob says, and with an almighty grunt the sledge starts to slide forwards—then drops down into even deeper drift. 'Again! One ... two ... and *three*,' says Bob, and we are on our way.

We have not waited for our support party to start with us, but it is not long before they catch up with their smaller sledge. We move slowly as the snow is deep and our boots plunge down one or two feet before finding traction. The sledge runners remain out of sight, buried several inches beneath the snow. It is backbreaking pulling through soft snow. After some hours the névé, or compacted snow, hardens in patches and when I step forwards my boots temporarily find support on the icy crust, though as my weight transfers they unpredictably drop further down into the snow. This is energy-sapping even without the sledge. Later the névé hardens and the sledge sits on top of the ice. It is as if the burden has been halved.

I keep my head down to minimise the ferocity of the drift smacking into my face. It no longer stings, as my face is totally numb, but I know my skin will be red raw by the time we stop. I concentrate on the snow ahead of each step, only occasionally looking up. Progress is imperceptible and our destination is obscured in the drift. My goggles are clogged with ice, but if I tilt my head down I can still see through a little gap at the top. At times it is a complete white-out. The drift swirls in the wind and plays tricks. The wind changes direction just enough to send you off course until the next compass check. Then, when I can no longer see my legs at all, I lift and shake my goggles and miraculously the air is clear.

My companions are only a few yards away but we are each locked in our own thoughts. Conversation is impossible and so my mind wanders over matters both basic and bizarre.

I think of our next food stop and how long before I need a comfort stop. I speculate about soreness in my back and legs and whether it is getting worse. I think about home, and the summer weather in Sydney, and the hotels and refreshment houses selling iced drinks along George Street. I think about Ma and wonder if my pa is somewhere watching me trudge along. What would he make of what I am doing now?

It is 9 p.m. when Bob calls a halt. It has been hard going and our mileage wheel says we've only travelled five miles. I am thick with snow and ice. It is packed around my face and hood, it is lodged between my mitts and the sleeves of my Burberry jacket, it is glued to my boots and wedged above my ankles. It is solidly encrusted on all straps and lanyards and will not simply shake off but hangs in icicles from my clothing and hair. We put up the tent, throw in all the gear we need and crawl in. The temptation is to collapse, but this would be a mistake. The iced-up clothing must be removed and dry or dryish clothes put on before we lose body heat. I force open my sleeping bag and shove my legs in. There is no feeling in my feet. The sleeping bag is cold and hard but gradually warms to become soft and damp.

We sleep on and off for twelve hours, such is our exhaustion and reaction to the cold. But the next day the wind is up to seventy-five miles an hour and it is a miserable forty-eight degrees below freezing. Ripped seams and tears have appeared in the tent. I take off my mitts and gloves to grip a sewing needle to fix these before they worsen. Azzi holds that part of the tent still and Bob stands outside the tent, using pliers to grip the needle and pull it through and push it back into the frozen calico. It takes hours, but a tent torn apart by a blizzard means death. Our fingers are frostbitten and take the rest of the day to recover. I am unable to hold a pen to write up my diary and instead lie in my sleeping bag shivering, with my hands clasped between my legs.

At noon on 16 November the wind abates and we quickly head south, followed by our support party. The surface is rock hard with sastrugi, wind-carved ice ridges, between six inches and two feet high presenting a series of solid obstacles for the sled. As we pull we look back to steer the runners in between these blocks which otherwise stop us in our tracks. Bob calls to us to look up and there to the south, rising above the plateau, are dark heavy nimbus clouds rolling towards us. We stop and secure the sledge, and no sooner is the tent up than the wind stops altogether and for the first time ever the tent walls are entirely limp. All is quiet. It is as if the wax has been cleaned from our ears. Hunter, Murphy and Laseron have put up their tent several yards away and when they converse their voices seem to be booming. We prepare our evening meal in this suspenseful silence. I have a sensation of being watched from afar. I ruminate it may be our Maker watching us, testing our resolve. After eating we are dog tired and we hop into our bags, but, unusually for me, I can't drop off.

'Hey, Hunter, Murphy, Laseron!' Bage is sitting up alongside me, calling out to the other tent. 'You chaps are the bloody support team. Get out here and throw some snow against our tent or we'll never get to sleep!'

An answer comes back suggesting Bob should go somewhere. I hope God is not listening too closely. Things must be getting to Bob, who is usually very calm.

It is early when we wake. The wind is light and there is barely any cloud. We are soon away and without the wind the temperature rises rapidly to a startling nine degrees above freezing. After an hour my clothing is drenched not from melted snow but from sweat. We call a halt and pack away our Burberry outer jackets, woollen helmets and mitts. Within another half-hour we are forced to stop again to pack away jumpers and balaclavas. We also retrieve and open our sleeping bags and drape them inside out across the sledge to dry.

We eventually are hauling in our underclothes and feeling very light at heart. When we stop we have done almost twelve miles.

Conditions remain favourable for three days and we haul till late each evening.

On the third day Bob is having trouble with snow blindness. He has been leading and has had his goggles off for extended periods. That night I put zinc and cocaine tabloids under his eyelids. It is not only Bob who is suffering; a couple of our supports are in real trouble after this solid push. Murphy is snow blind and is forced to sledge with a blindfold over his eyes. Johnny Hunter is going well, but Laseron is done in. That evening after dinner we all squeeze into one tent and Bob announces we will establish Southern Cross Depot, our first supply depot for the return journey, right where we are, sixty-eight miles from winter quarters at Commonwealth Bay. We have climbed to more than four thousand feet above sea level. The support party is to head back.

In the morning we cut up blocks of ice and erect a mound ten feet high with a flag at about twenty feet. It should be visible within eight miles of the depot if the weather is clear. Even though the support party would have slowed us down, I feel incredibly lonely saying goodbye.

It is Azzi's birthday. The blizzard blows without pause and we spend all day in our sleeping bags. Azzi surprises us with cigars, which we smoke around the cooker. Bob and I reciprocate by singing 'Happy Birthday' and 'Freeze a Jolly Good Fellow'.

I ask Bage how many days it will be till we reach the giant magnet.

'I'm afraid, Hoyle, the South Magnetic Pole is a more subtle concept and more elusive than the South Geographic Pole.' Bob continues, 'The magnetic poles have a restlessness to them, they are forever shifting. Even more confounding is the fact that wherever on earth you are gives a different indication of magnetic north. So you can only know where it is when you are there. That's when our dip circle points straight down.'

'I'm sorry I asked. I won't be able to sleep now.'

'I shouldn't worry about it. These forces are generated beneath the earth. No one knows much about them.'

Next day, the wind drops to thirty miles an hour and we head south again. The sastrugi are bigger, often about two feet high and very uneven. The sledge drops off the side of these ridges and either digs in or overturns. When the wind lifts to sixty miles an hour we have had enough and make camp. In the tent the walls shudder and crack with the wind gusts. I had previously taken comfort in the fact that if the tent burst we had our support party nearby, but now we are in a more perilous state. Even though I have achieved relative warmth in my bag, I am unable to sleep while worrying about the tent. I announce to Bob I am going outside to build a wall. I start the slow process of getting back into my outside gear. Bob joins me outside and together we break off large pieces of sastrugi and cut blocks of ice. It takes longer than I expected, but after a few hours we have a five-foot-high wall along the windward side of the tent. Back inside the tent our abode feels more secure and I fall asleep from exhaustion.

The gale continues the following day and we stay put. Two snow petrels take a liking to my wall and make a resting place out of the wind. I have seen no birds since leaving Commonwealth Bay. I can't imagine what they are doing here or where they are going. They are equally bemused by me and let me approach. With great difficulty I manage to get photographs of them. To set the shutter I first have to remove a number of tiny camera screws and bend the mechanism into shape. This must be done and the photo taken within a minute of taking off my mitts, after which my bare hands are useless. As it is I do not get sensation back until much later, when I am in my sleeping bag.

In the cold conditions our bodies crave sleep and it is 10 a.m. when we rise and see the wind has dropped considerably. We convert the wall into a mound to assist navigation on our return journey. It takes four hours for Azzi to complete his magnetic readings and Bob his meteorological measurements. Azzi says there are magnetic storms playing havoc with his observations.

It is my day to lead the sledge and I find it hard getting started and timing our combined efforts to lift the sledge over obstacles. The first mile exhausts me and I start to worry that the other two must be expecting me to hand the lead back to Bob. However we clock up a second mile and, after a ration of barley sugar and chocolate, we soon have five miles, at which point we huddle together in the lee of the sledge for a lunch of hard Plasmon biscuits with a slab of butter. Usually at lunch we dig a hole a few feet deep with an ice windbreak and sometimes a tarpaulin roof. This provides shelter for longitude observation and Azzi's magnetograph, but also for melting ice and making tea on the primus. Not today, however. Within five minutes of stopping the cold really sets in and the only thing for it is to keep going to warm up. It is after 11 p.m. with the sun about to disappear, when we call a halt, having clocked up our best day yet—over twelve miles.

Our hopes to repeat this mileage the following day are dashed by a wind over sixty miles an hour. We don't make a start till after 2 p.m. I am unsure whether we are overtired or if the blizzard is just plain vicious, but we struggle for every yard and at 6 p.m. pull up short without having done even five miles. We construct a windbreak and put up the tent. Both Bage and Azzi's cheeks have white pinch marks, telltale signs of frostbite which neither has detected due to their faces being numb. My own lips are split and my eyes stinging. The temptation as always is to collapse, but we crave food, and after melting snow we soon have a steaming hoosh, which revives us. Afterwards Azzi disappears completely in his bag. Bob is propped up on one elbow smoking his pipe with a distant look in his eyes and apologising for the acrid smoke in the tent. It is impossible to begrudge Bob this pleasure.

The wind does not abate overnight and we wait in our finnesko bags with the tent shaking as the gale roars above us until after midday, when we decide to make a go of it. Based on Azzi's readings and Bage's sun compass we alter course slightly to head due south. Being close to the magnetic pole my own compass has become lethargic and of little use. This section of the plateau starts rising again and we find ourselves negotiating a difficult slope. Between each spurt we pull the brake down to enable a small rest. We started off today with a small quantity of water but it has now frozen. Sucking ice does not quench the thirst and burns the inside of my mouth.

The next day is worse with the wind blowing down on top of us and penetrating every gap in our clothing. With each step we first hold the weight of the sledge and then lean and push forwards. The sledge has no forward momentum and regularly snags on sastrugi, which rise up to oppose progress. We only make four miles. Our axe and theodolite are missing. They have been left behind and Azzi walks back to find them.

The controls on my plate glass camera have become frozen and are almost impossible to move, especially after being in open air for any length of time. I have developed blisters on both hands from forcing open and adjusting the mechanism. The fluid in the blisters has now frozen, which is extremely painful. Only in the warmth of the tent can I lance the blisters to drain the fluid. I need good hard calluses on my fingers not just for photographic work but for tying and untying knots and toggles on everything from food bags to the tent.

It is now December and the sun is still shining at midnight. It is disorientating not to have darkness call an end to our daily sledging efforts. As we climb the plateau, the ice has changed and is here deeply furrowed by the wind. We pass over undulations gradually leading to the top of a rise, only to see the next ridge several hundred yards away. Time and time again the sledge slides sidewards and turns over. Righting the sledge necessitates removing most of the load and saps our energy.

On 3 December we find ourselves in a valley running east-south-east. Facing us are three large mounds of ice which rise up a few hundred feet. As we drag the sledge over the southern edge of the valley we see a maze of large crevasses, between which are lengthy ramps of accumulated ice. The crevasses are bridged with snow. The snow bridges appear solid, though many have sunk below the lip of the crevasse. Bage names this area 'the Nodules'. This evening at camp we raise our flags to celebrate the dowager queen's birthday and and Bob and I use the occasion to light up a cigar each.

As we sledge south from the Nodules the next day we are unable to avoid a series of crevasses. Again it is my day up front. After checking our leads, harnesses and quick releases, I extend my lead rope so as to be fifteen yards ahead of my companions. My job is to select the more reliable-looking snow bridges to cross. Having chosen a route, it is up to me to test each snow bridge with my own weight. Bage instructs me to do some stomping and jumping as I cross. Some of these crevasses are over twenty yards wide in parts, although we always find narrower sections to attempt our crossings. Stopping on a snow bridge is forbidden. When I do look down, the crevasses are quite beautiful, with shimmering ice crystals and luminous blue walls dropping into black nothingness. I lead the way across more than twenty of these snow bridges before the day is out. Three or four times the snow bridge collapses, dropping me for a nerve-racking split second before my harness pulls me up against the crevasse wall. Above my head the rope cuts through the soft snow like a fretsaw. Inside the crevasse I spin slowly in the harness as I listen for the voices of my companions. Bage and Azzi pull me back to the surface and, after shaking myself off like a dog to remove the ice from my clothes, I scout for a better option, then try again.

We continue further south across the 69th parallel. The weather improves a little, but the surface is worse than ever. It is like a turbulent choppy ocean has been snap frozen and my feet slide on the hard icy surface of each little slope. My shins and knees take a hammering and we are fearful of breaking a bone. The sledge, meanwhile, tilts and drops and jars its way over these corrugations. Azzi takes observations with the dip circle, a vertically held compass, which shows our magnetic dip to be eighty-nine degrees, just one degree away from the South Magnetic Pole.

Each day now we are conscious we must average ten miles a day if we are to achieve the distance planned. It is extremely disheartening when this proves beyond us. On days I am leading I regularly lift off my goggles to see ahead and keep up our pace, but my eyes are pelted with drift and become so sore they start to close over. Eventually I can only look down at my feet with just one eye open and an occasional upwards glance. We are now accustomed to walking on frozen feet, our mitts and woollen helmets frozen stiff and a mask of ice beneath our Burberry hoods. Sweat makes dry clothing an impossibility. My full-time preoccupations are food and maintaining body heat. I constantly weigh up whether the trauma of removing a cold damp item and the time taken to put on another slightly less damp item will improve my overall warmth.

We are smarter now about changing and packing. When we remove our wet Burberrys inside the tent, we stuff the arms and legs with equally damp socks and other gear before the Burberrys freeze solid. This way we can put them on the next day without having to thaw them first. Similarly, in the evening we stack our harnesses and straps one inside the other so they are pre-frozen into shape for putting on the next morning. The socks and gear we remove in the morning from our Burberrys we shove into the opening of our sleeping bags so that night there is a readymade hole we can fit our legs into. Getting my legs all the way down through the frozen twisted knots of the bag can sometimes take an hour. Once in our sleeping bags we literally shiver to warm up. The hoosh cheers us up enormously, but afterwards I am still hungry. I am ravenous for steak, onions and potatoes. Once we have warmed up, we talk about food and our favourite meals. I have had to stop making diary entries that 'today was the worst'. There has always been a worse.

Azzi needs to conduct a full twenty-four hours' continuous magnetic observation. To do this properly we dig a cavern in the ice eight feet square and five feet deep. We put down a canvas floor then lie in our bags, jammed together for warmth, with our frozen Burberrys above keeping off as much snow as possible. We take turns watching the instruments and otherwise shiver and try to sleep. It is much colder than in the tent, but Azzi gets his readings. We are encrusted by a lid of snow and ice and joke about whether this is how we will finish up. We are very glad the next day to leave our sarcophagus, even if it does mean a return to sledging.

At two hundred miles from Commonwealth Bay, we overhaul our gear and prepare for a last dash south. We establish a depot of food stores and equipment not required for the next few weeks. Our sledge weight drops to two hundred pounds. We leave a snow mound some nine feet high with a black flag above. We call this Lucky Depot. We then head south for several miles, and when we make camp Lucky Depot is still in sight. Our altitude is now five thousand feet, but the way south is still an ascent.

Our days elapse with relentless pulling of the sledge with our heads down and our faces iced into our hoods. Speaking is an effort with our lips split and faces numb from the stinging drift, our throats invariably dry as we have no way of keeping water from freezing once we are underway. Sucking small amounts of snow is not enough to help. Even with companions it is lonely for most of the day. I wonder as to the significance of any scientific work in this miserable place. Despite my initial excitement at exploring this unknown continent, I am now questioning if there is any point to our southward march. The world already has its Antarctic heroes with Scott and Shackleton. Will anyone really care what is achieved by us, wandering unseen and often unseeing through this alien land? There are no Arcadian pleasures to be had in this hellish place. There seems little value to a photographic record of the barren Antarctic plateau. And, overwhelmingly, it is easier here to die than to live.

After a number of miserable days, 16 December proves to be a fine day and greatly lifts our spirits. We do two days of over fourteen miles each, and again have the chance to dry our clothing and sleeping bags. But despite the sun the temperature drops to fifty degrees below freezing. The sastrugi here stand up to five feet in height and are maybe twenty to thirty feet long. These sentinels of the blizzard are carved into ghostly shapes that now catch the pale light, but for half the year sit perched like gargoyles in the darkness.

We enjoy a third day of sunshine. The wind stops completely and again we become so hot sledging we strip down to our undergarments. Goggles are essential to cope with the glare. Our faces, pinched by frostbite, are like blackened and cracked leather. Our beards and hair thaw out on these days. There is a decent ration of congealed biscuit in my beard which can now be picked out without pulling the hair from its roots.

When I look at Bob, who is normally such a neat character, I can only imagine the appearance of my own thick wiry hair, which is almost impossible to disentangle from my clothing. Meanwhile, without the howling wind our surroundings are even more eerie, and again I have the sensation our slow progress across the planet is being observed. I sense shadowy figures off to one side, but when I swing my head to see there is nothing. When we pause there is absolute silence across the lonely plateau, broken only by our exhaling. And as we start up there is just the squeak of the wooden runners on snow and the crunching of our own steps.

We continue to haul up undulating slopes and on 20 December, with a much lighter sledge, we do fifteen miles. On 21 December our sledge meter indicates we have travelled three hundred and one miles from Commonwealth Bay. We are at latitude 70.37. We have climbed to just under six thousand feet. Ahead of us the land continues to rise.

Azzi does a further set of readings. I crouch alongside him, writing up the figures he reads off to me. It is twenty-five degrees below freezing. I am careful not to breathe on the logbook as condensation makes an immediate film of ice on paper which pencil will not penetrate; ink pens are, of course, useless.

Bob becomes impatient and makes his way over to us. 'What is it, Azzi? What's the dip?'

Azzi is quiet for a moment. 'Magnetic dip is at eighty-nine degrees, forty-three and a half minutes. That's just a quarter of a degree off magnetic south.' He pauses, then continues, 'Right now, we are within forty-five miles of the South Magnetic Pole.

Bob thinks for a moment, then says, 'We've already gone past our rations provision for the outwards journey. Time to turn around, lads, and make for home. What do you say, Azzi?'

'Another day's tempting, but there's no guarantee a further day of sledging will make any difference. Bob, we are the closest anyone has ever been. We are certainly closer than the Doctor got in '09.'

'The Doc's orders were to bring you fellows back alive. It's taken us forty days to get here and that leaves us only twenty days to get back. I'm marking this place on my map "Turn Back Camp". Frank, you'd better get the camera out.'

I take our flags—the Union Jack and the Commonwealth of Australia Ensign—off the sledge and plant them firmly alongside each other in front of the tent. As explained by Azzi, ninety degrees of dip means the flags and I are vertically aligned with the geomagnetic field lines that point to the North Magnetic Pole.

'Three cheers for the King!' cries Bage. My camera records the occasion. There is not much to see in a photograph of the South Magnetic Pole—flags, men, sledge and ice—but it tells a story.

I am wistful as to what lies beyond the furthest line of ridge but another part of me feels we are a very long way from safety. We are now to turn our backs on the frozen heart of this continent, the home of the blizzard, and flee to the coast before rations run out. Of course the great compensations of turning for home are that it is a gradual descent and the wind will be on our backs. We hoist a canvas sail on the sledge and are soon on our way north.

Our sledge meter has had such a rough trot that Bob decides to remove it. The measuring wheel has only a few spokes left and we will need the meter later when we have to rely on dead reckoning. With fifty square feet of canvas and thirty-mile-an-hour winds, we find our sledge running faster than we can control and soon have to reef the sail. Even then we cover over eighteen miles our first full day and twenty miles the next. On Christmas Eve we keep sledging till well after 8 p.m. We have been talking of a special Christmas feast, but Bob is sensibly concerned about rations and decides to postpone this until we reach the depot at Lucky Camp.

Christmas Day is particularly hard as we find ourselves in piecrust snow which holds our weight in sections then, without warning, collapses beneath us so we are dropped to our knees. The wind shifts to our starboard quarter, causing the sledge to skid sideways and making it hard to stay on track.

By 27 December we know we should have reached the depot, but by lunchtime there is still no sign of it. The three of us stare through thick drift to where the horizon should be, looking for a snow mound. Mid-afternoon comes and visibility remains poor. Without the sledge meter we have no way of knowing if we have overrun the depot. None of us speak; the consequences are unthinkable. Then suddenly the depot looms in front of us. We are overcome with relief.

I am commissioned by Bob to prepare the postponed Christmas feast, 'to lift our spirits', while he and Azzi take observations. With the depot found and the threat of starvation gone, my confidence is restored, and I know Bob wants me to make a special effort. For a start, I decide to clean the Nansen cooker and tableware—namely the same three mugs which serve for every meal. Fresh snow and a knife help me to scrape out the glutinous food scraps and reindeer hair (from our sleeping bags) stuck firmly in the corners of the cooking pot. My inventory of ingredients can be numbered on one hand, but despite this I write an elaborate menu card.

Hors d'oeuvres are my Angels on Gliders, which look a lot like single raisins on fried bars of chocolate. These are a hit. The entree is biscuit fried in Sledging Suet. For the main course I serve Frizzled Pemmican on Fried Biscuit, which Bage remarks is vaguely reminiscent of the entree. To satisfy all tastes, I serve my pièce de résistance, an extra thick and greasy Antarctic sledging ration.

'And now, chums,' I say, 'it wouldn't be Christmas dinner without plum pudding for dessert.'

'Hang on,' says Bage suspiciously. 'We haven't been lugging tins of plum pudding all this way.'

'I didn't pack any tins,' says Azzi.

Fortunately it is darkish in the tent as I serve dessert and it is eaten by all with great gusto (which is how we eat everything).

'Hoyle,' says Bage, 'you are a magician. How did you conjure that?'

'Recipe, please,' says Azzi.

'Chef's secret.'

'No secrets on this camp!' replies Bage.

'Alright,' I say. 'My plum pudding recipe. Grate three sledging biscuits with a hacksaw. Then, by hand, extract pieces of fat out of pemmican ration. Mix together. Throw in glaxo, sugar, raisins and one fistful of snow, and just three or four drops of methylated spirits. Then boil for five minutes in a sock. Presto!'

'Whose sock?' says Azzi.

'One of mine, of course—it needed changing anyway,' I reply.

There is an uncomfortable silence at this explanation, and conviviality is temporarily lost. I save the situation by serving up our Christmas wine, which I insist be downed with a suitable toast. Bob obliges with a toast to the King, and there is much coughing and spluttering. I had made the wine by stewing raisins in pure alcohol from the primus cooker. No more toasts are proposed as we gradually get our voices back. The atmosphere improves after I reveal that I had actually used a spare food bag to boil the pudding.

Unfortunately, Bob has endured a stressful few days. He had removed his goggles in the search for Lucky Depot. He is in considerable discomfort with his eyes that evening of our belated Christmas feast.

I too have a restless sleep that night at Lucky Camp. I dream I am with my younger brother Eddie and we are being chased by the engineer of a steam locomotive that has pulled up to avoid hitting me as I stood taking an action shot in the middle of the tracks. Eddie is carrying my tripod and camera and laughing like crazy but he's going to be caught and I'm calling out, 'Run, Eddie, run,' but he doesn't hear me.

The next day we leave Lucky Camp in good weather with a following breeze and a firm surface for sledging. By our 5 p.m. lunch stop we have covered twelve miles, and by 11.30 p.m. we have covered twenty-two.

Bob, no doubt worried about rations, summonses Azzi and me as we start to unpack. 'Lads, these conditions are still good. If you are up to it, why don't we go for a sledging record? We could have some dinner but then keep going.'

Refuelled by a steaming-hot hoosh, we push on. The sun is sitting on the horizon, providing no heat and only gloomy light. The temperature drops and drops, making any interruptions to sledging unpleasantly cold. Maintaining steady exertion is the only way to generate warmth. I am leading and setting the pace, and soon am in my own world, unconscious of the others, unable to see or hear them. I drift into a trance-like state, my mind flitting from changes in the ice ahead to the Doctor and the other sledging parties. They should all be back at winter quarters by now, waiting for us. I think of my ma—she alone might be anxious as to my return—and my father; he would be proud and amused to see I was on the cusp of becoming an experienced polar explorer.

At 5 a.m. we stop, somehow put up the tent, and collapse for a mere two hours before setting off again. At 11.30 a.m.

we finally stop and camp. I am utterly exhausted, but none of us has frostbite. I stay in my sleeping bag for seventeen hours, waking intermittently with the cold and painful leg cramps as I roll over, trying to get warm.

We rise at 7 a.m. the next day, our bodies stiff and aching, and on checking our location find that we have achieved forty-one miles between camps. We manage twelve miles that day, feeling quite sore, and each of us with bad blisters from our record-breaking effort.

The following day is New Year's Eve 1913, and in the morning I lie in my bag waiting for the others to move. It seems extraordinary that I am really here in a tent with two first-rate scientists on our way back from the South Magnetic Pole. If my body wasn't so numb I would have pinched myself. The painful spasms in my legs are real enough though and the patch of ice on the finnesko where I exhale. I feel quietly confident that in a week and a half we will be back at the hut with Mawson, Mertz, Ninnis and the others. We'll barely have time to pack before returning with Captain Davis to Australia. I will have to do most of the developing on board *Aurora*. Many of my best glass plates—especially the wildlife photographs from Macquarie Island—should already be safely back in Hobart. Mawson has talked about producing a book and giving illustrated lecture tours using my photographs, which would gain wide circulation. The grind of running a postcard business seems a lifetime ago. Before the year is out, I could be famous.

Two more days of hard marching and we reach the hundred-and-nine-mile mound. It is only a little over forty miles now to our supplies at Southern Cross Depot. Once there we will have fresh supplies to sustain us for the final sixty-seven miles to our winter quarters. We badly need to reach the hut at

Commonwealth Bay to attend to our frozen feet. For most of the day our feet are numb and each evening in the tent we check each other for frostbite. Our faces also are frozen all day, but at night in the tent they burn as they thaw out. My nose and cheeks are scarred with frostbite and rough to the touch. The satisfaction of the hot hoosh is tempered by the stinging of my lips, which are cracked and split with no chance of healing while we sledge each day.

As we continue northwards, nimbus clouds roll overhead and soon there is heavy snow falling and the sledge loses glide as its runners clog up with soft snow. Bob keeps tripping and falling on the jagged sastrugi. Azzi and I confer. Bob's eyesight is completely gone. If he gets a bone fracture we'll all be in trouble.

'Bob, Azzi's got your sleeping bag out and we want you in it and on the sledge just for this next bit.'

'Thanks, Frank, but I'll just walk behind on my rope.'

'Don't think so, Bob—we can't afford a broken bone.'

'I won't be carried.'

'Then you'd better get on the sledge. If you don't, you'll force us to camp now and we need to get a few more miles up today.'

I have to first get into Bob's bag myself to force an opening and then together Azzi and I shove Bob's legs in and make him a space on the sledge.

After a few days of travelling like this, I recognise a large pile of ice ramps: one of our bearings for Southern Cross Depot. Bob's eyes improve a little and he is able to resume walking.

On 5 January the clouds remain low and the conditions stay gloomy. It is impossible to check our present latitude, but the depot must be very close. The compass remains unreliable due to the closeness of the magnetic pole. We reach agreement on a bearing and set off, but after four miles there is nothing. We discuss changing direction but Bob decides to stay put and camp. We have halved our rations and should have enough for another two days. Bob directs us to get into our sleeping bags as quick as we can to maintain body heat and save energy.

On 6 January it is snowing and visibility is down to several yards. Bob again decides we should stay put. I find it hard to lie still in my sleeping bag for a whole day. Azzi is nervy and jumps up at any lift in the gloom, hoping to secure an accurate latitude bearing, but the sun stays away. I am nervy too, but I manage to occupy myself by making up rhyming doggerel about our Christmas Day feast in the snow:

There was Azzi Webb and old Bob Bage, and me they nicknamed 'Hoyle',
No better chums I've had, who didn't mind the toil . . .

My poem gets a good laugh. I'm sure Bage and Azzi are surprised at my ability to string these lines together, though not as surprised as me. I fancy it must be due to our dire predicament. Bob then replies with his best Browning, but changing the names:

I sprang to the stirrup, and Azzi and he;
I galloped, Hoyle galloped, we galloped all three;
'Good speed' cried the watch, as the gate-bolts undrew;
'Speed!' echoed the wall to us galloping through;
Behind sank the postern, the lights sank to rest,
And into the midnight we galloped abreast.
Not a word to each other we kept the great pace
Neck by neck, stride by stride, never changing our place . . .

The wind dissipates to nothing, but snow continues to fall through the night. The seventh remains dark and gloomy with low cloud. Our sledge is buried under thick snow, though at least without the wind it is relatively warm lying in our bags in the tent, where we stay until 5 p.m. We have a quarter of our usual ration of hoosh, and then break camp, digging out the sledge. Within an hour we are moving east, looking for the depot. But it does not emerge through the low cloud and fog, and we are using up energy looking for something we will never find in these conditions. I feel a niggling anxiety start to grow.

'Bob, we're wasting our rations here. We need to go north to the coast before we have nothing left.'

Bob responds calmly, 'Frank, if we can't find this depot, which must be within five miles, how can I be confident we will find the hut? There are seventy miles between us and the hut, and no supplies on that route.'

'But you're just punting on the weather,' I argue. 'If tomorrow's the same, we're as good as dead.'

'Frank, we'll stop here. If tomorrow's the same, we'll make a run north.'

There is not much said that night; we each keep our own counsel. I am a bit shocked by the plummeting of my mood. Bob and Azzi go through the ration bags and reorganise what we have. Importantly, we still have fuel to make water, about a pint of alcohol and a small amount of oil. We have just over one ration of pemmican, five Plasmon biscuits, four ounces of sugar and a small amount of cocoa mixture. Bob and Azzi conclude this is enough food to make Cape Denison on a straight run. We go to sleep hungry.

At 3.30 a.m. Bob is up and the tent illuminated by sunlight. Azzi goes straight out and obtains a good latitude bearing. Surely we will now find the supply depot. However within minutes heavy nimbus clouds again roll up from the south, threatening more blizzard conditions. Bob doesn't wait. He starts removing from the sledge any equipment not critical for survival. The dip circle, thermometers, hypsometer, camera, wet and spare clothing and much of the medical and repair kits are left behind, but we keep Azzi's and Bob's logbooks and records and my exposed glass plates.

We give up on Southern Cross Depot and head north. Bob's aim is for us to do three days of not less than twenty miles each. We repack the sledge and Bob has Azzi lead off in conditions which would normally see us calling a stop. The blizzard whips up all the recently fallen snow, but at least it is on our backs. Without the sun or a compass or any horizon or landmarks we rely on the wind to point us northwards. Azzi is just several yards in front, but I can't see him, only the rope disappearing into the drift. Every so often the wind feels it is swinging around to the east. We put crampons on to stop ourselves being blown off course. It feels like the sledge is dragging sideways and one of the runners is constantly catching on sastrugi.

Bob sets a schedule by which we go nonstop for an hour on his watch, followed by a five-minute break. We do this till we agree ten miles have been done, and then stop for a 'lunch' break. Late that day, when we are confident we have done twenty miles, Bob calls a halt. Our dinner is watered-down hoosh, followed by alcohol in warm water.

The next day the blizzard continues, with the wind about sixty miles an hour. All our eyes are suffering badly, but when we camp we can make out the ocean in the distance ahead of us. It seems we have underestimated our mileage—but where exactly are we? In the morning Azzi and Bob decide we have come too far east. We tramp west for five miles then turn north, looking for a way to the coast. Before long we find ourselves in badly serrated and churned ice with crevasses. This slows me down to a virtual crawl as I have lost all sight in one eye, which I have bandaged for protection, and the other is little better. It is as if I have sand stuck in my eyelids. I am using hands and feet to feel my way forwards and am slowing down the other two.

Bage calls back to me that we are climbing up and over a pressure ridge. I hear him call out again and the rope connecting us jerks taut and pulls me forwards. He has fallen, and I hear Azzi sliding forward and calling out to Bob. I stay put, keeping tension in the rope, and let Azzi do whatever he can. Then I hear Bob catching his breath as he clambers back towards us and excitedly cry out, 'I saw the islets, Mackellar Islets.' Soon Azzi is calling out and I move up alongside them, but I am snow blind and see nothing.

Bob and Azzi are very excited, and despite my protests they pull out and cook up in advance our evening ration of hoosh.

After lunch we are in trouble straight away with crevasses which I am unable to see. Bob has to talk me over each one. Progress then stops completely as Bob and Azzi reconnoitre, leaving me wrapped in a groundsheet, shivering, alongside the sledge. After they return we have to retrace our steps and find another way down off the plateau. We keep tramping. On the downhill slope I am forced to glissade out of control on my backside. I am physically and mentally done in. I am doubtful of where we are and our distance from Cape Denison. I have the doggedness to keep going but nothing more.

About midnight I hear Azzi call out he has seen a marker pole for Aladdin's Cave, our Five Mile Camp where we know there is shelter. We are soon there, and Bob is hugging me and Azzi. I would cry, but my tear ducts are frozen dry.

Azzi finds dog biscuits and offers them to me, but the effort to eat them frozen is too much. Bage then finds a tin with chocolate inside; this at least melts once in your mouth. Azzi locates a shovel and excavates the entrance which I slide through. Snow is melted on the cooker and something is added to it and heated till I feel the steam rising. Azzi puts zinc and cocaine tabloids in my eyes and I sleep the sleep of the recently saved.

In the morning I have partial sight but Bob has overdone it and is completely snow blind, and we have to bandage both his eyes. Because it is a reasonable downhill slope and we hoist a smallish sail, he agrees to sit on the sledge. Azzi and I have a lot of difficulty keeping it upright.

Before long our dilapidated craft has been spotted and we see the hut and figures emerge from it.

Bickerton and Dad McLean are the first to reach our sledge. It is hard to describe the feeling of being greeted by friends after believing we might perish in the blizzard. We have dragged the sledge some six hundred miles across the Antarctic plateau and are now safe. I can't help but cry a little at their kindnesses; their help with removing our harnesses and crampons, and being given dry warm clothes and served hot chicken broth while Dad McLean examines our frostbitten feet and faces. We had been overdue and are the second-last party back. Dr Mawson's party is yet to return and so far there has been no sign of *Aurora*.

•

It was 10 January 1913 when we reached the safety of winter quarters. The following day Captain Davis unexpectedly walked in the door without anyone having observed the arrival of *Aurora*. Davis was dismayed to learn that Mawson was not present because of the uncertainty this created.

By the eighteenth there was still no sign of Mawson, Mertz and Ninnis, and a search party was organised. I had recovered and volunteered, as did Hodgeman. Dad McLean offered his services as doctor. Davis ordered we return in five days. We set off in a blizzard, but the temperatures were comparatively high, the surface soft and mushy, and the drift soon drenched us. Soft snow made crossing snow bridges quite perilous. We could not see anything in these conditions and could easily pass Mawson's group.

On our fourth day out, with twenty-five miles covered, the blizzard began to lift and we built a cairn of ice above a box of rations. With binoculars I could see a few miles to the east, but saw nothing human. It seemed so long ago that Mertz, Ninnis and I had shaken hands at Aladdin's Cave. They were out there, but who knew how far away, and if were they alive. Their rations would have been exhausted, but they had dogs and, if near the coast, seals and penguin meat. Crevasses were a concern, but surely could not wipe out three men.

On our return to the hut, decisions had been made. Captain Davis had to leave to find Frank Wild and his party at the Western Base before the sea froze. He had brought ashore fresh provisions for a group to stay through the coming winter to await the return of the Mawson party. There was much anxiety and unspoken sadness. Madigan, despite not being Mawson's biggest supporter, agreed to stay on. He would be in charge. Bage, always dutiful, also offered to stay, along with Bickerton, who was needed for any mechanical maintenance. Dad McLean volunteered, knowing a doctor was required. Hodgeman agreed to stay, and Jeffryes, the wireless operator on board *Aurora*, volunteered to stay in place of Hannam. Jeffryes was the only person who showed any enthusiasm for the prospect. The rest of us were all anxious to escape this hostile place.

Madigan cornered me. 'Hoyle, we would like you to stay and do more photographic work. Your cine camera and projector could help with morale.'

'But it will soon be winter,' I objected.

'Exactly. Bage and I thought we could do with your clowning to lighten the mood.'

'I'll think about it,' I said reluctantly, and made my escape.

From the beginning of February, an extraordinarily fierce gale hit Commonwealth Bay and did not stop for a week, threatening to destroy *Aurora* and halting any chance of loading. I could not help but think of my friends still out on the ice in the blizzard. Their empty bunks were a sombre reminder. On the eighth the gale eased, and Davis ordered those departing to board immediately. I was torn. My staying could do nothing to save Mawson, Mertz and Ninnis. The Doctor's party was now a month overdue, and if they were dead, there was no benefit to my being here another year. It was intolerable that my photographs and film, which had already been loaded on board *Aurora*, should reach home without me and be exhibited by someone else. They were the key to my future. Any accolades would not wait my return in a year's time. The role of unreturned hero was not for me and there was no fame here. Madigan had a hide to ask me to stay, I fumed. I felt bad about leaving Bob behind—but he had volunteered. Azzi was returning. I told Bage I was leaving. He accepted my decision without complaint. I said a quick farewell to those staying. They were taking on the burden of waiting in a desolate place which they were heartily sick of, for three companions who in the unspoken truth were not expected to return, likely already dead and of whom nothing more might ever be known.

I busied myself aboard *Aurora*, but could not shake a sense of guilt; I was returning and Douglas Mawson was not. What would we say on our return, and what was I to do with my photographs and film? It was all so unresolved and must remain unresolved for another year. Davis had been very close to Mawson, but was now thoroughly preoccupied. He had one and a half thousand miles to cover to reach the Western Base and then must head north before *Aurora* became frozen in the ice.

The one improvement at Cape Denison winter quarters was that wireless masts had been successfully erected to withstand the blizzard and contact was established with Macquarie Island. Hannam, in the meantime, had erected a makeshift aerial on *Aurora*, and as we steamed westwards that first evening he received a message from Jeffryes at Cape Denison.

'Mawson returned: Ninnis and Mertz dead: return immediately and pick up all hands.'

The news went around *Aurora* in minutes as Davis turned and headed back to Commonwealth Bay. We arrived next morning. No sooner was a boat made ready to go ashore when the wind started to freshen and soon was gale force as the barometer plummeted. Captain Davis looked highly agitated. *Aurora* struggled to maintain position and avoid drifting bergs. One quick shore trip would see Mawson and the whole party safely on board, but permission to launch was not forthcoming from Davis.

Our anxiety continued till early evening, when Captain Davis called a meeting in the wardroom.

'Gentlemen, it has been a difficult day. The winds have made it impossible to launch a boat to bring on board the shore party without risking loss of life. However, all members of the shore party are accounted for. The seven expedition members ashore here are all safe and have adequate supplies to last the winter. As to the Western Base party under Mr Wild, their predicament is unknown and their available supplies are unknown. Every hour we wait here in Commonwealth Bay makes it less certain we can reach them without being trapped in the ice. *Aurora* has just enough coal to reach the Western Base and complete the homeward journey. The barometer has shown no sign of rising. Accordingly, I believe I have no alternative but to immediately resume the relief of Mr Wild's party.'

There were numerous mutterings until finally Azzi said, 'We are in your hands, Davis.'

Gloomy Davis was not the type to invite further opinions and with that he left the room, and *Aurora* steamed to the west.

Our trip westwards was both hazardous and spectacular. I spent a lot of time on deck. It was hard to feel too excited, despite the imposing cliffs and icebergs we passed. Though I had been expecting the worst, I was nonetheless shocked by the loss of our friends Xavier Mertz and Belgrave Ninnis.

Davis told us Amundsen had reached the South Pole ahead of Scott and that word had not yet come through from Scott's expedition. We certainly kept a lookout for icebergs after Davis dourly told us of the loss of over a thousand souls on the ocean liner SS *Titanic* in the North Atlantic. This news of the outside world left me numb.

Davis suggested I set up a darkroom, which I did without enthusiasm. I talked a little with Azzi, but I wanted now to be home and I mostly kept to myself. It was almost three weeks of steaming before we spotted a flagpole and small human figures at the top of an ice cliff some hundred and fifty feet high. Wild and his party were all alive. Their existence on the ice shelf must have been more desperate than life at Cape Denison. Within a few hours they were aboard and we turned north. Our return voyage was uneventful save for Gloomy Davis interrupting Azzi, Frank Wild and me in the mess room one morning with some news.

'*Terra Nova* has arrived back in New Zealand,' he told us. 'It seems Captain Scott did reach the South Pole after all, one month after Amundsen, but Scott and four of his party died on the return journey. They died in March 1912, two months after we first reached Cape Denison. The bodies were actually found last November. They had run out of food and fuel.'

I spent a few days in my bunk with a head cold and fever. My thoughts went back to the excitement of first setting foot on the Antarctic continent. I looked through my diaries and was surprised by my boyish zeal of just one year earlier. I had experienced what I craved: the adventure that accompanied the discovery of new horizons. But it had involved a degree of hardship that, naively, I had not expected. It had at times been touch and go between surviving and perishing. With Bob and Azzi I experienced something I had never felt before, a rare sense of oneness, that despite our differences we strived for ourselves and each other. I had learned something of my fellow man; there was much I admired about certain of my AAE colleagues,but others I had little time for. Looking back, I was proud of how I had handled myself, but had no immediate desire to repeat the experience.

On the other hand, to return in the absence of our leader seemed a hollow victory. What would the public think of our efforts? Mawson's absence would limit the use I could make of my photographs. I was going to need an income immediately, but Mawson couldn't raise funds to pay expeditioners when he was stuck in Commonwealth Bay. Most of the scientific staff had university salaries to fall back on, but I was not so fortunate. I did not want to take on the burden of running my own photography business, and in any case I did not have money to do so. The more I thought about it, the keener I was to travel back with Captain Davis to 'rescue' Mawson and the rest of the expedition at the beginning of summer. That would be the real homecoming; this present trip was doomed to be an anticlimax. The public would only respond to Mawson's return.

My mind turned to the future beyond Mawson's recovery. The small kernel of expedition experience made me a more determined person than ever, but to do what? Frustratingly, I still did not know, even though I was now twenty-seven years old. With every nautical mile *Aurora* left in her wake, I thought more and more of the camaraderie of the hut and being on the trail with Azzi and Bob Bage. It seemed a lifetime ago I had filmed our departure from Hobart. I remembered *Aurora* sailing out the Derwent and my first meeting with Mertz and Ninnis when they came aboard with the dogs. I had been stirred by their dedication and enthusiasm in those early, heady days. With that thought I went to the only place I would now find them: my darkroom.

5

Back to Antarctica, November 1913

Shortly after returning to Australia in mid March Captain Davis agreed I could accompany him back to Commonwealth Bay, but could not say when that would be.

'Unless we get funding,' said Gloomy, 'Mawson won't be coming home this year. I am hoping we can count on you to exhibit AAE photographs at fundraising dinners in the state capitals.'

However, not long after my return to Sydney, the Royal Dutch Steamship Company engaged me to do a series of travelogue and tourism photographs throughout the Dutch East Indies. It was an opportunity too good to refuse, even though it meant I was unavailable for AAE work.

Davis, meanwhile had to travel to England in search of donations. It was only after Chancellor of the Exchequer Lloyd George gave him a thousand pounds that the Australian prime minister, Joseph Cook, came good with five thousand pounds.

I made it back to Hobart by November 1913, just in time to embark on *Aurora* for my second voyage to Antarctica. I was glad to be on board. There were few opportunities at that time which could compete with a voyage offering exclusive access to a field of photography my peers could only read about.

But Davis baulked at my request for extra time to take photographs on Macquarie Island.

'Mr Hurley, I'm anxious to reach Commonwealth Bay at the earliest opportunity—and I'm afraid it won't be soon enough.'

'What do you mean?'

'Something's amiss down there,' he said, frowning at me. 'In late August, we started receiving a flurry of wireless messages all times of day and night. There was mention of threats. Then we received a message sent by Dr Mawson himself that he and Jeffryes, the wireless operator, were leaving the hut and that the other five had lost their senses. The next day we received a message from Mr Bickerton telling us to ignore the previous messages, that it was the wireless operator Jeffryes who was insane. Then all messages just stopped.'

'But that could just be the blizzard bringing down the radio mast.'

'And the threats?'

'Well, in life there is constant threats.'

'Mr Hurley, someone is causing trouble,' said Davis with conviction.

I thought about this before observing, 'Bob Bage is solid as a rock, Dad Mclean, Bickerton, Madigan, Hodgeman—you couldn't get better.'

'And I recruited Jeffryes,' said Davis. 'There's no doubt about his ability and he's only been there since February. Actually, the person I'm worried about is Dr Mawson.'

On 13 December, in the early hours of the morning when there was no darkness to discriminate night from day, *Aurora* pushed carefully into Commonwealth Bay. As we passed the Mackellar

Islets, the ramshackle ice-framed hut of the Australian Antarctic Expedition came into sight. No one there stirred. Back from the hut, and quite prominent on the brow of a nearby hill, stood a newly erected wooden cross, a symbol alien to the landscape and defiant of the blizzards which ruled this place.

Aurora was jostled by the gusts that swept down the icy hinterland and fiercely struck the water. It was more than an hour before Captain Davis was confident his anchor had an invincible hold on the Antarctic continent. He launched a boat to shore.

John Hunter and Davis were with me in the boat, along with my Macquarie Island companion Les Blake. Davis led the way up to the door of the hut; there was still no sign of life. We paused and listened but the only sound that could be heard was the wind buffeting the hut. I stood alongside Davis as he pushed open the door and we both peered into its dark interior.

'Hello, Davis, back so soon?' came a voice I could scarcely recognise. It was Mawson. I could not see him but knew him well enough to recognise his cold sarcasm.

There was then a massive clamour from inside and, as I followed Davis in, there were shouts of 'Hoyle' and 'Johnnie'. We had literally caught them napping. They had seen *Aurora* early on, but grew tired of waiting for her to anchor. I found myself hugging each one of my former companions: good old Bage, pipe in hand and totally unchanged, Bickerton and Dad Mclean, Alf Hodgeman, even Madigan—and, of course, the good Doctor. I confess I was strangely misty-eyed to see my friends and to stand again in the hut where we had lived an almost monastic existence so close together for so long. Mawson was very composed but greeted me warmly. He had lost much weight and the bones in his face stood out. It was only when he stepped outside into daylight that I saw the full impact of his ordeal. He had turned old. He had lost most of his hair and that which he had was silver-grey. His face was gaunt, his eyes deeply inset and his brow quite furrowed. Most of all, he had lost his impressive fitness, and now looked quite frail. When Mawson alone had finally appeared on the hill above the hut in February, he was unrecognisable. Bickerton's first words to him were: 'Which one are you?' But our questions were suppressed for the time being, and Mawson promised without prompting to give a full account of things once we were on board and away from Commonwealth Bay.

Within a day everything considered of human value was taken on board *Aurora* and the hut was boarded up to keep out the blizzard. One last time *Aurora* slipped her anchor to depart Commonwealth Bay. The polar wind raced down from the plateau across the shore, darkening the water as it hastened us away. The hut was soon lost from view and my gaze fell upon the cross which stood on the very crest of the hill. Erected as a memorial to the two not returning, it was the last sign of our sojourn in the now-uninhabited landscape. I believed that as a result of our endeavours the hut would soon be home to new visitors. In fact, with the South Pole reached and an imminent crisis in Europe there were new fields for man's imagination. It was not just one year or several, but some decades before the door of the AAE hut was reopened.

To my surprise, once on board Dr Mawson insisted that, instead of proceeding straight home, Captain Davis head west so as to chart further sections of the Antarctic coastline. There was no enthusiasm on board for more surveying. Our route was perilous as we skirted icebergs in gale-force winds. I watched Gloomy shrink with exhaustion; he stood at the helm when I retired in the evening and was still there when I rose the next morning. No doubt sleeping only gave him nightmares of the disaster that befell the *Titanic*. He and the Doctor, normally firm allies, were plainly at odds as to the ship's course. The Doctor's dry humour had been a casualty of the expedition. His relations with Davis were icy to start and did not improve. And among the seven rescued expeditioners there was little conviviality. They had had enough of each other. The absence of Mertz and Ninnis hung heavily with us all. Jeffryes, the wireless man, would not shake my hand. He avoided all conversation and my camera. He had a wild and frightened look. I gathered from Bage that after some months in the confines of the hut, working through the night trying to make contact with the outside world, Jeffryes became delusional. Eventually he was removed from the position as he could not be trusted. Bickerton took over, though he was not as proficient.

After dinner one evening, Mawson gathered us together in the mess and presented in an almost formal way an account of his eastern sledging journey. It was as if he was practising for lecture halls at home. He explained how Mertz, leading the way on skis, followed by Mawson with the first sledge, had successfully passed over a snow-filled crevasse. Ninnis was in the rear with the second sledge. Shortly afterwards Mawson saw Mertz had stopped and was looking back. Mawson turned around to find Ninnis and his dog team and sledge had vanished. The snow bridge had collapsed.

'We stayed for hours calling out for Ninnis. We could see one of the dogs on a ledge some hundred and fifty feet down. It was alive, most likely with its back broken, and whimpering, though mercifully not for long. That sledge had the bulk of our food, the food for the dogs, our fuel and our tent. We could see the tent wedged in the ice. My sledge meter showed we were three hundred and fifteen miles from Commonwealth Bay.

'Mertz and I turned for home. We slaughtered the dogs one by one. Each dog pulled until it dropped. Malnutrition was our worst problem, along with frostbite. We both suffered stomach cramps and gastric complaints. Mertz became ill, very ill. He had bad diarrhoea and stopped eating. He said eating dog did not agree with him. He became delirious and could not continue. He died in his sleeping bag on 8 January. I covered his body, still in the sleeping bag, with blocks of ice. I made a cross from broken sledge runners and read a burial service.'

The Doctor explained how he had then struggled on alone for a further three weeks. There was no doubt his suffering was intense and his will to survive almost superhuman. As it happened, he found the cairn where Dad McLean, Hodgeman and I had left food and directions. He reached this cairn the same day we departed from it to return to the hut.

Mawson ordered Davis to steer *Aurora* back into the ice time and again through Christmas and New Year and all of January. I was content enough, but the others were impatient to be home. We all breathed a sigh of relief when, in mid-February 1914, *Aurora* finally turned north for home.

On the return voyage I had a number of long conversations with Mawson. He wanted to know how I was going with compiling the photographic records and what had been done to raise funds to meet the expedition's debts. He was surprised to learn I had been away to the Dutch East Indies. It certainly had been a contrast to my Antarctic experience, I told him.

'Do you remember how, in the middle of those winter blizzards, we talked of going to a tropical island? I went from fifty degrees below zero to a hundred degrees above. Instead of freezing, the cinefilm was melting in the heat. What got to me most were the hordes of natives and no one speaking English. I tell you one thing I discovered, Doc: I prefer the isolation of the icecap to the crowds of the East Indies any day.'

'Is that right? Well, I suppose there is now no corner on the globe that can hide from your camera. As for me I have had quite enough of the rigours of the frozen world.' He sighed and when I looked at his sunken eyes and weary figure I could see he had decided his adventuring days were over.

6

Australia, 1914

Aurora made a triumphant return to Adelaide, Mawson's home town. He must have been heartened by the crowds that came to the dock in the summer heat: such fanfare and speeches and press photographers. Then he was whisked away to a private dinner and the next day to the university. There was a public reception at the town hall, which Mawson's young fiancée, Paquita, attended with him. I thought her very pretty. But the fanfare was for Mawson alone; there was no opportunity to gather all the expedition members together. Bage and I and the others one by one went our separate ways. Wild was back in England, Azzi was in New Zealand. We remained unknowns.

There was talk of Shackleton leading a new expedition across Antarctica. Frank Wild had signed up apparently. Bickerton was keen. Mawson told me Shackleton's backers had seen my work and wanted to engage my services—but Shackleton, he warned me, could not be trusted. 'And don't forget, Hurley,' he added, 'I need you here in Australia until we have collated all the photographs and cinefilm.'

•

In early March I arrived by myself at Central Station in Sydney with several boxes of glass plates, film and equipment. With nowhere else to go, I landed on my mother's doorstep.

'I was wondering when my bad penny would turn up,' she said, as she kissed me on the cheek.

At Kodak's offices I worked on developing, printing and labelling. Mawson arranged a small advance from AAE funds to tide me over. I wrote to Shackleton, but his plans sounded very up in the air. There were invitations to speak at camera clubs, but the audiences were full of buffoons. The adventure was over. I struggled to work out why things didn't seem the same and yet everything was the same. I had become accustomed to a way of life that could not be had in my family home. Life back in Glebe was for the time being both inescapable and intolerable.

It was during one of our customary long silences over dinner that my mother quite startled me. 'And I 'ave read you are going back there with Shackleton.'

'The Antarctic, you mean? I may be. I really don't know if he is going.'

'Your pa would not approve, even though Mr Shackleton's an Irishman. He's more crazy than Mawson and Scott put together. No good has come of their antics but mothers weeping for lost sons and husbands.'

'I think you're wrong. Pa would have been proud. Which is more than I can say for the rest of the family. Didn't write me a single letter between 'em. And when they're here, barely a question as to what it was like.'

'Don't you be feeling sorry for yourself,' she peered at me and raised her voice. 'Just because you've got no money, no job and no wife. Jamie, it breaks my heart to see you—thirty years old and sleeping on your mother's couch.'

'I'm not thirty!'

'Near enough. Your brothers and sisters are busy with their own families, that's all. They mean no harm. But you must know *I* care about you. If I didn't care, why would I have written to Dr Mawson?'

I stopped chewing and looked up at her.

'What are you talking about?'

'You know,' she said. 'I wrote Dr Mawson when he first appointed you saying that he shouldn't take you to the Antarctic. I didn't think you should go. Your pa worked so hard on the postcard business you walked out on.'

'It was *you* who wrote to Mawson?! What on earth did you tell him?'

'I told him you had poor lungs and suffered the cold badly, which was true enough.'

'Holy Mother of God, Ma, surely you're not serious? That letter almost cost me the whole expedition!'

My mother was unmoved. 'I did what your father would have done had he been alive. You was always too wilful for your own good, Jamie.'

'So have you written to Shackleton now?' I demanded.

'There's no reason to be like that. I have not written Mr Shackleton. You're a man now, be it on your own head what you do. But why would you go back there? You have all the photographs you need. I read in the paper Dr Mawson is getting married next week—you should do the same.'

'Mawson is a damn sight older than me, and while he's off getting married he's still got me working away on his film.'

'No one says you're not a hard worker, Jamie, but you *are* almost thirty years old.'

'I'm in no hurry to get married,' I snapped.

She glowered at me and I decided to reveal some of my own news. 'But as it happens, I *am* planning on going away—not to Antarctica, but the Gulf of Carpentaria. You can read about it soon enough in the papers. I'm going with Francis

Birtles, and no, we are not going on his bicycle, we're being given a car and cameras to make a film on the outback. And there's good money in it for me.'

'When's this happening?'

'Easter. We'll be leaving from the Royal Easter Show, actually. Birtles likes a crowd.'

'Well, you will be in the papers, won't you, with Francis Birtles and all—why, he's more famous than Dr Mawson. I'll be there, Jamie, but don't you ignore me now—you 'ave to come and talk to your ma, you'll have to look out for me.'

I was gone some three months with Birtles. We clocked up six thousand miles at a whirlwind pace in an open-top Ford with a twenty-horsepower engine. Birtles taught me how to drive. And we didn't just stick to roads; Birtles knew all the stock routes. It was hard to believe the ease with which the Ford carried my equipment across areas that had taken the explorers Leichhardt and Burke and Wills months to tramp on foot. It was the best introduction to the outback a city boy could have. It was desert, but not as forbidding as the desert of the Antarctic plateau.

I learned a lot from Birtles; he lived the life I wanted to lead. He was a man of surprises and resourcefulness. He had set records, written books and made a film. He was a true adventurer. Although not a scientist, he had an appreciation of the land. He had spent time with the Aborigines and learned bushcraft. He was a good shot and kangaroo was our staple meal.

I was fascinated by Aboriginal hunting and fishing methods using the crudest of weapons. I found myself wanting to film the people more than the landscape. They made good subjects for my camera, despite being as black as the ace of spades. It was something special to see the toughness of the men, their cheeky lubras and piccaninnies. Birtles said their way of life should be filmed before they died out. The footage it occurred to me would then prove quite valuable. There were however the challenges of the heat, dust and flies.

We stayed a while in an idyllic spot on the Nicholson River in Arnhem Land only a few hundred yards from an Aboriginal camp. Birtles had been negotiating for several days for permission to attend a corroboree, but nothing was happening, despite gifts and inducements.

Birtles returned to camp one morning, furious. 'Hurley, if these niggers are not going to show us their witchcraft, I'll have to show 'em some of mine.' And with that he took a full tin of benzene from the car and walked off towards their camp. I followed with some apprehension. He entered the water just upriver of the blacks' camp and poured out the benzene. Then, leaving the empty tin in the bush, he walked into the camp, which was no more than a series of campfires and bark shelters. Once he had the attention of the blacks, he took a burning stick from their fire and tossed it into the river at the spot where the gasoline had now gathered. There was a wall of flame followed by screams as the natives fled the camp.

I thought the exercise a cruel failure, but next day they were back. That evening, by the light of several large campfires, I filmed the ochre-painted bodies of the men in a spectacle of dancing and chanting which few white people could ever have seen. Birtles was ecstatic.

Not long after, a black walked into our camp and handed over a crumpled grimy envelope with a letter from my mother. She must have been trying to make up for her previous interference, because she told me Shackleton had been sending cables to confirm I would join his expedition, but I needed to be in Buenos Aires in several weeks. Shackleton had previously announced a 'Trans-Antarctic' expedition, but I had no idea what this meant. It didn't matter; it was Shackleton. With Scott gone, Shackleton was the most famous Briton alive. I cabled my acceptance from the tiny police station at Burketown.

Birtles and I arrived back in Sydney with the Ford full of spears, shields, kangaroo skins and other trophies of our journey. He received a lot of publicity. I was busy arranging passage on a ship to South America.

My mother had that same surprised look on her face as she opened the front door to see the pile of boxes I had stacked on the verandah. She let out a little cry and, stepping outside, threw her arms around me, cameras, parcels and all. I couldn't move and couldn't return the hug without risk of dropping fragile lenses and glass plates.

Just one cup of tea later and I was out the door on my way to Harrington's and Kodak's offices for cinefilm reels, boxes of glass plates, colour dyes, flash powder, battery packs, bottles of chemicals and other supplies for Shackleton's expedition. While at Kodak, I found the AAE negatives and colour lantern slides that Mawson had been on my back to give him.

It was late by the time I made it back home and my mother was in bed. I fell asleep in the lounge room and didn't wake until midday. The next few days were spent unpacking from the Birtles trip and working out what Harrington's and Kodak were able to supply. Amazingly, they were willing to supply me on credit just on the basis of the Shackleton name, even though they were still owed monies from the AAE.

Birtles insisted on us putting in long hours together looking at the glass plates and film from our outback journey. He was keen to have photographs for a book. After labouring all night under the ruby lamp, I emerged from the Kodak building in the wee hours of the morning and was taken aback to see broadsheets at the newsstands emblazoned with the headline: AUSTRALIA AT WAR. Others, who had not been absent from civilisation as I had, were expecting this announcement. Britain was going to stand up to Germany and send troops to defend little Belgium.

The mood in the street following the declaration of war was different to anything I had experienced. The conversations I listened to over the next few days at Harrington's and Kodak were charged with an intensity I could not fathom. Britain was mobilising its armed forces for a war on the continent. It seemed so remote, though I was drawn in by speculation the British navy would not allow the Shackleton expedition to leave England for some months, at least until the crisis in Europe was resolved. Colleagues my age and younger, mild-mannered fellows, counter jumpers and office clerks, were pledging their enlistment to serve overseas in a British Empire Force that our politicians were promising the mother country. Meanwhile, I waited anxiously for a cable from Shackleton.

Within days newspapers announced an Australian Imperial Force would leave for Europe as soon as it could be assembled, lest it arrive too late and the war be over. The following week there were reports Australian forces had raided and occupied German territories in New Guinea. Before I had time for misgivings, I received word that *Endurance*, Shackleton's main expedition vessel, had left England bound for Buenos Aires, and I was expected to meet it there by mid-October.

Ma put up with my comings and goings. She had enjoyed reading the excited newspaper reports about Birtles and our adventures in the outback. Now over dinner she looked nonplussed as to whether I should be taking my chances with Shackleton or enlisting.

'Your pa would have none of this recruiting young Australian men to fight for all those kings and kaisers in Europe!'

During these hectic days, Birtles and I were feted at a series of dinners and public functions. These were not my cup of tea, but I was impressed at how well Birtles brushed up in a white shirt, stiff collar and dinner jacket, and how he could string together a few well-received words. Invariably someone would start singing 'God Save the King' and people who barely knew each other would be shaking hands and back slapping with great gusto. I became used to saying a few words to accompany my lantern slides.

It was on such an occasion that I found myself conversing in a small group that included Elsa Stewart. I saw her again at another function, and then another. She did not actually converse, but she was there. Only after a number of these encounters did she tell me very quietly that her name was Elsa. She often accompanied her father to public talks and knew who I was, she said. I ventured to think she was actually interested in me. She was as pretty and perfect a picture as could be composed with very fair skin and short wavy brown hair. Elsa was tiny; when we stood alongside each other she came up no higher than my chest. Elsa had once worked as an assistant in a photographic studio and thought the photographs of mine which she had seen in the newspapers were fabulous. Though I had precious little time for a day off, I asked her if she would meet me at Watsons Bay and help photograph some harbour scenes. To my delight, she agreed. She looked immaculate in the photographs I took and bore patiently all my tinkering and fiddling with the camera and tripod while waiting for the right light. My hobby had always been a solo activity, but here was someone who actually enjoyed our time together and was a pleasure to be with.

Being part of the Shackleton expedition gave me renewed sense of purpose at a time when all the talk was of war. I was going to the Antarctic and I was going with Shackleton. These were heady days and with time pressing in on me, I became obsessed with the idea that Elsa and I should become engaged before my departure. The papers were full of young army recruits announcing their engagement. Once this idea had occurred to me, it just grew and grew in my head. But I wasn't sure how to achieve this. There was no one I could discuss this with—certainly not Ma, who was rarely even-tempered—about what I was doing, who with, and why I was never at home. In the end, after rehearsing it a thousand times in my head, I spoke with Elsa in a teahouse in Hyde Park.

'How do you think we do together, you and I?'

'Frank, we do fine. That is, if you enjoy being with me.'

'Who wouldn't enjoy being with you?'

'Well, you are awfully busy. I might be in your way at times, but if ever you need someone to help with your cameras, you know you can ask me anything—and you said I was a quick learner.'

'I enjoy it when you're in the way,' I assured her. 'And you look after the glass plates a lot better than some of those camera-club clowns. But I bet your folks don't like you spending too much time with me. I don't exactly have a regular job, do I?'

'Daddy doesn't know you; they've hardly met you. They do think you are awfully clever, though.'

'Clever for someone who hasn't had much of an education.'

'That's not what they think.' She raised her head from her teacup to meet my eye. 'You could come for dinner so they could get to know you.'

'I'd like that—but there may be no time. Between Mawson's demands and Shackleton I hardly have time to sleep. Ma says she never sees me. I say, Elsa, if, um, if I write letters to you when I'm away, will you write to me care of the expedition?'

'Yes, Frank—of course I will.'

'But you may have to write even if you haven't heard from me for a while. We'll be out of port for several months.'

'I'm not a very good letter writer, Frank, and I won't have much news that you'll be interested in, but I can write if you tell me where to send letters.'

'And, Elsa . . .' I paused, not quite sure how to say it. 'Do you think we get on?'

'Oh yes, Frank. I'm quiet, that's all. All my friends say I'm quiet as a mouse.'

'My friends say I'm as quiet as an elephant. In our expedition hut everyone complained it was my voice and stomping around that woke them up.'

'I think you need a loud voice when you are showing films.'

'Elsa, the films from this Shackleton trip, I think they could make quite an income, quite a steady income. They'll do better than the Mawson film. I think your father might be surprised. Elsa, do you think . . . what if we were to become engaged?'

'Engaged?' Elsa looked quite startled.

I drew a breath. 'To be married, I mean. Would you marry me? I mean, not right now, we would just be engaged until I return. Then we could be married. We could spend more time together after the expedition.'

There was an awkward silence, during which Elsa's eyes stayed fixed on her teacup.

I was too shy to reach for Elsa's hands, which in any case were clasped firmly in her lap. I stared at my own rough calloused hands with brown chemical-stained fingernails. I needed to go to the barber and my hair, I knew, was springing out everywhere. My shirt had not been starched and my collar was too tight. I was a stupid ignorant oaf.

But Elsa's head was nodding and, when I looked closer, I realised she was wiping away tears with her handkerchief. At last she looked up and spoke, but all I heard was a squeak. What had I done to cause this? Our eyes met and, unnerved, I looked away. Then I heard her whisper, 'Yes, Frank,' and I realised that she was accepting me. Now I was able to move from my seat; I stepped around the table to kiss Elsa on the cheek, the first time I had kissed a girl.

Elsa lived on the other side of town from me in Double Bay. Her parents were very kind and I expect were relieved when they realised there could be no wedding for at least two years. Elsa came home to meet Ma and they got on well together. I purchased a ring but it was too large for Elsa and had to be altered.

Elsa happily agreed to take on my correspondence with the AAE and the suppliers of my photographic equipment. This was a far safer proposition than relying on Ma. In a short time I was needed back in the Kodak darkroom, where I worked with the scent of Elsa's perfume lingering on my jacket. The future was looking bright.

•

In mid-September 1914, I boarded SS *Remuera* bound for South America. Only when I was inspecting the vessel's wall charts did I realise Buenos Aires was on the eastern coast of South America and that I would be sailing around Cape Horn. The ship's captain was keen to meet me.

'And don't you worry about Admiral von Spee,' he said.

I had no idea what he was talking about. 'Who is Admiral von Spee?'

'You haven't read the papers? The German navy has been sinking our merchant ships in the south-east Pacific. We're going to have to give him the slip.'

Part III

7

With Shackleton, 1914–1916

After SS *Remuera* steamed out through the Heads of Sydney Harbour I slept solidly for two days. I had the rare luxury of a cabin to myself. Stretched full-length on my bunk, I read the Imperial Trans-Antarctic Expedition Prospectus, which Shackleton had sent me. He was seeking to raise sixty thousand pounds! This was a phenomenal sum, even compared to the debts Mawson had run up. I was beginning to understand the advantages that came with the fame of a Shackleton. What possible return could there be for investors advancing these sums for others to risk their lives in remote parts of the globe?

The stated object of the expedition in the prospectus was little help: 'To cross the Antarctic from sea to sea securing for the British flag the honour of being the first carried across the South Polar Continent.'

The prospectus explained: 'This expedition is the natural sequel to former British expeditions which sought chiefly to attain the South Pole such as that led by Sir Ernest Shackleton in 1907–09 and that which resulted in Captain Scott's great achievement and tragic end.' It did not mention that Amundsen had reached the South Pole first.

According to the prospectus, the vessel *Endurance* would land a party on the Weddell Sea coast of Antarctica, from where six men would sledge to the South Pole. My jaw dropped as I read on. The same party would continue across the continent to the Ross Sea, from where Scott had reached the pole. As the official photographer, I would be one of the six accompanying Shackleton. This was fifteen hundred miles—almost three times the distance I had covered with Bage and Azzi! And I was done in at the end of that trip. Of course, Shackleton was taking dogs. This was the only way such a distance could be achieved. Scott had fallen short, though Amundsen had shown that with dogs it could be done. But there could be no support crew or food depots on Shackleton's plan, at least not until well after the pole had been reached. The food needed for six men and dog teams over that distance would be enormous. A separate party coming from the Ross Sea would lay supply depots for the return journey. It occurred to me the six-man polar party could have no certainty, at least not until it was too late, that the Ross Sea party had even landed, let alone established any food depots.

I thought back to the agony of running out of food with Bage and Azzi, and being unable to find Southern Cross Depot, a depot we had ourselves established several weeks earlier. How would you find a depot when you were uncertain it even existed? More worryingly, while rough maps now existed of the area between the Ross Sea and the South Pole, there was no knowledge whatsoever of what lay between the pole and the Weddell Sea. No one had ever been there.

It was a little late to be giving these practicalities any thought. *Remuera* was not going to turn around. I wondered what on earth had compelled me to cable Shackleton, a man I had not even met, to say I would go with him. I only knew two of the crew, Frank Wild and Frank Bickerton. No one else from the AAE was going. Frank Wild's reason for going

I could understand, as he was a thoroughly rugged seafaring type who knew Shackleton and had spent more time in the Antarctic than any living soul. The aptly named Wild was out of place in civilisation.

The more I thought about it, the more certain I was that Shackleton's plan had Buckley's chance of succeeding. It sounded as doomed as Burke and Wills trying to cross Australia on foot. In fact, our journey would be a greater distance, required climbing several thousand feet, was a more arid desert than that of Central Australia with not even a witchetty grub to eat, and without fuel there was no water.

I couldn't see the importance of crossing the centre of the Antarctic. If we were unable to achieve this goal, it would not concern me. My pictures would still be unique and, photographically, the coast was of much greater interest. But I was going to need to look after myself to make sure I got back with my photographs. My friends on the AAE, Mertz and Ninnis, had not returned at all, and they'd had dogs to pull sledges and Mertz was a champion skier. Alone in my cabin I began to feel that Ma had been right: I *was* irresponsible. I should have canvassed the Shackleton plan with Mawson.

When I'd told him of my intention to join the Trans-Antarctic Expedition, he said he had doubts about Shackleton. I had figured his lack of support was due to my not having finished the pictures for his lecture tours, but it now occurred to me he might have had good reason for his concern.

While I had been away in the outback, my mother had collected the frequent newspaper articles on Shackleton and I had bundled these into my trunk to read on the *Remuera*. Reading the stories, I realised I was part of something bigger than I could have imagined.

If Sir Ernest succeeds he will have added a new glory to the record of British Polar Exploration. He will have achieved the last great geographical feat that it remains for man to accomplish.

As anxious as I was, it was hard to resist being part of something as exciting as this, and with such a revered figure as Shackleton.

I had ample time on board to rehearse my first conversation with the great explorer. I would not be 'cap in hand' as I had been with Mawson in 1911. Without my cinefilm and photographs, there was no prospect of any financial return for Shackleton's backers; in fact, there might not be an expedition at all. They had requested my services. There was no one else with my experience at capturing sharp landscape and action photographs in polar conditions; certainly no other photographer who could sledge that distance. And, I would tell Shackleton, I needed control over the developing and editing stages. Additionally, I would demand a share of the profits. It was his expedition, but they would be *my* photographs. I had not travelled halfway around the world for wages only. What could Shackleton say? The more I thought about it, the more determined I became to negotiate a satisfactory arrangement, and the more surprised I was that on such a vital matter Shackleton had appointed me without submitting written terms.

There was a lot on my mind as the *Remuera* made its way across the Pacific. I wrote a letter to Elsa to be posted in New Zealand. I was relieved that, while away, I would receive letters from Elsa just as Mawson on the AAE had the pleasure of mail from his Paquita. Now Mawson and Paquita were married. With my twenty-ninth birthday approaching, it would be embarrassing to receive no mail from a lady friend. But would Elsa wait eighteen months? I had promised I would return as soon as possible, but I had not dared tell her what I suspected—that I was likely to be away considerably longer than this.

The warehouses lining the Buenos Aires waterfront were grimy and monotonous. Behind lay a smoke-stained sky with low cloud. I had been expecting something more colourful. There were however bustling crowds and a diverse assortment of vessels and not far away the masts of *Endurance*, were pointed out to me, just visible behind a row of dilapidated cargo ships.

Endurance was a barquentine-rigged three-masted wooden ship, like *Aurora*, but smaller. She looked a dainty ship to be heading into Antarctic seas. Her hull was jet black and slender, but her nice lines were spoiled by a miscellany of unstowed cargo and a superstructure of dog kennels built along both sides of the upper deck. She was strewn with crates, hessian sacks, drums of fuel and water, and had snow sledges strapped to the gunnels and side stays.

My dockside reconnoitring ended abruptly when I was grabbed from behind in a wrestling hold. 'Hoyle, we've been bloody wondering if you would make it!' It was Frank Wild, who had sailed out from England on board *Endurance*. He was small but strong as an ox and his warmth and easy confidence was a tonic to me.

'And where is Bickerton?' I asked.

'Bick enlisted. He was on board until just before we sailed out of West India Dock in London. Once war was declared there were soldiers everywhere. I think he fancied himself in uniform. Truth is, we were all a bit torn. I wasn't sure if coming away was the right thing to do. But we're here now.'

I was surprised. 'So Bick chose soldiering over exploring?'

'Well, the pay is more reliable,' Wild joked.

'If he's not here, who's looking after the motorised snow tractors?'

'The boss recruited a colonel in the Royal Marines, Orde-Lees. Loves all the latest inventions. He's a bit of a toff, but he's fit and he can ski. He's an odd bod, though; insisted on bringing his bicycle.'

Wild showed me on board and took me to Shackleton's cabin to meet the great man, who had arrived in port and boarded

Endurance only two days before me. I had learned from Wild that he had already cut two troublesome sailors from the crew. To all on board he was simply known as 'the boss'.

The meeting was brief. Shackleton was seated at a small writing desk. He made no effort to get up but eyed me closely and shook my hand with the firm grip expected of an explorer of his ilk. He was swarthy, and stocky like a boxer, with a broad brow and a square chin. Despite the cold day, he had a light sheen of sweat on his forehead.

'Settle in, Mr Hurley, and we'll talk later.' He was certainly a change from the professorial Mawson.

As we left, I noticed he had a large tattered poster of Rudyard Kipling's 'If—' on the back of his cabin door.

If you can keep your head when all about you
Are losing theirs and blame it on you,
If you can trust yourself when all men doubt you,
But make allowance for their doubting too . . .

He could, I would discover, recite the whole poem at the drop of a hat, and many more poems besides. I could readily believe that 'If—' was his personal manifesto, and it would prove quite prophetic as things turned out:

If you can meet with Triumph and Disaster
And treat those two imposters just the same . . .

And I confess the poem found resonance with me:

If neither foes nor loving friends can hurt you,
If all men count with you, but none too much . . .

I had lost contact with my colleagues from the AAE; I was not a letter writer nor one for social chitchat. Not being much of a drinker, I found myself bored if dragged to the pub. I enjoyed my work and I yearned to travel. Ma said I was a rolling stone that gathered no moss. But only one person can look through a viewfinder.

I was very much the newcomer on the expedition and so it was a relief to have Frank Wild, who was second-in-command, to introduce me to the men I would be in close quarters with for over a year. They were almost uniformly young, with English or Scottish accents, and consisted of a good number of scientific types, educated at famous universities like Oxford and Cambridge. I was expecting them to be snobbish and some of them were, but they were quiet rather than rude. They had heard of me and were curious about the AAE. They were mostly smaller than me and didn't look too used to working on board ships or doing physical work at all. At least three of them—Wordie, James and Macklin—needed spectacles even for outside work. 'You'll be in trouble in a blizzard,' I said, and they looked most unhappy.

Wordie was a geologist and James a magnetician, like my friend Azzi. Macklin and another fellow, McIlroy, were doctors. I met a quiet Scottish biologist, Clark; a smallish fellow, Hussey, who was a meteorologist, though quite a contrast to the serious Madigan of the AAE; and the 'odd bod' Orde-Lees, whom Wild had mentioned was the motor expert. A young man called Marston joked shyly that as expedition artist he hoped I did not make him redundant. The captain of *Endurance* was a New Zealander, Worsley, whose manner was far less daunting than that of Gloomy Davis. One of the ship's officers was a big chap, Crean, who had been on Scott's second expedition and looked a handy fellow to have in a scrape. As we shook hands, I realised Crean had been in the party that found the bodies of Scott and his companions. In fact Crean,

Wild, the boss and I were the only expedition members with polar experience. I was not introduced to the sailing crew, but from what I could see they looked an unlikely, uninspiring lot for Shackleton to have handpicked.

I had equipment to stow and sadly did not get to explore Buenos Aires. The Argentine women were very attractive and groups of young women were interested in *Endurance* but kept their distance. Shackleton hosted local dignitaries on board *Endurance* and occasionally disappeared to civic functions. After several days in port, there was a small but enthusiastic send-off. Our last mailbag included a letter to Elsa. *Endurance* slipped away from the dock and was escorted by the Buenos Aires tugboat fleet out into the Río de la Plata.

•

A freshening nor'-easterly breeze has us well out to sea. I am working with Crean, lashing cargo on the forward deck, when our attention is drawn to an unexpected movement and I see first one boot and then another behind a pile of loose boxes and stores. Fearing the worst, I lean over to see who it could be. A voice cries, 'I'm coming out, I'm coming out,' and the boots are followed by a boy of slight build whom I've never seen before, and he in turn is followed out of his cubbyhole by a black and ginger cat. There is quite a commotion as a barrel falls over and with the roll of the ship gets away from Crean and me. Order is restored and all eyes are looking back to the bridge, where Shackleton stands motionless, having watched the scene unfold. Crean leads the boy aft and I follow. This young stowaway has done what I would like to have done when I was his age, but not on this boat, not on this voyage. Could he have any idea about our destination? Shackleton is looking very stern as the boy mounts the steps onto the bridge. Worsley and Wild arrive as Shackleton questions the stowaway.

'What's your name, boy?'

'Perce Blackborow, sir,' he replied respectfully with his head down.

'And how old are you, Mr Blackborow?'

'Eighteen, sir.'

'You are friends with some of my crew?'

'I know some of the men what joined in Buenos Aires, sir.'

'And are they the only ones who knew you were on board, Mr Blackborow?'

'I don't know what you mean, sir. I snuck on, sir.'

'I see . . . And do you know where we are bound, Mr Blackborow?'

'Antarctica, sir.'

'And do you know, Mr Blackborow, that in those parts it is not uncommon to be marooned and run out of food, and that the first to be eaten is any stowaway?' The boy raised his eyes from Shackleton's boots to his solid-looking waist.

'They won't get much from me, sir.'

At this Wild and Worsley smile, but not the boss.

Much to my surprise, the boy is not put off at the first opportunity, but is engaged by Shackleton as ship's steward. This, I come to realise, is not untypical of how the boss has selected the sailing crew and scientists. We are now twenty-nine men and a ship's cat, Mr Chippy. Mr Chippy will be the first cat in Antarctica.

Within several days we are receiving a battering as the wind changes direction and the overladen *Endurance* makes her way through the southerly squalls and wild seas of the Roaring Forties. My new scientist friends turn various shades of green. I am blessed for a voyaging life and do not suffer seasickness. Nor do heights worry me. I hope Shackleton is impressed when I happily climb up into the crow's nest to film.

After ten days of sailing, a range of mountain peaks rises up through the clouds ahead of us. This is South Georgia Island, but as we draw closer its coast is shrouded in fog and no safe passage can be seen. Worsley directs regular siren blasts into the fog, and shortly we hear a horn replying in the distance. A small tug, *Sitka*, emerges and comes alongside to inspect what manner of humankind we are on board. We have been expected, and within a short time *Sitka* has led us safely into King Edward Cove, a large sheltered harbour on the north-east coast of South Georgia.

The seas flatten as we enter, and there is an eerie silence as the wind in the rigging, which has been so constant, is now but a whisper. One hears instead the creak of deck timber and sighs of shipmates as the prospect of land approaches. The mist swirls and lifts, and I borrow Worsley's binoculars as civilisation comes into view. Through the glass I spy a pleasant prospect. Boats are moored on the water's edge, near a large wooden building with a high A-framed roof designed to withstand heavy winter snowfalls; a series of chimneys signify this building is industrial in use. Beyond and ranging up the hillside are small wooden houses, and above these I can make out against the snowline a white-painted church and steeple. This settlement is the whaling station Grytviken. South Georgia is an English territory, but it is the Norwegians who have established whaling operations along its coast.

Grytviken nestles at the very end of King Edward Cove. To the south lies a valley, at the head of which a powerful glacier can be seen discharging snow and ice from mountains that rise up to nine thousand feet and run the length of South Georgia. Despite the grey day, the entrance into Grytviken is truly spectacular. The settlement is reflected in the still waters at the end of the cove against a stunning backdrop of alpine peaks. Along its northern shore rises Duce Fell, a peak of a mere four thousand feet.

It is only as *Endurance* draws closer that we observe the penance Grytviken pays for its occupation by man. The reflections off the waters of the bay are enhanced by a surface layer of oil and blood and gore. The small bow wave of *Endurance* turns red. From her stern she trails hundreds of yards of intestines which have wrapped around the rudder. By now, all on board have begun to choke at the stench of rotting whale corpses—and there is to be no respite. Not far from where we drop anchor are several moorings; each has tied to it long lines of whale carcasses which have been pumped full of air and towed into port to await processing. The large building I saw through the binoculars is the main processing plant. Between it and the water is a broad flat landing, across which a number of whales have been winched for flensing. In both directions, the entire shoreline is a graveyard of skeletal remains. I count over one hundred skulls. The shallows along the edge are red with blood and awash with intestines and offal.

I busy myself with getting the dogs ashore. There are seventy sledge dogs and they prove hard to control, so excited are they at being on land strewn with whale offal.

Word soon spreads that our Norwegian hosts are saying it is one of the worst-ever seasons for ice. Pack ice fills the whole Weddell Sea. Shackleton's trans-Antarctic crossing depends on establishing a base on the southernmost shore of the Weddell Sea. To reach the starting point will involve sailing through a thousand miles of pack ice. No one can do this, say the whalers. Shackleton is cautioned to wait till next summer.

Next day the word is we will stay here in Grytviken for some weeks. Wild says no way Shackleton will wait longer than that. Thank God for Wild. Relations between Shackleton and I have been cool after I refused his offer of wages only and insisted on a share of film rights. He said he would have to sort this out with the expedition backers, but after all it is my reputation that makes their film rights more valuable.

In the meantime, I get to work recording scenes of South Georgia. I would like to get panorama shots of *Endurance* from the surrounding peaks, but I doubt if any of the scientists are up to helping to carry my equipment on the climb. Worsley, however, has a hardy constitution and has time on his hands in port. He is good company and I am glad when he offers to join me, along with his first officer, Greenstreet. We plan to find a route to the very top of Duce Fell.

We set out early next morning. It is hard going above the snow line. The final sections are quite sheer and ropes are needed. It is bitterly cold, but the day stays clear and I get some exposures which make *Endurance* seem tiny against the mountains. The energetic figures of Worsley and Greenstreet are overwhelmed by the grandeur of the South Georgia landscape. I am very excited about getting the plates into a darkroom.

When I do, the negatives from Duce Fell are perfect. When Shackleton sees the plates he is impressed and I know I have earned his respect, even if all is not yet forgiven. *Endurance* was built with a darkroom and I soon have plenty of developing work to do. If I am not out exploring, then it is in the darkroom I am happiest. With the door shut and red lamp on, I could be anywhere. I have my negatives and do not notice the passage of time.

Mail arrives and there is a letter from Elsa written the day after my departure from Sydney.

Dearest Frank,

This is the first of many letters I promised I would write you. I will try to write as often as I can, though I still can't think of things that you will find of interest compared to your adventures. I am sure wherever you are there will be news of the war. But that is all people here talk about. I am so very proud of you and what you are doing.

Your ma has invited me to tea at your sister's house. I am afraid they will think me very shy, but I do want to meet your family. I am just a little nervous, that's all . . .

The letter was signed 'Your loving Elsa'. Reading and rereading the letter evokes the strangest of feelings. I am embarrassed by her confession of feelings for me. It is, I think, a feminine trait. I doubt men would have these feelings and I am unsure how to reply. There is nothing from Ma.

During our stay at Grytviken, Shackleton, the scientists, the ship's officers and I are invited by the station manager, Fridjhof Jacobsen, to a special dinner at his home in honour of our expedition. I have developing work to do, including some prints intended as gifts for our Norwegian hosts, and I am not in the mood for drinking. I ask Shackleton to excuse me until later in the evening.

When I emerge from my darkroom it is as dark without as within. The dinner will have started. On deck, all is still. I hear drunken cries and laughter coming from shore. The main entertainment in Grytviken is imbibed, and there are few women to curb the worst excesses. Norwegians, I am told, are big drinkers. They work hard by day but once it is dark they have little else they want to do and expect us to be the same. I am surprised Sir Ernest wants to carouse with Jacobsen, but the boss is a big Irish fellow and I daresay handles it as well if not better than the whalers. If nothing else he is a businessman based on the amount of credit Jacobsen has given him.

There's no one else on the deck of *Endurance*, but in the fo'c'sle I find Blackborow, who agrees to row me in. We climb down the side with a hurricane lantern. The yellow light illuminates concentric oily ripples as I step into the dinghy. The smell of offal at water level is even more offensive. The boat strains as it moves in a sea thick with entrails and blood. Rowing requires restraint to avoid oars being tangled in tentacles of whale gut.

We bump against the shore and I plant my feet firmly before letting go the dinghy, which quickly disappears. Without my coat it is cold and the ground is slippery as I head off in the direction of the station manager's house. I figure if I walk towards the light with the glistening black harbour on my left I will get past the flensing plant and onto a pathway. Shortly, however, the light from Jacobsen's house disappears inexplicably. I realise a large object looms in front of me. My path is blocked by a fresh catch, a large blue whale, hauled up onto its back in the flensing yard for a grisly dissection on the morrow.

Unimaginable that the blasted Norwegians should choose to sail to the opposite end of the world to slaughter such extraordinary creatures and to do so in such a barbarous fashion. They have turned this pristine harbour into a bloodbath. It is not their country and there are no civic requirements on the conduct of their butchery. They have no concern at living in the squalour of their own abattoir. Great strips of blubber are guillotined and thrown into huge steamers to extract the precious oil. Here at Grytviken they take only the oil. The waste is sickening; it is like slaughtering herds of cows for jugs of milk.

I make my way down the flensing yard to the head and beak of this spectacular creature, but the incoming tide makes this route impassable. Walking back to the tail I realise this giant must be ninety feet long, and even as it lies prostrate it is more than double my height.

The tail lies in a pile of guts and offal extending from the flensing shed, which I am disinclined to explore. Spying a timber ladder alongside the carcass, I am reminded of my misspent youth evading nightwatchmen in the factories and warehouses around Glebe. I brace the ladder and ascend the girth of the leviathan. But as I am retrieving the ladder for the descent, my feet go from under me and I realise this mammal has already been sawed open along its gut. I plunge backwards into an abyss.

I fear my neck will be broken, but the back of my head smacks against a flap of blubber and I am tossed over further into what I realise is the bowel and intestines. I let go the hurricane lamp. It falls and goes out. Darkness is complete. I am smothered and unable to draw breath as I choke on what I imagine is undigested krill. I am grabbing and clawing at whatever I can, but all that I touch is slimy and gives way. It is an enormous effort to bring myself upright in the pitch-dark, but I manage it. Lifting my head above the blood and gore, I gasp for air. In seconds I am climbing and leaping the ribbed walls of my prison, but to no avail. I am drenched, and inside this once warm-blooded creature it is now below freezing.

At the top of my lungs I call out, 'Hello,' and then, 'Help!' but I hear nothing in reply. My predicament seems bleak and I regret my unkind thoughts about our Norwegian hosts. I continue to call out hopelessly from the belly of the beast.

After what seems an eternity I hear footsteps and see a glimmer of light and then a face wearing a look of incredulity. It is one of the whalers. With ropes and lamps, I am saved. I can't hide my relief, but nor can I join in the laughter and cries of 'Jonah'. I am taken to the manager's house for a hot bath. My best clothing I never see again. My mortification is complete and I will not be sad to leave this place.

However, first I have to endure being dressed in my host's clothing and returned to the company of my colleagues and the Norwegians in a large dining room, its walls brightly painted red and blue. Each of the Norwegians insists on shaking my hand. I sense Shackleton watching me. Eventually I find a seat next to Wild, who is listening intently to our host Jacobsen recounting previous attempts to enter the Weddell Sea.

'Ten years ago,' says Jacobsen, 'my father-in-law was master on *Antarctic*. His ship is designed for ice but is crushed to matchsticks . . . and then two years ago, before Germany and England decide to have this crazy war, Wilhelm Filchner wants to go exactly where you want to go, because the map says the Weddell Sea takes him furthest south. But the map is only what people think is there, of where they think there is land. And the map does not show ice. The Weddell Sea ice takes his ship, *Deutschland*, in a circle for a year. Filchner is lucky and survives. Now he is exploring the French countryside with the German army.'

Jacobsen takes a puff of his cigar. 'And the ice this year, I tell you, is far worse than 1912. That is why you should wait and try next spring.'

Shackleton leans back and sticks out his jaw. 'If I had known the war would drag on, I would not have come. But now I am here I cannot wait a year. This is when I am here. This is when I will go. If the ice stops us, then we will make camp and wait out the winter. What we can achieve in Antarctica will be of such importance it will outlast a war in Europe. But for Antarctica, you know, every continent in the world is occupied.'

'*Ja*, and by the time you come back,' Jacobsen interrupts, 'they will mostly be occupied by Germans.' Shackleton ignores this quip.

'We will be the first to cross the Antarctic continent. No one before us could hope to do this. We are the ones to do it. Besides, Britain already has many war heroes, but the world also needs explorers.'

'Like Scott.'

'Yes, Fridhjof, like Scott—but, unlike Scott, I plan to bring my men home to their families.'

Jacobsen puffs contentedly and smiles across at Shackleton. '*Ja*, the plan is good. But the ice is real. Here is how you will know I am correct. In summers past we do not see icebergs near South Georgia. But this summer they are there. When you leave South Georgia and turn south, I suggest you keep a sharp lookout.'

I am a mere photographer, yet I can't help but reflect that Jacobsen has lived here on the edge of the Weddell Sea for many years. Shackleton has dismissed Jacobsen's concerns not because they are open to question, but because the boss has made up his mind. It is plain also that neither Wild nor Worsley will challenge him. Worsley is no Davis and Frank Wild is one of those incredibly talented people who latch on to a charismatic leader and follow without demur.

Shackleton had been waiting for a ship due in from Buenos Aires, hopefully with mail from civilisation and the latest war news—and, I hope, perhaps a letter from Ma or Elsa. But when at dawn on Saturday, 5 December 1914 there is still no ship in sight, *Endurance* hands its mailbag to *Sitka*, raises anchor and sails out of Grytviken. Within the day the scientists on board are seeing their first icebergs, just as Jacobsen had predicted.

Endurance was at war, although I did not realise it then. It was more like an elaborate sport, just how far south she could reach, how much of the polar world she could conquer. It was the start of a struggle *Endurance* could never win. She was on her maiden voyage. She battled gamely, but the odds were overwhelming. She had not been built for the Antarctic. *Endurance* was designed for sightseeing tours of Greenland, made redundant by the tensions in Europe. She was strongly built, with a steel prow for brushes with icebergs, but her hull was designed for comfortable cruising, not rounded and reinforced for wintering in a frozen sea.

On Sunday 6 December I record in my diary that *Endurance* is at latitude fifty-six degrees south, longitude twenty-seven degrees west. She is pushed southwards by strong nor'-westerly winds and a high following sea. Her scientists are fascinated by the infinite variety of weathered icebergs that she passes.

The bergs are in constant collision with the rolling southerly swells, which crash and spray spume across the ice monoliths. Progress is rapid, and a day later *Endurance* is at fifty-seven degrees south. Broken fragments of bergs and icefloe accumulate, and soon we are in pack ice which looks to be thickening. *Endurance* turns nor'-east to escape back into open water. By the ninth, *Endurance* has had to retreat north and is at latitude fifty-four degrees. She sails east and, when she can, south-east, skirting the edge of the pack. Eventually the line of the pack falls away to the south and we start to make headway.

Saturday 12 December and *Endurance* reaches sixty degrees south and longitude seventeen degrees. This far south the longitude changes quickly. The sea is again littered with loose icefloe. As we progress, the ice forms extensive plates. Worsley navigates around the more solid-looking pieces till these are unavoidable and *Endurance* is forced to bump her way through. The wind is favourable and all square-rigged sails are set to drive the ship through the pressure of the pack. Occasionally she cops a heavy blow on her propeller and stalls and even spins a little in the ice. Worsley stays constantly at her helm and is visibly anxious as he guides her through. He heads straight downwind to the sou'-east to build up momentum, then pulls the wheel hard to starboard to strike the icepack in hope of forcing an opening. Once he breaks through, he straightens up to regain speed. Above the sound of the wind is the now-constant grind of ice on the timber hull. The ice claws at *Endurance* from bow to stern, but lets her through.

Below decks the scraping noise has everyone on edge. Shudders vibrate through the hull as the bow of *Endurance* collides with unseen icefloes or rises up momentarily until its solid weight crashes back down through the plate ice.

Sixty-one degrees south and the wind goes round to the south-west, full of sleet and snow. Visibility is poor. *Endurance* pauses, stops, drifts sideways. Square-rigged sails are furled. There is no steerage. An anchor is dropped onto the ice to keep head to wind. Engines are run to stop ice forming around the propeller.

The next day, the wind shifts to the west and sails are hoisted. *Endurance* breaks through into open water and good progress is made. The low clouds are driven away and, when the sun comes out, the brilliance of sunlight and reflection from the ice is overwhelming. Our sleek black vessel enters a world of dark blue ocean and floating islands of plate ice which stretch to the horizon. Alongside ancient honeycombed bergs, the ocean turns aquamarine and turquoise. Bergs are dotted with sleeping seals, sea leopards and my old friends, Adelie penguins. The Adelies at least are curious at the entry of *Endurance* into their pristine frozen world, which until this century had withstood the ambitions of man. I hoist my full plate camera and cine camera to the highest point in the rigging and up I go to perch by myself for hours, far away from the personalities and hectic activities on board. As far south as I can observe from my vantage point, all that I see is ice.

The Grytviken whalers have not exaggerated. It is a bad season for ice. But we are committed to our voyage. There is no turning back for *Endurance*. The engine alone now does most of the work. Worsley has come to enjoy using his ship as an elegant battering ram. Despite the seriousness of our predicament, he is childlike in targeting floes that are the most populated by sleeping seals and groups of chattering penguins. The seals are oblivious until tipped unceremoniously into the water and the penguins scatter port and starboard of the bow, cluck-cluck-clucking furiously in disbelief. Worsley calls for Scottish biologist Robert Clark to come to the helm, and then berates Clark for not answering the penguins that are calling out his name. Even Clark, a man of few words, manages a smile. Fortunately he is good-humoured, as this becomes a frequent jest.

Every so often *Endurance* is brought to a halt by a solid section of floe. The engine is reversed, then Worsley chooses the most likely point and gives it full steam ahead. We all brace for collision, and as the ice shatters and gives way we breathe a sigh of relief. Occasionally, however, the ice holds and the bow of *Endurance* rises up on the floe. We wait in suspense to see if we are to be repelled. Gradually the weight of the keel forces a crack and the ice fractures in a line of water ahead of us into which *Endurance* steams before the lead closes over.

Tuesday 22 December and we are sixty-three degrees south. It is slow-going. Every so often a new lead in the ice opens that takes us several miles further south. I look out for icebergs to film. They have the advantage over many subjects in that they fill the viewfinder, are stationary, and are luminescent and infinite in variety. The living wildlife, of course, is more elusive. I have seen a number of blue whales, but with rare exception I am unable to capture them on film. Most days Frank Wild shoots one or two seals to add to the larder as their steaks are a popular item on the menu. Overhead, *Endurance* has a regular following of petrels and terns which swoop on any scraps.

Life on board *Endurance* has fallen into a routine of three eight-hour watches under Shackleton, Wild and Worsley respectively. Each shift is a mix of scientists and sailors, no matter how incompatible. Orde-Lees confides in me he has never before peeled a spud nor scrubbed a floor and thinks it a poor allocation of resources by Shackleton. I have to show him how to take the eyes out of a potato without losing a finger. He is particularly unhappy the morning he and I have to shovel coal into bags for heating the planned expedition hut.

'But this is work the sailors should do,' he says, holding the bag open as I am, apparently, better at shovelling.

The days pass quickly as *Endurance* continues to push south. Blackborow has tacked up a calendar in the mess and draws a black cross through each day that passes. Without this the days and weeks become indistinguishable. There is now barely any night to segment each day. It is still light at midnight. I sleep whenever I am too tired to work in the darkroom. My rest is disturbed by the comings and goings of the crew, and the shuddering of *Endurance* as she continues her odyssey southwards. And at all hours of the night and day there is the clawing and scratching of ice on the hull, sometimes raucous and sometimes subdued whispering: 'This far and no further, this far and no further.'

Christmas Day finds Endurance at latitude sixty-five degrees south. Christmas luncheon is a special occasion for which tablecloths are turned over to hide their worst stains and a great variety of tinned delicacies are served, including mock turtle soup, whitebait, jugged hare, mince pies and figs and dates. Hussey entertains with a banjo and later on, outside, he entrances an appreciative audience of Adelie penguins on a nearby floe.

I feel I do not know the other expedition members as well as I did on *Aurora*. It may be because I am the only Australian. I sense I am a little too loud for their liking and they don't appreciate my clowning around. There are none I would call close friends. As a result I am more subdued, not the practical joker I was with the AAE.

Boxing Day sees the start of a four-day south-westerly gale that stops all progress and forces *Endurance* back, losing many miles of hard-won gains. On 29 December, Worsley ambitiously rams *Endurance* between two floes, but they resist, causing minor hull damage. *Endurance* is wedged and can move neither forwards nor back. More sails are hoisted and the engine driven at full steam, but the ice has a firm grip. Frank Wild leads a work party overboard to attack the ice with picks and shovels. The cold conditions are conducive to vigorous work, and after an hour or so *Endurance* twists free and we quickly scramble up the side before we are left behind.

By New Year's Eve, having traversed several long leads, *Endurance* crosses the Antarctic Circle. The sun does not set at all but, despite this, the evening produces a most spectacular 'sunset' with gold and crimson light reflected between the clouds and icefloes. The scientists—Wordie, James and Clark—are good companions and have invited me to a quiet celebration in Clark's cabin which, being near to the boiler, is not as cold as elsewhere.

'Here ye go, lads,' says Jock Wordie, as he places a brown paper parcel on the table. 'Ye must hae a piece of me mother's Hogmanay cake.'

'But Jock, ye bin saving it all this time,' says Clark.

'Well, tis auld lang syne today, I'll gie ye a wee piece each.'

'It's got icing,' I observe as he cuts the string and unwraps the cake.

'Not usually,' Clark replies.

'Och, lads,' says Wordie in dismay. 'It's not icing; it's mould. Ye better hae two pieces each!'

The first and second of January 1915 see *Endurance* in thin, newly formed ice crust which she easily cuts through. I have suspended a small timber platform from the bowsprit and secure cinefilm of the steel-edged prow carving up the floe, the ice lifted and tossed port and starboard. I also take pictures looking down on the deck from the foretop yardarm. On Saturday 2 January, the ice providentially opens and *Endurance* covers one hundred and twenty-four miles by noon.

Our latitude is now sixty-nine degrees south and Worsley estimates we are a hundred miles north-west of land. But the favourable conditions don't last, and the next day it is again gale-force winds from the east-sou'-east. Worsley tucks *Endurance* in behind a berg some hundred-and-twenty-feet high to which we attach an ice anchor. On the fourth, the ice anchor is taken up to avoid collision with large moving bergs. By now the snowdrift is so thick it is impossible to see anything beyond the rigging. When the drift clears *Endurance* is walled in to the south by high pack ice and is forced north and nor'-east.

This morning climbing down from my bunk I accidentally waken Clark in the bunk below when my stockinged foot steps on his face.

'Wha tha fook! Hurly-burly,' he cries out.

'Bloody hell, Clark, have I broken your jaw?'

'It's nae my jaw I'm worried aboot. Ye haven't washed ye socks since ye came aboard!' Luckily he is a good sport. Before the day ends we sight blue whales and sperm whales in the distance. Endurance reaches 70 degrees south.

By the sixth adverse winds again have *Endurance* moored to a large icefloe. Conditions do not look like improving and the dogs are taken down on the ice for exercise. They are very excited. They have been losing condition chained up on deck and snap at passers-by. They have been teased mercilessly by Mr Chippy, who delights in strutting along the tops of their kennels, just beyond the reach of their chains.

The following day sees little improvement. *Endurance* is surrounded by heavy coastal formations of ice, which have been pressured into large hummocks well above the height of the bulwarks. Shackleton and Worsley decide to lift the ice anchor and look for an open lead heading south. As *Endurance* detaches, the once-pristine ice floe is now strewn with cans, boxes and rubbish, the detritus of our life on board. We are no better than Grytviken whalers.

Endurance is back at latitude 69 degrees. On 10 January we catch glimpses of Coats Land. An offshore breeze opens up a wide sea channel to the south which *Endurance* charges down. She is surrounded by hundreds of seals attracted to her wake. A week later *Endurance* reaches latitude seventy-four degrees south. Worsley announces we are just one hundred and ninety miles from our destination, Vahsel Bay. But two days later we are stuck in a southerly blizzard and forced again to moor in the lee of a large iceberg. The winds are over fifty miles an hour and the best place to keep warm is my bunk. I curl up with *For the Term of his Natural Life*, a book about convicts by Marcus Clarke, which causes me to contemplate the good fortune of my own existence.

Like *Aurora*, *Endurance* has a fine library. In it I find a small but invaluable travel book, *Polar Exploration*, by William Bruce, who led the Scottish National Antarctic Expedition of 1902–04. Bruce wrote the book in 1911, just before Amundsen declared his intention to race Scott to the pole. I am surprised by Bruce's forthright opinions. They accurately sum up the view I have formed of Shackleton:

> *What the mass of the public desire is pure sensationalism, therefore the Polar explorer who attains the highest latitude and who has the powers of making a vivid picture of the ... hardships involved will be regarded popularly as the hero and will seldom fail to add materially to his store of worldly welfare ... The general rule, however, is that the man of science opens the way and reveals the treasures of the unknown, and the man of business follows and reaps the commercial advantage ...*

It strikes me this is exactly why Mawson, the man of science, does not trust Shackleton. Shackleton is too desperate to be a hero. There is every chance he will bring about a tragedy of epic proportions. How is he going to bring the Weddell Sea expedition members home if he pushes *Endurance* south until she is locked in ice? As to the party crossing Antarctica to the Ross Sea, how can they know what they will find? What is Shackleton really expecting to achieve?

Whatever Shackleton achieves, it is my job to be there to create the images. My photographs may be all that endures, and they will be what I make them. Shackleton may not like it, but he must know it is I who holds the power of the 'vivid picture'.

8

76 Degrees South

Endurance is now seventy-six degrees south and less than eighty miles from where Shackleton wants to land at Vahsel Bay. I dash off letters to Ma and Elsa to accompany *Endurance* back to South Georgia. The letters are only a page each and I wonder momentarily if and when I will write again, and if the letters say enough—but there is nothing more. We will soon be on our way, that's all.

There is a growing level of excitement on board. On Saturday 23 January, the clouds roll back from the east. For the first time land is visible, twenty miles away to the east and south. It can be seen rising up some three thousand feet. The scientists and crew mill on deck, and to escape the hubbub I climb to the crow's nest on the mainmast, where I enjoy the isolation. Up here I am as remote as *Endurance* in the endless icepack.

Two days later the wind swings to the west, and just two hundred yards in front of us a broad lead opens in the ice. All sails are unfurled and the motor is at full speed, but *Endurance* does not respond. The ice surrounding her is in parts some twelve feet thick. Crean leads a group who, with picks and crow bars, try to loosen the grip of the ice, but without success. I take photos of *Endurance* 'sailing' while held rigid like a model toy ship in the ice.

After a few days of being stuck fast, Shackleton allows us to stretch our legs on the surrounding floes. Orde-Lees offers to carry the camera in a rucksack, and so we venture out on skis. I set up the tripod and experiment with new Paget Autochrome plates for colour photographs, keeping a record of exposure times for each picture. I take shots of *Endurance* and of Orde-Lees manoeuvring among hummocks of ice. He is very accomplished on his skis while I am a rank amateur. My elbows and backside take a pounding. After one of my falls, I find Frank Wild standing above me.

'The boss is livid. He's worried we'll get a break in the ice and be stuck waiting for you two. You'd better get back there and take it on the chin.'

Orde-Lees is excessively apologetic, but I am not accustomed to being the object of the boss's flashes of temper, especially when I have been attending my photographic duties. Orde-Lees is an easy target and my sense is that Shackleton is not unhappy to link me with him. It is as if the boss thinks I am also an odd bod.

Orde-Lees scampers ahead and I trudge back with Wild.

'Do you think we'll get breaks in the ice to make it further south?' I ask.

'One decent blizzard is all it would take to clear this ice,' he answers. 'Vahsel Bay is just twenty-five miles away. But I think the boss will try Orde-Lees's motor sledges tomorrow, to see if they can move stores across the ice and up onto the Barrier. Otherwise, I don't see how we can haul the hut that far along with fifty tonnes of supplies.'

But the motor sledges turn out to be next to useless. Orde-Lees has never been to Antarctica before and there was no time to trial the motor sledges in Norway as had been planned. Orde-Lees' stocks take a tumble. I could have come up with a superior design for the variable Antarctic surface, but it's way too late now.

That evening, being Saturday, we have musical entertainment from Hussey and Seaman Cheetham on banjo and fiddle, and our regular toast to 'wives and sweethearts'.

Not everyone relaxes together easily and the sailors are openly rude to some of the scientific staff, of whom they think very little. Worsley is called out to deal with a fight among the crew which the carpenter, Chips McNeish, has stirred up in the fo'c'sle.

The boss knows activity is needed and games of football are encouraged to let off steam. I see little point in joining in. Both sailors and scientists are more able than me at kicking a ball. I take my camera onto the ice, but photographing a football match in Antarctica is difficult. The field is not defined and the players appear as black silhouettes on a glaring white background. Orde-Lees protests the non-observance of rules until he is silenced by big Tom Crean sitting on his chest.

I am keen to explore our surroundings. There is an iceberg several miles away that dominates the horizon. We have named it the Rampart Berg as it resembles a fortification. Worsley offers to climb it with me. He has the standing to persuade the boss to grant permission, and so at eight o'clock next morning Worsley, Wordie and I set out with a sledge of cameras and gear. We reach the berg by noon and it is quite imposing up close, even though it is only a few hundred feet high. What is particularly unnerving is that all around the berg the icepack is moving with the surface current, and to actually step onto the side of the berg is like jumping from a moving train. The surface ice is pushed inexorably against the steep edges of the Rampart Berg. The ice groans and scrapes and shifts and folds and jumps and is altogether frightening to stand near. I retreat three hundred yards to capture the massive berg within my camera lens.

After three weeks in which *Endurance* has remained firmly stuck, everyone on board has grown a little testy. Breaks in the ice appear but, more often than not, by the time the crew mobilises, the open water closes over. Worsley and the boss call for all hands to 'sally' the ship. With the engine running full astern, we all stand on the starboard gunnel and, on Worsley's command, run to the port side then, on his call, all run back to starboard. The intent is to break the grip of the ice, but once again we fail. Worsley then has all hands gather on the poop and has everyone jump up and down in time. I detect little if any movement in the ice and suspect this activity is sponsored by Shackleton to invigorate everyone on board. There is much merriment and the activity warms us up.

Over breakfast on a mournful Valentine's Day, *Endurance* shudders as her weight cracks the ice around her and, four hundred yards away to the south, a lead opens up. All hands take to the ice with picks, chisels, sledgehammers and saws. We dissect the ice plate in front of the bow and, with a full head of steam, Worsley propels *Endurance* forwards to open a gap. He has little distance in which to gain momentum, but some headway is made. We work at this all day and gain but thirty yards.

Overnight the open water we have created freezes over, and the next morning we start again. At day's end the boss calls a halt. We have made one hundred yards, but there are hundreds of yards to go to the open lead and a brief survey shows the ice plate ahead of us is in parts more than ten feet thick.

The open lead remains in sight but out of reach. It becomes the domain of killer whales, which blow spume and push their sleek black-capped bodies out of the water until they are sitting on the edge of the ice. They are looking for seals and are very curious about us. Their white eye patches stare back at me as they lift their heads tauntingly and cast an evil eye in all directions before disappearing beneath the floe. They certainly make me ill at ease when working alongside open water or on thin, translucent ice. Killer whales, like ourselves, are enthusiastic predators. With winter approaching we are looking to find and slaughter as many seals as we can for our own larder before the killer whales take them. I have become quite adept at killing and butchering seals and penguins.

On 24 February, Sir Ernest announces the end of the ship watches. Instead we work during the day and take turns as nightwatchman, whose job it is to keep the bogie fires alight and take meteorological observations. *Endurance* has become a shore station.

The boss wants the dogs off the ship and they are mighty pleased to go. All hands are busy building canine igloos—or, as we call them, 'dogloos'—which extend in a ring around *Endurance*. The dogs are secured by pouring water on the end of their chains in a small hole in the ice.

Over the next few weeks, Chips undertakes carpentry work in preparation for wintering-in. New WC shelters are constructed over the poop. The stove that was intended for the shore hut is installed in the main hold to create a living and dining room for the scientists and officers. This is dubbed 'the Ritz'. Around this, Chips has built a series of small cubicles to serve as living quarters, each with three or four bunks. Hussey and I are allocated a room with the doctors, Macklin and McIlroy. I wonder how Shackleton determines these arrangements. Macklin has barely said a word to me the entire voyage, though he and I are both in the shore party for the polar crossing. I get in early and nickname our cubicle 'the Billabong', and without too much objection soon have it decorated with an Australian flag, a boomerang and my photographs. I had expected to experience again the camaraderie I had enjoyed with Bob and Azzi but it seems unlikely. Our quest has slipped away from us and there is a tension in our enforced cohabitation with the sailing crew. The chaos of moving accommodation distracts from the overwhelming issue of what is to become of the expedition.

Winter clothing is issued by the boss to all hands, including finnesko mittens, Burberry boots, woollen helmets, Jaeger sweaters and so on. On 14 March, the boss starts winter routine with breakfast at 9 a.m., lunch at 1 p.m., free time in the afternoon and dinner at 6 p.m. The days grow shorter. The sun now lives on the horizon, often hidden, then coming out and casting long shadows and tingeing the ice with golden light. The atmosphere is laden with rime crystals. Refraction and the glimmering of light off the ice cause mirages on the horizon in all directions.

Perhaps it is just the cold and gloom, but our small civilisation seems to belong to another world, remote from homes and families. My sense is that God has lost sight of us; we are faraway objects, as if seen backwards through a camera lens. Even the sun shrinks, diffuses and splits into two, then three suns, which my naked eye gazes on, each sun linked by a halo as depicted in picture books of the holy saints. I blink and rub my eyes but there are still three suns glowing above the horizon. Mock suns, Hussey educates me, are a parhelic phenomenon. This comes and goes during the morning and reoccurs on subsequent days. Then, at the end of April, the sun sets and does not rise at all the next day. Hussey says we will not see the sun again until the end of July, and who knows where on earth *Endurance* may be then, if she can be found at all? Until that time, it is long days of blackness interspersed by several hours of twilight. This limits me severely as to what I can achieve with a camera. However, we put this time in the netherworld to good use, training the dogs to pull sledges.

On the AAE, Mertz and Ninnis looked after the dogs from the time they left England and developed a close bond with them. Knowing the importance of dogs to my survival in an Antarctic crossing, I am keen to work with them. Six dog teams of eight to nine dogs are formed, and as I am in the polar party I am designated master of one of the teams.

Shakespeare, Hackenschmidt, Rugby, Rufus, Bob, Jerry, Martin, Sailor and Noel are my team. I am exclusively responsible for feeding and caring for them. Over time I learn much about them. Shakespeare is the natural leader of the team. He has the noble appearance of an English sheepdog and is both brave and wise. Bob is the brother of Shakespeare and a hard worker. Rugby is much like Bob, but has no tail to wag. Rufus is a revered elder of the pack, but still a good worker. Sailor is a cunning rascal who looks to be pulling hard, but a close check shows his trace is not quite taut. Hackenschmidt is in lean condition, but likely to become the biggest dog in the pack. Noel is the smallest, but has a rivalry with Hackenschmidt and attacks him at any opportunity. Noel stands on his hind legs to beg for food and comes with me on all my walks. Jerry and Martin are brothers. Martin is a terrific puller, but often in trouble for pinching other dogs' food, and Jerry is too friendly with people for his own good, frequently jumping up on me when I am busy adjusting the camera.

The part of a photographer's work that has never interested me is the taking of ordinary everyday portraits. There is far too much vanity involved, for which I have no patience. However Shakespeare and my dog team are free of vanity. They are diverse in their breeding and their faces are full of personality. I use the quieter days to obtain a series of classic portraits to reveal their unique characters, which range from Saint Bernard to pure wolf.

The dogs have had some sledging experience, but not for some time, and they have not worked together nor with me. First I train just with Shakespeare and a small bobsled until he and I have an understanding. Then the whole team must learn to behave in harness. Each dog learns its position along the main hauling trace. I teach the dogs to listen for my voice and to be ready to move together at the instant they hear a command. Time is short and I use the whip to expedite the learning process. 'Mush!' and the team steps forwards, 'gee' and Shakespeare leads them to the left, 'haw' to the right and 'hoah' to stop. For all their differences, my team quickly learns to combine well together. They have a natural leader in Shakespeare, who instinctively finds the best way around hummocks and thin ice, and puts a stop to any fights within the team.

In no time, my favourite activity is taking the dogs out to exercise and practise pulling a sledge. Worsley or Greenstreet often accompany me on the sledge. We dress warmly, for the temperature is below freezing. Despite wind and sleet stinging my face, I know I am alive on these hair-raising rides with the dogs, chasing the moon through a purple sky above the ice. The visibility is often abysmal and I rely on Shakespeare to lead us home to *Endurance*. In darkness he somehow finds long stretches of white powder snow and avoids the dull blue glow of wind-polished sastrugi.

By mid-June, all the trainers are boasting about their dog teams. A sledge race is organised and bets placed. Wild wins, but is only ten seconds ahead of my team. I challenge him to a rematch, but once again Wild is the fastest home. However Sir Ernest was part of his crew weight and had been thrown off, so my team wins by default. I make quite a few pounds, but collecting the winnings is another matter.

Progress with the dogs has been swift and they will be in good shape to pull heavy loads by the spring. But their unquestioning service and loyalty are a stark contrast to the increasing irascibility of Sir Ernest and my other companions. By choice, I spend more time each day with Shakespeare and the team than any of my fellow expedition members. With winter just starting, we are all wondering what is to become of us, of *Endurance* and of the expedition. No one dares ask the boss. But I have heard the crew talking: 'Should have listened to the bloody Norwegians. We're in for it now.' At night-time, especially as I lie in my bunk trying to get warm, I am kept awake by ominous sounds, like distant cannon fire, of ice breaking and falling or, closer at hand, the groan of ice floes being pushed together.

More fights breaks out in the fo'c'sle. All hands point to the bosun Vincent; he is a powerful-looking man and rough as they come. He has been badgering and striking the other crew. The boss demotes him on the spot to trawling hand. Vincent lets it be known he has been unjustly accused and is especially aggrieved by the pay cut that accompanies his demotion. I would not like to be one of the sailing hands sharing the fo'c'sle with him.

Among the officers and scientists it is Orde-Lees who becomes the butt of all jokes and derision. He is store master and his cutbacks are unpopular. He abolished the supply of bread in the evenings, which is entirely sensible, but this has not gone down well with the sailors. They say he has his own secret stash of delicacies. He is a complete toady to Sir Ernest—'Yes, sir; no sir; three bags full, sir'—which I find sickening to watch. I'm sure the boss is onto him.

We have our Midwinter Feast in traditional style, with hilarious dress-ups. I organise a stage and lighting, and we put together over three hours of entertainment, singing and dancing. Sir Ernest plays a pompous lord, Orde-Lees is a clergyman, Hussey a black minstrel with banjo and so on. Fortunately, Sir Ernest leaves the sailors to their own devices in the fo'c'sle with an extra portion of rum and tobacco to celebrate; they would otherwise inhibit the wit and entertainment of our celebration. We raise glasses with our regular toast—'To our wives and sweethearts . . . and may they never meet!' We conclude with 'God Save the King' and 'Auld Lang Syne'.

More often now the weather does not permit sledging trips. The temperature is around minus-thirty degrees. Blizzards rage across the ice without warning. They strike savagely at

Endurance so that she vibrates and trembles. The ropes and spars are solid with rime and resonate in a discordant ringing such that we are forced to shout to be heard. One morning I wake and immediately know something is missing. There is no sound of squabbling from the dogs. I put on my layers and emerge on deck to see all the dogloos down the port side of *Endurance* have gone; the blizzard has completely covered them with fresh snow. It is some hours before we find and extricate the dogs. They are not at all stressed by the experience and wonder what the fuss is about.

The blizzards come and go, often lasting a number of days. There is constant work shovelling snow from *Endurance*, as she would otherwise disappear save for her three masts. Around us the crusty icefloe is transformed. Fallen snow has been carved by blizzards into snow ramps and cornices. After one prolonged blizzard Rufus does not emerge from his dogloo, and on checking I find he has died and frozen solid.

Most days now we see no animal life. It is as well that we have taken in plenty during the autumn. We have cut a small hole in the ice near *Endurance* to tempt wandering seals or penguins, but there are none. Every so often the plate ice cracks and a lead of water forms, sometimes staying open a few hours or sometimes a few days. The ice groans day and night with pressure from the pack and the movement of bergs. Mostly the sounds come from afar, like the sound of surf on a distant reef. At times the movement is close, the ice shudders beneath my feet and my dogs whimper, raise their shaggy heads and look at me. I too look up, expecting to see a foaming wave racing towards us, but there is nothing and stillness resumes.

'*Endurance* cannot live in this.' It is Worsley passing on what the boss has said to him. 'It is only a matter of time. We may have months, but then again it could be over in a few weeks.'

Looking at the horizon I can see movement in the ice. Floes push into each other till one buckles and lifts upwards.

Great Stonehenge boulders of ice appear overnight, projected at perilous angles till they crash back down. One morning I emerge to find the landscape around *Endurance* transformed. Pressure ridges have risen upwards, rafting blocks of ice higher than the gunwales of the ship and threatening to topple on board. The dogloos are pitched at hysterical angles. Arrangements are made so we can bring the dogs on board at short notice. Chains for the dogs are fitted on deck. The boss directs all sledging stores, tents, paraffin and sledging equipment be stowed on deck, readily accessible in the event *Endurance* were to be crushed. Unnecessary excursions are put on hold. The boss directs an hourly watch be maintained at night. We sleep with our woollen helmets on and our finnesko boots and Burberry jackets alongside our bunks, ready for a quick departure.

On 26 July a long-lost friend, 'Old Jamaica', peaks over the horizon, sending shafts of light into collision with showers of condensation crystals falling around us. *Endurance* is brilliantly lit but in less than a minute the sun is gone and we are in the afterglow. Tomorrow I will be ready with my camera.

Sunday 1 August is a nervous day for us. Without warning the floes advance on us and tongues of solid ice push up along the port side of *Endurance* and threaten to roll her over to starboard. *Endurance* cries out at the grinding lateral forces and wrenching strain on her rig, but she holds together. She rides the pressure wave and eventually the shifting ice heels her over to port. Outside the ship is chaos. The dogloos are rolled over and crushed by a wave of ice. The dogs are brought on board and gangways raised. At the same time we make ready the lifeboats, such is the uncertainty of our predicament.

Then, as stealthily as the pressure wave had hit, the pressure recedes and all is quiet. An inspection of the hull reveals damage at the very stern. The cast-iron gudgeons into which the rudder pintles are fitted to enable rotation have been twisted up, and the pintles are now kinked. The rudder has been forced hard to starboard and the after part of the rudder has been shorn off.

Life as we know it returns almost to normal. Scientists return to work with their observations. Meanwhile, Worsley reports that *Endurance* has drifted north to latitude seventy-two and longitude forty-seven degrees, and inexplicably the ocean depth, within the space of a day, has gone from four hundred fathoms to twelve hundred fathoms. Over several days it deepens to nineteen hundred fathoms, over a mile deep, which is disconcerting for no good reason.

I explore our new hinterland of raised hummocks and ice pinnacles. Through the camera viewfinder, the uninhabited icefloes are a meaningless jumbled landscape without perspective. Worsley obliges by stepping into the frame, a stark black silhouetted figure, sometimes on all fours, clambering amid the reflected glare from the blue and white frozen outcrops of rough-hewn ice. I capture *Endurance* on a full glass plate. Photographed over a foreground of ice ridges and boulders, she is stoic in a turbulent sea of troubles. She represents everything that is dear to our fragile community. In the absence of penguins, and having now photographed all the dog teams, it is *Endurance* herself that becomes the focus of my craft. From what Worsley has said, I gather she may not be with us much longer.

Having come through such a long winter without seeing the sun for three months it is a moonlight image of *Endurance* I want most to capture. Many sledging trips, I was guided home by the rime-encrusted masts rising in a black starry sky above the floes. Night-time photography is by necessity hit-and-miss, and only in the darkroom do I ever find out what, if anything, is on a negative. With Worsley's help I set up several pans of magnesium flash powder. I place one each on either side of the bow and down the port side of *Endurance*, and a few more on the ice hummocks between the camera and the ship. We dig small recesses in the ice so the flash will be out of sight to the lens and reflecting up onto the hull. Under Sir Ernest's supervision I place flash powder in pans on deck to illuminate the rigging. A number of crew stand by with buckets of snow lest the explosions start a fire on board. I then run electrical wire to each flash pan. Care has to be taken to stop the explosive from freezing. From thirty yards away I frame the shot. I open the shutter and flick the switch. Muffled explosions rip through the air and night briefly turns to day. *Endurance* seems to leap into the sky and a great cheer goes up from those patient souls waiting on board. I stumble backwards as *Endurance* disappears from my sight along with my camera and tripod. I lose my balance and, totally blinded, I stagger, then trip and plunge face first into the ice.

Later, in the darkroom, the boss is happy with the results. He knows the difficulties of developing glass plates and film in these conditions. He has observed my struggle to keep enough water above freezing point to wash the glass plates so they do not turn into giant ice blocks. He is particularly impressed by the darkroom table I have fashioned from a flat metal box with constantly circulating warm water to keep the dishes of chemicals at a workable temperature. So limited is the supply of water that I resort to attaching strips of exposed film to racks which I dangle overboard in the sea before doing a final rinse in fresh water. The ends of my fingers split from the cold.

September sees the arrival of warmer weather. The others play hockey and football alongside *Endurance*. I record in my diary a snow petrel heading north, the first bird for months. Opportunities for sledging are starting to look more promising. However the last day of September gives us a scare. Around *Endurance* pressure cracks have formed in the ice running south-sou'-east to north-nor'-west. In the afternoon these cracks start to grind and push sideways and there is an enormous squeeze on the forward section of the ship. I watch, expecting the hull will collapse inwards. The lower cabin areas and flooring are buckled and beams start to bend. Tongue-and-groove joints in the deck planking start to spring apart. *Endurance* is literally shivering with the strain. There is then a gut-wrenching crack and the ship shifts; the floe cradling *Endurance* has split in two and the pressure dissipates.

The tension of being stuck in the ice spreads to all on board and causes odd behaviour all around, from which I am not exempt. Orde-Lees has no interest in the dogs but has the nerve to ask me to get their water and as a result I swear profusely at him. The next day he interrupts me cleaning my cameras.

'The boss is pleased with your flashlight shots.'

'Well, he ought to be—they're perfect. I used enough flash powder to sink the bloody ship.'

'Listen here, Hurley, you called me an unseemly name a day ago.'

'What of it?'

'Well, I take it you didn't like my asking you to bring ice on board for the dogs.'

'So is there something else you want?'

'Well, look, it's just that there's not much room on this boat for spats. I've no grudge against you. We should try to get on.'

'What are you after, Lees?'

'Just trying to keep the peace, Hurley.'

'Well, that's fine, keep out of my business, that'll keep the peace.'

He is, I decide, a very odd bastard. He has no good reason to butter me up that I can see.

October sees greater numbers of seals and penguins close to *Endurance*, and we quickly slaughter them to replenish the larder. The weather grows warmer still, and woollen helmets and gloves are no longer necessary. It is startling after many months to see again the haggard, grimy faces of my companions, and I suspect my appearance is no better. On the fourteenth there is movement in the ice around *Endurance*. We are just finishing dinner when there is an enormous crash outside. Emerging on deck we see that, for the first time in nine months, *Endurance* is free of ice and floating in a newly formed lead of inky-black water. This is the cause of much excitement. It is our first chance to inspect the hull around the waterline. The helm has been damaged, but nothing looks irreparable. The mood lifts and Wild, in his deep baritone voice, leads the sailors in a sea shanty. Very privately I thank God that He has saved us. I go to my bunk that night much lighter of heart.

The next day is a propitious one. I let a few souls know it is my birthday and tell them I am twenty-eight (I am not yet ready for twenty-nine). While mostly I prefer my own company, I do not want to miss out being toasted by my fellow expeditioners.

Endurance remains in an open lead. A small spanker sail is hoisted and she actually sails a hundred yards or so. A whale surfaces and blows, the first I have seen in several months.

Two days later is Sunday. In the absence of clergy there is no observance of church practices on *Endurance* like Mawson's services on the AAE—though, for the most part, we all put our trust in the Almighty. Certainly we know our Maker is close at hand. The officers and scientists are quite religious at least in their observance of our Sunday evening gramophone concerts in the Ritz. The sailors are not invited to these occasions. After the meal is cleared away, out come the pipes and tobacco, and favourite recordings are played. As we listen we are each transported to our lives back home. This Sunday, as the gramophone needle descends, the whispery sound of its journey to the first song is overwhelmed by a scratching noise outside that increases until it becomes a roar. The lead has closed in on both sides of *Endurance*. The vibrations of the hull drown out the sound of the gramophone as the ship has the breath squeezed out of her. Then upwards she rises, stern first, and we too rise from our seats and rush outside to observe her drive shaft and propeller lifted clean above the ice.

Overnight *Endurance* subsides and we have a fitful rest. The following evening, just before dinner, the compressive power of the ice is renewed and in a matter of a few seconds it is as if the hand of God has lifted *Endurance* from the ice and laid her on her side like a child's plaything. True to my calling, I set up the tripod outside and take photographs of the once-elegant *Endurance* now pitched over at an angle greater than from any gale.

The boss introduces sea watches again, but we are all on watch all the time. We know not when to sleep. Individual days are blurred by our descent into chaos. Two killer whales take up residence in the lead alongside *Endurance*. They cruise back and forth, and snort and lift themselves up onto the ice. Their malevolent faces seem to enjoy the wild hysteria they create in the dogs. The killers make us wary whenever we step near the edge of the floe.

Endurance is taking water through unseen apertures. The boss orders what little coal reserves we have to raise steam to run the engine-room pump. The pump now runs clickety-click, clickety-click throughout the short nights and long days. The widest girth of *Endurance*'s hull has now sunk into the floe and I do not see how she will lift herself out at the next assault.

Antarctic ice is no neutral power. It opposes the very existence of *Endurance*. She is the epicentre of surge upon surge of pressure waves determined to remove her. The ship groans as her cast-iron floor plates in the engine room detach, as her stern post is wrenched sideways and as her deck timbers buckle and spring apart. The dogs are intuitively aware of the impending crisis and maintain a chorus of unnerving howls.

On 26 October, at latitude sixty-nine degrees and longitude fifty-one degrees, the three lifeboats are lowered onto the floe and manhauled a hundred yards from *Endurance*. The boss announces his plan is to construct sledges for the boats, to load them with bare essentials and sledge towards Paulet Island some three hundred and fifty miles away. I am directed by Shackleton to pack just my albums of expedition photographs, and no cameras other than a compact box brownie.

The next day the battle for *Endurance* is lost. Chips the carpenter reports the water is gaining on the pumps. The dogs, the main stores and essential equipment are moved onto the floe. In the galley a last supper is prepared and the order given that we abandon ship. We are dumbstruck. The timber panelling in the wardroom still exudes a comforting 'don't leave' feeling. The ship's clock is tick-tocking away on the wall, accurate as ever. Downstairs in the Ritz, water is well above the floor. My glass plate negatives in the inundated darkroom are bound for the deep.

At one o'clock in the morning of 28 October, it is forty-seven degrees below freezing. We have set up tents on the ice and have had to move them twice already due to the floe splitting underneath them. No one dares sleep.

Hoosh and hot tea are served from a makeshift stove at breakfast. The boss gathers all hands and announces, '*Endurance* won't be sailing any further. She is beyond saving. We will not be making a trans-Antarctic crossing. Tomorrow we will turn around and go home.' He does not say how.

That *Endurance* is lost was already known to all. But the crew needed to hear it from the boss. It is a relief to hear Shackleton say there will be no crossing. It means my own chances of survival are improved. There is, of course, no way of getting word to the Ross Sea party that they need not risk their lives to establish food depots. Shackleton now distributes garments that had been intended for members of our polar party. Unfortunately there is not enough of the best outdoor clothing for everyone. Wild draws lots for the reindeer-fur sleeping bags, which mysteriously all go to the non-officer sailing crew. The boss then gives a talk about what each man is allowed to bring. Sir Ernest sets the example by starting a pile of personal possessions he is tossing out. Soon there is a heap of oddments that have made it off the ship but must now be left behind on the ice: spare clothing, hats, dress suits, cufflinks, coins, mirrors, combs, hair oil, brushes, Bibles, books, chess sets, cigarette boxes, portmanteaus and many other things of personal value, but now entirely useless. That evening, sailors who have not accepted their predicament scavenge through the pile. Unfortunately the weight of my cine camera and plate glass camera requires they be abandoned. Gone is the prospect of filming history-making events; it is now a matter of returning home any way we can. Hussey is asked to bring his banjo, however. The boss knows morale is more important than cameras. Shortly afterwards, Mr Chippy and four recently born pups are shot.

Next afternoon, we are underway, heading north across the ice like a caravan of gypsies, leaving behind what has become known as Dump Camp. A working party leads off early to clear a trail and remove the worst hummocks. Then follow seven sledges, pulled by seven dogs each, with several hundred pounds of gear. Eighteen men have the job of manhauling the main lifeboat, which Shackleton has named *James Caird* in honour of an expedition benefactor. A dubious honour it seems to me. *James Caird* is a twenty-three-foot-long wooden whaleboat. With supplies on board she weighs a good tonne. The sledge on which she sits soon cracks with the strain as she rises up and over sharp ridges of ice. In between the ridges men sink to their waists in moist soft snow. Each of the dog teams has to double back to haul up more gear in the smaller lifeboat, *Dudley Docker*, also named after a benefactor.

After two days of adverse weather and poor visibility, we have only shifted a mile and a half across the ice. Most of the men have had no experience sledging heavy loads in these conditions. Loud, uncouth remarks are made by sailors about the futility of going on, and equally loud and aggressive rejoinders are heard about who is not pulling their weight and the dire consequences that will befall them. The boss asks me to accompany him, Wild and Worsley for a scout ahead. I am pleased Shackleton has at least acknowledged my sledging experience. Together we conclude the route is impossible. There is no flat, hard surface, it is instead a labyrinth of hummocks and ridges. The decision is made to set up a semi-permanent camp on the thickest piece of ice floe we can find and await the thaw and break-up of the ice pack.

The expedition does not actually have the equipment needed for an outdoor camp for twenty-eight men. There is, however, an opportunity now to salvage whatever else from *Endurance* will provide shelter and comfort. Sections of decking are removed so that the remaining boxes of food and supplies can be fished out with boathooks from the icy water in the hold. Sails and spars are taken to be used in construction of a central mess and cooking area in our new encampment. The whole timber wheelhouse is lifted off *Endurance* to be converted by Orde-Lees to a storeroom. A lookout platform is constructed so seals and wildlife can be easily spotted. Shackleton accepts my suggestion that deck timber be stripped from *Endurance* for use as floorboards beneath our tents, so we can sit without contracting piles.

Our predicament means my metalwork and handyman skills come to the fore. Trawling through *Endurance* I can see that the brass case for the ship's compass and its Flinders bar can be fashioned into a workable bilge pump, which Worsley has said is desperately needed for the lifeboats. The cooking stove being used is a nightmare to operate outside, but I am able to convert an empty fuel drum into a specialised cooker that burns seal blubber, of which we have an indefinite supply. Over a few more days I construct a galley cooking range from a steel chimney chute stripped off *Endurance*. I also teach the men how to make workable crampons from scrap metal.

While I have lost my darkroom, I am able to retrieve my glass plate camera and continue taking photographs a little longer. I also rescue playing cards, my own collection of books and several volumes of the *Encyclopaedia Britannica* from Sir Ernest's cabin.

My mind moves from survival to having the photographs to tell the story.

All my glass plate negatives are lying underwater in the *Endurance* darkroom. I am determined to retrieve them. They are in canisters which are zinc-lined and soldered shut. Orde-Lees offers to help. We harness up my dog team and sledge across to *Endurance*. Clambering through the wreck is a disconcerting experience. If she rolls and sinks there will be no time to exit. We chop through the darkroom wall with an axe and rake through the icy slush with a boathook, but are unable to see the canisters. The boathook yields nothing and we become more and more anxious to decamp. There is nothing else for it; I strip to the waist, plunge into the water and shove my arms where I believe the film cases should be. I am desperate to find them before I lose sensation in my hands. My arms seize what must be the cases and, as I stand up, Orde-Lees grabs the tins and pulls me up out of the water. As I scramble to pull on dry clothing, *Endurance* shudders and ominous sounds chase us from the hull. Our adventure is not quite over, though, as on the way back a killer whale breaks through the ice directly in the path of our dog team. Shakespeare reacts instinctively, pulling the team to safety but almost spilling Orde-Lees and me into the open water.

On our return, we find the boss fuming at the risk taken to retrieve the photographic plates.

'Mr Hurley, you think you are above my command! You put in jeopardy the life of someone whom I'm responsible to bring home.'

'Boss, it's because we'll make it home I rescued the plates. We'll need them; they tell the expedition's story better than any one of us.'

I talk him round and he agrees we can keep one tin, which amounts to a hundred and twenty of the five hundred plates.

'I'll get the best plates into one box.'

'No, Mr Hurley, we'll do it together.'

Sitting alongside each other, we pull out the glass plate negatives, hold them up to the sky and peer into the milky light. One by one, we select the pictures we wish to save. The boss is the final arbiter. One hundred and twenty are resealed in the box. Then, whether through lack of trust in me, Shackleton smashes each rejected plate with a hammer. I watch as the images are forever fractured and the shards of glass fall into the snow.

9

Ocean Camp

Our new base we called Ocean Camp. It was just a mile or so north from *Endurance*. We could see her masts in the distance. Here we awaited the thaw with the prospect of a lifeboat journey to islands frequented by whalers. There was simply no telling how long the ice surrounding Ocean Camp would take to break up, or if it would break up at all in the coming summer.

Every few days I made my way back across the ice to *Endurance*. She was our crippled loved one, abandoned by her erstwhile companions. Her sails and spars could no longer obey Worsley's commands, but she was still a fine-looking ship and a rare sight wedged in the pack ice. I lugged over my glass plate camera and tripod as if I was off to a portrait sitting. On suitable days I took the cine camera instead. Each day, as *Endurance* came into view among the ridges and boulders of ice, I felt relieved to see her, to know she was still with us.

I looked for changes in the ship and how she was held in the vice-like grip of the ice plate. I watched for warping in the timbers in the hull, but they still looked strong and impregnable. The masts and spars stood tall against a grey featureless sky. The ice had pushed up hard on the stern and starboard side, and she now heeled ever so slightly, as if there was a wind in her furled sails or she was a model ship on a pedestal.

I always checked the light carefully. Most days there was low cloud. With high levels of reflection and glare, *Endurance* was a black silhouette through the eyepiece, a shadow puppet against a brilliant white backdrop. I wished then she had been painted any colour but black. Nevertheless, I applied my craft, adjusting the aperture and shutter to pick out the detail of timber, hawsers, chains and pulleys, though many of those deemed useful had already been stripped by Chips the carpenter.

There were rare days of sunshine which sculpted the ice in soft blue shades and shapes of infinite variety. On these days I used my limited supply of Paget colour plates and framed *Endurance* with a mixture of icy foregrounds both turbulent and serene.

I found different ways to approach *Endurance* from the camp, and each of these cast the ship in a different perspective. Facing her bowsprit jutting up into the sky she looked fine and brave, as if nothing could stay her. She was stayed, however, frozen like one of my photographic plates, captured in a moment in time. She had been caught and held, tossed on the frozen sea but not yet at rest.

On some days, before I thought better of it, I climbed in *Endurance*'s rigging. I felt like a young boy comfortably perched in a favourite backyard tree. To the north, the Weddell Sea was still frozen as far as the eye could see. I would leave the camera on deck, hitched securely to a halyard. If I deemed it worthwhile, I would string up some pulleys then haul up the camera to capture the icy vista through the boat's rigging.

Spring loosened the grip of the icepack on the southern continent. As the floes flexed and heaved, *Endurance* rose one day and fell the next, riding and enduring the mounting pressure waves that radiated from the pack. One morning I found the ice had wrenched the entire sternpost and rudder from their cast-iron fittings. *Endurance* now heeled dangerously to port, more than if the fiercest gale was blowing. The massive weight and solid carpentry of the ship were as nought to the icepack, which was now very much on the move. Groans came from the hull below the waterline. Timbers buckled and twisted. Joints severed irreparably. Water entered and moved through the hull. Wooden planks in the solid decking first bowed then popped, leaving gaping holes. It was unnerving to be on board in what had once been home to us all.

Worsley was a regular visitor, mulling on repairs he might undertake, but otherwise he kept his own counsel. Despite the gloom I saw his face wet with tears. This had been her maiden voyage. It seemed unnecessarily cruel that, having survived winter, it was the spring that should wreak such havoc on *Endurance*. I knew little of the forces at work and did the only thing I could do, taking photographs to record her passing. I knew from the twisting and straining of ropes that the rigging must soon collapse. I set up the tripod for the cine camera in the ideal spot, and after three days came the catastrophe I had been anticipating. I saw the early signs of movement and started hand-cranking through the motion picture film when, with a mighty crack, the top half of the mainmast snapped and toppled, dragging spars and rigging to the deck.

The boss came up shortly after, and I told him what I had just filmed. Shackleton nodded in a self-absorbed manner and, scarcely moving his lips, said deadpan, 'What the ice gets, the ice keeps.'

Beneath the prow of *Endurance* and running back from where the bowsprit extended there was some fine timber carving to which I had previously paid scant attention. Now I could walk alongside and inspect the patterned handiwork just above eye level. I would have loved to keep this carving, but it belonged to the ship, and the ship now belonged to the deep. I drew up my camera so at least an image of the carving might be retained.

The timber masts were now puppets for the ice that gripped the hull. The masts and rigging twisted and turned and tangled. Spars crashed to the deck. Canvas sails unfurled, shook off the ice of winter and flapped noisily. Over several days the hull became a mangled wreck, smashed and crushed beyond belief, but all before my eyes and recorded by my camera. The images I had taken were safe for the time being, but *Endurance* herself, our link with civilisation, was as good as gone. Our small fraternity was well and truly marooned on the now-melting icecap.

On the morning of 21 November 1915 I saw the wreck had stirred further. The funnel had rolled over. The bulk of the hull had dropped below the surface of the ice. The stumps of the three masts with horizontal cross spars stood out against the sky. I had raced across from Ocean Camp without my Burberry jacket and now shivered with cold. There was a roaring sound. The wreck shuddered. I saw three twisted crosses pushing skywards before drunkenly cavorting as the ice shifted around them, and then they sank and were swallowed whole. Then all was still.

Ocean Camp is a small settlement barely afloat on the ocean's surface. We do not belong here. How can we survive here when our bulwark *Endurance* could not? If we are still here when winter comes, we will surely perish. Our flimsy canvas tents will not withstand winter blizzards and we only have enough decent winter clothing for several men. Chippy's idea of building a sailboat from the wreckage of *Endurance* was rejected by Shackleton. Instead we are to drift northwards on the ice until it breaks up, then take to the lifeboats. Some three hundred miles now to the nor'-west is Paulet Island. Though uninhabited, sealers frequent the seas nearby.

Wild explains, 'The boss wants to sledge the boats further westwards while we still can. If we don't, and we launch the boats in westerly winds, we run the risk of missing Paulet and the South Shetland islands.'

In the meantime, the ice protects us from the turbulent swells and cold depths of the Weddell Sea. The ice is our world. We walk on the ice, we sleep on the ice, we build with it, we drink from it, we defecate on it. The iceshelf provides the game for our survival, food to eat and fuel for our stove.

Ocean Camp has the appearance of an old prospector's settlement: a series of grimy tents, scattered boxes, tins, building materials and rubbish. A black greasy smoke comes from the blubber stove and soot covers everything. The trodden-down pathways between the tents are black with ash from our boots. The blackened snow fast absorbs heat from the sun's rays and gradually the path melts down until one is in danger of slipping through to the ocean beneath.

Soon it is the height of the Antarctic summer. The surface snow is soft and moist. My boots are permanently damp. The sun does not set and in the middle of the day the tents heat up inside, condensation forms and drips on our sleeping bags so they are heavy with moisture. After only a few weeks we have to move a hundred yards before the whole camp sinks into the ocean.

The boss has allocated us to five tents. He has selected Hudson, James and me to share his tent. I am unsure what to make of this. I would like to be flattered, but I think he sees me more as competitor than companion. Reg James is our bespectacled physicist, completely inept in the outdoors and, in Shackleton's eyes, the most likely to meet with an accident. James has become withdrawn since the loss of *Endurance* and says little. Hudson, the first officer without a ship, is in my opinion and the opinion of the others quite mad.

Within several days, Orde-Lees has so aggravated the occupants of his tent that they eject him. In the middle of the night they forcibly carry him outside. He is left to sleep by himself in the tiny wheelhouse storeroom. There is only enough room for him to lay his bag across the top of the stores, so he is unable to lie straight. His crime is his snoring. I am surprised the boss allowed his eviction, but I figure the boss is happy to see Orde-Lees isolated, as he has become a doom-and-gloom merchant and pessimism is infectious.

And still the ice surrounds us. I struggle with the boss's copy of Browning, but greatly enjoy *Nicholas Nickleby*. There is competition for respective volumes of the *Encylopaedia Britannica*. One day I learn all about rope making.

'Hurley, what is your stove doing here?' Shackleton has emerged from our tent, where I know he has just groomed himself with his hand mirror.

'It's going to be in our photograph,' I explain.

'You said it was a picture of me you wanted.'

'Yes, boss, but the idea is to show life at Ocean Camp. Orde-Lees is going to take the shot and I'll be alongside you skinning a penguin.'

'I see, a picture of domestic bliss. And are those skis meant to suggest you're a champion skier?' He sits down in front of our tent and puts on his favourite black hat. He looks fierce but is quite accommodating about having this photograph taken even with me, and even with his expedition now reeling from catastrophe.

It is clear to me that, if we do make it home, our survival on the ice will be a big part of the story. I am keen to capture some idea of what life is like in our frozen camp suspended above the ocean. One morning, when there is ample sunlight, the boss gives permission for me to interrupt chores and photograph our group at Ocean Camp. I call the boss and Wild into the foreground. Orde-Lees creeps forwards and I send him back to where I have lined up several of the men. No one minds too much the standing around for a photograph when the weather is mild. I call out, 'Goggles off, everyone,' and I get my shot.

Chippy is the busiest among us. He has been directed to improve the seaworthiness of two of our three boats, *James Caird* and *Dudley Docker*. With timber from *Endurance* he rigs a mast for *Dudley Docker* and raises the height of the gunwales of both boats.

Hussey, like a wandering minstrel, plays banjo and leads singsongs every night in our tents.

'Does your banjo know any new songs?' I ask him.

'Och, 'tis only Shackletunes now,' says Clark, keeping a straight face.

'My banjo,' says Hussey, 'is under orders from the boss to keep the orcas away.'

I laugh. 'My singing does that.'

The boss, meanwhile, is struck down with a mystery illness and is unable to get out of his sleeping bag. He says it is a cold. Macklin says it is not warm enough here for bacteria to survive, so it must be rheumatism or exhaustion or both.

By the time the boss rises from his sickbed, there is a strong sense of desperation across the camp. Christmas Day is approaching and there is no sign of the ice breaking up to enable the launching of the boats. None of us want to be on the ice for the onset of winter. Inactivity feels like a death wish.

One month after the sinking of *Endurance*, the boss accompanies Wild on his sledge and I take Crean on mine to survey the ice surface. It does not look promising, but that evening the boss announces we will make a start dragging two boats westwards across the ice shelf to reduce the distance between ourselves and Paulet Island. Worsley leaves a note in a pickle jar inside the bow of the third boat, *Stancomb Wills*, which records our sorry state: 'Endurance crushed and abandoned in ice 69 degrees S, 51 degrees W. All hands tomorrow proceeding to Westward. All well. December 23 1915. EH Shackleton.'

A massive effort achieves just over two miles, and on Christmas Eve progress is stymied by leads opening in the ice. Even travelling at night the surface is soft and unreliable. We start again Christmas Day and find it tough going, clambering over hummocks and falling through cracks in the ice. My dog team pulls magnificently, but it is the eighteen men hauling the full weight of *James Caird* who are quickly exhausted. We have all lost condition and it is backbreaking to pull the lifeboat over the slightest rise. In some sections the men plunge down into the sea beneath the icecap until yanked up again by their harnesses. The brine means their clothing never properly dries out. After a mile they retrace their steps and attach themselves to *Dudley Docker* to drag it up to *James Caird*. On Boxing Day we manage less than two miles.

Conditions are worse the next day. We set off before midnight and Shakespeare leads the way through the worst obstacles. The dogs are a joy to work with and handle the conditions far better than men. I avoid thinking of what will become of my team when we launch the boats.

The men with *James Caird* are struggling. Their sledge sinks a foot or more into the snow, and momentum becomes impossible. Several hours of effort sees a gain of only a few hundred yards. Around 4 a.m. I pass *James Caird* and hear an altercation between Worsley and Chips, who has undone his harness trace and is refusing to pull any further. The boss is fetched and Chips, who is a big fellow, unleashes his complaints.

'It's feckin' madness, and I for one am not going to see these boats ruined. It's not just the sleds breakin' up! The men are done in and we hae na done a mile. An' wha' for? The feckin' ice is doin' five miles a day!'

There's a substantial audience to this outburst. The fo'c'sle crew stand in their traces in sullen support. All eyes look to the boss.

'If we don't go west, Mc Neish, we'll miss Paulet completely. You've been ordered to get back in your harness.'

'I'm not obliged to obey his orders, nor yours for that matter. Worsley is no feckin' captain 'cause he ain't got no feckin' ship! No one's paying us when we is marooned.'

Only the boss's eyes show his fury. Wild is sent to fetch the case containing the ship's articles. The dog teams are tied up and the whole crew is gathered. Shackleton speaks so all can hear.

'I am in charge of this expedition. I am responsible for the expedition members and for the ship's crew. When I joined *Endurance* at Buenos Aires I signed on as master of the ship. The ship's articles—I have them here—provide for loss of the ship. You've given your oaths to obey my command. The articles expressly give me that authority on board ship and onshore and in the lifeboats. Anyone who does not obey lawful orders, the usual punishments apply. Anyone who is mutinous . . . so help me, God, I'll not be bringing them home. Ship's articles have not terminated and wages continue until we reach port.'

Chips backs down. He is probably right, though, I think, about sledging the boats.

A break is taken and hoosh is served. Wild walks through camp brandishing the shotgun. He shoots a dog that has been injured by a sledge.

Dragging the boats continues. One day later, just ten miles from Ocean Camp, the boss orders a stop, the going only being worse. We set up a third, hopefully final camp—Patience Camp, the boss calls it.

New Year's Day 1916 is spent at Patience Camp. The usual toasts are made. The boss and most of the fellows are homesick for their families. There is murmuring among the sailors they'll never see another Christmas. As for me, I have now been in the Antarctic for five Christmases in a row. It is not a special day for me. I have only distant memories of being excited as a child at Christmas. I do remember the dreadfully hot Christmas day after Pa died when Ma, having had too many sherries, burned a rabbit in the pot as she slept through the afternoon.

However, in light of the expedition's predicament, I make some personal resolutions on New Year's Eve. One, I won't make the mistake again of abandoning my films and photographs on a sinking ship. To think they almost went to the bottom and I may have returned to civilisation as impoverished as I began. They should never have been abandoned. Shackleton's judgement can't be trusted. Two, I am going to have to look after myself to ensure I am there at the end. Not everyone will return home. Many of the sailors and some of the scientists will not cope with winter conditions. They have no idea how to look after themselves on the ice, let alone help anyone else.

Our northward progress on the drifting ice is at the mercy of wind and currents. We like southerlies as they break up the ice and blow us homeward. Our camp is no longer connected with the main pack where *Endurance* was abandoned. The surface remains soft and walking anywhere is perilous. Leads constantly open and can cut you off from camp. Orde-Lees is the only person allowed any distance from camp as he can travel more safely on skis. Each day he scouts for seals to supplement our stores. He is fanatical in his belief that fresh seal meat keeps off scurvy, and Macklin and McIlroy agree, though without bread and cereal it plays havoc with our bowels. To save bullets Orde-Lees stuns the seals with a blow to the head then cuts their throats. If a seal or penguin comes up near the camp, we do the same. We each carry a pocketknife at all times. Likewise, we carry with us and lick clean our own spoon for mealtimes.

One morning, Orde-Lees excitedly rouses our camp, having discovered that overnight large numbers of Adelie penguins have come up to rest on our floe. These birds have no reason to be afraid of man and show no fear. Their dark eyes ringed in white bands record astonishment and consternation at our violence. It is an unfair contest, by the end of which we have killed over three hundred Adelies. This is two weeks of food for us and their blubber will fuel our stove even longer.

The ice further deteriorates and it is obvious our camp will not be moving again until we take to the boats. As the dogs are unable to come with us, they have completed their service to the expedition.

I hear Orde-Lees complaining to the boss, 'They eat a seal each day. They're now competing with us for food.'

There is no argument I can make. Shakespeare is not my dog. The dogs belong to the expedition. There is no room in the boats even for one dog. They will not survive if abandoned on the ice; Wild says they would turn on each other. But there are several expedition members I would rather leave behind.

My team is the first chosen. I have no say in this. Wild takes the pack behind a nearby ridge. I have fed them and said my goodbyes. I have a camera to clean.

A gunshot reverberates through the camp. I know Wild has killed Shakespeare, the pack leader, first. A minute later a second shot rings out. I carry on cleaning my equipment. A third shot and I clean the same lens again.

One by one the dogs are dispatched with a bullet to the head. The boss has agreed to this, despite bullets being a precious resource. It is the most humane way, said Shackleton. He is, I surmise, thinking more about Frank Wild than the dogs.

I count through the eight shots. I try to concentrate on anything else, but by the end I am completely distraught and storm off so I don't have to face anyone. I tell myself it's a necessity but it hurts in a way I haven't experienced for some years, and I realise I was closer to my dogs than my expedition colleagues.

That evening, my foul mood is made darker when Orde-Lees pipes up, 'I say, Wild, have you added the carcasses to the larder?'

I leap to my feet, but Wild steps in and pins my arms before I can knock Orde-Lees's head off.

By the end of January we are only one hundred and fifty miles from Paulet Island, but Wild tells me confidentially we have drifted too far east and have no chance of reaching it, though we may come close to the South Shetland Islands. With the movement of the icepack, Ocean Camp has, ironically, moved a few miles closer to us. The boss must be having doubts that twenty-eight men can fit into two boats, as he now orders retrieval of *Stancomb Wills* from Ocean Camp.

This is just in time, as the ice is dangerously soft with many cracks and leads opening. Killer whales regularly appear in the narrow pools to observe our travelling circus. Eventually the boss bans all further excursions. Since the loss of *Endurance* our icy raft has floated some two hundred and fifty miles northwards. It is now a roughly circular island about twelve hundred yards in circumference. Frustratingly, the ocean remains clogged with ice floes, making boat navigation impossible.

Life on an iceberg is disorientating. On the morning of 15 February—the boss's birthday—we wake to discover that the wind, accompanied by foul weather, appears to have swung to the north, reversing our progress. It is only later in the morning, when Wild checks the compass, that we realise our ice floe has pirouetted and the wind has remained steady.

At the end of March we are still stuck on our ice floe, with the weather getting colder as winter approaches. Game has become scarcer, and the boss puts us on half rations. Our floe starts to split in half and we madly scramble to move sledges and food supplies across to where the tents are. The boss introduces four-hour watches. Soon our floe is not much bigger than our camp. It moves with the swell and constantly bumps and grinds against surrounding floes. In all directions I look out on thousands of bergs, rhythmically rising and falling like an embroidered white quilt across a huge bed. But to us sleep seems like a gamble. Our floe sinks lower in the water and looks ready to split again.

The boss orders camp be struck and all equipment that's coming be stowed in the three boats. In the early afternoon we launch. I am in *James Caird* with the boss and Wild, as well as Clark, James, Hussey, Wordie and the sailors Vincent, Green and McCarthy. Chips is also with us, no doubt so the boss can keep an eye on him. I glance up from my oar and there, left behind on the ice, are the scattered boxes and rubbish of Ocean Camp, and my abandoned wooden tripod. All I have is a pocket Kodak and three rolls of film.

Despite having craved escape from the clutches of the icepack for over a year, the sensation of floating in a small wooden boat is unsettling. Even heavily laden, *Caird* rolls and pitches as men climb over each other to swap positions. More than once, the oar handles punch me in the jaw as they seesaw up and down with the motion of the boat. The scientists have little experience in rowing. It is in any case impossible to row, as the oars jam up against the ice. Wild takes charge, standing at the stern wielding an oar first against this floe, then the other, pushing us clear.

'The bloody sledges are dragging on the ice,' cries Wild. The boss had directed that the boat sledges be strapped and partially suspended off the stern in case of future need.

'Alright,' calls Shackleton. 'Cut them off.'

Their bindings are slashed and they drop below the waves. We are now committed to ocean travel. After four hours we half push, half row ourselves into open sea, followed by Worsley in charge of *Dudley Docker* and Hudson in charge of *Stancombe Wills*.

Hours after emerging from the ice, I look up and rub my eyes at what I see—the ice pack is now bearing down on us. We are caught in a tidal surge that is sweeping us straight back into the icepack. As fast as we can row, we are being sucked back to the ice, in front of which there is a foaming pressure wave.

The boss calls for a mighty effort.

'Stroke . . . and stroke . . . and stroke,' urges Wild.

All three boats gradually pull away and manoeuvre across to an outlying berg, where we tie up for the night. We are exhausted, our hands blistered, none of us having laboured at oars in such trying circumstances. We have had almost no carbohydrates in our diet now for many weeks and have no reserves of energy. The boats are hauled onto the floe, tents put up and my portable stove gets a workout cooking a hoosh to restore some sense of wellbeing.

Just before midnight I am awakened by the boss crying, 'She's splitting up, she's splitting up!'

I sit bolt upright in darkness. The boss is not in the tent, and as I emerge I see collapsed tents and hear people in the water. The boss is lying flat on the ice, pulling a dark lump out of the water. It's a finnesko sleeping bag without its occupant. Again he reaches down, and this time he grasps an arm. Up out of the black soup comes Clark, his eyes bulging and a look of terror on his face.

Others clamber along the edge of a two-yard-wide crack, retrieving what they can before the bergs have a chance to crunch back together.

'Pull *Caird* across,' calls the boss as the split in the floe leaves our tent and the boat at risk of drifting away in the dark. The tent and our belongings are thrown into *Caird* and a dozen souls drag and propel it across the crack in the floe. One by one we then leap across the water to the main part of the floe. The boss insists on going last, and by then the gap has widened and he does not jump. We stand facing him across the open lead. The boss disappears into the night, his cries muffled by falling snow.

Wild runs back to launch *Stancomb Wills*, but the sea is awash with jostling icebergs pushing and grinding. Launching a boat in darkness between bergs on the move is to risk being crushed. Fortune intervenes and the newly calved berg is shunted back towards us. The boss finds an opportune moment and leaps across safely.

Our hearts are pumping and there is no interest in returning to the tents. A rollcall reveals all are safe. The stove is lit and pieces of dryish clothing are volunteered to stave off hypothermia for those who were plunged into the drink. We huddle around the stove and wait for morning.

As soon as it is light and a lead opens, we launch the boats, leaving behind heavy boxes of food, as the boats have been sitting dangerously low in the water. In *James Caird* we take hourly shifts at rowing until we emerge from the pack. An easterly is blowing, so we take advantage by setting sail and heading nor'-west, but around midday snow squalls hit us from the nor'-east and the wind increases to gale force. *Dudley Docker* and *Stancomb Wills* are unable to make headway and bash themselves uselessly into the foaming swells. *Stancomb Wills* did not have its gunwales raised and ships a lot of sea. Its sail is too small and it is unable to sail into the wind.

Spray drenches the boats and freezes solid in our clothing, and ice gradually builds up inside the hull and on the deck. The boss directs Wild to turn and run south, leading the other boats back into the pack, where the bergs flatten the sea and shelter us from the rollers. That evening we again haul the boats onto a large iceberg and set up tents. Our camp remains intact overnight, despite the berg splitting and being eroded down to about a hundred feet long. We remain surrounded by churning ice, and it is not until afternoon that we are able to launch into a small lead. *Caird* navigates westwards through the pack, followed closely by *Dudley Docker* and *Stancombe Wills*.

That evening we are too nervous to sleep on the ice, so instead the three boats tie up to a reasonable-sized floe and Green, the cook, goes ashore with the blubber stove to prepare hot milk and Bovril. No sooner is food served than we are forced to cast off to avoid being holed by unstable bergs eddying around us. We are compelled to spend the night in the boats, sometimes rowing, sometimes pushing off bergs, sometimes resting and trying to keep the three boats together. We slump across the rowlocks and huddle together for warmth. Clark and James are horribly seasick and lie prostrate under a canvas sail. I am shivering with cold; sleep is impossible. Throughout the night we listen to a pack of killer whales which take a close interest, surfacing and blowing their spume over us.

At noon on 12 April there is enough sun for Worsley to check our position. He stands up straight in *Dudley Docker*, braced against the mast, and somehow, despite the boat rolling in the swells, he looks down at his sextant and takes a reading while all eyes are on him. The boss leaps across to *Docker* and he and the captain check their calculations.

'Not as favourable as I wanted,' the boss says as he rejoins us.

Shortly after, Wild whispers in my ear, 'We are no nearer land than when we started. In fact, we've gone bloody backwards. We are sou'-east of Patience Camp.'

It is a bitter blow. Our hopes of reaching the South Shetland Islands are dashed. Instead, due to the persistent nor'-easter, the boss determines to head for the northern tip of the Antarctic Peninsula, Graham Land. I feel bitter disappointment, as few whalers go that far south, but the alternative of missing all landfalls and being adrift in the Atlantic Ocean does not bear thinking about.

We steer west-sou'-west in a heavy following swell, and about 9 p.m. a solid-looking floe provides a mooring for *Dudley Docker*, with *Stancombe Wills* attached to its stern and *Caird* attached to *Stancombe Wills*. However, during the night the wind swings south-west and Worsley has to cut the mooring line to save the boats being dashed against the ice. The boats stay tethered together, with the poor crew of *Dudley Docker* directed by the boss to row into the breeze throughout the night so as to keep the three boats head to wind.

The temperature is minus-seven degrees and sleep is again impossible as the boats jerk and pull against each other in the swells. We huddle together in the middle of the boat for warmth. In the morning our Burberry coats have a white covering of snow and frost. My companions' faces are haggard, with cracked lips, red eyes and ice frozen in their beards. I have developed painful boils on my buttocks and feet from constant wetness and chafing. Like the others, I have been eating uncooked pemmican and have diarrhoea. Consequently I spend time sitting uncomfortably, my nether regions exposed, over the edge of the gunwale while I hang on grimly to the side stays.

Overnight each of the boats has become heavily laden with ice and Wild takes to it with an axe. The oars are too heavy to lift until the ice is removed. The wind having changed in our favour, Shackleton, after conferring with Wild and Worsley, decides to have an attempt at an island to our north, Elephant Island. We hoist sail and head west and north through the floes, and after some hours we again emerge through the pack into open ocean. The wind picks up until we are forced to reef the sails. So excited are we by our favourable progress and escape from the ice that we forget to secure any ice for drinking water. That evening Worsley fashions a sea anchor from oars tied together, and he lets this drag from the prow of *Docker* to keep head to wind with *Caird* and *Stancombe Wills* tied in a row behind.

Elephant Island is no more than a pile of jagged cliffs, glaciers and mountainous rock rising up over half a mile out of the South Atlantic Ocean. It appeared to us after dawn that morning of 14 April like a saintly vision, even though it was still more than thirty miles away.

We had survived another night at sea, although my companions were by then seriously incapacitated. Frostbite and hypothermia were the main concerns. We were all fighting to keep circulation in our hands and feet. Blackborow's feet had gone and he could no longer row. Greenstreet was the same. My own hands were in agony from the cold, but at least I could feel them, which was a good sign. Orde-Lees was out of sight, dry-retching on the floor of *Docker* and apparently unable to row. I heard much dreadful abuse heaped on him. In *Stancombe Wills*, Hudson had been hallucinating and collapsed. Crean had taken over. The day was fine, however, and winds stayed favourable until fading away at midday, when it again became necessary to take to the oars. Now we regretted our failure to secure ice for drinking. We were all parched and had not slept for over three days. How did Coleridge know all this so well?

Stancombe Wills continued to lag behind, so we took it in tow. I spent most of the day at the oars, constantly shifting my weight to find a less painful way of sitting. When I could,

I would glance over my shoulder to make sure Elephant Island was still there. By 5 p.m. I was still seeing the same outline of ridges and glacier.

'How far now, Frank?' I asked Wild.

'Ten miles.'

'You said that hours ago,' I said, and Wild and Shackleton glanced at each other.

'Hoyle, there's a current,' said Wild. 'We are holding our own.'

Alongside me, Chips McNeish cried out, 'Holy Mother of Jesus, what are yer sayin'? We been rowing for nought! We shoulda bin restin' while we can, before the wind comes oop . . .'

'Chips,' responded Wild, 'I've been at the helm for two days straight. You take over and I'll row.'

Darkness fell and snow squalls arrived from the south-west so we could no longer see our destination. *Dudley Docker* disappeared into the gloom. The wind turned gale force with fifty-mile-an-hour gusts bringing a large cross sea broadsides on our port bow. Spray from the waves lashed everyone in the boat, then turned to ice. By this time, Clark, James, Hussey, Wordie and Green had each collapsed from exhaustion and were lying under a sail in the bottom of the boat. As I still had feeling in my hands, the boss asked me to take the sheet, which even with a reefed sail was hard work. I held that rope for several hours, half sitting, half lying on the floor of *Caird*. My hands were locked frozen with the rope wrapped around them. Unable to play the rope, the wind gusts pulled me bodily towards the ratchet block.

I was swaying back and forth with my eyes shut when freezing water poured across my back and swamped the boat. Looking up, I saw Chips had fallen asleep at the helm and was now sprawled below the tiller. Wild leaped up and pushed the tiller leewards to force *Caird* into the wind. We bailed to save ourselves. Wild resumed the helm.

I looked back and could see white rollers breaking off the bow of *Stancomb Wills*, its black shape sitting low in the water, riding the crests then being swallowed whole in the following troughs. The boss thought he could hear a surf breaking but it may have been nerves.

Dawn brought blessed relief. There, but a mile off, was Elephant Island. *Stancombe Wills*, though low in the water, was still afloat. *Docker*, however, was nowhere to be seen. We sailed into the lee of the island and took to the oars. Dark forbidding cliffs towered above us.

For some twelve miles of coast we rowed, seeing no beach, nor cove nor even a ledge at the foot of the cliffs that would provide a landing. We rounded a glacier and took ice on board to quench our thirsts. Eventually, a small shingle beach was spied and the boss transferred to the smaller *Stancombe Wills* and navigated in over a shallow reef. Stores were taken ashore and *Caird* was then guided in until she scraped and stranded in the kelp. It was all I could do to straighten up and clamber over the gunwale. It was such a long time since I had known solid ground, the shingle beach swayed beneath my feet. I clung to the boat to avoid collapsing.

We were ashore. There was relief in that. But what sort of refuge was this and where were our companions on the *Docker*?

10

Elephant Island

More than half the crew on board *James Caird* and *Stancombe Wills* were utterly useless in getting the boats up on the beach. A number of men had to be carried. Our spirits lifted when, around the headland, *Dudley Docker* hove into view. I walked stiffly to the water's edge to assist her.

Blackborow was lifted over the gunwale and carried ashore. Greenstreet was next. He was lifted over the side but was able to stand, although shaking as if with palsy. He stumbled through the wash onto the shingle and stood transfixed watching Green the cook who, wanting blubber for fuel, was walking through the seals wielding a cast-iron poker. Greenstreet approached the nearest stunned animal and dropped to his knees. He pulled out his knife and sliced the seal open just below the ribcage. He thrust his bare hands through the incision up into the seal's chest cavity and rested in that position with his head embracing the seal for several minutes, hoping to restore sensation and save his fingers.

Docker was pulled up and Green soon had a fire going in the blubber stove. Wild, Worsley and the boss embraced. I lay down on the bare rock some distance away. A wave of sobs took me by surprise and it was some time before I could stop shaking and return to the group.

Tents were raggedly erected on stones at the foot of the cliff, and in our stupor we fell asleep. We slept the sleep of the almost-dead until the cold morning light, the rising tide and threatening waves told us this was no haven. We had to move.

Wild was dispatched westwards with several others in *Stancombe Wills* to find a landing that offered shelter. The boss and I took a climbing rope and clambered eastwards along the foot of the cliff, squeezing between basalt spires and edging across thin crevices above the waves. We craned our necks to see through sleet and snow past jagged headlands, only to see more of the same.

Night fell and Wild had not returned. A large blubber fire was maintained with the stove door open and facing out to sea. Hours later a cry was heard, and out of the darkness *Stancombe Wills* streaked ashore with phosphorescence in its wake.

In the morning the boss is anxious to move. 'Boats in the water, everyone! Mr Wild has found a landing seven miles along the northern shore.'

At least half the men do not shift at all. I can understand this of Blackborow, Greenstreet and Hudson, who are genuine invalids, but it is contemptible of the sailors who think only of their present comfort.

The boss directs himself to a group from whom the most grumbling is heard. 'If we do not leave before the bay fills with ice, there will be no chance of survival here.'

Meanwhile, Wild and Worsley have laid down oars as makeshift rollers between *Caird* and the sea. The boats reach the water, but three oars are shattered. There is a toll exacted for every gain.

We row as close to shore as we dare to avoid being blown out to sea. Above us the cliffs rise vertically over a thousand feet. There is a constant stream of snow blasting off the tops and eddying down on us. At Cape Valentine, however, we are unable to hide from the squalls that come screaming down the glacier in a headwind against which we bend our backs but make no progress. *Docker* is loaded with extra bodies and, with only three oars, is blown sideways.

We steer closer to shore and it is almost evening when Wild guides us in. The keel of *Caird* bumps between shallow rocks and runs aground. We are all done in and are raked by snow and sleet as supplies and belongings are heaved onto a narrow gravel spit. Seaman Cheetham stumbles out of the water and faints, falling heavily on the shingle. One of the crew has had a heart attack and McIlroy too has chest pains and is carried ashore. I am shaking and numb but able to help haul up the boats. Many of the others are oblivious or, worse still, simply ignore the labours of those few who empty the boats and drag them up the beach.

Green is incapacitated, but others cook up a hoosh. Tents are erected on the highest part of the beach. Gear has been dumped in the snow and sleeping bags are wet but the men are beyond caring.

No sooner do I sleep than I am awakened by canvas hurling and cracking over my head. Wooden tent poles fly through the air like clubs. A storm has hit our little camp and nothing is secured. Two tents have ripped and come down, and ours is about to take off. The boss and I drop the poles and flatten the tent on the ground, weighing it down with rocks, and then crawl underneath. Others have climbed into the boats to escape the gale.

Daylight does come, but there is nowhere to hide from wind or rain. Wild has brought us aground on a narrow spit of snow-covered gravel that juts out due north and connects what would otherwise be a rocky islet some two hundred yards out from an unclimbable precipice. This rocky hillock, which we name Penguin Hill due to its numerous occupants, rises only a hundred feet and would be a good lookout point, but its view of the ocean to the north is impeded by a much larger rock, which stands a further hundred yards offshore. Penguin Hill, from its smell, is a long-established rookery for penguins and seals. The spit itself, which is our only walking area, is forty yards at its widest. On either side to the east and west are exposed rocky bays which will choke with ice at the onset of winter. To the south-west a large glacial tongue descends into the bay and has formed a collar of ice on the base of the spit.

'They're about to leave! Quick, they're about to leave!' It is Orde-Lees. He is pointing out along the spit and is almost in tears as he raves at the boss.

Through the sleet and early morning gloom, all the penguins have come down from the rookery and are gathered on the beach. They actively inspect the water's edge.

'Alright, Lees.' Shackleton waits for Wild as he gathers tent poles, sledge runners, hammers and other instruments to use as clubs. Meanwhile Shackleton has pulled the remains of a tent off a huddle of bodies wrapped in drenched sleeping bags.

'Get up, I say! Every one of you form up in line with a club or else these penguins will be gone and you will starve on this godforsaken rock.'

The grimy faces of the sailing crew emerge from the bags. 'We can't, boss. We ain't got proper clothing and our hands and feet are frostbitten. We can't even stand, let alone walk.'

'I'll not have the same men doing all the work. Where are your mitts and hats?'

'They're gone, sir, last night in the storm, sir—we're all fucked.'

'Holy Christ, you blaggards can't e'en take care of yourselves. Get up, man, before I take to you with a club.'

The boss drags one of the sailors by the scruff of his neck over rocks and onto the shingle.

'Mr Orde-Lees wants every one of those penguins in a pot. There's a couple of hundred now, but there's about to be none if you don't move.'

Green speaks up. 'The aluminium cooking pots have all gone, boss. Whoever was on watch . . . a fair lot of the stores and spare clothing have blown away in the night.'

Shackleton's face is dark. 'Only Blackborow, Hudson and Greenstreet are excused. Every other hand, get down to the beach.'

He and Wild kick and push the sailing crew from where they lie prostrate on the ground. Crean then leads the men in single file along the edge of the spit to cut off the penguins from the sea, but the penguins are already leaping, first one, then another disappearing in the black waves.

We run now to get into them, lashing out on either side. Careless of whether we kill or maim, we strike them down, crack their skulls. It has dawned on us that this hellhole is now our home; there is nothing else. Better to be a penguin in such a place. But we are humans and we slay them. Most escape, but some turn back and retreat up into the rookery and are killed there.

'Seventy-seven, boss,' says Orde-Lees. 'We have seventy-seven. That's a good three or four days of food and fuel.'

The fury over, the truly appalling part is now the butchering and flensing away the blubber in the freezing cold, using small pocketknives in our bare, frostbitten hands.

Later, Shackleton assembles the whole group. 'This place is named Cape Wild, in honour of the man who found it.'

'It's a wild bloody cape!' retorts Hussey.

'We could easily stay put here till the spring. As you see, there are seals and penguins in good numbers. The glacier provides fresh water. However, I do not propose waiting for the spring.

Mr Blackborow needs an operation in the next several weeks. I intend to take *Caird* to South Georgia, where I will arrange for a vessel from Grytviken to bring our whole group off this island. Mr Wild will be in charge in my absence. I will be asking for volunteers to accompany me. Captain Worsley has already agreed. Lastly, as I have told you, I brought you here—and I am determined to get every single one of you home.'

Next morning, Chips is again hard at work strengthening *James Caird*.

Wild tells me, 'The boss is taking Chips. He doesn't like him, but he needs him to make sure *Caird* is seaworthy. He's taking that other troublemaker, Vincent, off my hands and Crean has twisted the boss's arm to go and that other Irishman, McCarthy, too.'

'You disappointed?'

'I'll tell you in a few months. It's eight hundred miles to South Georgia. The wind blows straight from Cape Horn and if they miss South Georgia, well there's nothing else really and there's no coming back against the westerlies. But, you know, it's the boss we're talking about; I think he can do it.'

'And if he doesn't make it?'

'If we're still here in the spring, then it's my turn. The boss has told me I'm to take *Docker*. There are bound to be whalers up around Deception Island.'

'They might come past here.'

'No, no one's been here since the 1830s, when they finished off the last of the elephant seals. Have you noticed there're no rats? Not even they can survive here!'

So not even whalers come near the island. And no one will know to look for us here. Nor is there a resident seal population as a food source during winter. That means starvation. To stay here can only mean death, unknown and unrecorded.

'Frank,' I say, 'if it comes to that, I'll come with you in *Docker*.'

'Oh, I wouldn't be worried about that, Hoyle. Shackleton will save us.'

•

Caird was twenty-two feet long. To avoid rolling over in the swells, which were expected to be sixty to eighty feet, she needed ballast, and a lot of it. Bags sewn from blankets were filled with stones to be laid down along the keel. Chips used some two thousand pounds of stones, which could only be brought on board after the boat was launched. To strengthen the keel, Chips took *Docker*'s mast and lashed it along the floor of *Caird*. The sailors used a mixture of wax and Marston's oil paints to caulk the seams between planks. Knowing seas would regularly wash over the whole boat, Chips used timber and canvas to fashion an almost complete deck cover.

During preparations, the boss took me aside. 'Hurley, if I don't make it, I want you to get all the cine film and photographs to Ernest Perris at the *Daily Chronicle* in London. Perris runs the business side of the syndicate and he'll work out what's required. You just need to hand over the films to him. Frank Wild will do the lecture tours with the photographs and be in charge of fundraising. He's met Perris.'

'Boss, I can do the lectures synchronised with the photographs, and there's the film, also. Really, Wild knows nothing about all that.'

'Perris will help Frank with all he needs to know.'

I'd been thinking about this already and was surprised by Shackleton's insistence.

'Boss, if you're serious about raising money, you need me involved. There are too many things that can go wrong—and with all respect to Frank, he can't be expected to fix 'em.

The slides and film have to be put together properly if you want to get the crowds in.'

'I tell you what, Hurley: I'll agree you can do lecture tours in the United States, but Frank is to do Britain and the Continent, and you have to do everything in your power to cooperate with Perris in terms of developing and editing and so on.'

'I'll do that, but it means a commitment of my time and, well, it's disappointing I won't be involved in presenting my own work the way I want to present it. Why can't I have that opportunity?'

'Blast it, man, so long as the syndicate's debts are paid and my debts are paid and my wife is not a pauper, then you can have your bloody films!'

'Well, that's how we should do it. Look, there's one other thing: I haven't met Mr Perris. He may be good at what he does, but I can tell you Mawson's syndicate made a right mess of *Home of the Blizzard*. The footage was excellent, but they didn't edit it properly, they didn't show people what they wanted to see of Antarctica. They didn't do proper titles. They didn't make anything near the money they could have.'

'Well I expect you won't make those mistakes.'

'I won't. That's why you chose me. But, boss, we're assuming the worst, which we don't believe will happen. But, assuming it does, you'll need to give me something in writing saying I am to have control of the cinefilm. Mind you, this is only if you're . . .' I hesitated. 'If you're not able to be there yourself.'

Shackleton agreed and I wasted no time finding a blank page in my expedition diary to record the terms and have the boss's signature witnessed. While Shackleton was a genius at raising money, he was not a great one for detail, and with the stroke of a pen he passed ownership of the films to me.

Shortly afterwards, *Caird* was ready to launch. In a gap between storms, but with a moderate swell still breaking along the spit, all hands except those incapacitated heaved the boat into the shallow surf. *Stancomb Wills* was alongside, loaded up with ballast and supplies to be transferred into *Caird* once out past the breakers. I stood on the beach with my pocket Kodak like a tourist, trying my best to record the scene, but all the time thinking what the caption would be: *Last photograph of the Great Shackleton* maybe.

'How long, boss?' someone called.

'Two weeks' fine sailing to South Georgia is what I expect,' replied Shackleton. 'Once we've a ship, the six of us will come straight back to get you all.'

'Lucky there's no sheelaghs wanderin' the streets of Grytviken, else Crean might fergit about us.'

'Too right, and McCarthy too. Doan you go feckin' any sheelaghs till you've picked us oop!'

'Too many bloody Oirishman on one feckin' boat, if you ask me!'

They had to yell now to be heard, and excited voices carried in the wind back to where I stood on the spit. I watched with apprehension as the undertow grabbed the stern of *Caird* and dragged her out till she was side on to the incoming waves. Standing on the upper deck wielding the oars, Chips and Vincent desperately tried to straighten her up. A white roller struck the port side and *Caird*, without ballast, rolled ominously to starboard, throwing the hapless Chips and Vincent into the sea. There was a collective groan from those on shore.

Soon, however, *Caird* was in deep water, and over successive trips *Stancombe Wills* loaded over a tonne of ballast and supplies into her till she sat down neatly in the water with just two feet of freeboard. I took another shot of the men in the foreground on the water's edge with their backs to me, arms raised as they waved to the ever-more-tiny boat, which all too soon disappeared below the swells on its way to the horizon. I hoped this simple shot of the farewell to our rescue mission might one day become famous for the right reasons. As things turned out, of all the days for the Irish it was Easter Sunday, 24 April 1916.

With no shelter from the weather, we spent days digging a snow cave into the ice foot of the glacier. However, so damp was the cave inside that no one was prepared to stay in it.

Wild then directed construction of two low stone walls some eighteen feet apart on the Penguin Hill end of the spit. We upturned *Dudley Docker* and *Stancombe Wills* and suspended them alongside each other from bow to stern on the stone walls. The remnants of the tents and tent floor cloths were then draped across the whole structure and formed walls held down by stones and ropes. An old tent doorway was sewn into place as an entrance that could be opened and shut.

As the ground was part of the rookery, the stench was considerable, and being only several feet above sea level, it looked to be impossible to have a dry floor. So we excavated and removed layers of slimy guano, and then used beach rocks and gravel to lay out a new floor. It was less than five feet high inside, so not even Frank Wild could stand upright. But it was about twelve feet across and there were twenty-two of us needing shelter. A number of sly sailors quickly seized on the idea of making beds above ground in the thwarts of the boats by improvising additional decking and stretchers. Eventually twelve men slept on this mezzanine level and the rest dossed down on the ground. The blubber bogie stove I had made was brought inside and a small chimney added.

I did not fancy being at such close quarters with the whole sailing crew. They were an illiterate bunch, coarse in their language and personal habits, and passed their time talking only about their stomachs. I still had the tent I had shared with the boss. I set it up in the most sheltered place I could find, but storms again brought it down in the middle of the night and I had to barge into the hut in the pitch-black and sleep where I could. No tent could survive on the exposed spit and I was forced to make my home with all the others in what became known as the Snuggery.

•

The Snuggery is a stinking miserable hovel. We are trapped here like rats. I am lying cheek by jowl to men with infected boils, pustules, gaping ulcers and weeping sores. We can make no more boat journeys without first destroying this, our only shelter. In any case, the bays on both sides of the spit are now iced in. The boss left in the nick of time. He has taken the best boat, the skipper and the most able of the sailors, and I for one feel their loss keenly. Over half our group already have severe frostbite. I would not like to be the young stowaway Blackborow in these conditions, for despite his pluck he is the most likely to go first. The weather is appalling and winter has not yet started. God knows how long this is to be our home. Amid this grimness I resolve to myself that I will survive.

In the evening Wild seems his usual self and doles out serves of hoosh while Hussey, with his back turned to avoid accusations of favouritism, selects the recipient by calling out a name from us survivors. Even with this system there is nasty bickering. After the meal, washed down with weak black tea, Hussey pulls out the banjo which the boss insisted he bring from the wreck of *Endurance*. Accompanied by the wind ripping though gaps in the canvas, Hussey picks at the chords while Wild sings slowly in his rich baritone:

Nita, Juanita, ask thy soul if we should part
Nita, Juanita, lean thou on my heart.

Just two weeks later, on a rare day with sunshine, Wild finds me studying the horizon.

'Hoyle, can you take a photograph of the men today? I'd like to have one shot of them all together before the boss comes back or, you know, if anything else happens. Even Hudson is up today.'

Wild wants a record of the souls for whom he is responsible.

The occasion causes some merriment, the incongruity of the dishevelled men gathering together in front of the Snuggery. Before I can stop them, a number have wiped their faces with snow. They would otherwise be unrecognisable. Only Blackborow is missing, as he remains laid up in his bunk. He declines an offer to be carried outside.

I sense the occasion will make an extraordinary photograph, but I only have the pocket Kodak to work with. The morning light reflecting off the sea ice behind me is intense, and the men are squinting and looking away. Their nervous smiles are for the camera only. None of them know if they will make it back home.

I bring the men together so they form a single dark amorphous mass in their grimy Burberry jackets and greasy woollen hats and mitts. There is massive reflection from the glacier in the background, too, but I persist, deliberately overexposing the shot so the men are not too dark. Afterwards, I get Orde-Lees to take a shot of me leaning against the Snuggery, one for posterity.

The sun does not stay around long. Within a few days we are being lashed by winds gusting up to eighty miles an hour from the west-south-west. The ice in the bay is blown offshore and the waves whip up and send a constant shower of sea spray across the spit. There is no shelter outside and we are driven into the Snuggery, where only a few can cluster around the bogie stove and the rest lie in sleeping bags all day, trying to get warm. The constant babble and arguments about space are quite draining. Even in the daytime, the light in the Snuggery is often too dark for reading. Our *Encyclopaedia Britannica* is down to five volumes: A, E, M, P and S. We have increased our general knowledge on automobiles, engraving, manufacturing, photography and sexual reproduction, but have many gaps in other areas.

The moisture and temperature changes in the Snuggery mean it is far from ideal for storing my cinefilms and photographic plates. And there is an ever-present risk of large waves flooding the spit and washing our settlement into the sea. So I select a spot halfway up Penguin Hill and dig a hole in which to store these valuables, along with the boss's bag containing logbooks and scientific records. Orde-Lees takes a great interest and offers to help.

'I daresay, Hurley, no one will ever find this if the boss doesn't make it.'

'I dunno about that, I'm not done for just yet. And whatever happens, I want my negatives to survive.'

'Are they yours?'

'Well, twenty percent of the earnings is mine, and in the long run the films are mine. I wouldn't be here just for what the boss pays.'

'I suppose I didn't think about money when I agreed to come,' Orde-Lees says thoughtfully.

'Yeah, well, I'm here because his backers insisted he get me for the photographic work. It's the only way they make a commercial return.'

'Right now,' says Orde-Lees, 'any return would be acceptable to me. But I suppose you're not an amateur; you're more the professional, a commercial man.'

'I am not interested in going broke, if that's what you mean.'

The weather stays bad and there is nothing for it but to stay all day in one's sleeping bag. The sailors on the mezzanine level are now rueing their choice of bunks, as they have no headroom and are unable to sit up during the day. This does not help their tempers. They complain bitterly and never give thanks they are still alive. Every day there is constant griping. At least the lack of exercise reduces our appetites.

Fuel for the stove is the problem. We are fast running out of blubber. We are down to using strips of penguin skins which, when heated, drop just enough melted blubber to keep a fire burning, despite everything being so damp. I have plenty of time in my sleeping bag to study the bogie stove and set about an innovation to capture more of the heat that disappears up the chimney. I mould an empty oil drum to make a horizontal extension to the flue which we can use as a second cooker. As a result, and with the shortage of blubber, we only run the stove in the morning and cook two meals of hoosh at the same time. We now have just one hot meal a day, and the evening meal we keep from freezing by shoving it in the end of someone's sleeping bag.

The bogie stove requires constant attention to keep the fire burning—in order to save our last matches—and at the same time to avoid flare-ups. The penguin skins and blubber produce greasy smoke and fumes which make our eyes water and at times have everyone coughing and choking. Bowls and eating utensils have been lost and meals are eaten by hand or gobbled out of filthy mugs. The finnesko sleeping bags of those above me are rotting from exposure to saltwater, and there is a continuous shower from above of moulting reindeer hair. The hair, along with penguin fur and other rubbish, invariably gets into the hoosh.

Four weeks come and go without sign of Shackleton. No one really believed he would reach South Georgia in two weeks and be able to come straight back. Even if he made it to South Georgia, the whaling fleet are all steel-hulled and would be unable to risk coming into the pack ice that now surrounds

Elephant Island. Snowfalls have completely covered the spit and the icefloe, so it is now impossible to see where is ocean and where is land. Other than our flagpole, which consists of an upended oar on Penguin Hill, our habitation is invisible from the sea. The thick sea ice portends badly for the supply of blubber from seals and penguins over winter. A few snow petrels are caught but are all feathers and bone.

June arrives and the temperature drops to twenty degrees below zero. Blizzards from the south hit without warning, as the cliffs prevent us seeing from where the weather comes.

The blizzards threaten to blow us off the spit. The sound of the canvas walls motoring noisily in the wind prevents conversation, and I lie in the darkness wondering when our shelter will be ripped to shreds.

Overnight the blizzard breaks up the icecap and drives it north. Groups of gentoo penguins are washed up on the spit, and in the morning a raiding party manages to kill over one hundred birds. Thank God we have fuel again. These gentoos are taller than Adelies and provide twice the blubber. Our spirits are lifted. Orde-Lees is ecstatic that Wild agreed not to put a halt to the slaughter. This, however, was on condition Orde-Lees himself gut every bird. This is a stinking filthy business, but Orde-Lees doesn't seem to mind; he says the entrails keep his hands warm. The gullet and stomach are cut to remove any undigested fish, which add variety to our meals. Orde-Lees says with many of the penguins he finds their hearts still beating. It sickens me that they have not been killed properly.

'On my arithmetic that is the one hundredth,' I hear Orde-Lees call out, as with a thud another penguin carcass is tossed against the Snuggery. Skinning the carcass is also a dirty job, but Wild allows the men to do it in the entrance to the Snuggery to avoid frostbitten fingers.

Shortly afterwards, the flap opens and an exhausted Orde-Lees crawls inside, looking very pleased with himself. But his expression soon changes. 'Oh my Lord, what is this then? Who has done this to my bed?'

There is silence.

'What beastly scoundrels have left this bloody mess across my bedding?'

Those skinning the gentoos have been stacking the blubber strips on Orde-Lees's sleeping bag.

'Wild, who has done this? My bag was wet enough, but now it is putrid!' Wild looks up but says nothing.

'Who is responsible for fouling my bedding?' Orde-Lees demands.

He is met with less-than-helpful responses.

'If the smell keeps you awake, then the rest of us can sleep.'

'Aye, and you wouldn't want the feckin' penguin blubber dirtyin' the nice stone floor.'

The sailors are rabble enough but I would not want to be Orde-Lees; his fortunes take a turn for the worse the next day.

'I've sacked the colonel as store master,' Wild tells me. 'The crew think he is smuggling supplies. They say they've seen him taking things and heard him eating sugar in his bag at night.'

'I can't believe he'd be that foolish. The bastards should be happy if he's not snoring.'

'Well, I'm bringing in the sugar and milk powder and nut food to keep alongside me. Lees kept an inventory and there doesn't seem to be anything missing. But I can't change what the crew believe, so he's sacked. It's best for him really.'

A few days later, Wild, who is usually so calm, loses his temper with Orde-Lees over the bartering in food. This has become rife and is generally tolerated to deal with likes and dislikes. Orde-Lees, however, is a hoarder, and has built up a stash of goodies in the bottom of his sleeping bag. He now acts like the Bank of England. Stephenson is loud in his complaint that in exchange for a single bar of Streimer's nut food he has bound himself to pay Orde-Lees six lumps of sugar every week until rescued or the sugar runs out. Streimer's nut food is our most prized delicacy. It is a mixture of ground nuts, sesame oil and sweet nougat. Stephenson, having gluttonously eaten his nut food, is now moaning aloud that Shackleton won't be returning at all and the deal unfairly favours Orde-Lees.

Wild will not allow any negative talk about Shackleton's survival and gives Orde-Lees a blast.

'Colonel, there is no such deal, you blasted Shylock. Why, it could be eight weeks before the boss returns, so you make fifty lumps of sugar and a man collapses from lack of carbohydrates! God knows McIlroy and Macklin have told us we all need sugar. The boys need their rations; that's the end of this gambling with lives!'

Orde-Lees looks very put out.

Later, when we're out walking the spit, Orde-Lees tells me the remaining supplies will soon be finished.

'Wild keeps pandering to the sailing crews' stomachs. They expect the same rations as if they were working, and they don't have the sense to plan ahead for tomorrow, let alone for next week.'

'I expect Frank is keen to keep up morale.'

'There's no morale. The day Wild runs out of food he runs out of authority. All those men do is lie about arguing. They are like caged animals living in the smell of their own fart.'

June is a dismal time for us. It is too cold to be outside for any length of time. The men spend the whole day lying in their sleeping bags. Relieving oneself outside is avoided. Instead, there is a two-gallon petrol can which most of the men urinate into. But the sailors are careless and unsanitary and spillages occur frequently. Wild marks a line above which the user is required to empty the can. The sailors know by sound when this point is to be reached, and then steadfastly abstain until someone can be prevailed upon to go outside.

For several hours each day there is light from the sun, but it is barely above the horizon and mostly hidden by clouds. In the Snuggery it is now too dark to read. I feel this hardship greatly. But it may be as well we do not see the squalor in which we live. One June afternoon, as I am lying in my bunk, I find myself staring distractedly at reindeer hairs which come wafting down in waves from the thwarts of the upturned boat above me. They are coming from Stephenson's finnesko sleeping bag. It is then I see through the dim smoky light his greasy face, his open mouth, eyes shut and his head jerking back repeatedly. I should turn away, but I do not. I am amazed at his baseness and lack of shame. His eyes open and it is a few seconds before I realise he is staring straight at me. He reads the expression on my face. I look away, shaking my head in disgust.

Hours later I am outside on the spit when I am grabbed by the shoulder from behind. It is an angry red-faced Stephenson.

'Yer feckin' Australian convict bastard! Who d'ya tink y'are? Yer tink ya feckin' better 'n us? Yer tink yer important? Yer carry on like yer one of the officers, but yer not. Yer no feckin' scientist neither!'

I am taken off guard. 'Don't be a fool,' is all I can manage.

'Coom on then,' he says, and pushes me back across the snow-crusted shingle.

I am shocked at his intensity. 'Leave off,' I respond, and this time he throws his left fist, which connects with my right shoulder.

'Coom on,' he says again.

I lose my temper then and we grapple, and I manage to club him around the ears. By now we have stumbled down to the bay ice and we each try to throw the other. We are both unfit and breathless and are locked together a full minute before I finally push him off and scramble to my feet.

'You're a bloody mongrel,' I call out as I stride away.

Wild's orders are that every man except those invalided must have an hour's exercise outside each day. Wild and I have just turned at the end of the spit on one of our many laps when we are joined by McIlroy and Macklin.

'Frank,' says McIlroy, 'the gangrene markings on Blackborow are quite clear now. We should wait no longer. Blackborow has asked us to operate, says he feels up to it.'

'Could he wait just a week or two? The boss promised he'd get him to a hospital.'

'Macklin and I think he will have more chance if we amputate now, here, in the Snuggery. Frank, he may not make it back anyhow. But he won't last the winter unless the gangrenous tissues are removed now.'

'Do you have what's needed?'

'There's enough chloroform to knock him out for an hour, and we can boil up the instruments. But we want the whole mob out of the Snuggery. Hudson and Greenstreet will have to stay inside. Hurley, can you work on the stove to keep the temperature up without smoking us out? It has to be warm enough so chloroform will vaporise, at least fifty degrees.'

In the Snuggery an operating table is constructed out of Streimer's nut food boxes and covered in blankets that don't look too clean. Blackborow is lifted up and given a wash. He is just a young boy and this morning he is excited and won't stop talking.

'Do you think the Streimer's bars really are German? Not very patriotic, is it, the boss bringing so much of it? I like it anyhow, German or not.'

Meanwhile, I am stoking the fire and selecting the best pieces of penguin skin I can find, each with just a good quarter-inch thickness of blubber. The men have all left now to find a cave out of the rain. McIlroy and Macklin are in their undershirts, which are not exactly clean, but are at least free of guano and greasy reindeer hair. Wild stays to lend a hand. I have had the medical instruments boiling in the same pot as yesterday's hoosh. Not long after arriving on Elephant Island it became necessary for our only saucepan to be used as a commode for invalids.

Macklin does the chloroform and hovers around Blackborow's head, listening to his laboured breathing and watching the coat draped across his chest rise and fall. By the flickering light of a hurricane lamp, McIlroy starts methodically to cut and peel back strips of skin from the toes of Blackborow's foot. McIlroy is good with the scalpel and I watch it all very closely. He removes all the toes on the left foot and after two hours is stitching across the wound. Blackborow wakens and obviously has pain as he grimaces and smiles at the same time. They put him back to sleep with morphine. For once it is peaceful in the Snuggery, and Wild and I are in no hurry to let the others know they can return.

Midwinter's Day arrives, and there is nostalgic talk about last year's festivities on *Endurance*, the variety of delicacies and bottles of rum. We were stuck fast in ice, but at least with a proper roof over our heads. This year we make do with mashing up the dwindling supply of Huntley & Palmers wholemeal biscuits with the now-mouldy Streimer's nut food to make a pudding. To wash it down, Wild has requisitioned the remainder of Clark's preserving solution. Clark had this for biological specimens, usually deceased, on which the ninety-percent-proof methylated spirit could do no further harm. Wild dispenses it with a little sugar and water for his toasts to 'the boss and crew of *James Caird*', 'the King' and, of course, 'wives and sweethearts—though,' he adds, 'I have neither.'

Then our concert begins, with each man sitting upright in his sleeping bag and singing or reciting some doggerel he has memorised for the occasion. Orde-Lees bears the brunt of the wit. Macklin, a learned doctor, is surprisingly vicious towards him. The two had fought over space in the Snuggery and had to be separated. Macklin reads aloud a cruel verse he has composed, 'The Colonel's Lament'. If it were me I would not have let Macklin finish, but Orde-Lees just shakes his head and mutters, 'Oh, dear me.' As it happens, I have composed a piece which makes fun of Orde-Lees for his snoring and Macklin for his farting, but at least I have been even-handed.

Despite the abuse, Orde-Lees does nothing to curb his night-time snoring. He is regularly kicked and punched awake from his noisy slumbers, and I confess I have thrown stones at him if the tempest fails to drown him out. One evening Wild has to intervene before violence erupts.

'That's enough. Now, Colonel, here is how we restore peace. In the evening you will wear this rope looped around your arm. Hurley will help me rig up some eyelets along the roof to my bunk. If you are causing offence, I will pull until you stop. If it turns out you are not the offender, then you are relieved of the rope for the rest of the night.'

Amazingly, Orde-Lees agrees to this and the rope is fitted into place, but still this does not satisfy the sailors. 'Put it round his feckin' neck!' they cry.

A few days later we all get a fright as the winter storms worsen and waves come licking at the edge of the Snuggery. The saltspray permeates our clothing and bedding. The storms however do bring large numbers of gentoo penguins washed up on the spit. The colonel is quickly outside to lead a party of those with a stomach for slaughter. I find myself increasingly reluctant to take up arms against the hapless penguins and seals despite our dire necessity. One morning the squalls are particularly unpleasant. Huge white rollers rush up on the spit and eighty or more gentoos are unceremoniously and bruisingly bundled and bounced off bergs and rocks and tossed up on the shore. When their bellies hit shingle they leap to their feet and with barely a shake they nonchalantly waddle to higher ground. Within several minutes Orde Lees is leading a party along the water's edge to discourage the gentoos from returning to the surf. The gentoos reach the end of the spit and rock hop up the side of Penguin Hill. The men, weapons in hand stretch in a band between the gentoos and the sea. By now half the gentoos have been slain and lie where they have been felled. Lees and his party are now confident they have cut off the remainder. There is no rush. The gentoos with little complaint retreat up Penguin Hill. The men take time to enjoy the antics of the gentoos. Despite being exhausted from their long sea journey they waddle and hop and only occasionally stumble as they ascend the icy rocks and snow of Penguin Hill. The killing pauses as the men slowly converge on the penguins at the crest of the hill. Up here the wind is stronger and snow and sleet lash the men who pull down their hats and balaclavas. They do not try to talk above the fury of the storm. Soon the men can see over the crest to the south where Penguin Hill drops in a steep cliff not far from the Snuggery. In the background through the gloom, the forbidding spires and crags of Elephant Island are visible. The men look down at their feet where the gentoos are now huddled several deep along the edge of the cliff. The gentoos look around, curious of the strangers crowding them. The penguins converse and show no fear. Then, first one and then another, leap off the steep cliff without, or so it would seem, any thought for their safety. The other gentoos all follow.

There are men waiting at the bottom of the cliff. Most of the gentoos are dead or unconscious. The men finish them off.

June comes to an end with no sign of rescue. Inside the Snuggery, I can't avoid hearing the talk.

'Wild said the boss would be here by now.'

'It can only mean one thing.'

'Did you really think a wee cockleshell of a boat could sail hundreds of miles in those seas?'

'You've seen the feckin' waves, man, some are more'n eighty feet high.'

'But if anyone could do it, the boss and the skipper could.'

'Well why ain't they here then?'

'The boss wouldn't give up. They had food for a month or longer.'

'They didna' hae water for a month, I know that. You believe what you like.'

Wild intervenes. 'Stop that rubbish talk, you lot. Your brains must be frozen. Say the boss does take until June to reach Grytviken. He won't want to take the risk of coming here and getting stuck in ice in an iron whaler. He knows he needs a wooden boat and you know there are nonesuch in South Georgia. So where's he going to get one? Well I suppose he could try the Falklands, but he'll be wanting *Aurora*, which has to come all the way from New Zealand. So he has to cable, but there's no cable in South Georgia, so he has to go to the Falklands anyways. It's at best seven weeks' passage from New Zealand to here, so that would mean the end of July. So for God's sake give it a rest!'

It is only a few weeks later, as I am lying in my sleeping bag reading Nordenskjöld's account of his ship being trapped in the Weddell Sea ice, that our forced hibernation is disturbed by the sound of a loud cannon firing.

'Ship!' cries one voice then another, and there is a mad scramble for the tent flap.

'Stand by, stand by!' Marston, who was already outside, is yelling and running towards the Snuggery, but as I emerge no one is looking out to sea. Marston is pointing back across the spit to the west. 'It was large as a cathedral, I swear.'

The glacier has cracked with a loud boom and a huge section has fallen into the bay. Snow and ice is still avalanching down vertically in a cloud of mist and spume. Some four hundred yards away, a long black line emerges from the base of the cliff and advances towards Cape Wild, where we stand on our low-lying spit of shingle.

There is less than a minute, no time to move Blackborow and Hudson. The waves gather height and are at least twenty feet high as they hit the pack ice surrounding the spit. The waves first lift then crack the ice like a bedsheet in the wind as an invisible submarine force propels towards us. Slabs of ice are lifted skywards and thrown forwards in a churning maelstrom. Thank God my films are stored high up on Penguin Hill, so I know they are safe as the first wave rushes up along the spit and inundates the Snuggery.

The next wave goes no further. The icepack has acted as a damper. Ice boulders are left stranded on the spit but our home has survived with only a dunking.

The incident is unnerving and strips away any sense of security I had in our abode. We may have been more secure on the icecap. Our tiny strip of land is no more than shingle and guano pushed by current and wave action into a spit joining Penguin Hill to the prison-wall cliffs of Elephant Island. The island itself remains inaccessible, but by appearance its hinterland is a forbidding combination of precipice and glacier. For much of the time our shingle spit is covered by snowdrift up to twelve feet deep in parts. We constantly shovel snow to prevent collapse of the stretched canvas roof of the Snuggery.

•

From mid-July onwards we experience increasing problems with the volume of water produced from snow thaw and the heat generated by the cooker. One night my slumbers are disturbed when I shift my arm and find it plunged into icy water. Our floor is lower than surrounding snow levels and heavy rain has formed an undercover lake, luckily still an inch or so from my bag. I wake Wild, James and McIlroy, and together we bail out some sixty gallons of evil-smelling water and guano sludge. At 5 a.m. we do the same again, and every three or four hours for the next day. High tide aggravates the problem. We excavate the hut interior and construct elaborate drains, which help, but do not eliminate the need for bailing.

The winter gales are terrifying but they have a beauty I admire even though I am unable to capture them on film. They are very much part of our daily experience. If I happen to be outside during such a maelstrom I will sometimes linger. Only in the midst of the elements at their wildest do I find an escape from our crowded abode. The wind howls and the sea rises up until Elephant Island and Penguin Hill disappear, as does the ocean itself. Instead there is just spume from crashing waves and constant pelting of ice fragments and spray that flies across the spit like shrapnel. Eventually self-preservation kicks in and drives me back inside the Snuggery. Fearful as these storms are I have come to prefer a wild sea to the deathly quiet of being iced in and surrounded by a frozen vista. The sea brings food and hope of rescue and the tides and currents are my connection with other lands and the rest of mankind, marooned here as I am on this most desolate piece of rock.

July runs out of days and there is still no sign of Shackleton. The unavoidable conclusion is that we have not been rescued because the boss, Worsley, Crean, Chips, McCarthy and

Vincent have all perished. There is really no other explanation. Even Wild now accepts this. He issues orders for gathering the items needed for another sea voyage.

It is now the two-year anniversary of when *Endurance* was first commissioned and the expedition left London. It is also two years ago that the war in Europe started. All the men have friends and family that were expecting to join up.

'Be all over now and we'll hae missed our chance.'

'Aye, they'll hae forgotten aboot us.'

Orde-Lees pipes up. 'I don't believe that. It could only be over by now if it was a draw, and Britain would never accept a draw with Germany.'

The conversation is interrupted by an outbreak of coughing caused by acrid smoke from the latest tobacco substitute. The sailors, all nicotine addicts, have consumed their entire tobacco ration. Cheetham, as chief tobacco scientist, has persuaded them to remove the sennegrass padding from their finnesko boots, never mind they will have frostbitten feet. He has then boiled this in water with the remains of several broken-up old pipes in the expectation that the sennegrass, when dried out, will be infused with tobacco flavour. Other additives include lichen, seaweed, navel lint, reindeer hairs and any other hairs and flammable detritus from the sleeping bags. Cheetham has much scorn heaped on him for his efforts. I am pleased I have never succumbed to being a regular smoker.

Orde-Lees for once gets it right with his protest, 'Good Lord, it smells like a cross between a fire in a feather factory and a third-class smoking carriage on a working man's train!'

Monday, 7 August 1916, and Wild insists we celebrate the bank holiday with a biscuit pudding. It's very nice, too, although Orde-Lees insists on reminding us there is only another four or five weeks of biscuits left. These are our last treats, as the milk powder has all gone and the last of our Streimer's nut food will be gone in a week.

The following Saturday, our regular toasts are accompanied by our final ration of methylated spirits, a tablespoon each. Wild is particularly mournful at this. We have two cases of Bovril rations left for making hoosh, along with some sugar cubes. There are still twenty-two mouths to feed.

Three or four days later, in the middle of a violent storm, I am startled by Orde-Lees bursting through the Snuggery entrance.

'Gentoos!' he cries. 'Lots of them! Wild, I can lead a party and get them now before they go.'

Wild looks up. 'Where, Colonel? Where and how many?'

'About thirty, I should say, on the rocks at the foot of the hill.'

'Show us, Colonel. Hoyle, will you come too?'

Outside it is bitter, but worse than that is the heavy drenching rain. My Burberry is almost worn through in parts and, while effective against snow, it is useless once wet.

We are lifted and virtually blown to the water's edge, where we see a group of penguins huddled close together above the rock platform at the base of the cliff.

Wild says, 'No, Colonel, I'm not sending men out in this. Wait till the weather's better.'

'But they'll be gone by morning,' Orde-Lees protests.

'It's a good sign, but we should soon start to see seals. I'm damned if I'm going to slaughter thirty penguins when one seal will give us five times the amount of meat and blubber. Leave them be, Colonel. I'm giving the penguins a day off.'

With that Wild was gone.

'You would have had to gut them yourself in the rain.' I have to yell my consolation to Orde-Lees to be heard. 'No one was going to come out in this.'

'I've done it before.'

'I know, but why should you? Don't say you don't feel the cold.'

'Feel the cold! Is that all you feel, Hurley? Do you know how close to the edge things are here? I thought you would know about starvation. What do you think is holding things together here? It's not Wild. The men don't respect him like they did the boss. And it's not God's law! There's no religion holding things together on this island. The only thing that counts with those sailors is food in their bellies. That's all they think about. Run out of food and they'll turn into cannibals. I've heard them talk about me. I'm the one who's going to meet with an accident. I understand that.'

'Nonsense,' I say and turn to head back in.

'Hurley, it's Wild who let the larder run down, but it's me that will pay. It's me they want!'

For much of August, the spit is surrounded by pack ice. Few penguins arrive and fewer seals. Orde-Lees does a stocktake of frozen carcasses and informs Wild there are only twelve penguin skins left for fuel, penguin meat for four days and seal meat, much of it putrid, for nine days.

Within a short time, it becomes apparent this information has reached the sailors.

'No rescue means we starve to death.'

'We'll eat the first to die, that is what it means.'

Wild interrupts. 'Colonel, you are a God-fearing man; surely you do not believe the Almighty God, after all our sufferings, will let us starve here without a soul knowing.'

Orde-Lees responds, 'Believing in Almighty God is no excuse for being improvident, Mr Wild.'

Wild shot a leopard seal in August but we were unable to prevent it swimming off. The rifle has only fourteen cartridges left.

We have better luck a week later, when a pregnant Weddell cow wanders up on the spit and is quickly butchered. And on the positive side, we have by experimentation found that if Elephant Island seaweed is boiled for several hours it forms a palatable jellylike substance. However the process uses up considerable fuel and we are very low on blubber.

The real challenge is clearing snow and ice from the rock platform. The rock pools, we discover, are lined with limpets which, if collected in sufficient volume, add welcome variety to our diet. Fifty limpets are a worthwhile snack, but they are often deep in the pools and difficult to collect before losing sensation in your arm.

For some time I have been wondering whether I will have a choice to leave by boat with Wild on a rescue attempt or stay in the relatively safe, although dismal, landfall of Elephant Island. Conversation in the Snuggery is now so openly desperate there is no longer a façade that we are waiting for the boss to return. When Wild asks me to accompany him, I readily agree. Macklin is to come, along with two others. Deception Island is two hundred and fifty miles away against the prevailing south-west headwinds. Sealers should arrive in those waters from early November. Wild figures it could take up to six weeks rowing in *Dudley Docker*. *Docker* is smaller than *Caird* and sits lower in the water. We have five oars left, one of which needs to be converted to a mast. The remnants of a tent will be cut into a mainsail. It will be a wet voyage. Of course, I already know my films cannot be risked and I am going to have to leave them cached on the island. They are more important than me.

11

Rescue, September 1916

It says somewhere in the Bible that you know not the day, nor the hour. That's how it was for us. August had come to an end. I had spent the morning in a working party shovelling snowdrift away from the Snuggery. The tide had dropped, so we quit clearing snow to fossick in the tidal zone for limpets and seaweed. 'Hoosh-oh!' had been called for lunch, and the sailors and all had trooped back inside. Despite the anxiety of being fed, it was my wont to tarry at times like these and delay my return to the crowded squalor of the hut. Marston, too, was lingering as he finished shelling his morning's haul of limpets.

'I say, Hurley, have a look at that, will you?'

I looked. It was unmistakable, yet it was unbelievable. Marston rose to his feet.

We both rubbed our eyes. It was a ship—not an iceberg that looked like a ship (of which there were many), but a real ship. As if from nowhere this small black object had just rounded the rocky island that stood offshore from our spit. It was a mile or so off, and just before the horizon. I shook my head and looked again, It was still there and it was moving. It was not a sailing ship, but a small steamboat.

Marston's shelled limpets fell across the rocks. 'Ship ho!' he called as he turned and ran to the hut with me hot on his tail. 'Wild, Wild, there's a ship!' he yelled.

The hut exploded with great commotion from within. One by one, bodies came out through the flap till the flap was no more, and the more impatient pushed through the canvas walls.

Since there was no certainty as to the boat's purposes, I retrieved our last tin of paraffin, put a pick through it and poured its contents onto a small bundle of sennegrass and added some rather frozen strips of blubber. I struggled to induce flames, and the sennegrass was so dry there was little smoke. At the same time, Wild, Macklin and Orde-Lees made a dash up Penguin Hill, only to find our flag was a frozen lump at the base of the oar which served as a mast. Instead, Macklin's Burberry jacket was quickly hoisted, but the lanyard jammed when it was only halfway.

By this time it was clear the steamboat was heading straight for Cape Wild. Orde-Lees, Clark and Hudson carried Blackborow outside in his bedding so he could behold the wondrous sight. The four of them were in tears.

The boat, which was flying a Chilean naval ensign, dropped anchor some hundred and fifty yards offshore and a rowing boat was lowered. I immediately recognised Shackleton's solid features. I retrieved my Vest Pocket Kodak and quickly captured the scene, the final shots on the roll and my last photographs on Elephant Island.

As they drew closer ashore, Worsley and Crean were recognised. Shackleton in the prow of the boat called out to us and Wild answered, 'All well, all well.' We would learn later that the boss had been troubled when he had looked through the binoculars and seen Macklin's Burberry flying at half-mast.

With small waves breaking along the spit, Wild signalled the boss to come alongside a rocky outcrop. Shackleton declined point blank Wild's invitation to step ashore and inspect our quarters, and so the first of three boatloads of castaways clambered aboard, one of whom asked, 'Are you all well, boss?'

Shackleton paused and replied, 'Don't we look alright now that we have washed?', and those being rescued looked at their greasy destitute selves seated among their clean-shaven and clean-faced Chilean rescuers and laughed heartily.

I retrieved the logbooks, photographic plates and cinefilm from Penguin Hill, Hussey carried his banjo. An uneaten hoosh was left still warm in the cooking pot inside the Snuggery. I was in the final load as we pushed off and commenced rowing back to the steamboat when a cry was heard from on shore and a figure came running furiously across the spit. We rowed back to the rocky point. It was an emotional Orde-Lees who dived headlong into the boat. He had gone back inside the hut. I could only imagine he had been having a quiet moment with his Maker.

Our rescue boat was a Chilean navy tug called *Yelcho*. Once on board, the sailors went straight to the downstairs mess to enjoy a meal, and in short time had drunk themselves silly on Chilean wine. The scientists and officers and myself, along with *Yelcho*'s Captain Luis Pardo, stayed on deck to listen to Shackleton, Worsley and Crean tell the story of their voyage in *Caird* over eight hundred miles to South Georgia. They then had to cross the mountains of South Georgia to reach a whaling station. This voyage to Elephant Island was their fourth attempt to reach us after being defeated each time by the icecap.

We also listened with open-mouthed amazement to learn that the European war was still being fought, despite modern weaponry taking an unbelievable toll in human lives. We heard that soldiers lived like rats in the ground to escape constant artillery bombardments directed by observers in zeppelin airships. There were stories of poison gas, machine guns and bombs dropped from aeroplanes. German U-boats were sinking all merchant ships. Yet despite horrendous casualties, the war showed no sign of stopping. We heard for the first time names such as the Somme, Verdun and Gallipoli, and stories of the sinking of *Lusitania* and the murder of Nurse Cavell.

In the midst of these stories I leap to my feet to take my last view of Elephant Island. Despite the great height of its peaks, it has gone. The icecap and icebergs have all gone. Out of sight below the horizon, it is as though that world no longer exists. But for the images captured on my film, the quality of which is still uncertain, who would believe what we have experienced? And what is this strange feeling of emptiness welling up inside me? I feel numb. Having heard enough of the catastrophic events in Europe, and feeling overwhelmed by a strange sense of exhaustion, I seek out a small corner, where I lie down alone on the deck wrapped in charcoal-coloured blankets. I should be warm, but my body is shivering. The deck below me vibrates with the deep loud throbbing of *Yelcho*'s engines. Soon my whole body is racked by sobs as my mind relives its suspended disbelief at the loss of *Endurance*, our escape in the boats, our entombment on Elephant Island, and the survival and return of the boss. Whether it is the swells or the strangeness of the food I have just consumed I know not, but I am sick right across the deck where I am lying.

•

On arrival in Punta Arenas we were treated as heroes. Shackleton, being Shackleton, had gone ashore several miles before the main port to alert the local governor and the press. By the time we arrived, a crowd lined the jetty and a Chilean naval band was playing stirring music to greet us. Within a short time the crowd had swelled to some several thousand people cheering in Spanish, tooting whistles and waving flags.

The boss had forbidden us to shave our beards or change clothes, so the populace could see what real castaways looked like. Shackleton preceded us as we walked down the gang-plank in our rags, and one by one our names were called and we were introduced to the governor. The Red Cross carried Blackborow away on a stretcher.

There followed the strangest of street parades as, led by the governor, Shackleton and Captain Luis Pardo of *Yelcho*, we marched into the town square with crowds lining the foot-paths. After a few words from the governor and the boss and photographs by the local press, and despite our odorous state, it was open slather as we were greeted warmly on all sides. The men of Punta Arenas kissed us on both cheeks, women wept and children snuck up to touch our filthy garments. Well-to-do families and citizenry came forwards and insisted on having one or two survivors each to care for as their houseguests. I refused several entreaties from disappointed dignitaries and eventually an arrangement was made for Wild, Clark and I to have rooms at the Royal Hotel. What I craved more than anything else in the world was escape from my fellow man.

It is hard to explain the pleasure of those moments of closing a door behind me and having a room completely to myself. The room had a bed and two chairs to sit on and running water from a tap. Most extraordinary of all, the hotel rooms had electric lighting so that, at the pull of a cord, there need be no night-time. Night had brighter light than day. Most unnerving was a large vanity mirror. Who was the frightening, dishevelled man that stared back so suspiciously? I inspected my appearance closely, then ran a hot bath and removed the clothing I had worn for a year. Applying a sharp razor,

I rediscovered my face beneath tangled hair and matted beard. My delicious solitude was eventually disturbed by Wild delivering fresh clothing and requiring my presence at the British Club for the first of innumerable celebratory functions.

The morning papers told our story—ALL SAVED AND ALL WELL. Shackleton's reputation as a popular hero now knew no bounds. The world took respite from its utilitarian politics and war-obsessed front pages to revel in the heroism of men who were explorers for a common good, not soldiers of a nation state. Having been offered the darkroom of a local photographer, I again found solace under the ruby lamp, developing and checking the glass plates and cinefilm and making a series of lantern slides. With the exception of the small Kodak film taken on Elephant Island, which suffered from overlong storage, all the photographs were fine. The glass plates taken over a year ago, and which had been underwater, sealed in a tin container in the wreck of *Endurance*, proved to be excellent.

The genuine warmth of the Chileans was overwhelming and I was at my wit's end devising excuses to escape their constant offers of hospitality. Luncheons, dinners, theatre boxes, drinks, midnight cocktails—the celebrations went on and on. Fortunately, the demands of my work as expedition photographer provided an excellent reason for my absence. Despite the comfort of my room at the Royal Hotel, I had trouble sleeping and found myself staring at the patterned tin ceiling and listening to the banter in Spanish from the hotel corridor. I dealt with this insomnia by spending long nights working in the darkroom until eventually I could lie down and sleep.

Three days after our arrival, Wild turned up at the photographic studios where I was working with an 'order' from the boss that my presence was required that evening for a reception at the Magellanes Club. This proved to be a most magnificent affair, attended by the leading citizens of Punta Arenas. We were guests of honour in a large banquet hall festooned with flowers and blazing with electric lights. An orchestra played popular songs, as well as the British and Chilean national anthems. I was captivated by the dusky beauty of the women-folk, richly attired in vivid dresses and shawls, their olive-tinted complexions aglow. In between numerous speeches in Spanish and English, course after course of Chilean dishes were served.

Festivities continued through to the early morning. I found myself avoiding eye contact as this led immediately to a cry of 'Salu!' and the obligation to drain my glass. Champagne flowed like water and I could not help but wonder at the number of bottles consumed. My enquiries revealed the cost per bottle was not insignificant. The result was much gaiety and bonhomie as alcohol papered over the contrasting social positions between the *Endurance* crew and our generous hosts. An inability to understand the crew's language spared the Chileans from some of the worst crassness. I was forced to endure being dragged to a table where that vulgar greaser Stephenson, dressed in a starched white-collared shirt and borrowed dinner jacket, was arm in arm with two Chilean millionaires who good-naturedly filled his champagne glass while he puffed luxuriously on a cigar.

As a result of the lateness of the evening and close quarters with our hosts, especially being kissed on both cheeks by the men which I could not get used to, I was not surprised when I felt poorly the next day. I caught my first cold in over two years, after being protected all that time by Antarctic temperatures. Having tolerated my *Endurance* companions throughout the deprivations of Elephant Island, I was now heartily sick of them. Drinking and womanising became an obsession with them all. Wild was frequently incomprehensible from the grog and I feared for his health.

In short time, a number of the sailing crew were in gaol for drunk and disorderly conduct. To preserve the reputation of the British in neutral Chile, the boss wisely arranged for the crew to be shipped back to England on the next boat. This left just the officers, scientists and myself to enjoy a celebratory tour to the national capital, Santiago. I was pleased to have an opportunity to see the coast and countryside, but the Latin American hero worship of Shackleton was nauseating. The boss said the tour was to encourage the Chileans to side with the Allies in the war, but in reality it was a blatant Shackleton publicity tour. I had to admire his ability to charm an audience, however, and armed with my lantern slides he gave a number of successful lectures to packed town halls in Valparaíso and Santiago. I could readily see his Irish blarney was more entertaining than the dry, though more accurate, Mawson monologue.

A week after our arrival, there was much cause for excitement when a mailbag for *Endurance* arrived. There were several letters from Elsa, but none from my family. The first letter I opened was over a year old, posted by Elsa in August 1915:

Dear Frank,

I hope this letter finds its way to you and that you are safe and well.

My parents and I are well. I think of you often, of course, and when I do I wonder just where you are. I received your letter from South Georgia. I have read and reread it so many times. I hope you don't mind, I read it aloud to my parents. My father was very excited and has told everyone at his work about you. Just about everyone here has now read Sir Douglas Mawson's book The Home of the Blizzard, *with all your wonderful pictures.*

The newspapers, however, have space for nothing but the war. I do not know what news you have received. I am sorry to tell you that the newspapers here have reported that your friend Lieutenant Robert Bage was killed by enemy fire in the first fortnight of the fighting at Gallipoli. The newspaper mentioned his Polar Medal. There was no other information about the circumstances. Australian casualties have been high . . .

That was the end of my excitement. I had no more stomach for reading letters. How could this be? And what was Bob doing in Turkey? Without Bob, I would not have made it back to Cape Denison.

There seemed to be little good happening in the civilised world. All of us who received mail had similar news of friends and family. Frank Wild told me he learned that Harrisson, with whom I tramped the length of Macquarie Island, had been lost at sea.

The business of the Imperial Trans-Antarctic Expedition was sadly not complete, and on 8 October the boss left for Australia and New Zealand to participate in a rescue of the Ross Sea party on the other side of the Antarctic continent. While Shackleton had been quaffing Chilean champagne, those expedition members whose job it was to lay food depots from the Ross Sea to the South Pole were still stranded on the ice, waiting and no doubt wondering what had become of our Trans-Antarctic party. This meant Shackleton had to deputise me to get the films safely to Perris in London. I was keen to do this, despite reports of indiscriminate U-boat attacks on shipping. Any thought I had of returning home to Ma and Elsa in Australia was now vanished. I had said to Ma and, more importantly, had promised Elsa I would return to Sydney as soon as I could. But there was no doubt in my mind I had to go to London rather than going home. Everything I had achieved, everything I had endured, would be wasted if I did not take this chance. But still I could not bring myself to write and tell Elsa until mid-October, shortly before boarding the England-bound RMS *Orissa* in Montevideo.

> *. . . of course, Elsa, I know this decision means it is only right that you be released from our engagement, and from waiting any longer for your languishing, travel-weary correspondent—and a poor correspondent at that. I will be several months at least working in London, and Shackleton insists I am the only man who can do the job, so vital for the expedition finances . . .*

Spending almost four weeks at sea on board *Orissa*, without any opportunity to work on the films and liberated from the boss and the entire *Endurance* crew, was a most restorative experience. I was at last my own man again. No one was dependent on me nor I on them.

I was honoured to be invited to join the captain's table for meals, and soon found myself in the centre of a pleasant circle of travelling companions. French, Italian, American—the cacophony of foreign tongues and accents was quite exciting. All the talk was of U-boat 53 and its whereabouts. Curiously, I felt no anxiety about the risk of coming under attack, notwithstanding my companions rattling off the names of ships sunk in the last several weeks.

In the civilised society on board ship, I was fascinated by the number of stylish and engaging female travellers, married and unmarried. They were endlessly inquisitive about how I lived on the ice, and much time was spent bringing me up to date with the events and fashions of the last two years. I found my services in much demand for playing deck golf. Unbeknown to my shipboard companions, I had turned thirty-one years of age on the very day I boarded *Orissa*. I was aware that others would be thinking I should be married, but it made no sense to me, despite my affection for Elsa, that I should rush back to Australia with this purpose in mind.

Anxiety on board about U-boats and mines in the shipping lanes increased sharply as *Orissa* reached Lisbon and then La Rochelle. But I was too excited to be nervous. At that time I did not really believe my fellow man could be so deadly. And I had the strangest sense that in going to 'old England'—with all the picture-book images of patchwork fields, ivy-covered stone cottages and, of course, Buckingham Palace—I was going home.

12

London, November 1916

In mid-November *Orissa* eventually found a berth in the crowded port of Liverpool. Everywhere were troop transports and barges full of khaki-clad men.

'Mr Hurley, sir, Mr Hurley!' I was accosted before disembarking by a bespectacled balding man in a grey suit and red bowtie. 'Allow me to introduce myself. I am Mr Bussey from the *Daily Chronicle*. Mr Perris has asked me to meet you, sir, and help you through customs. Did you see any U-boats, sir?'

Bussey turned out to be very helpful, as there was a lot to carry. To my surprise, uniformed customs officers weighed my films to estimate their length, and then charged five pence a foot. Bussey handed over a cheque for one hundred and twenty pounds and rushed me through. He collected the bags and together we boarded the 4 p.m. London express.

It was darkish as we left the station, and I did not get to see the patchwork countryside as the train noiselessly reached an astounding speed well over fifty miles per hour. Within a little more than four hours, the train arrived at Paddington Station in London. Bussey whisked me into a cab and it was about

9.30 p.m. when I first met Ernest Perris in his office on the top floor of the *Daily Chronicle* building.

Perris had weary eyes and neatly combed dark hair, though it was more hair oil than hair and I couldn't help but notice crumbs on his waistcoat which several weeks earlier I would have been glad to consume. He left me in little doubt he was sizing me up, and I guessed Shackleton had been in his ear about me. After a lengthy dialogue about the extent of photographs and film which I handed over, he had Bussey drop me at the Imperial Hotel in Russell Square with instructions to bring me back to the *Chronicle* at nine the following morning.

I had no complaint with the Imperial Hotel, which soon became my London home. In fact I felt that hotel life suited me. The next three days I spent with Perris and his staff, going through the entire footage and all the glass plates. Afterwards, Perris called me in for a meeting in his large office, from which there was a fine view of Fleet Street and the busy London traffic.

'Hurley, the glass plates are excellent. We will start using some of them in the *Chronicle* immediately. Most of them, though, will have to wait for Shackleton to get here, and we can then book a London theatre for travelogue lecture presentations. We will do an illustrated book of the expedition, but that could be several months away.'

'I am quite used to narrating my own lantern slides and would like to do some of the shows,' I told him.

'We can talk about that. Do you know Ponting? Went with Scott?'

'Of course. I intend to meet him if I can.'

'He has some London shows coming up. Get along, will you, and see what he does.'

'I certainly will. And about my cinefilm?'

'Yes, well, I'm afraid there is a problem there, my dear fellow.'

He sat back in his chair. 'Hurley, we need a moving picture that tells a strong story. Shackleton's story is very good, mind you, and you have plenty of film—and it's good film; your camera work is first class. But it has to entertain. This war has been so depressing and drawn out. People—the public, that is—need some relief, some escape from it all.'

'What do you mean?'

'What do I mean? I mean, Hurley, there are not enough penguins!'

'Penguins?! There are penguins.'

'Not nearly enough penguins and penguin antics. Not enough seals and seal antics. Not enough wildlife, generally—but, mainly, not enough penguins.'

'But we didn't go to visit penguin colonies. And you know I had to abandon most of my glass plates on the ice. For goodness sake, Perris, we were stuck on the icecap. Penguin and seal colonies are on land. Most of the time we were the only living creatures. If we saw penguins, we ate them!'

'My good fellow, I'm not blaming you. But your Mawson film had lots of penguins.'

'Mawson had a land base at Commonwealth Bay. I could use some of that footage, if you like.'

'No, no, I'm not paying anyone else.'

'Well, what do we do?'

'What do we do? Well . . . we can't risk filming in the zoological gardens. There's nothing else for it. You'll have to go back.'

I could hardly believe my ears. 'You want me to go *back*?'

'Well, you don't have to go *all* the way back do you—to Antarctica?'

'I suppose South Georgia has some seal and penguin colonies that haven't yet been wiped out.'

'Well, that would do. I can organise the equipment. Damn the U-boats! How much time would you need?'

I was halfway out the door when Perris called out, 'Oh and, Hurley, I liked the dogs, especially the cinefilm of the puppies. Did you eat the dogs too?'

'No, we didn't eat the dogs. We shot them, though.'

'Yes, that's what I thought. Anyway, I've organised two Pomeranian puppies for you to take with you. Maybe you can get them in some shots with the penguins.'

I walked back to the hotel not unhappy, but wondering how I would explain this to Ma and Elsa.

I soon had no doubt I had been right to come straight to London. Perris looked after my accommodation and arranged a modest advance. The return to South Georgia would take several weeks to organise. There was, of course, an enormous amount to do on the Imperial Trans-Antarctic Expedition film and photographs if they were to make a financial return. More than that, however, London was the focal point of the war effort, and many of my expedition colleagues were here or coming through here on their way to the front or to go on leave. There were huge numbers of 'colonials' in London from all over the Commonwealth: Canada, Australia, New Zealand, India and Africa.

In that first week, Perris took me to a packed Philharmonic Hall to see '90 Degrees South: With Captain Scott in the Antarctic'. I was spellbound by Herbert Ponting, the photographer who had travelled with Scott's expedition in 1911. His photographs were projected on a huge screen and were stunning in their detail and perfection. He personally narrated the story with such delicate poignancy there were many in the audience in tears. But there was humour, too, and one emerged with an overwhelming sense of pride at the achievement of this British expedition. Ponting presented what his audience wanted to see and hear; they came with handkerchiefs at the ready. And of course the most moving photographs were not taken by Ponting at all. They were the grainy enlargements from the camera found in Scott's tent. I could see what I needed to do with the Shackleton film.

While working at the *Chronicle* I was visited by my *Endurance* colleagues Clark, James and Wordie. Also Mawson—who by then was Sir Douglas Mawson and had been commissioned as a captain in the British Army—was a regular visitor to London. We had a lot to talk about, but my asking about the chance of royalty payments from the AAE struck a raw nerve.

'Hurley, you must have heard I am struggling to clear the debts of the expedition. The film was not all it should have been, and proceeds in Australia and here have been very disappointing, frankly. And America has been a disaster.'

'I could have told you that would happen.'

'Well honestly, Hurley, it was not helped by you disappearing with Birtles and then with Shackleton. That's when we needed your help. We never received the Paget colour plates you promised to send and we couldn't find all the Macquarie Island plates you said were at Kodak's offices.'

'But, Doc, the money that has been raised is from my photographs and I have received nothing for them. And why should I assist with AAE lectures if I am to get nothing for it?'

He gave me a dark look but did not lose his temper.

'Well, you are Shackleton's man now. I assume you are committed to getting his film released. Look, I daresay the war has not helped with any of this.'

Mawson put me in contact with other AAE expedition members in London. 'You must visit Bickerton,' he said. 'He is not long out of hospital and lucky to be alive.'

'What about Dad Mclean?' I said. 'I gather he worked closely with you on the expedition book.'

'Well, he's just married my stenographer, if that's what you mean. Actually, he's been a great support. He spent months working on the proofs of *Home of the Blizzard*—including, of course, your photographs.' He added rather pointedly, 'I haven't been able to pay him anything.'

Dad McLean invited me to dinner at his home in the London suburb of Shepherd's Bush and it had a remarkably salutary effect on me to see two lovebirds enjoying domestic bliss around the hearth of their tiny flat. Mrs McLean was both beautiful and very intelligent.

In those first weeks in London before Christmas, I often walked through Hyde Park and I could not help but notice the number of soldiers arm in arm with their sweethearts. It must be something to do with being a soldier in uniform, I thought. Then out of the blue one morning, Clark turned up at my hotel and to my astonishment asked me to be the best man at his wedding the next day. He was such a shy fellow, I had no idea he was capable of any romantic achievements. I was quite taken aback and had to explain I had appointments.

'But, Hoyle, my fiancée would be so pleased if ye could coom along fer a wee drink. And och, she has a fine-looking sister.'

The thought of Clark matchmaking for me was too much.

'I'd love to, old chap, but I am really jammed.'

A few days later I met up with Bickerton, who had left the ITAE to enlist in the British Army at the end of 1914. I knew he had been wounded, but was not prepared for the sight of his disfigured face. A line of white pulpy skin ran like a geological fault line from his jaw to his temple. An anti-aerial gun had exploded in his hands. His thumbs hung down uselessly on both hands. He was a sadder version of his old self.

'I'm here, aren't I? Not quite "unbowed", but there's others a lot worse,' he said.

My good friend Azzi Webb returned on leave from the front at the end of November 1916. He had enlisted with the Australian 7th Field Engineers. We spent a number of days walking the London streets, and in the evenings went to the theatre. Azzi opened up about how ghastly things were at the front and just how frayed his nerves were. Only after spending time with Bick and Azzi did I realise what little consideration I had given to the horrendous war on the Continent and the personal sacrifices made by Bick, Azzi and Bob, and others like them who had felt compelled to enlist.

One of Azzi's officers had been with Bob Bage when he was killed at Gallipoli.

'It was the second week after the landing at Anzac Cove,' Azzi said, 'in a salient they called "the Pimple". The Australians had succeeded in forcing back the Turks. Bob was given an order to go out into no-man's-land and mark out a new trench with survey posts and string to straighten up the Australian line. The Turks were just a few hundred yards away. You can imagine Bob; he doesn't suggest it wait till after dark. He's under fire the whole time and just as he's finishing he cops a burst of machine gun fire that brings him down. He's then stuck in no man's land till a Turk sniper finishes him off. It's all so stupid, isn't it? I mean, he was a scientist—what's he doing marking up frontline trenches in Turkey, of all places?'

I pictured Bob in a soldier's uniform. He would have his pipe firmly clenched between his teeth. I could not picture him being shot by anyone. He was such a gentle soul.

'It *is* stupid . . . Bob of all people—it's just so unfair.' I remembered how I wouldn't have made it back to Commonwealth Bay without him. I had been completely snow blind, crawling across the ice, listening for his voice calling out what was in front of me.

Together we visited Bob Bage's mother and sister, who were also then in London. Bob had told them quite a lot about us both. Azzi was good and spoke about Bob and our trip back from the South Magnetic Pole. I felt very uncomfortable talking about it all with these two ladies over a cup of tea. Mrs Bage cried into her handkerchief the whole time until I felt I could not stand it any longer and we just had to leave.

In general, though, getting around London with Azzi cheered me up enormously. I discovered I liked musicals, especially big musicals with big orchestras, and music revues with comedy and variety. Azzi and I obtained excellent seats to see George Robey in *The Bing Boys Are Here*. As we emerged the whole audience seemed to be humming:

Sometimes when I feel low
And things look blue
I wish a girl I had . . . say one like you.
Someone within my heart to build a throne
Someone who'd never part, to call my own
If you were the only girl in the world
and I were the only boy.

Robey had the audience in the palm of his hand. He made them laugh and he made them cry. I wondered how he did that and I wondered why they liked it so much. Azzi said with the war on everyone wanted to laugh and cry. This soon became my favourite London show. I went back many times. London had any number of concerts and performances. There seemed to be an insatiable need for music revues and romantic comedies to help forget the war. There were also many shows I found vulgar, though this did not detract from their popularity with the masses.

On one of his London trips, Mawson promised to introduce Azzi and me to Lady Robert Scott. We met Mawson beforehand in Hyde Park.

'She's expecting you,' he said. 'I have told her about you both.'

Mawson set a cracking pace and Azzi and I hurried along on either side of him. It was a delight to be together again and to be, if only briefly, men of leisure and to walk unimpeded in normal clothes in the bracing but snowless winter. Thankfully, Mawson and Azzi were in their civvies and so I felt less conspicuous. It seemed nearly all the other men we passed were in khaki. They stared at us, wondering—or so it seemed to me—who these three tall colonials might be.

Just on dark we rounded a corner into Buckingham Palace Road and presently Mawson mounted the steps to an impressive-looking home and rang the bell before Azzi and I had time to scamper.

'Lady Scott will see you in her bedroom,' said the butler.

Azzi and I sheepishly followed Mawson up the staircase and along a hall lined with fine statuary and paintings, and were shown into a large well-lit room. Sure enough, sitting up with a tray of books and papers in the middle of a rather grand bed was a most attractive woman—beautiful, actually—in a white satin gown. Mawson kissed her hand and before I knew it she was warmly shaking mine.

'Sir Douglas has told me of your daring exploits with the camera. And Mr Webb, a true scientist and so loyal throughout.'

'Lady Scott saw your photographs in the *Daily Chronicle*, Frank,' added Mawson.

'We would all be the poorer without your pictures, Mr Hurley,' said Lady Scott. 'I had grave fears for your expedition after two years without news from Sir Ernest. How relieved I was when news came through that you were saved—and all alive. And now we have your photographs to show the world the hardships you endured.'

'I think the papers were pleased to have a break from the wretched war, ma'am,' I replied. 'My photographs were an all-too-brief distraction.'

Our hostess bade us sit down around her bed and asked Mawson to pour four glasses of whisky from a nearby cabinet.

Our conversation was very convivial and Lady Scott proved well informed on matters of polar exploration. She asked me quite directly, 'How do you compare Sir Ernest's venture to your expedition with Sir Douglas? Never mind that Douglas is listening, I am sure you have already had this discussion.'

In fact we had not. Mawson smiled sheepishly as I paused before answering,

'Strange as it may seem, the expeditions are not readily comparable,' I said. 'With Sir Douglas we had a base and did sledging and mapping. We brought back fossils and specimens. As you know, with Sir Ernest we were so soon trapped by ice we had no chance of achieving our goal.'

Lady Scott looked at me quite intently. 'You explorers are all the same; you are quite obsessed. Do you know, Mr Hurley, to achieve your goals can be quite disillusioning. And as I know only too well, it is not so much about reaching your goal as the returning. Sir Ernest did not reach his goal . . . but he returned and got you all home safe.'

'That he did, ma'am—though we are yet to hear from the Ross Sea party.'

'I'll tell you what gave me great comfort,' she continued, 'was that when Sir Robert knew he would not return he made sure that his diary would. He left a note that his diary was to be recovered. Without that, his death would have been a far greater tragedy. And you have your photographs. They are very special; they are better than words. I think you are all heroes, like Jason and his Argonauts—and what's more, like Jason you have returned to your loved ones.'

'My loved one has had to be very patient,' said Mawson. 'And now, with this war, who knows when we will be home?'

'There are too many, Douglas, who do not return home from this war, and those that do have nothing good to say about it. I'm afraid your achievements in Antarctica have been overshadowed.'

Mawson replied drily, 'Yes, sadly war bonds are more important these days than raising money to pay the expenses of old explorers.'

Lady Scott returned her attention to Azzi and me. 'And are you both like Sir Douglas, happily married but separated by vast oceans? Who do you write your letters home to?'

'I'm afraid the only Mrs Hurley is my mother, and she says I am a poor correspondent,' I confessed.

Mawson chipped in, 'Frank's mother loves him so dearly she wrote to me after I first offered him the AAE job. She told me he had consumption, was unsuited for the life of an Antarctic explorer, and should be discharged. Well, that cost us a bit in medical tests!'

This caused much hilarity.

'You do not look one bit like you are dying of consumption, Mr Hurley.' Lady Scott stared at me and I ducked my head shyly as she went on, 'If you stay away from France, you can marry and live to a ripe old age. Forget about being an explorer. The poles have been trampled on by men; the age of heroic discovery, I am afraid, is gone. Instead you men are now obsessed with killing one another.'

Mawson responded, 'But you ignore the increasing discoveries in science.'

'Radioactivity? I have been reading about it; a cure for consumption would be more useful. And as for the benefits of scientific discovery, Sir Douglas, I know you are only doing your duty, but I cannot approve your current occupation. Supplying poison gas to the Russians, of all people, makes us British no better than the Germans.'

As we left, Lady Scott counselled Azzi and I to find sensible wives, not as opinionated as her. 'And if you must go on long expeditions, remember to plan your return carefully lest you make her a widow. Though 'tis not so bad; I was a widow for a year before I knew it.'

The weather grew colder and more dismal. It was dark by mid-afternoon. In the evenings a combination of the famous pea soup fog and wartime blackouts meant I frequently lost my way walking the London streets. Several times, bombs dropped by zeppelin airships fell close to my hotel. Waking and half waking from my sleep on these occasions, I often found myself in a place which could only be Elephant Island. I am lying in foul oily liquid and try as I might I can't get up. I am held down by a weight which I cannot lift. Somehow I know that my companions have all left and I am stuck in this place alone. When I wake, I am clammy with sweat.

Most days I spent at the *Chronicle*, working on the glass plate negatives and cinefilm, and afterwards I dined alone or with friends who were passing through London.

Perris and I had a tense week arguing over the terms of my agreement to return to South Georgia, which ended in him accusing me of being greedy. This was a bit rich coming from him. He and Shackleton had still not paid my wages from the *Endurance* expedition. Still, I could not help but admire him as a businessman.

A week or so before Christmas I was woken after midnight by a persistent tapping on my door. I opened it, and in walked Leslie Blake, one of my first friends from the AAE and who had been in the Macquarie Island party. Azzi had given him my address and I was pleased to see him—at first. Blake seemed to misapprehend my bachelor status and assumed I had the same proclivities as himself; namely, to importune any attractive young woman who passed by. We soon argued and I told him his behaviour was immoral. He stared at me disbelievingly.

'Immoral! Hoyle, have you any idea what things are like? Do you know what I do at the front? I am a captain of a battery of howitzers. I have killed more men than I will ever know. My own men have died in my arms. But I'm still a bloody virgin! I have hardly kissed a girl. I am not going back to the front without having a go!'

Even allowing for the time he had been at the front and the shortness of his leave, Les Blake's conduct left a lot to be desired. He drank heavily. I told him I didn't drink and was engaged, but he was incorrigible. On our first evening at the theatre, to avoid becoming his partner in crime I was forced to dash out saying I had another appointment. Next day he called me a 'bloody wowser'.

•

Christmas Eve. Blake, thank God, has gone back to the front. My head is crowded with memories of Christmases past, but my hotel room is empty of both company and conversation. I have spent the last five Christmas Eves on the ice or at sea, but I had my fellow travellers as companions. Now I am here in the middle of this congested city, in the heart of so-called civilisation, and I am alone. And I am coming down with a bout of influenza. Ma and Elsa are on the other side of the world and I wish I could be with them. The crowds outside the hotel have disappeared indoors to their private celebrations. I think with envy of those soldiers on leave who have girls under their arms.

Christmas Day is worse. The theatres are all closed, and the shops too. London is grey and damp. I pride myself on my stoicism, but I cannot stop a few tears in the quiet of my hotel room as the voice of George Robey warbles in my head:

I wish a girl I had . . . say one like you . . .
If you were the only girl in the world
and I were the only boy.

It is a relief when Christmas festivities are finished and life returns to normal—well, normal for London in wartime that is. Thick fog means the German army could be on the other side of the street and you wouldn't know. And inside the restaurants and even my hotel lobby there is a stench of cigarette smoke. On the crowded tube and in the theatre there is constant coughing. And everywhere I look there are ladies of the night, outside all the theatres and clubs. There is deplorable immorality among a certain class of women in London, and it is the Australians and colonials that swarm like bees to the honeypot. Just outside my hotel there is an attractive young woman who stands alongside the same column every night and who now nods to me and says, 'Evening, guv'nor.' Blake assumed I knew her and asked to be introduced. So numerous are the prostitutes, it is safest not to let my eyes wander and to keep to myself and certainly not risk starting a conversation with a stranger.

This London winter has already gone on too long for me. Better to be living under an upturned boat. I am terrified by the London cab drivers, whose madcap antics on icy roads are a greater threat than the German zeppelins. I go for longer and longer walks; Hyde Park, Regent's Park, St James's Park. I am saddened by the disrepair of these once-proud gardens. Overgrown hedges, unkempt lawns and weeds tell me the gardeners have all gone to France; the iron railings and gates have all gone to cannons.

Even my hotel and the London theatres lose their lustre. I am driven mad by the habitual tipping that is expected and obsequious fawning behaviour it induces in waiters, waitresses, barmen, barmaids, lift attendants, doormen, porters, chambermaids, cloakroom staff, bathroom attendants, cab drivers, newspaper boys, ushers and so on and so on. It is utterly contemptible they are not paid a decent wage. The only reliable wages are in the army. And that is to say nothing of the divide between the upper and lower classes which the British education system churns out. The trenches are the great leveller.

•

The date of my departure for South Georgia was to be mid-February. By this time the U-boat situation had worsened considerably. Perris, however, remained optimistic the German blockade of British ports would fail and that Germany's sinking of neutral ships would bring America into the war.

'I tell you, Hurley, that is the only way this war can be won. The *Chronicle* has just reported that the US has severed diplomatic relations. A declaration of war can only be days away. And it can't come too soon; in two days last week U-boats sank twenty-seven ships.'

'What should I do about my trip to South Georgia?'

'What do you mean what should you do? Have you made your will?'

'No. Should I?'

'Irresponsible not to, in these times. But I shouldn't worry too much; the ship we've booked you on will have a special anti-U-boat gun fitted.'

'Well, that will be handy for the daytime.'

'Oh, I've had a cable from Shackleton. They've rescued the Ross Sea party, but they weren't in good shape. Three dead, I'm afraid.'

It was a few more days before there were any details. It sounded a total disaster. They established food depots for our trans-Antarctic party, which never even set foot on the Antarctic coast. They suffered starvation and quite likely scurvy, and all the time the poor bastards were just waiting and waiting for Shackleton.

In February 1917 I travelled to Glasgow, where I boarded *Pentaur*, a filthy old oil and coal transport. I was her only passenger, and to make my journey legal I signed on as a purser at one shilling sixpence a month. I had my two Pomeranian puppies for company—I named them Blizzard and Blubber—along with fifteen hundredweight of photographic equipment. Our departure was held up by the mounting of a twelve-pound gun to the stern. Having previously had no interest in being an active participant in the conflict that gripped the world, I found myself suddenly quite excited by this small artillery piece. I insisted that, as I was part of the crew, I be trained in its operation. I was champing at the bit to see a U-boat in the same way one might hope to see a blue whale. I would have loved to have written Azzi to tell him I too had fired a shot in anger. After the dull monotony of London I was thrilled by the prospect of running the gauntlet of the U-boat blockade; I did not pause to consider the mismatch between the ancient *Pentaur* and a modern well-armed submarine.

On our first day out of port I volunteered to act as sight layer and had the dubious satisfaction of firing practice on a floating target at five hundred yards and then at one thousand yards and fifteen hundred yards before the target disappeared, untouched, in the swells. We then spent nervous days and nights peering at every whitecap as we hugged the Irish Coast before heading out into the Atlantic.

After a week I lost patience watching for submarines. As the tension on board eased and my own excitement abated, I retreated to *Pentaur*'s saloon, where there was nothing for me to do but read and await the next mealtime with the captain and steward and whatever argument they were having that day. Apart from Blizzard and Blubber, I was wretchedly lonely for the six-week voyage. Tragically, Blizzard, who was constantly escaping outside, failed to return one day and a short time later Blubber pegged out after coming down with distemper. That was the sad end of Perris's special effects.

We reached South Georgia at the end of March, very late in the season to start filming. I found myself back in Grytviken and all those memories returned from the early days of the Shackleton expedition. This time, however, I was my own boss. I was free of the petty rivalries and boorish behaviour of an overcrowded party. A small coastal launch, aptly named *Matilda*, was made available for my peregrinations to the penguin and seal colonies. *Pentaur*'s second mate volunteered to accompany me and help lug the cameras, cinematograph and tripod up hill and down dale as I searched out the best shots.

For four weeks we tramped the foreshore, camped overnight on shingle beaches, walked the valleys, traversed glaciers and climbed small peaks. The weather was wild, constantly changing, and at times threatened to blow us and our small tent out to sea. But in between storms I captured a thousand feet of cinefilm and hundreds of photographs, including Paget colour plates of penguin and seal rookeries and spectacular scenery. I was in my element. This was the life I loved most of all. I captured plenty of penguins for Perris.

•

By late June I was back at the *Chronicle*'s offices in London, thoroughly refreshed. As Perris had predicted, America had declared war on Germany and was sending troops.

I handed over the film. 'Here are your penguins,' I said. 'I can start putting it all together.'

'That's marvellous, but I think the penguins are going to have to wait now for this damn war to finish. I'm afraid the only explorers the public will pay money to see are dead explorers, and Mr Ponting already has that film.'

Perris had that way of taking the wind out of my sails. Nevertheless, I had my work cut out for me in the darkroom and editing the cinefilm.

And then the war came to me by way of a letter shoved under the door of my room at the Imperial Hotel. In July 1917, some two and a half years after hostilities commenced, I was invited to make an appointment at the London headquarters of General Sir William Birdwood, whom even I knew to be the commander-in-chief of the Australian Infantry Forces in the British Army. The AIF wanted to appoint an official photographer and Mawson had put my name forward. 'Insist on some rank,' he advised. 'A lieutenant at least.'

To me, the war was an inexplicable madness that I hoped would pass. I had never considered joining up. But not so many receive an invitation from the commander-in-chief—and I knew no one else willing to pay for my services while the war dragged on.

Sir William Birdwood was remarkably charming and intrigued by my Antarctic expeditions. By the time I left our meeting, I had agreed to depart for France and report to Captain Charles Bean, Australia's official war correspondent. Charles Bean's reporting on the Australian soldiers had made him a household name. He went ashore with the Anzac troops on the first day of the Gallipoli Campaign and witnessed their heroic deeds there and later in France at

Pozières, Bullecourt and Messines. He, more than anyone, was responsible for their reputation for courage and daring.

What I was cock-a-hoop about, however, was that despite my never having served in the Army Reserve, Sir William Birdwood agreed I was to have an immediate honorary commission of captain, and would earn a captain's pay.

Part IV

13

Menin Road, September 1917

I bought all the London papers and began reading voraciously of the war I was about to experience first-hand. I examined the grainy black and white images reproduced on the front pages. There were photographs of soldiers, but I saw no photographs of a 'war'.

The fighting had been going on since before I joined *Endurance* and throughout the whole time we had been stranded and drifting unawares in the icepack. On arrival in Punta Arenas we had been dumbfounded at the stories of zeppelins and aeroplanes dropping bombs on cities, U-boats sinking passenger ships, machine guns, poison gas and liquid flamethrowers. And we thought *our* lives had been in peril! Before our departure I had no idea that such things could happen, but on our return the unspeakable had become the commonplace. I struggled to grasp what had changed in our absence. While in Chile I had shaken hands with both expatriate British and expatriate German businessmen. The whole thing seemed a madness that would surely pass by the time I reached England, if only because of the deadly nature of the conflict. But now the word on the street in London was it would drag on through yet another winter, although for all the casualty lists there seemed little movement in the newspaper maps of opposing armies.

The Chileans had revelled in their role in Shackleton's rescue of his crew, but after we departed Chile we received little in the way of fanfare for what we had endured. World events made our failed voyage insignificant to the public imagination. The conflagration in Europe made trivial that we had survived when so many had given up their lives. Not being soldiers, we couldn't be heroes. Shackleton, however, *was* seen as heroic for having rescued his own disastrous expedition. I realised the truth of Lady Scott's words: that the time of great polar explorers like Mawson and Shackleton belonged to another age. Scott was talked about only for having died a noble death.

Most of my *Endurance* colleagues enlisted as soon as they reached home, despite being scientists by trade and having no experience fighting wars. They enlisted as if it was the most natural and normal thing compared to the merely idle madness they had engaged in with Shackleton. The younger members felt guilty they had cheated death when siblings and friends made what they called 'the supreme sacrifice' for their country.

And now it was my turn to depart for Europe wearing the uniform of a soldier—though of course I was a non-combatant. From Charing Cross Station in London, the military train was full of officers. I had never seen such a concentration of the best of British in uniform. My captain's uniform seemed drab compared to the bright red tabbed collars of the general staff officers. I was seated in a compartment with two colonels who pointed out various majors and a general. I felt an imposter just as I had when joining the Mawson expedition, that I did not belong, that I was no more a soldier than a scientist. I dared not look up for fear of missing a salute.

At Folkestone I boarded *Princess Victoria*. She was full to the brim with subdued soldiers returning from leave. Somehow I found George Wilkins, who had been appointed my assistant photographer. He was from South Australia, a little younger than me, and had a bright impish grin. Wilkins was my soulmate if ever I had one. While I had been drifting in the Antarctic, he had been wandering in the Arctic with the Stefansson expedition, and before that he had been a photographer in the 1912 Balkan War. He did not have my photographic experience, but I had to admit he was more modest and he knew how to fly an aeroplane.

As our boat came into Boulogne, I was taken aback by the picturesque beach, colourful parasols and large numbers of men, women and children bathing in public. The pale sand and translucent green water brought back memories of hot February days on the other side of the world. But in my last Australian summer I had witnessed nothing like this scene of gay abandonment. I pressed against the railing and was transfixed by the sight of a young man and woman holding hands on the edge of the deep, near naked it seemed to me as they plunged into the water. I watched their brown shoulders bobbing above the gentle motion of the sea. They laughed at the attention they attracted from the mass of khaki alongside me. The couple embraced and turned away so that *Princess Victoria*, her decks crowded with British soldiery, could not spoil their pleasure. It all seemed so incongruous, knowing the deadly purpose of those around me. Surely there could not be a murderous war within a day's journey from this scene.

On shore, George and I were busily gathering our equipment when I heard someone say, 'Captain Hurley, Lieutenant Wilkins.'

I turned to find a tall thin officer with bright carrot-coloured hair, a pointy nose and spectacles.

'I'm Captain Bean, welcome to France.'

Bean looked older than I'd expected. But for his uniform and slouch hat, he looked like a professor, very fair-skinned and frail-looking—though he grabbed his share of luggage.

Bean had two cars with drivers, one of which we filled with equipment. From the other, George and I had our first look at the French countryside as we exchanged stories with Bean. This was my first time on the Continent. I may have been an experienced traveller in the remote uninhabited world, but here in this ancient cultivated land I was a complete novice. The road was lined with poplars and ran through small fertile fields. The villages were attractive with old solid stone cottages and churches. The inhabitants were industrious, though elderly. In the fields, labourers wielded ancient sickles into the late evening to reap the harvest. Golden sheaves of wheat were bundled, tied and raised into a series of great conical ricks scattered across freshly cut fields of stubble.

It was several hours drive to army headquarters at Hazebrouck, and darkness fell before we had reached Saint-Omer. Being close to the front we drove without headlights. We rounded one corner at some speed, and there in front of us on the road was a flock of sheep. There was a frightful noise and some ominous thumps. The driver pulled up, and by torchlight we found all but two of the flock had disappeared. Our vehicle had inflicted a mortal blow on one and the other had blood coming from its forehead and was bleating hideously. A herdswoman arrived and commenced an even louder wailing, at the same time running back and forth between the two beasts. It was a piteous scene as we lifted both sheep clear of the road and laid them in the field. Bean apologised to the herdswoman in his best schoolboy French and handed her a roll of notes, but this did not appease her. He went back to the car and returned with additional notes, which she shoved in her dress while still maintaining her lament. Bean searched his pockets for coins and proffered these, but in her agitation they were scattered in the dark across the road. Unable to do more, we left her there alone in the night and continued our journey.

Nearing Hazebrouck the western sky was lit up as if by an electrical storm. As we drove into that storm and I heard the dull thunder, it was then I knew for the first time what it was to hear the sound of a thousand heavy artillery guns. From the pit of my stomach an uneasiness grew, until all my senses were on edge. We drove on into the night as the flashes of light were followed more closely by the increasing roar. Wilkins and I fell silent.

After midnight we came across an encampment. Sentries emerged from the dark as we pulled up. Bean showed us to some stretchers under a large canvas awning, and we tried to fall asleep to the sound of the now-intermittent artillery barrage. This eerie night-time arrival marked the end of my naive ignorance as to the gobsmacking callousness of the combatants. I woke to a vivid nightmare from which there was no escape.

I was up before first light, taking in the different sights, sounds and smells. There was a distant crackle of rifle and machine-gun fire, and the intermittent thump of something bigger. Closer at hand in the dark was the sound of coughing from nearby stretchers.

Bean joined us early with three steaming mugs of tea. 'We're off to Hill 60 this morning,' he said in a jolly voice. 'It's a good place for your first look at the frontlines.'

'Will we be based there?' asked Wilkins.

'Good heavens, no. I have organised one of the cylindrical Nissen huts for you at Steenvorde, about ten miles from the front, just inside Belgium. It will have a darkroom and all you need. And I've organised a car and driver so while it's quiet you can get around the different Australian brigade headquarters.'

'Was last night quiet?' I asked tentatively.

'Oh, our artillery has been building up. Noisy, aren't they? But believe me, it is far better to be giving than receiving. It's a sign there'll be action soon to break this deadlock.'

We set out in the car, Bean in front with the driver, and almost immediately joined a procession of military vehicles; troops crammed in motor lorries and open trucks, horse-drawn wagons laden with artillery guns and shells, ambulances and truckloads of supplies needed to keep a modern army in the field. Bean leaned over the back of the front passenger seat and continued his briefing.

'The Australian soldier has already made a name for himself in this war, but our photographic record is non-existent. Your job is to create that record. You are going to see trench parapets and German pillboxes, scenes of heroic struggles that have taken a toll in lives. Those scenes and the units that fought there need to be recorded with your cameras and preserved for future generations.

It was hard to suppress our excitement. Bean's impressive knowledge gave my confidence a considerable boost. He knew almost every officer we met and all of the generals.

'And of course,' he added, 'of more interest to Prime Minister Hughes is propaganda, anything to keep up enlistment, front-page stuff for newspapers. Hurley, I'll leave the propaganda photographs to you. And one other thing to keep in mind is that Australia House in London will hold a photographic exhibition of the Anzacs early next year. Your work will be on display.'

I could hardly believe this. Despite all my work on the Shackleton pictures, my first international exhibition would be photographs I had not yet taken of the AIF in France.

Away from the military traffic on the road, rural life continued unabated. The stone villages and farmhouses were, I imagined, unchanged in the hundred years since Napoleon. Then our car entered the town of Voormezeele. Not even Napoleon could have matched the carnage wrought upon this place. No building was undamaged. That which could catch fire had been burned, and that which would not burn had been toppled. No habitation remained. Homes, churches and public buildings were but crumpled masonry and stones. There were no roofs or windows. The road through had been cleared of rubble and the inhabitants had fled.

From Voormezeele, the Bosche had been forced back some three miles over the last three years. In this corridor, civilisation as I knew it had been banished. Grassy meadows, ploughed fields, gardens, shrubs and trees ceased. Constant shelling from both armies had remoulded the landscape to a more desolate wilderness than I had ever seen. The road remained as an essential artery to maintain the beast. It was a pathway between the wreckage, broken vehicles, carts and other detritus of war.

We turned off the road, having driven as far as we safely could, and continued on foot.

'Sling these gas masks over your heads,' said Bean, demonstrating. 'Like so. And keep your shrapnel helmet on at all times. I stirred up so much trouble to get you fellows appointed, I'm not about to lose one of you through carelessness.'

We had soon walked to where Bean informed us we were now in front of the Australian artillery. The Australian howitzer batteries sent shell after shell screaming over our heads some three thousand yards to the German lines. There was an ear-splitting din such that I could not suppress an involuntary crouching as I walked.

We arrived at an unimposing mound and Bean informed us that this was the remnant of Hill 60, which had been blown up in June by underground mines. The trenches here were waterlogged and I gave up trying to keep my boots dry. Around the clock, soldiers operated water pumps—not unlike the bilge pumps on *Endurance*—to relieve the flooding of the underground tunnel systems.

We had been following a connecting trench for some distance when suddenly Bean disappeared from before my eyes. Seconds later he bobbed out from behind a hessian door and called Wilkins and me to come in. All was blackness inside, until I made out a trail of candles leading down a damp tunnel. There was a series of stairs and ladders by which we descended some two hundred feet. We turned a corner and found ourselves in a damp candlelit room being introduced by Bean to the Australian colonel in charge of this section of the line. I had the presence of mind to salute.

Soon we were sipping tea from white china cups as the colonel explained the intricacies of the Australian artillery battery operations and the thousands of yards of telephone wires which communicated directions and distances of enemy targets. Our artillery gunners aimed their deadly missiles, but could not see the death and destruction caused. I found myself distracted by the framed family portraits and homely furnishings of the colonel's subterranean office, and the convulsive shudder of candle flames each time the Australian guns rumbled above our heads. As we made our way back through the clay catacomb tunnels there was something horribly familiar, and it was some time before I realised it was the smell in my nostrils of lamps burning whale oil.

'Hoyle? What the devil are you doing here?' The uniformed figure emerging from the gloom was Blake, Leslie Blake from *Aurora*. We grabbed each other, quite stunned by our chance meeting in such a place. Bean and Wilkins were surprised to hear that Blake had been a geologist with Mawson's expedition.

Bean shook hands with Les. 'Well done, Captain Blake, on your Military Cross,' he said.

'What's this about?' I said in surprise. 'Have you been taking risks?'

'Surveying work.'

'Marking out the front line,' added Bean. 'And I heard you were wounded.'

'Only in the buttocks. I was so busy keeping my head down I forgot about my arse.'

Blake brushed off further questions, and instead offered to show us his digs and give us a tour of Hill 60.

Blake was fluent with the numerous tunnels and caverns. He directed us to a trench which, by a series of cramped steps and ladders, led to a small observation post at the crest of Hill 60. This was my first view of no-man's-land. It was a land the like of which I had never seen before and could never have imagined. No matter how many eyewitness accounts I had heard, no matter how many grainy photographs I had seen in the newspapers, I was unprepared for what lay before me. To the east for about two thousand yards was a wasteland bordered by long zigzagging lines of German frontline trenches, and reserve trenches further back. I could see into our own trenches and the hessian-covered squalor in which our infantry lived. This desolate corridor extended both north and south as far as the eye could see.

Nothing lived in no-man's-land. Colour plates would be wasted on its grey and grimy pockmarked churn of earth and debris of war. There was no living vegetation. Trees were but shorn stumps. Barbed wire coiled wickedly in thickets tangled and clumped by constant shelling. Misshapen slabs of concrete marked collapsed German fortifications. Everywhere was broken or abandoned equipment; remnants of wagons, ammunition boxes, gun mounts, artillery shells, rifles, bayonets, helmets, fragments of uniforms and of men.

Directly in front of where I stood, an enormous crater had been gouged out by one of the explosions set off by Australian tunnellers. Lying way down in this pit were the decomposed remains of three German soldiers. Exposed to the elements and in full view, there could be no concern for these corpses, their identity or burial. It was, I gathered, an unremarkable scene even for a photographer.

Framing this scene, a mile behind each of the lines of trenches, were barrage balloons, from which tiny occupants suspended in baskets were observing what life there was and directing artillery fire here and there.

My gaze took it in, horror upon horror. The countryside had been churned and raked into a landscape unrecognisable to its former rural inhabitants, and even more desolate than the icefields that had swallowed *Endurance*. There was little prospect for explorers who dared venture into no-man's-land. Just as on the Antarctic plateau, it was easier to die here than to live. Better to be adrift on an iceberg in the Antarctic. To have survived only to return to this! And to think of my erstwhile companions on *Aurora* and *Endurance* who had already been killed and maimed by this uncivilised conflict.

By the time we tramped back to the car at Voormezeele then drove on to headquarters at Hazebrouck, it was almost midnight and we were exhausted. George did not say too much on the way back. I gathered he had seen terrible things in the Balkan War, though surely not on this scale of devastation. Despite my tiredness, I was unable to sleep. I realised I had little knowledge of the background to this conflict, partly because of my absence from 'civilisation', but more because I had never taken an interest in politics. Frankly, for the job I had taken on, it mattered not. I was expected to be a seasoned professional. Opinions and emotions played little part.

I started to think about what photographs could be taken. What I had just seen was grim and featureless, but was the very heart of the beast. I could more easily photograph scenes away from the front, scenes of soldiers parading and training, but for what purpose? They might satisfy an army censor but would not satisfy me. And in the back of my mind I remained confused as to what I should think about the wanton killing of men. Could this killing, this war, be photographed? There was undoubtedly a moment of time between parading soldiers and bloated corpses that was called action. How close I could get to that action I had no idea.

As to the horror around me, I had no darkroom to retreat to, and instead reverted to my diary to set out what I had seen:

> *Until my dying day I shall never forget this haunting glimpse down into the mine crater on Hill 60, and this is but one tragedy of similar thousands and we who are civilized have still to continue this hellish murder against the wreckers of humanity and Christianity.*

Blake had told me the Australian 7th Field Engineers were at Renescue, so a few days later George and I called in there and I asked after Captain Eric Webb. Shortly Azzi emerged, wondering who the hell was the army captain wanting to see him. He could hardly believe his eyes when he saw who it was. We embraced, and slapped each other on the back marvelling at the strangeness of our circumstances and me being in uniform. Azzi looked aged, even more than when I had seen him in London. His face was gaunt with bags under his eyes. But it was terrific to be reunited.

That evening, Wilkins and I dined with Azzi in his mess in a well-concealed dugout. He introduced me to his fellow officers as if I were a celebrity, and against a background of the *crump*, *crump* of artillery fire, we told stories from the frozen world.

Before the end of my first week, Bean collected me in his car to photograph a visit from Sir Douglas Haig, the British commander-in-chief. Haig was to review his Australian soldiers, which Bean said was an honour the Australian infantrymen would long remember. I hoped he was right about the latter.

The entire Second Division was assembled in one location for Haig's convenience, and as a precursor to marching to Ypres to take part in Haig's latest plan to achieve a breakthrough. It was a unique event and Bean asked if I could devise a way of taking a single photograph of one whole battalion.

The division was bivouacked outside Renescue in a series of wheatfields over some fifty acres of flat farmland. Harvesting of wheat in these fields had just finished and the men now stood in rows where the golden wheat had stood. These men were in their prime: tall, well fed and rested, having just completed furlough during the European summer. From the feathers of their slouch hats to the puttees strapped above their boots, they were proud soldiers, trained to make an impact, ready and willing to test themselves. There would be casualties, but there were no conscripts here; these were volunteers who had travelled around the world to fight for king and country. They were responding to the call I had ignored when I sailed off to join Shackleton. This was their great adventure away from the humdrum of the cities, the quiet country towns, small coastal dairies, rolling wheatfields and dusty sheep stations. A soldier's life was their great escape from the expectations of being breadwinners toiling away in factories, shops, offices and farms.

I devised a bosun's chair just as I had on *Endurance*, and was soon hoisted with my equipment some sixty feet, courtesy of an ancient yew tree and a dozen infantrymen. In the front rows were the young lieutenants and captains, whom I was told were most certain of being among the casualties. Their buckles and buttons shone a little brighter than those of the khaki masses behind them. Despite my elevation, I could not capture all that humanity in my viewfinder. Not being in a position to ask over ten thousand men to walk back one hundred steps, I did the best I could in hazy conditions. It was an imposing sight to see these Australians assembled in their battalions, a multitude of youthful upturned faces squinting into the morning light, too many to identify individual faces in the image I would create. As I held open the shutter, I could not help but wonder how many of this proud formation would return from Ypres.

•

Our build-up to a major offensive is plain to all, including the Bosche. In the meantime, horrific slaughter and devastation is wrought by the artillery of both sides. My senses have been pounded day and night with the thundering roar of our heavy guns sending their shells screaming overhead to the German lines. I am both fascinated and horrified by this constant shelling. The howitzer guns rest on haunches of steel, their barrels pointing to the sky. These huge gargoyle-like beasts with up to fifteen-inch-calibre guns send projectiles of metal and high explosives weighing some fourteen hundred pounds thousands of yards through the air to the enemy lines. These beasts have an insatiable appetite. The arteries of the frontline are clogged with carts and trucks bringing forwards stockpiles of artillery shells.

The Germans return fire with deadly accuracy. The only saving grace is that, due to our build-up of troops and munitions, the Germans have so many targets I have come to accept not every shell is aimed at me. Still, when I hear the familiar whistle of German howitzer shells coming my way, I instinctively duck and sometimes drop to the ground. I have learned the hot spots. The men I speak to who are required to work throughout the barrages in these areas have a fatalism about them and accept that death is a simple matter of chance.

•

Not long after setting up our quarters on the edge of Steenvorde, the village was subjected to an aerial attack. I woke in the dark to the sound of exploding bombs from German Gotha bombers. In the morning, smoke was rising from the ruins of old stone houses and the traffic on the roads was in chaos. Bean arrived to view our digs and escort Wilkins and me to the old city of Ypres.

'You may as well see what we have been fighting to defend these last two years,' he said as we bundled ourselves into the car.

As we approached Ypres from the west, the pleasant road-side fields became increasingly filled with the necessities of war; army camps and stores, munition dumps, field hospitals, ambulances, truck depots and all manner of wrecked vehicles.

One mile before Ypres, we entered a broad tree-lined avenue. Driving closer to the town, green foliage gave way to misshapen pockmarked trunks and bare branches. On the city outskirts all tree branches had been severed by artillery fire and only scarred stumps remained.

Bean explained, 'The first battle of Ypres was where the German advance was finally stopped in 1914. The Germans tried again to take Ypres in April 1915. I was in Gallipoli then. They couldn't capture the city, but they pretty well encircled it, close enough to shell it to smithereens. Haig now wants to push the Germans back. You fellows have arrived just in time.'

•

A traffic sentry pulls us up before Ypres and we have to proceed on foot. He checks our passes and admonishes me, 'Tin hat on, sir, and gas mask in the "at ready" position.' Our artillery batteries near Ypres maintain a constant bombardment on the German lines and the Bosche return shot for shot, aiming for our batteries and supply dumps. Every so often they send another shell into the Ypres ruins. Masonry, stones and brick dust fly into the air. The Bosche have the exact bearings of the main roads and intersections around Ypres and can at any time land a shell where they choose. Sometimes their shells land on an empty stretch of road, sometimes among a team of horses and equipment, and sometimes amid a group of men. Artillery is impersonal. Those firing the guns do not see what they destroy. But a couple of miles away their observers in barrage balloons press binoculars to their eyes and peer through the smoke and mist.

The main roads through the city have been cleared of rubble and we are able to stroll between what were once fine buildings but are now mere remnants of their former selves.

Roofs and top storeys have been blown away. Windows are shattered and stone walls contain huge gaping breaches. Building frontages are now just piles of masonry, and private rooms and apartments are exposed to the elements, wallpaper and furnishings telling something of the former inhabitants, who either fled or lie beneath the wreckage. Brass bedsteads are twisted into skeletal shapes, kitchen stoves are riddled with shrapnel, books, pictures and toys are no longer cherished but scattered and abandoned. We clamber carefully around beams poised precariously on walls almost completely shot away. In relatively sheltered alleyways we come across Royal Artillerymen merrily cooking rations and living out of cellars that have so far survived the onslaught.

'And this,' says Bean as we round a corner, 'is what remains of the Cloth Hall.'

I am struck by the sight of what was obviously at one time a most impressive building and is now an even more impressive ruin.

Bean sees my interest. 'I can tell you it was built in the thirteenth century, when Ypres was the centre of the textile trade, but was destroyed within a few weeks in 1914.'

It has the appearance of a huge cathedral, well over three-hundred-foot long, and even now the battered remnants of its imposing tower stand some hundred feet. The main building has several floors, all of which have caved in, along with the roof. The entire archway façade had been intricately carved with historic figures now headless and pockmarked from shrapnel. Columns and archways lie like fallen giants.

With Bean's agreement, Wilkins and I return the following day, determined to photograph the tragic destruction of this ancient walled city. I have never seen anything like this, a whole metropolis destroyed. I am, I suspect, more taken by the macabre appearance of the Ypres ruins than I would be were the city intact.

We stumble through rubble and adventurously climb the five-storey walls of the old post office. The huge oak beams which made up its ceiling are now just matchwood. The walls visibly shake with concussion from the nearby twelve-inch artillery gun batteries. We look to the east of the city, where a historic gateway once led across a moat onto the road to Menin. The breach in this ancient wall now leads to the frontline trenches. The Second Division of the AIF, which I photographed at Renescue, will shortly pass through here. Just past the city walls I can see the intersection on Menin Road known as Hellfire Corner, one of the most dangerous places on earth. The road has hessian curtains erected to spoil the German artillery observers' view of the constant traffic. As I watch I see our supply wagons gallop gamely through Hellfire Corner, dodging shell bursts at breakneck speed. It is a game of chance.

I feel strangely guilty at my enthralment with everything I see. It is all new. Away from the front, the countryside is the stuff of picture books. Autumn has now arrived, leaves have turned red and are about to fall. But I am fascinated by the advanced mechanisation of the war effort, especially the power and numbers of howitzer and artillery batteries, the sheer volume of shells fired and their devastating effect on the combatants and the landscape. I can't believe the mix of aircraft, from large German Gotha bombers to the small biplane scouts and fighters which regularly perform aerial gymnastics for the benefit of incredulous trench dwellers. I am determined to have my chance in the air as soon as I can visit an Australian squadron. And, though I keep it to myself, I remain unable to understand the folly of those who want to be involved in this murderous conflict, for that is what it seems to me: sheer wanton murder.

Our curved iron Nissen hut at Steenvorde proves quite comfortable, despite the chill in the air. In addition to Wilkins and our driver, there are two other staff who help with the carrying, developing, printing of photograph titles and chores like the cooking. I have christened the hut 'the Billabong', as a reminder of the *Endurance* expedition. In fact, the round sides of the Nissen hut reminds me of an upturned boat, not unlike the Snuggery. Unlike *Endurance* days, though, I am the only one who sleeps inside. The others have an army tent just outside. After my *Endurance* experience I value privacy perhaps too much. But the arrangement works well, notwithstanding the early start of winter rain. Our cameras, plates and film are out of the weather and there is a spacious darkroom.

•

Just before 5 a.m. on 20 September, Wilkins and I were approaching Hellfire Pass on the Menin Road. In pre-dawn drizzle we were carrying our full kit of equipment, cine and tripod and other cameras. Menin Road was for the briefest of intervals unusually quiet as the monster drew breath.

Lining both sides of the road, at times head-high, was a dark twisted mass of machines, wagons, equipment, malodorous bodies of dead mules and horses, busted guns and munitions of all sorts.

Bean had given us the heads-up a stunt was on, and so we had spent the night at the Red Cross dressing station in the ruins of Ypres, and had been glad to leave. We had been unable to sleep due to the constant roar of our own gun batteries. The dressing station had been emptied of its wounded and was in full readiness, with orderlies nervously fussing like hosts not knowing how many guests are coming.

We knew the clock had struck five as, with a flash of light and a deafening roar for several miles in both directions, the whole of the British batteries opened up. The ground beneath our feet shuddered. Any attempt at conversation ceased. The gun crews were working nonstop on unseen targets, shells whizzed over our heads and the individual roar of each battery was lost to a cacophonous wall of noise that swelled and resonated in my head.

With heavy loads we plodded on as our sense of hearing was overwhelmed by the constancy of the din. There was no backing away now, no saying stop to the guns. With our cameras at the ready we were part of whatever was about to happen, and in any event nothing could be heard even if we were to give voice to our apprehension. My mind wandered back to those days in the bush at home when prehistoric cicadas in their thousands simultaneously emerged from years of cold silence under the earth to torment all living creatures with their relentless fever-pitch drumming. Their shrill sound was impossible to escape as they beat their bodies senseless.

Shortly, we reached the mine crater at Hooge. Bean appeared and led us down into brigade headquarters, where we descended some thirty feet, through passageways of running water and caverns leaking from the overnight rain. He introduced us to General Bennett, who was in charge of operations on this sector. Wilkins and I were glad for some respite from the crescendo above ground.

Then, without warning, the guns stopped. The general looked up and all in the room fell silent. This was zero hour. Above us, line upon line of soldiers from the Second ANZAC Division that I had photographed at Renescue would already be out of their trenches, through the barbed wire and now running at the German positions. The phone stayed silent. I went back to the entrance, but it was still dark and there was nothing to see and nothing I could photograph. But I heard the *tacca-tacca-tacca* of Bosche machine guns; they would have plenty of targets.

Within ten minutes our artillery started up again. The barrage had been lifted forwards to the next line of Bosche defences.

Presently a message came down the wire that the first line of German trenches had been secured with light casualties. I received a nod from Bean. Wilkins and I made our way back outside. This was our chance to move up, even though we would be well behind the Australian attacking line. I emerged through a canvas flap and straightened up, dizzy with the rush of blood and noise, and blinded in the morning light. There was a terrific thud just yards from me. The ground shook and I was tumbling forwards through the air. Pieces of timber boardwalk were flying over my head. Curiously, I had time to notice the trench was upside down before I landed on my side with the camera pressed into my ribs. I was in one piece. George was lifting my pack off my back.

'Frank, are you alright? Can you hear me?' George's voice sounded very distant.

Other soldiers stood around looking at an enormous hole in a timber balustrade along one side of the trench. A Bosche shell had hit, but failed to explode.

My heart was racing and I must have been whiter than a sheet by the look on George's face. No blood, nothing broken, I felt slightly foolish sprawled across the ground. There was nothing else to do but move. I jumped up on the duckboards and ran on ahead with my gear before George could gather up his equipment.

I must have been in shock, because I brushed past several soldiers coming the opposite way before realising they were wearing grey uniforms. They were Bosche. Wilkins caught me up and we both took in the sight. The Hun did not seem to notice us. Looking straight ahead, they trudged along to our rear lines. These were the first live German soldiers I had seen; unarmed, mostly terrified boys, and with barely any escort, prisoners of war to be interned. Ironically, they were the lucky ones, now free of the battlefield.

More Bosche prisoners followed, carrying stretchers with the first wave of injured Australian soldiers. Other prisoners were holding and guiding the walking wounded, both Australian and German.

Looking ahead into the German lines, the Bosche observation balloons had all come down or been destroyed. This morning the RAF dominated the sky, with no German aircraft to be seen. Our planes hung above the Bosche defences and regularly bombed and strafed the German positions. They ignored crisscrossing tracer bullets and anti-aircraft guns which sent up puffs of black smoke. Before too long, I saw one of our aircraft catch fire and plunge to the ground in no-man's-land. Had my cine camera been on I might have captured this, but it was all over too fast.

Wilkins and I passed 'Stirling Castle', which was now just a mound of concrete and brick remnants from what had once been a heavily fortified hilltop. From this point, the Australian dead and wounded were everywhere. They lay in the mud and ooze across the war-ploughed battlefield. I could not help but stare at my countrymen, many of whom had horrific wounds, but we did not pause until we reached the first of the German trenches. Here we stopped.

The carnage along the entire length of the Bosche trench was more than I could ever have imagined. There were none living. The entrenchments themselves were waterlogged and had collapsed inwards, with arms, legs and torsos strewn throughout in a macabre broth. I did not see how I could capture a credible photograph of this scene. I was nauseous. Images of the horror of Grytviken whaling station were here emulated by human slaughter, with 'civilised man' as the pawns in this evil game.

The noise was horrendous; shells whizzed overhead and there was a constant *tacca-tacca* of machine-gun fire from a further line of German defences. We kept our heads down.

On the way back to brigade headquarters, Wilkins and I followed six Bosche prisoners carrying one of our wounded on a stretcher. A German shell landed among them and killed the whole party. There were no remains to be seen for three of them. The others were frightfully mutilated. We scurried past. We did not stop. There was nothing we could do.

We made our way back along Menin Road, past row upon row of stretcher cases waiting for field ambulances, and then to Ypres by dusk and on to our hut at Steenvorde. That night we were up after 1 a.m. developing our photographic plates of the day's efforts. I went to my bedroom dog-tired, shut the door, and before I could reach the basin I was retching on the floor, shaking and sobbing uncontrollably. I had to struggle to prevent my distress being heard by the men outside. How could God, to whom all on the battlefield prayed, be they British, German or French, allow the generals and politicians to carry on this obscene conflict? At headquarters they said we had won a victory and captured over five thousand prisoners. But no one told me our casualties. Our dead could not be any less. How was it my friends Azzi Webb and Leslie Blake participate in this killing?

Eventually, I fell asleep, slept deeply and woke refreshed.

That morning I completed my diary entry for 20 September with something Bean had said to me, but which I regretted even as I wrote:

One of the most glorious days in the annals of our history.

Glorious . . . glorious . . . What on earth was meant by this? I had seen nothing glorious. Bean would undoubtedly know more of what had been achieved, but the cost in lives would need to be worth it. The more it played on my mind, the more offensive it became to me, and I scratched my pen through the words until they were indecipherable.

We learned that during the prior evening, at the same time as we had been developing our negatives, fierce German counterattacks had taken place across the ground we had photographed. By morning, the Bosche had been repelled, though no reference was made to our casualties being light. The Second Division men were by then digging in to their new positions, not having slept for at least two days, and having nowhere dry or safe to lie down amid the churned-up mud. Casualties capable of walking had made their way back to dressing stations. Only a small number of our soldiers were required as prisoner escorts, and these struggled to keep pace with German prisoners anxious to get to the rear, away from the shelling. As for the dead, they lay where they fell, with no immediate prospect of burial parties. Our soldiers moved around them as if they were not there.

Bean took Wilkins and me along to meet the British army censors, who were more reasonable to deal with than I expected. General Kitchener was apparently now so desperate for public support and more recruits that he had reversed the policy of banning journalists and was now actively seeking favourable propaganda stories and photographs. Even so, the censor's concerns were misplaced and bureaucratic.

One of the censors lifted a negative to the light. 'Captain Hurley, this is the sort of thing we won't allow,' he said. 'If the Boche saw this, they could identify the village in the background.'

'I understand,' I replied politely. 'But the Germans already have their own photographs. Each morning I see their aeroplanes taking photographs of the build-up. Their artillery have the precise coordinates they need for each day.'

'Aerial photographs don't identify which units they are looking at,' the censor responded sharply. He tossed the negative back into the box.

I bit my tongue. 'Let me show you a good way to hold negatives,' I replied with a deliberate look of horror on my face.

Bean smiled. 'Captain Hurley and Lieutenant Wilkins will pop in once a week for clearances. They know the ropes.'

A few days later, Bean called in to brief us on plans from headquarters to continue the push to remove the Germans off the high ground east of Ypres. Zero hour was set for 5.50 a.m. on 26 September. The First and Second Australian Divisions were relieved from the front, and in their place the Fourth and Fifth Divisions made their way through the mud into the newly taken positions. Others crossed Menin Road and assembled overnight in Chateau Wood and Glencorse Wood.

On the twenty-fifth, Wilkins and I set out early to photograph the build-up, only to have a most nerve-racking and frustrating day. It was apparent the German artillery knew exactly when and from where our attack would come. Heavy shelling continued nonstop. The Bosche concentrated on our communication lines with uncanny accuracy, finding and destroying a number of ammunition dumps. In short time, the heavy traffic on Menin Road was a long line of blazing wrecks, between which a trail of mustard-gas victims with bandaged eyes and all holding hands were guided back through the mud.

All day, stretcher parties streamed back from our front as the barrage took its toll. The casualties from shellfire were so horrendous I did not see how our attack could proceed.

It was impossible to take any satisfactory pictures. Half the day was spent lying in shell holes with the camera strapped to my back, waiting for a chance to move about. But there were no chances, just moments of running madly across unprotected ground. Through the lens, the landscape was a dark, featureless mire. Nothing in the open stayed still long enough to be photographed. Men huddled all day in trenches and dugouts. Chateau Wood was not even a wood, just tree stumps and shredded branches. It gave no cover to our men. But they knew how to dig. Shovels, tin hats and gas masks kept most of them alive amid the onslaught.

The bayonet and rifle were nothing compared to the destructive force of artillery assembled on both sides of the frontline. I was not so much afraid as dismayed by the random murderous force of the constant shelling. In the afternoon, a nearby dump of howitzer shells took a direct hit with a concussive reverberation that flung Wilkins and I to the ground. It seemed a full minute before the clods of earth, wood and metal debris ceased to rain on us. We were winded and deafened, but unharmed. But it was the end of both stills and cine cameras for the day.

The next morning was another early start. An intense British cannonade opened with a giant thunderclap before dawn. Their work done, the guns fell silent at 5.50 a.m. Within a minute came the *tacca-tacca-tacca* of the German machine guns. Then our artillery started again. The Fourth and Fifth Divisions, with English infantry on their left and right flanks, advanced along a six-mile front. They found the German trenches and pillboxes pulverised by the shelling. Many Germans surrendered.

The Anzacs advanced through Polygon Wood and captured the ruins of Zonnebeke village. Wilkins and I were allowed up into our new frontline positions, although only after they had been secured. The fighting itself had stopped, other than regular sniping. The real action was over. We were left to photograph the carnage. The German dead lay strewn across the floor of their pillboxes and scattered at their entrances and in shell holes and dugouts. Every scene was redolent of the firestorm that had passed through. But the firestorm had gone. I sensed the inadequacy of the photographs I had taken to date. The scenes I was photographing showed devastating destruction. But they did not show the fighting, nor did they show the certainty of imminent death for anyone moving above the parapet.

Wilkins and I frequently moved in sight of the German lines, and to take a decent photograph we invariably spent time fussing around in one spot. Nearby soldiers complained we attracted attention. I walked on the wrong side of a pillbox with camera and tripod, and a bullet pinged off the wall beside me. I dropped to the ground and slid around the nearest corner. I felt sure the same sniper followed me all day.

Counterattacks were expected at any time. We were still taking pictures of the heavily shelled pillboxes when a deadly Bosche barrage began. Wilkins and I set ourselves the task of photographing the shell bursts. This proved enormously difficult, not to mention life-threatening. Working from an old German dugout, I worked out as best I could the German targets and set up the camera and tripod in the open and framed the shot. At the sound of a shell I leaped out to take the photograph. Anything that sounded too close I dived back inside.

We had better luck when we returned to Menin Road. We hid behind tree stumps and dived into ditches, but eventually secured some useful plates. Wilkins cut things too fine and landed heavily, cracking a rib and collecting a piece of shrapnel in the leg. By the time his wound was seen to, it was well after dark when we made it back to Steenvorde, totally exhausted. At the aid post the talk was of a successful day, though there were many casualties.

Bean arrived at the Billabong not long after us. 'You two are making a name for yourselves,' he declared. 'Headquarters have received reports of two mad Australian photographers doing their best to be blown up on the Menin Road.'

'Can't disagree with that,' replied Wilkins. 'But I think we succeeded in photographing some shell bursts today.'

'You're lucky you didn't succeed in having an end to yourselves,' admonished Bean. 'You are no good to me in a field hospital or worse!' With his thinning red hair and glasses, his army uniform falling off his beanpole figure, he looked very much the schoolmaster.

'You're right,' I said. 'Wilkins and I took chances today—but it paid off. We'll now have photographs showing the shellfire our lads cop every day.'

'But they don't go looking for it.'

'We have to go after it—otherwise we'll have nothing worth seeing. When there's an attack, we're not allowed near the front, and the rest of the time our soldiers are in trenches or underground . . . The actual battleground is just a featureless mess with concealed trenches and camouflaged artillery posts. These shell bursts will help show the danger.'

Bean stiffened. 'You are not adding these shell bursts into your other photographs, are you?'

'My oath, I am. I can show you, if you like.'

Bean looked at me for several moments, then addressed me in his formal schoolmaster's voice, 'Captain Hurley, it's not a case of what I like. It's not to be done, not with any photographs you take with the AIF.'

'But you want decent shots for the London exhibition, don't you?'

'The exhibition is to have photographs which accurately show the contribution of the Australian forces. I don't want fakes! That's the sort of thing Lord Beaverbrook and the Canadians do to sell newspapers. Your photographs are part of our historic record.'

'Listen here, Bean, I don't do fakes!' I was angry now. 'I can assure you, the German artillery today was very real. Be serious, man. You know Wilkins and I can't just stand up in the middle of no-man's-land and wait for everything to line up in the viewfinder! I've got no way of knowing exactly when a shell will explode, or if the explosion will be fifty yards on my left or ten yards on my right.'

'Captain Hurley, I'm sorry if this wasn't made clear, but your appointment was approved as official AIF photographer, and the photographs have to be cleared by censors. It's not for you to be adding things later or changing the photographs. You owe it to the diggers to show things truthfully without cropping things in and out.'

'I owe it to the diggers!' I raised my voice. 'I owe it to the diggers to show why so many are being killed and wounded without even seeing a German. You've told me no photographs of Anzac casualties. No photographs, you said, that show 'em in a bad way. Well I happen to think their families ought to see the conditions they live in. And die in! And now you are not even going to let me do that. You and your bloody rules!'

Bean's face was flushed. 'They are not my rules, Hurley. It's the bloody war and the censors have a job to do. We don't need to stoop to distorting things! The public don't want fairies in the garden!'

'Bean, I am not the one distorting things. I've read your dispatches. Light casualties in the battle for Menin Road! You wrote that!' I excused myself and went to my darkroom, slamming the door behind me.

14

Passchendaele, October 1917

There were ominous signs of the build-up to another large battle and the Bosche were surely ready and waiting. Having had a gutful of being shot at, and still fuming over my argument with Bean, Wilkins and I escaped the front and took off in the car to see last year's battlefields at the Somme. I had been told to photograph the Leaning Madonna in a basilica in the town of Albert.

Heavy shelling had destroyed the besieged town and the ruins of the basilica had been boarded up. The basilica had a tower and spire which had been shot away in large part, but miraculously was still standing. Shell holes left bricks and masonry suspended in mid-air, and at the very top was a statue of the Virgin Mary, her arms extended to the heavens and holding aloft the baby Jesus. The shelling had struck the Madonna and she now was almost horizontal, and yet she did not fall nor drop the child Saviour. As the battle of the Somme raged, the tower continued to be shelled, because it remained a prominent vantage point. But the Madonna refused to fall. A rumour took hold among the soldiers of both armies that whichever side brought down the Madonna would lose the war. The Madonna and child had remained suspended precariously for over twelve months now.

On the way back in the car, I muttered to Wilkins, 'You know the censors are banning the very photographs the public need to see; the photographs that would be an end to the case for conscription, maybe an end of the war.'

'You mean photographs of men killing men.'

'Yes, and the horrible ways they die. Seeing that Madonna suspended reminds me of a photograph I stared at as a kid. Do you remember seeing picture books of the siege at Glenrowan? Two of the Kelly gang were burned beyond recognition, but though Joe Byrne was shot dead, his body was pulled from the fire. A Melbourne photographer jumped on the train to Glenrowan but when he got there the siege was over. So he strapped Joe Byrne upright against the door of the Glenrowan Inn, put a gun in his hand and took picture after picture. There were no rules with Irish bushrangers.'

'You're not suggesting we do that!'

'No. We're not going to do that. We can't even photograph an Australian corpse. But that's why this war keeps going. Folks at home got no idea.'

I could see that my plans for the London exhibition would be thwarted by Bean's restrictions. I crafted a letter which I decided to send not to Captain Bean, but to General Birdwood:

> *... I conscientiously believe it my duty to illustrate to the public the severe hardships faced and bravery of the Australian soldier and to do this to the best of my ability. Unfortunately I am unable to do justice to them and produce pictures of quality if unable to utilise standard photographic techniques including composite printing. As I am unable to fulfil my duties I must regretfully resign my position.*

A day after sending the letter, I called in at General Birdwood's headquarters to photograph senior staff officers.

After I had done a series of portraits, he took me aside. 'Captain Hurley, after tomorrow's battle I will have a word with Captain Bean and see if I can fix things up.'

'That's very good of you, sir; not everyone understands what's involved. No photographer can capture what war is like on a single negative. These photographs of the AIF will be on display at the exhibition in London. They need to impress. And of course any composite photographs are always labelled.'

On my return to the Billabong, Wilkins had our equipment ready for us to move up to the front. He looked surprised when I told him about my exchange with Birdwood.

'You mean you were talking about the pictures for the London exhibition now? I would have thought he'd be too busy worrying about tomorrow's attack.'

'Well, yes,' I replied, 'but they're his soldiers we are photographing. It's his war.'

•

I wake with a start, my head reverberating to a loud booming sound. Moments—or is it minutes?—pass before I start to work out where I am. Nothing is familiar. My eyes, I think, are open, but the world around is black. I shiver at the cold in my bones, unsure if I am on the icecap listening to calving icebergs, or in the Snuggery on Elephant Island, or in the centre of London during a raid. My bedding is damp and there is moaning nearby. I draw myself up on one elbow. It must be well before daylight, but there is no returning to sleep. My dreams of times past wisp away like vapours, leaving only the reality of present darkness and tremendous crashing noise. Reaching out, I touch cold clay walls. Memory returns. Of course. I am in Flanders. Have we been bombed during the night?

The evening before, Wilkins and I found billets in an Australian artillery officer's dugout. We are presently twenty feet underground. Overhead a fifteen-inch howitzer battery has started sending its deadly projectiles, fourteen hundred pounds of high explosive, some two miles to the German positions. It is the commencement of the third stage to control the high ground east of Ypres, including the ruins of Broodseinde. The First, Second and Third Australian Divisions will emerge from their trenches in a wide three-thousand-yard front to attack the German defences.

I am anxious to observe what I can of this, but when Wilkins and I exit the dugout there is confusion and disarray. The Bosche have been shelling our lines heavily and we have sustained many casualties even before zero hour. It has been raining throughout the night and is mayhem in the darkness. How utterly dismal to wake up to a world such as this.

Wilkins and I get moving, but are well behind the action. In between the shelling, we hear machine guns and rifle fire up ahead. First ANZAC Division casualties are streaming back already, many of them stretcher cases. These were our assault troops, waiting in the pre-dawn for the signal to attack. A German artillery barrage caught them by surprise in the open. They crouched in shell holes under waterproof capes. If a Bosche projectile landed in their shell hole, they were killed or maimed. After thirty minutes of this, the survivors were only too glad to be allowed to advance into no-man's-land.

Despite this bad luck, for this is how it is described, the word coming back is that the attack has been successful. Our artillery bombard the German lines in stages, with the infantry ready to pour forwards as soon as the barrage lifts. Within a few hours, Broodseinde Ridge is captured, but our losses are high. Wilkins and I do not get close enough to see the fighting, but from what we do see, Australian casualties must again be in the thousands. And although the Germans have lost ground, it is a mere thousand yards, and their artillery remains active all day, causing constant losses in our supply lines.

It is a treacherous business trying to move about the battlefield, and due to ongoing rain the light is bad for photography. Wilkins and I are mighty glad to head back to Steenvorde, where, utterly exhausted, I have a hot meal and heat up a bath before falling into bed. How obscene it is that I do this while my brothers down the road stand unfed and knee-deep in mud, listening to the scream of shells overhead. I am just as bad as some of our red-tabbed British generals, many of whom never see the frontline.

A few days later, a note arrives from headquarters: I have permission to make six composite pictures for the London exhibition, providing they are clearly marked as to the number and details of negatives used. This is an enormous victory. Bean will be spitting chips, though Birdwood must have consulted him. I quickly send a note withdrawing my resignation. I will do these six composite photographs in large format. They will outshine everything else on display. Already in my head I have ideas for what these six photographs will portray. They will express my horror of this dreadful conflict. The exhibition will be my first chance to prepare and display my own work. It will have an international audience and be of a scale I could never achieve by myself.

Next morning, Wilkins and I leave the battlefield behind. I have had a gutful of it. Since Broodseinde, the rain has continued and the pockmarked ground is a dangerous quagmire. I have been champing at the bit to go up in one of our aeroplanes and take aerial photographs. So after our regular visit to the censors, Wilkins and I call in on the Australian No. 69 Squadron at Savy. However, gale-force winds and driving rain over the next few days mean there is nothing doing, and their RE8s are confined to hangars. But while waiting around I read an English newspaper report that Shackleton is about to leave London for South America. He has been ignoring my letters regarding payment of outstanding *Endurance* wages, some five hundred and thirty pounds. Shackleton knows I am in France and it occurs to me that, as long as there's a chance I might stop a bullet and not return, he has no intention of paying. If I don't front him, I will never be paid. I have to get across to London before he leaves. In the meantime, a message comes in from Bean to get back to meet him at Ypres.

We find Bean at Birdwood's headquarters. He is very polite. 'You can't be wandering off at the moment. Things are about to happen here. Our intelligence is the Germans may be about to collapse. Haig's staff are talking about a breakthrough in the next several days. Subject to this rain, the Third ANZAC Division will be asked to attack Passchendaele in the next few days. That's the final stage in forcing the Germans off the high ground. Bosche POWs say German morale is totally shot. There may be an uncontrolled retreat.'

'The rain doesn't look like stopping,' I said. 'Just now we passed a field gun being dragged by two mules. The mules were up to their necks in mud. They'll have to be shot. What's the ground like where the attack is?'

Bean took a deep breath. 'A lot worse since Broodseinde. Haig can't possibly know how bad it is. They'll never get the artillery up in time to protect our infantry. Monash wants to wait, but Haig won't call it off. Lloyd George wants a breakthrough.'

There is no mention of my resignation or its withdrawal, or headquarters' agreement to use of composites.

'Bean, I'm afraid some serious personal matters have come up that require me to be in London for a few days next week.'

'That will be difficult, I'm afraid. You may not be able to get away. If the breakthrough comes at Passchendaele, Haig won't stop till he's cleared the Bosche out of Belgium.'

•

The rain increased. Mud turned to ooze. Our artillery could not be brought forwards in time. Neither Haig nor Monash nor Birdwood came to the front to see the conditions. There was no postponement. On the morning of 12 October, the Anzacs went over the top and scrambled and slid their way towards Passchendaele.

The red tabs, a colonel and a major, were jumpy. The Third Division Anzacs had achieved their first two objectives, but Passchendaele was still in Bosche hands and the German pillboxes on Bellevue Spur had not fallen and were taking a heavy toll. The officers tossed their cigarette butts into the muddy pool below the map table and forgot Wilkins and I were there.

There were mules heading back to Menin Road from where we'd just come. They pulled carts with stretchers of the wounded. The carts were impossibly sluggish in the mud, but no motorised vehicles could navigate the flooded landscape. It was cold standing there and I wanted to move forwards. The red tabs said the front had advanced less than a mile from Broodseinde. We wore our helmets and had gas masks on our chests. Wilkins had the tripod.

'Let's go,' I said, tightening my shoulder straps and picking my way around the edge of several pools, though my boots were already soaked through. I walked up to what remained of the railway. 'We can follow the line.'

'Frank, don't we need permission?'

'Probably, so best just to go. They'd be thinking we want 'em to say no; you know what they're like.'

'But the German artillery must have the exact coordinates of this line.'

The Germans were still shelling, but they had a lot of targets to choose from.

The railway had long ago been destroyed. There were rails, but few sections were connected for any distance. Some rails were bent to remarkable shapes. Some were buried. Sleepers had been pinched for use in trenches and fortifications. The embankment was in parts over three yards high. It felt relatively safe walking along its southern side without crouching. I wanted to be closer to the new frontline by midday.

I wondered how our soldiers had been able to leave their trenches in the heavy rain and attack across the bog that confronted them. There was no prospect of running when the only way forwards was across slippery raised edges of water-filled shell holes. Wilkins and I juggled cameras to keep them dry, but were soon covered in mud from numerous falls. At times we sank to our knees and were lucky to keep our boots from the hideous, sucking slime.

There was a different smell here, a stench we experienced well before we saw our first casualties on the ground. It made me gag at first, and I had to hold my breath as I moved forwards, though I said nothing. It was not from heavy losses this morning, but an unpleasant remembrance of some weeks-old battle. We stepped over old remains exposed by the recent shelling. Pieces of greatcoats and uniforms caked in mud, and contorted limbs, from which army I could not tell.

The oncoming traffic was all casualties. There were few prisoners. Stretcher parties consisted of six or eight men to carry just one wounded soldier above the quagmire. The walking wounded struggled in the conditions. They were mostly silent, white-faced with exhaustion, their uniforms and bandages drenched through. I felt self-conscious with my captain's stripes but not even a side arm. However, the men were not the least bit curious about us.

We moved forwards as best we could, with a sense of purpose, but unsure how far we could safely go. After a couple of miles we passed the ruins of Zonnebeke railway station, from where we continued up to Broodseinde Ridge. Shells were now bursting all around us. I started to worry about losing Wilkins to a sniper bullet or stray shrapnel; it suddenly seemed irresponsible to have just taken off without really knowing where our lines were and whether there would be a counterattack. I wanted to get close to the action and Wilkins was willing. I didn't think too much about becoming a casualty, but I became awfully worried about losing my assistant, whom I knew Bean valued highly.

The corpses became more frequent. The uniforms, where discernible, were the German grey. It was no longer possible to hold one's breath. We inhaled the scent of death.

I spied a number of bodies up ahead that were not dead, but lying against the embankment watching our approach. They were Australian wounded. Within a few yards of them lay dead German soldiers; one was just a legless torso, caught out, no doubt, in the terrifying shelling of the last week.

The Australians had dug tunnels into the embankment. They reminded me of wombat burrows. I did not fancy them much as protection against the shelling, but they had some value against the rain. One young boy nodded to me as we drew closer, picking our way through the mud. From under the brim of his helmet, his watery eyes told me he was just holding himself together. His look told me of what I had not endured.

'You chaps alright?' I said.

'Yes, sir. But if you had some water, sir.'

I handed him one of our spare canteens and a pack of Capstan cigarettes. 'Keep them,' I said. 'Stretcher-bearers know you're here?'

'Yes, sir. They still have the serious cases further up to keep 'em busy. We're fine here. Who are you with, sir?'

'Australian Photographic Unit. My name is Frank, this is George. You've got such a beaut spot here, would you mind if we took some photographs?'

'Long as we don't have to stand up.'

George and I quickly dropped our packs and he set up the tripod.

'Sir, I'd be keeping your heads down—we don't want any extra attention from the Hun.'

I set up quickly.

'You photographing us or the dead, sir?'

'We'll get both, and I'd like to ask you to stay still. That shouldn't be a problem for these other fellows.'

'Oh, that Hun has been here since Broodseinde. He'll be still. What are the photographs for, sir? Do wives and sweethearts see 'em?'

'Depends on the censors. Our job is just to take 'em. You chaps are Third Anzac Corps?'

'Yes, from Victoria, sir. Sir, the folks at home, they know the casualties, don't they?'

Things could not have been more glum. The Anzacs had failed at what was to be the final hurdle. There was no breakthrough. The war would now go on past Christmas and into yet another year. The Anzacs would be stuck in their miserable trenches through the worst of winter. As best I could gather, we had lost several thousand in just one day at Passchendaele, slaughtered without any chance of a fair fight. It was a disaster, but no one used this word. Bean was very down about it but the dispatches I saw gave no clue of any of this.

The next morning I made for Boulogne and from there back to old Blighty. If Shackleton was a gentleman, he would honour his debts; if not, I would engage a solicitor to stop him in his tracks.

Neither Shackleton nor Perris wished me a happy birthday when I bowled into the *Daily Chronicle* on 15 October, but they were cordial. The following morning I received payment in full. It was a great relief to restore my financial position in one day. I knew in my bones that if I had not left Flanders and fronted Shackleton, I would be a poorer man. Lord knows the AIF would not make me rich, though at least it paid for my living expenses and, if it came to it, my funeral expenses. And Charlie Bean would have us all risk our lives for nothing more than love of country.

It was a whirlwind trip. London crowds milled in the streets, and theatres were buzzing. But for the khaki uniforms, you could be forgiven for not realising there was a war on. But that night, drifting in and out of sleep in my hotel bed, the now-familiar sound of high explosives took me back to the front. I was photographing a corpse in a muddy pool, a young German boy soldier who lay on his back as if asleep. His reddish hair was flecked with dried clay. It was the type of close personal portrait I usually avoided, only my camera seemed drawn to him and his face was bloated and too close and swelling in and out of focus. I pinched myself to check if I was awake or dreaming of Flanders. Air-raid sirens confirmed that it was German zeppelins bombing London streets. The red-haired boy disappeared.

I caught up with Azzi in a London tearoom. He was on leave and looking like a ghost. 'Dad McLean has been gassed,' he said. 'I don't think he's going to make it, and I thought we should visit his wife together.'

'I won't have time, Azzi,' I replied, knowing I would not be good in that situation.

I dined with Sir Douglas and Lady Mawson. They were rightly horrified by my stories of Ypres and Passchendaele. They had read nothing of the battle for Passchendaele in the papers. Paquita Mawson was like a delightful young schoolgirl compared to the dour Mawson. She was sweet and intelligent and very devoted to him. He has done very well, and with a knighthood to boot.

I came off the boat in Boulogne and was surprised to see Wilkins waiting with the car. Before we drove off he handed me an envelope. 'This came for you. I'm sorry, but I opened it before I knew it was personal.'

It was from Birdwood's staff. 'I've been given the sack!'

'It's a transfer.'

'I've been bloody sacked!'

'You're being appointed to the AIF in Egypt. You're still a captain, for God's sake.'

'Bloody Bean has played politics to get rid of me!'

'So what if he did? The whole of the AIF would give their eye teeth to be posted there—anywhere but Flanders. It'll be a whole lot warmer for one thing. And look, it's not for a few weeks yet. That gives you plenty of time to get killed here.'

Nothing Wilkins said could persuade me that this was anything other than the most shabby treachery on the part of Bean and his red-tab friends, after I had daily risked my life to get the photographs no one else could get. Wilkins, meanwhile, had been told he was to stay on as Bean's assistant. I had come to expect self-interest and unfairness on private expeditions, but here with our country's fighting forces, in the middle of the battlefield with thousands dying each day, I had hoped for something better. Instead, I found the army was a mismanaged bunch of string-pullers and bureaucrats. The good soldiers, and there were many, were the ones who bore the brunt of the misery of the trenches and were wantonly sacrificed.

I returned to the darkroom at Steenvorde determined to finish off my collection of photographs of Flanders for the London exhibition. Annoyingly, I found we had regular guests. Red tabs would just drop in to request a photograph be taken of them or their unit or to beg a print for themselves. I left these requests to Wilkins.

I returned to one of my favourite haunts, photographing the smoky ruins of Ypres. I even enjoyed the hair-raising races in the car along Menin Road. One cold afternoon in a dugout on Westhoek Ridge—part of our newly won territory—I watched the Hun artillery, undoubtedly assisted by observation balloons, shelling our ammunition wagons on the main supply road. The wagon drivers gamely galloped their horses as shells burst in front and behind them. A direct hit would send them to heaven. As they gambled with their lives, the men alongside me placed bets as each wagon approached.

From Westhoek, Wilkins and I crept across to the edge of the lake at Chateau Wood. I fancy it was once a favourite spot for lovers. Now, only death lingered in its forest of uprooted tree stumps, churned earth and duckboard track disappearing in the gloom.

I took photographs and we turned to make our way back to Hooge Crater and the Menin Road. As we did so, we found ourselves caught up in a bombardment that had us dashing from one inadequate shelter to another. The Hun howitzers whistled overhead as we ran. *Wiz-sh-sh-sh-sh-sh-sh-sh-boom!* A shell landed at my feet without exploding. A dud! It covered me with mud. We leaped to our feet and continued on our way. My legs felt like lead as we scampered for our lives.

Frustratingly, despite a number of attempts, Wilkins and I had not been able to arrange with 69 Squadron what would have been my first flight. Instead, I found an obliging lieutenant who allowed me to join him in his observation balloon from near the Menin Gate. We ascended to three and a half thousand feet, until we overlooked the vast necropolis that was Ypres.

Even had there been no war, it was the most fantastic and frightening experience to be floating so high above the earth suspended in a wicker basket with a highly flammable hydrogen balloon above my head. Was this what God saw when he looked from the heavens at this world of man? From this height, individual acts of valour were imperceptible. Certainly the haze made poor conditions for photography. The battleground ran to the horizon in both directions like an ugly scar across Flanders and the whole of Europe, consuming thousands of lives and seemingly endless industrial resources. A pall of smoke overhung no-man's-land and below us the grey sky was reflected in the muddy pools of a thousand flooded shell craters which pockmarked the ground. To the east, a constant flickering of artillery gun flashes marked the way to Passchendaele. Then out of the northern sky slightly above us we observed seventeen Gotha bombers approach. When they were about a mile away, I saw the ground rise up behind them in a series of massive eruptions as they dropped their bomb-loads of deadly high explosives. They disappeared from view above our balloon and we had a nervous wait, in parachutes, to see if we would be fired on.

Wilkins sat up suddenly brandishing a crumpled old newspaper. 'My, my, these are fancy words indeed. I say, Hurley, listen to this.' And then, in a pompous voice, he read aloud: '"To you men and women of Australia . . . When I arrived . . . I did not know what the word Anzac meant. But I learned it was a title of fame and glory . . . . . . I cannot imagine that you men are failing to realise your debt of honour to the men who have gone before, to the men who have died in that temple of blood and glory, Gallipoli . . . Death is a very little thing—the smallest thing in the world. I can tell you that, for I have been face to face with death during long months . . ."'

'What are you reading?' I said, but Wilkins ignored me and read on.

'"For this call to fight means more than ease, more than money, more than love of woman, more even than duty; it means the chance to prove ourselves the captains of our own soul."' Wilkins looked up. 'That's laying it on a bit thick, isn't it? But then again, you made captain by joining the army!'

'Who's saying that?' I asked.

'Why,' he said, 'it's your good friend.'

'Which friend?'

'Shackleton. He's been in Australia giving recruitment speeches. He spoke about your great white war in the south.' And again, in his pompous voice, '"I say to you men of Australia: Face the test of battle."'

'He must have given that speech on his way home from the rescue of the Ross Sea party,' I said. 'They'd be wishing they had not listened to his speeches.'

'Still, he went and got them.'

'He got those who were still alive, Wilkins. But, crikey, he hasn't been near the front. Would he give that speech if he had seen what we have seen?'

'Well, let's face it, we have seen and we've photographed, and those photographs will be used for recruitment propaganda, same as Sir Ernest Shackleton.'

Wilkins was right, there was little I could say.

'We have been employed to do a job as best we can,' I said. 'We are in Bean's hands as to what he does with our photographs.' Then I added, 'Shackleton was a bloody dreamer, heroics at any cost. He had a favourite poem about death. Browning, of course.' As I lay back I could hear Shackleton's voice.

Fear death?—to feel the fog in my throat,
The mist in my face,
When the snows begin, and the blasts denote
I am nearing the place . . .
No! let me taste the whole of it, fare like my peers
The heroes of old,
Bear the brunt, in a minute pay glad life's arrears
Of pain, darkness and cold.

On the Saturday before I left Flanders, Azzi dropped in for the evening. We talked about how much longer the war could drag on. Passchendaele had at last been taken by the Canadians. They succeeded where the Anzacs had failed. But there was no breakthrough, there was no collapse of the German army. The Americans were arriving and could help fill the trenches in the new year. Azzi spoke wearily, as if he would not live to see the end of it. In the morning, Azzi said he would go to the Sunday service. Wilkins and I offered to accompany him. We made our way to a sunken roadway where a crowd of soldiers were gathered in the shelter of a large earthen embankment.

'I am asked—must this war continue?' said the balding English minister, glaring fiercely at the few hundred heads bowed before him. 'May we not now join with President Wilson and negotiate for peace, is that not the humane path? And I am compelled to answer—look ye to the root cause of this conflict, has that cause been purged? That cause, we know, is original sin and the heathen forces in Christendom. Do not err by looking only to the moral condition of Germany, which as a nation has made a foreign policy of foul murder. Look, I say, to the impurity, the intemperance, the Sabbath-breaking that we see daily in our midst.

'So do not say, as President Wilson may well say, "Let this cup pass from me." The shedding of blood is not to be taken so lightly. For Christ died that we might live. This is the very crux of the sacrifice that our young men have made when they offered themselves as instruments of God's punitive justice. The fight against sin requires we see this terrible war through until the heathen renounces evil.'

This was foreign to me. Perhaps I had been away too long from churches and politics. The congregation listened patiently, however. What were they hoping for? I wondered. What good could come of this war? There was nothing redemptive in what I saw at Ypres. This religious dogma, along with Shackleton's brand of fatalistic patriotism, both seemed claptrap to me.

I did not want to be out of step with the world but to me Azzi looked no better off for the haranguing he had received. He was as flat as a tack. It all made me quite angry. The institutions of church and state had either gone mad or always been mad.

15

Egypt and Palestine, December 1917–March 1918

Guncotton and explosives were our cargo as we waited to depart Plymouth on P&O *Malta*. The only clue to our secret departure time was the sudden loading of mailbags. One by one, some twenty merchantmen raised anchor and headed out to sea. *Armada Castle*, a large auxiliary cruiser, was our main escort, accompanied by six destroyers. All the merchantmen had six-inch guns mounted. The rumour on board was that there were nine U-boats off Gibraltar, and we would have to give an account of ourselves.

After six days our convoy entered the Strait of Gibraltar. Even though we were entering the most dangerous sector of the Mediterranean, I was stirred by the sight of the rugged Spanish coastline to our north and the distant outline of Africa in the south. By the time we took shelter in Malta, two vessels had been torpedoed and sunk.

The U-boats did not get me, but I was struck instead by Nurse Jillian Loch.

The padre, with whom I shared a cabin, brought Jillian Loch to our table at dinner. The church has its uses, as I would otherwise never have had the gumption to introduce myself.

Even had she not been about the only young woman aboard the *Malta*, I would have been swept away by her lively, friendly manner. She was not at all overawed by the company of so many men, nor the conversation, which ranged from submarines to boxing. She had wavy nutbrown hair, did not wear make-up, and had a schoolgirl's mischievous smile. She did not wear rings or jewellery of any kind.

'I am afraid you won't have heard of my unit,' she said when I asked. 'I'm with Queen Alexandra's Royal Army Nursing Corps for India. A mouthful, isn't it? A group of us were transferred to England and France just before the Somme.'

'Looking after the Gurkhas?'

'No. We are not allowed near coloured soldiers; I'm afraid it's very old-fashioned.'

Jill Loch—or Jilloch, as I would sometimes call her—became my partner at cards that night, and deck quoits the following days.

A few days later we anchored in Malta and alongside came several brightly painted rowing skiffs with high prows fore and aft, just as I imagined Venetian gondolas. Their skippers haggled to take us ashore. Jill was excited at the prospect of an excursion. She proved to be a good walker and in quick time we had climbed to the top of the nearest hill and explored its fortifications, both old and new. We dined at the Westminster Hotel and I made sure we were back on board by 9 p.m.

In my cabin that evening I was so ecstatic I could hardly sleep. Our outing had been a success and Jill's company a refreshing change from the world of men. I couldn't wait till morning, when we had agreed to meet over breakfast.

Jill was again happy to go exploring, and before long we reached the top of Fort St Elmo, which had a commanding view over the harbour and out across the Mediterranean Sea. There were views inland of several walled villages, all tightly packed around the spires and domes of their basilicas. In the distance, we were beckoned by the dramatic outline of an ancient city.

We found our way by crowded train to Citta Vecchia, through a draughtboard pattern of fields of wheat and barley and once there we lost ourselves among ancient stone walls, ramparts, towers, domes and minarets. We were accosted by dozens of street urchins: *Mister, you need guide, you need taxi, I spik good Ingleesch, you give me coin, me have no father, me no mother, no aunt, no uncle* ... We escaped and strolled through markets, climbed well-worn stone stairways and turned up narrow laneways, until eventually we entered a square at one end of which was an exquisite Renaissance cathedral.

I had been to St Paul's in London, but felt I had seen nothing to compare with the beauty of the interior of this cathedral in Citta Vecchia, with its ornate marble walls, mosaic floors, statuary, vaulted ceiling, cupolas and frescoes. I could only account for my rapture as being due to the presence of my companion.

'A place as beautiful as this,' said Jilloch, 'makes it so much easier to believe in a caring God.'

My gaze moved from the ceiling to her upturned face. 'How you cope with the sick and dying I can't imagine,' I said.

'Oh, I cope with the dying,' she replied. 'There are any number of deaths each day. It's mourning the dead I can't cope with. During the Somme, there was a piper from a nearby regiment of Scot's Guards. He made a point of coming to us each time there was a funeral, and some days there were several. He would stand in ceremonial dress and play the Piper's Lament. All of us nursing sisters were constantly in tears. We had to ask him to stop coming.'

'I am afraid I have become very indifferent about corpses on the battlefield,' I confessed. 'I have learned to photograph without thinking too much. It's the wounded I get distressed about.'

'Yes. We are told to concentrate on the lightly wounded . . . to get them back to the front. Well of course it's the last thing they want. The bad cases just linger and, if lucky, they recover enough to get a boat home.'

An eight-mile walk back to the port did not diminish our mutual sense of freedom and escape from the world of war.

'Frank,' said Jill over dinner, 'is it top secret why you are heading to Cairo?'

'If it is, Jilloch, no one has told me. All I've heard is that with all of the setbacks on the Western Front, Lloyd George wants the army to take Jerusalem as a Christmas present for the British people. I'll be there so they can preserve a photographic record of it all. Trouble is, my photography can't preserve the protagonists.'

'No, I suppose that's left to the nurses.'

'And you, Jilloch—why are you returning to Bombay?'

'My mother is unwell and I'm told I am needed. The ANC has given me leave.'

'You are single then?'

'Why yes, Frank—of course, yes. What did you think? I am writing to someone, though: an officer I met in France. But it's all just so shocking, isn't it? This damn war. And India is so far. It is so far away, it's like being in another world.'

I have the U-boats to thank for keeping us in the harbour at Malta for five days, five delicious days when the two of us explored to our heart's content and forgot about the death and destruction that gripped Europe. I experienced the excitement of sightseeing for its own sake with a companion ready to laugh and share stories, neither of us feeling any urgency to reach a particular destination. However, I felt a strange anxiety inside, conscious our days together were both precious and numbered. Really, our friendship seemed quite hopeless. She was writing to someone else, and I was at the start of a new adventure. I did not want to make a fool of myself.

The night before we reached Port Said, I could not sleep. I rehearsed things I could say to Jilloch and wondered whether I should say them. She gave no sign that she was interested in me as a suitor. I was not interested in having a correspondence unless we could meet again, but how could we? I was reluctant to embarrass myself in front of her for nothing.

Our last day together came and that is where we got to and no further. I knew nothing more I could say. I disembarked at Port Said thoroughly occupied having to safeguard twenty pieces of luggage to the train station en route to Cairo. Jilloch kissed me farewell and stayed on board the ship and that was that. I was so damnably lonely and miserable, back on my own again.

•

Not only do I know no one, but I have arrived too late and missed all the action. The tide of war here has turned. The Turks and Germans are on the run it seems. Jerusalem has been captured by General Allenby after hundreds of years of Ottoman rule.

The Australian Light Horse are in reserve somewhere remote, no one knows quite where. After ten days of waiting at railheads and haphazard train journeys and being jammed in trucks surrounded by my boxes, I wake up on Christmas Eve on the floor of a goods train in a railway siding in the desert. Even with the train now stationary the rumbling in my head continues, and I realise there are lightning flashes and dark ominous clouds and a violent wind thick with desert sand that gets through all my clothing. I negotiate with railway wallahs for my cameras and equipment to be carried a half-mile to a small encampment. It starts to rain and there is literally no inn and certainly no rooms to be had, and I find myself sharing a tent with three strangers. I am wakened in the middle of the night by cold wet canvas across my face. The pegs have lifted from sodden ground and the tent has collapsed. The heavens then burst well and truly and soon there is two feet of water running across the clay floodplain where we are camped. I salvage my gear and manage to reset the tent on top of large trestle tables, where my companions and I actually manage to get some sleep despite having to clench and hold down the tent walls in the storm gusts.

My mind goes back to being flooded in the Snuggery on Elephant Island. I do not know what a normal Christmas is! When will I have a Christmas Day at home? I wonder.

It is almost New Year's when Henry Gullett, newly appointed Head of War Records, Middle East Section, tracks me down and finds me a billet in Khirbet Deiran, a small Jewish settlement where the Light Horse are based. Gullett is a younger, better-fed version of Bean, without the red hair and sharp proboscis. He is also a journalist by trade, but unlike Bean he actually served in the army before taking up his current position. After helping me stack my luggage in a fine house in the village, Gullett makes a pot of tea and we sit outside on a low whitewashed stone wall in the shade of Australian eucalypt trees, introduced here because of their ability to withstand arid climes.

'I'm afraid, Hurley, I should have got you here several weeks earlier, before Jerusalem fell. Nothing can happen now this rain has started. Can you believe we missed the chance to film a cavalry charge?'

'Beersheba?'

'Two whole regiments of Light Horse ordered to charge Turkish trenches, their rifles slung across their backs and just bayonets in hand.'

'I can't see how they weren't massacred. Coming from Flanders, you would need to see it to believe it. Would have been impossible to film unless I had been in the Turks' front-line. And the Turks, I hear, are good fighters.'

'They are tough bastards and they're used to the desert. Got their tails up after Gallipoli. They are a very superior kind of nigger. We've been fighting them now for two years, only this time *they* are the invader. Some of our lads think they are on an old fashioned crusade, throwing heathens out of the Holy Land.'

I can only shake my head. 'By God, no one who had been to Ypres would say that. But it's a different war here. Perhaps without constant shellfire I can actually get decent photographs of the conflict.'

'You'll get your chance. The Suez and Egypt are secure and the Turk has been cleared out of the Sinai, so now we're on the offensive. With the capture of Jerusalem, the way I see it, the fighting's just moved from the Old Testament to the New Testament.'

'I'm afraid that's lost on me.'

'I mean there'll be more action in Palestine once this rain stops.'

The following day I travel in a battered Box Ford to our front-line positions in the Judean Hills. The ground changes from sand and clay to weathered limestone, and the ancient hills are terraced and shaded by rows of olive trees and occasional fig trees. Most spectacularly, the rains have created an abundance of wildflowers; red anemones, blue marguerites, tiny white and yellow narcissi, orange ranunculi and bright yellow cyclamea scattered everywhere in a riot of colour. I peer at a nearby ridge, but see none of the enemy. Each outpost I visit is only lightly guarded. Occasionally there is the clatter of a machine gun and the ping from a sniper's rifle, but that is all. The Third Brigade Light Horse are here and having a quiet time of it. Even more laconic than their compatriots in Flanders, they do not follow the fashion of turning up on one side their broad-brimmed digger's hats, for they are horsemen and have little need of marching with rifles shouldered. But to a man they wear an emu feather in their hatband, no matter how battered and dusty their hat. They save energy by saluting only the officers in their own units. Their commanding officer is quite pleased to have them form up on horseback and parade for my cine camera.

•

A week later I returned to Khirbet Deiran and met Gullett for breakfast in the officer's mess of the Desert Corps, to which I am attached. With abundant fresh produce, the meals served are an embarrassment of riches compared to the shortages in France and England. But Imperial Yeomanry also based in Deiran frequent the same mess, and I find they are quite stuffy. Gullett seems quite chuffed I have started filming each of the Light Horse brigades and have met the Australian commander, General Chauvel. His eyebrows raise when I tell him, 'Chauvel has promised me thirty men and horses to film entering the streets of the Holy City.'

'Really? Well, that's splendid; we must have film of Jerusalem under a British flag. But of course, Hurley, the Light Horse were not at Jerusalem when the Turks withdrew. It was General Allenby who marched in.'

'I see. But the Light Horse fought near enough, at Gaza and Beersheba. And, after all, pictures of Jerusalem without Australian soldiers in the frame would be next to useless for Captain Bean.'

'I suppose so. Captain Bean is very enthusiastic about this photographic exhibition in London. Doesn't want to be criticised for ignoring the Light Horse. So you've got your work cut out for you and a lot of ground to cover.'

Before I could reply I was interrupted by a hand on my shoulder and found myself looking up at the chin of a smooth-faced English officer.

'Excuse me, Captain Hurley. You are likely unaware of the dress code in the mess, but you can't wear a beanie here. I'm afraid it won't do. You can wear your officer's cap.'

'Thank you, thank you,' I blurted and pulled off my old woollen hat feeling quite mortified.

'We're just on our way,' Gullett said as we both shoved handfuls of fruit into our pockets and retreated outside. 'And I hear,' he continued as we emerged into the bright morning light, 'you are to restage the Beersheba cavalry charge?'

The road to Jerusalem wound up to the east through narrow limestone gorges. At the top of the ridge there were fine views to the north-west some twenty-five miles to Jaffa, on the coast. We negotiated treacherous hairpin bends and soon came in sight of the Holy City, perched on a hilltop just over a mile away. We entered through the ugly surrounding sprawl of the densely populated modern city. With the sun about to set, I captured photographs of my small Light Horse contingent as they rode their mounts down to an ancient causeway outside the main walls of the old city. Fortunately, the Turk chose to abandon the city intact, so I was able to inspect the holiest of its sacred sites. My lack of religious education and biblical knowledge had never been redressed, and I was impressed but mystified at the overt reverence at the Wailing Wall.

Gaza was not so lucky. Between March and October 1917 there were three pitched battles to capture this city from the Turk. British artillery destroyed the ancient town. It finally fell after the capture of Beersheba, but not before several thousand lives were lost. I went there with two squadrons of Light Horse to take photographs. The route was picturesque, passing orchards and olive trees and fields of barley. The white dirt road was lined by green cactus hedges, but as we drew closer to Gaza they had all been slashed and used to corduroy the road for army vehicles. The troopers and their commanders were compliant to my every request, no doubt glad to have an easy day. At the ruins of Gaza's twelfth-century Grand Mosque I chose just one trooper to add human dimension by sitting on crumbled masonry inside the collapsed nave. I set up amid the rubble while he enjoyed the sunlight pouring in through the vaulted and now-open ceiling.

Meeting later with Gullett he explained, 'The Turks had promised neither Gaza nor Jerusalem would be used for military purposes. But of course they were never going to give up Gaza without a fight. Allenby said the mosque was being used to store munitions although I could see no sign of that.'

'Gaza,' I said, 'is the Ypres of Palestine. There is not a building intact.'

Some days later I set up the cine camera in a trench to film a re-enactment of the charge on Beersheba. At the appointed time, two regiments of the Fourth Brigade Light Horse, eight hundred horses and men, formed up in three lines some seven hundred yards across, with three hundred yards between each line. From one mile away I watched a long low cloud of dust rise up. Then a line of small dark centaur figures emerged, but at first appeared not to be moving as the cloud rose higher behind them. For a few moments the figures were suspended in midair, and only then did the drumbeat of thousands of hooves reach me like a low purring sound. There was a glint of steel as bayonets were raised and the purring turned to low thunder as horses and riders came belting across the plain. The ground trembled with pounding hooves as the Light Horse drew closer. At five hundred yards, grains of sand started to dance along the front edge of the trench. At three hundred yards, my hand winding the film through began to vibrate on the crank handle. At two hundred yards, my whole weight was leaning on the cine camera tripod to brace against the onslaught. And then the first wave of attackers were upon me and the furious dark glistening horses rose as one and cleared the trench, leaving me in a blinding, choking cloud of dust.

•

In Flanders fields the poppies grow
Between the crosses, row on row . . .

These lines are the best known of any poem from this terrible war. Yet I did not pause to photograph the flowers in Belgium at the end of the European summer. Here in Palestine time moves slower. Torrential deluges have flooded the Holy Land, ending the fighting and creating new life. I see so many red anemones that I am reminded of the graves in Ypres and the Somme. Colour images on the battlefield in Flanders were next to impossible, as even with the new Paget process the required exposure was several times longer than for black-and-white film. However, the light in Palestine in winter is the equivalent of an English summer, and without constant shelling there is time to compose. These hardy daisies, though, are so small that in a patch of several square yards it is difficult to find a central focus.

George, one of my Light Horse trooper assistants, offers to display a bouquet of anemones for the camera. He crouches on the desert sand, his face deeply etched by shadows from the bright midday sun. The emu feather in his slouch hat quivers slightly in the breeze while he holds his prayerful pose. Only later, when I am exulting in the colours achieved on the negative, do I see that George is an elderly man, more than twice the age of the other troopers. It caused me to think of my own father—what would he think of this war. Surely George must have lied about his age to enlist. When I later ask him about this, his answer amuses me greatly. 'The enlistment officer rejected me,' he explains, 'even though I was an experienced veteran of the Boer War, so I went back again with my son, who had to put his age up three years and I put mine down thirteen. The enlistment officer looked at us both and said, "I see. Well you'd both better go."'

•

Still there was no action and I was being driven mad by requests to do portraits of this and that smug red tab in their polished riding boots and on their favourite horse. I arranged my escape to the aerodrome at El Mejdel, where the newly established No. 1 Squadron, Australian Flying Corps, was based. I had no sooner set up my cine and stills cameras when one of the squadron's new Bristol fighter aeroplanes came into view with smoke billowing from the fuselage. I seized the opportunity and had the cine camera running as the biplane came in to land. As soon as it came to a stop, flames could be seen licking up around the engine cowling and the pilot leaped from the cockpit. Within seconds there was an explosion and the aircraft was engulfed in flames. The pilot was safe and I had some terrific action shots. I had to avoid crowing about my luck.

Then it was finally my turn for a long-awaited first flight. Captain Ross Smith was entrusted to find me something to photograph from the air and bring me safely back to earth. Smith had enlisted in the Third Light Horse but, dismayed by the dismal conditions at Gallipoli, he then volunteered for the AFC.

The Bristol had a very tight rear cockpit for an observer or gunner, which is where I squeezed in behind Smith. The roar of the engine was deafening and it was immediately apparent that vibration would be the problem for any airborne stills photography. The Bristol roared and bounced along the aerodrome until it was weightless. Smith pulled back on the stick and lifted us airborne. The hangars and vehicles left behind became toy models. I watched the altitude gauge over Smith's shoulder: one thousand, two thousand, three thousand feet . . . Below me there was a transformation of perspective the like of which I had never before experienced. The fertile areas cultivated after the rains became a very neat manmade patchwork. Streams, irrigation ditches and wadis became arteries and veins. Roads like white ribbons looped across a piecrust landscape on which there was occasional ant-like traffic. Extraordinarily, even though we were travelling at ninety miles per hour, the Judean Hills appeared stationary.

At seventeen thousand feet it was freezing, even in a full-length leather coat. Smith then dived down through the clouds until we were skimming above the stagnant surface of the Dead Sea, which is nestled so low in the Jordan Valley we were actually flying below sea level. Over Jericho on the way home black cloud puffs appeared around us, followed by sharp thunderclaps. The Turks' Archie guns followed us as we turned towards Jerusalem and then home. Back on solid earth I was ecstatic and immediately began planning with Smith to accompany the squadron on a bombing raid.

After almost two months in Palestine, Gullett at last gave me the nod that a stunt was on. I rushed back to Deiran. Gullett knew I was getting restless. He turned up at my quarters on dusk with bags of oranges and almonds which we devoured sitting outside with cups of tea.

'The Light Horse are on the move,' he said. 'There's to be an attack on Jericho. Chauvel wants to push the Turks back across the Jordan River.'

'Can I go with the Light Horse?'

'That may not be so easy. The main infantry assault will be east along the Jerusalem–Jericho road, but the First Brigade Light Horse are to head across the mountains to the south. That could be pretty steep and rough-going, especially with your equipment.'

Of course, he knew what my response would be.

The First Brigade Light Horse were stationed in Bethlehem, where I joined them. It was not hard to understand the excitement of the troopers as their horses filed one after another out through narrow Bethlehem laneways onto the surrounding plains where, long ago, three wise men observed the Star of Bethlehem and shepherds tended their flocks.

We rode the whole day past great limestone hills. We passed trucks of infantry and tractors hauling heavy artillery guns into forward positions. They cut a swathe through the anemones, narcissi and marguerites, crushing the wildflowers into the red clay soil.

The further we rode, the more the country increased in its desolation. The desert looked as dry and fierce as the remote parts of Northern Australia, but far from being flat it presented an endless array of roughly hewn plateaus, hills and ridges interspersed with broad valleys and a thousand steeply carved gullies, now bone dry after the rains. The few mature trees stood as withered relics from more favourable times.

We rode till well after nightfall, which tested me severely. My horse, I hoped, would not expose my inexperience as a rider. I led a packhorse in tow with my cameras and equipment. An hour before midnight we tethered the horses and were instructed to have a short kip. It was bitterly cold, my legs and backside were aching and sleep was elusive. We had been ordered to travel light so there were no tents or bivvies, just whatever blankets we carried.

It was 3.30 a.m. when we saddled up to lead off through a series of gorges towards Nebi Musa, where an attack was to be made on the main Turk defensive line around Jericho. Nebi Musa, I learned, was reputedly the burial place of Moses. Thick cloud blocked out the moon so, in pitch-black darkness, I allowed my mount to pick her way nose to tail behind the horse in front along narrow wadi banks and steep cliff faces. Our column stretched for a mile along the mountain pass. On the ridge above, I glimpsed silhouettes of the leading riders, while below me in the darkness came the sparks of horseshoe on stone.

Gunshots rang out well before dawn and were followed by the crump of cannon and mortar fire. At first light the brigade assembled behind low hills, with Nebi Musa directly ahead. The Turks held heavily fortified positions on top of two impregnable-looking hilltops. First Brigade was kept in reserve out of sight of the Turk artillery. A regiment of New Zealand Rifles dismounted under cover and threaded their way along winding gullies towards the Turk positions. The Turks sent down long strafing bursts of machine-gun fire and artillery shells. We stayed in reserve the whole day, by the end of which the New Zealand Rifles, joined by two British regiments, had started to climb the rocky precipice below the Turk strongholds, though the enemy remained in control of the heights.

In the late afternoon, three Bedouins were brought into camp. They told of a narrow trail which led eastwards out of sight of Nebi Musa down into the Jordan Valley. This was an opportunity to get behind the Turk lines. No one mentioned whether the arrival of three Bedouins was a propitious omen. Within an hour First Brigade, with the Bedouins in the lead, made its way in single file along a small wadi and disappeared into a narrow rocky canyon in the fading evening light.

Again we stopped not much before midnight to rest horses and attempt to sleep. By this stage my backside and legs were in agony. A cold whistling wind was dampened by drizzling rain. My sleep was broken by the noise of horses breaking their rope lines and pickets and whinnying their disapproval of our resting place. But I know I slept because I twice woke from a dream of standing on board a departing ship surrounded by my equipment and watching two figures on the dock disappearing in the distance. One figure was my mother. The other, I think, was Jilloch.

At 3.15 a.m., stiff with cold, I was glad to be up and on the move. To reach the plain below us we had to drop thirteen hundred feet of altitude in less than two miles of goat track, for that was what we were on. We descended through treacherous, slippery conditions which I would never have attempted in daylight. I relied entirely on the good sense of my horse and concentrated on staying in the saddle.

An hour before dawn the Light Horse moved into positions behind the Turk trenches outside Nebi Musa. Patrols were sent out to scout along the road into Jericho. By daybreak word came back the Turks had abandoned their positions on the heights and retreated back through Nebi Musa and to the north and east of Jericho. An advance party of the First Brigade galloped into Jericho and succeeded in cutting off and capturing a number of Turk soldiers. To their horror, they found several buildings full of dead and dying Turk soldiers suffering from typhus and left behind in the haste of evacuation. The Turk army had crossed to the eastern side of the Jordan River, destroying bridges as they went. By this time our horses had been without water for thirty hours and we were fortunate to find a small stream near the town. Jericho had fallen without fanfare.

•

A poor choice of evening bivouac in Jericho results in my sleep being disturbed by the groans of wounded Turk soldiers and typhus patients. I make plans for an excursion the next day to see the new frontline along the Jordan River and an Australian doctor offers to accompany me. In the cold air before daybreak, a Box Ford and driver take us east until I can see the distant dark reflection of the waters of the Jordan. From here we proceed on foot.

Knowing the road will be enfiladed by enemy fire in daytime, I find a small grove of gnarled olive trees and have the driver park under cover with the car facing home in case a hasty retreat is needed. With stills camera and tripod over my shoulder, we set off down the road as the sky begins to lighten.

I can see a patrol of some fifteen Light Horse to the south, on our side of the Jordan, and a smaller detachment to the north. We head towards the main group, who are only four hundred yards away, with the hope of including them in photographs. Suddenly the dirt sprays up behind us as a volley of rifle fire informs me these soldiers are Turk cavalry. My companion and I drop to the ground. The driver is still back at the car. From where I am crouching I yell to him to get the car out of range and back to Jericho. The noise of the car engine starting fills the still morning air. Unfortunately, the valley is now flooded in bright sunlight and the car and the great cloud of dust it creates is more than enough to attract the attention of Turk artillery batteries across the Jordan. The first ten-pounder shell lands well short. The second lands alongside the road, but again well behind the now-speeding vehicle. The commotion is the distraction we need. There is nothing for it but to abandon my camera. My companion and I take to our feet and sprint for cover, looking about wildly as we run. As I learned in Ypres, a fast-moving vehicle is a hard target for artillery, but it is still a few minutes before the driver makes it out of range. Meanwhile, we are in sight and in range, and there is no cover.

In short time I am completely winded. Spying a patch of saltbush no more than a few feet high, we go to ground. The Turks know exactly where we are and continue their firing, but do not advance on us. We crawl under cover as far as we can. My heart races with the whine of bullets over our heads and occasional ping off nearby rocks. Peering through scrub I see the two sections of Turk cavalry join up, all the time watching intently for us. Perhaps fearing a trap, they do not come searching for us.

Instead they use their artillery to flush us out. Shells commence falling where we have gone to ground. Our situation is perilous because in this countryside you can literally see for miles and there is little groundcover other than the saltbush and my precious wildflowers.

As the ground warms up in the sun, I remonstrate with myself at my own foolishness. How could I have been so daft, so bull-headed, as to go off without checking and without an escort? To have come through Ypres and risk losing my life here, of all places! Meanwhile, the Turks are conferring and seem reluctant to come after us. To stand up means the risk of taking a bullet, so we lie where we are on the baking hot sand for almost two hours. The cavalry patrol moves on, but several of their number are still in sight. We tear up sections of saltbush, shove it under the back of our belts and holding up other bunches as a screen we wriggle backwards some hundreds of yards. I have plenty of time to study the anemones, narcissi and marguerites. Eventually we make it back to the road to Jericho, where we are picked up by a rescue party of Light Horse. I am hugely embarrassed, but have a story to tell.

•

My time in Palestine was coming to an end. The photographs I had taken were needed for the AIF exhibition at Australia House, London, in May. One of my last commitments was to rejoin Captain Ross Smith at the First Squadron AFC for the promised opportunity to film a bombing raid. My memories of that day are a mixture of awe and regret: awe at the majestic grandeur of the Judean mountains bordering the rippleless blue of the Dead Sea, and regret that we were bombing Kerak—which, I discovered, was home to a twelfth-century castle built by Crusaders and besieged at one time by Saladin. It was a huge citadel perched on a hilltop, with impressive stone battlements and a moat on one side. It must have seemed truly impregnable in the twelfth century. But it had no defence against attack from the air. One after another, the Bristols dived on Kerak and released their hundred-pound bombs. Turk troops ran for cover as the bombs exploded on rooftops and in courtyards. Ancient masonry walls crumbled and smoke and dust rose heavenwards, soon obscuring the mountain top. Then it was our turn. The Bristol engine screamed as the plane descended at frightening speed. The bomb was released and, as the nose of the aeroplane lifted, my arms and shoulders were pressed down on the fuselage as I clung to my camera and wound the film through. Afterwards I felt very out of sorts in the mess as the pilots enthusiastically discussed the success of the raid and speculated on the number killed.

Despite my original misgivings, Palestine had opened my eyes to a beauty unexpected. There was much more I would have liked to have seen and so, after an exhausting time cleaning and packing all my equipment, I was in a sombre mood as I shepherded my boxes on the train journey back to Cairo. In early March I returned to the Continental Hotel, where I had stayed on arrival and which had the benefit at least of being familiar. It had been commandeered by the British forces and was full of red tabs. Arriving from the train station

I was ready to collapse, but there was a mountain of work in the darkroom and with military censors which I hoped to do in just over a week.

Cairo was a hive of activity and rumours. The news from Europe was dismal. With Russia out of the war, the German armies from the Eastern Front had now arrived in France. The British advance had ground to a halt after the slaughter at Ypres. As a result, the Belgian coastal ports remained in German hands, and so its U-boat campaign continued. And how many more times could I run the gauntlet of the submarines? I became convinced from what I heard that I would never make it out of the Mediterranean. Even if I made it onto a lifeboat, I would almost certainly lose all my work. In a fatalistic mood, I decided, despite a shortage of film stock, to completely duplicate the cine film and make one complete set of photographic prints to leave with GHQ in Cairo.

Gullett met me in Cairo and helped me deal with the censors. As a diversion we walked the ancient laneways of the old town, past the mosques, markets and bazaars, fruit vendors, wood-turners, jewellers and sellers of antiquities, ornate filigree and curios. After my two months in the desert, the noise, smells and colours of Cairo revitalised my senses. Camels overladen with sugarcane, olives and figs moved through crowds of Arabs wearing garments of every hue. The women, though, were dressed completely in black from their heads to their silver-braceleted feet, and all the time their eyes sparkling and darting mysteriously above their yashmaks.

At Gullett's insistence, I attended a 'soiree' hosted by Lieutenant Colonel Bourchier, who had led the Fourth Brigade in the charge on Beersheba. Bourchier introduced me to the usual gathering of red tabs and was especially gushing over my journey with Shackleton. Several guests were from the Bandmann Opera Company, which was then performing in Cairo. And so it was I met one of their lead sopranos,

Miss Antoinette Thierault-Leighton. She was tiny, raven-haired with dark brown eyes and a silky olive complexion. Her girlish smile melted away my usual reserve. Our introduction was brief, but I was very taken by her, and when I learned the company was performing the following evening at the city's Khedivial Opera House, I decided to go.

Despite many trips to the theatre in London, I had never seen a production of *The Yeomen of the Guard*. Before I knew it, the applause was dying down after the final curtain and I had bluffed my way inside the stage door and handed over my card to be delivered to Miss Thierault-Leighton. I waited what seemed an eternity. It was very hot. All sorts of people came and went. No one paid any attention to me. The flowers which I had clung to throughout the performance were now very much the worse for wear. What if she had other fellows waiting for her?

'Capitaine Frank 'Urley?'

'Miss Thierault . . .'

'Toni, please.'

'Toni. I hope you remember, I was at Colonel Bourchier's. Your singing was wonderful!'

'Of course I remember. You were with Shackleton.'

The Shackleton reputation proved of enduring value, despite the war. We stood facing each other until I noticed neither one of us was speaking and remembered what I had been rehearsing in my head.

'I wanted to ask if you would join me for supper?'

At this her face became thoughtful, and she was silent for several seconds before replying. 'There is a small restaurant we sometimes go across the square.'

That evening I forgot about U-boats and the war and was instead engrossed in my efforts to impress this young singer, made harder by her limited English and my complete lack of French.

'I sing in English,' Toni explained, 'but my speaking is not so good. My tutors were Gilbert and Sullivan.'

'I can think of none better. They are my favourite.'

'And sometimes if I am excited I start speaking Urdu.'

'Urdu?'

'From India, where I was born.'

Antoinette captured all that was exciting and mysterious about Cairo and the Middle East, with her French accent, dark hair and playful eyes. She was unlike the typical expatriate women of Australian or English society. There were a number of these very prim and proper matronly wives, who chaperoned their military husbands through the moral uncertainties of Cairo. Antoinette was a far cry from all this; she was cultured and captivating in a European way, and neither intimidating nor boorish. I became ridiculously infatuated with her and with the idea of her. At the theatre she held centre stage and all eyes were on her. Offstage she seemed carefree and vivacious, with no airs or graces. I was spellbound.

I saw *The Yeomen of the Guard* again the following evening, and on this occasion was able to concentrate sufficiently to follow the story. Antoinette played Phoebe, who is forced to endure the affections of an oaf so as to steal the key to a prison cell. Phoebe contemplates matrimony:

. . . of all the world of men, I wonder whom?
To think that he whom I am to wed is now alive and somewhere!
Perhaps far away, perhaps close at hand! And I know him not!

Antoinette's voice filled the theatre:

Were I thy bride,
Then all the world beside
Were not too wide
To hold my wealth of love.

Again I waited backstage with flowers, frequently mopping my brow to stop perspiration running down to my shirt collar. I had that day purchased a new Light Horse uniform complete with cream jodhpurs, but it was proving uncomfortably warm. Almost an hour passed before a young cast member informed me Miss Thierault had left to attend another engagement.

Undeterred, I sent a letter inviting her to lunch the next day at the dining room at Shepheard's Hotel. There I sat, shifting awkwardly at a white-linen-covered table for two, pondering if the heat had affected me. I thought of Les Blake, whom I had dismissed as having gone woman crazy in the turmoil of wartime London. Having become fearful he would not survive the war, it seemed to me he had lost all discrimination. Had the same happened to me?

My persistence had always been greater than my patience, and after half an hour I was rewarded by the arrival of Toni, dressed very simply compared to the gay costume of the theatre. She guided me through the menu, which she knew quite well, and questioned me about my family and my work.

'And, Frank, after the war, what will you do?'

I had given this little thought.

'If my exhibition in London is a success, I would like to take it to Australia. My mother is there, I have not seen her for over four years. And I've never had a chance to exhibit my Antarctic photographs.'

'And do you have moving pictures like *The Somme*? Last year, everyone in Cairo, they go to see this. More than see any musical.'

'Yes, in London too people flocked to this film. They wanted to have an idea of the war. But it was shot away from the front and before the terrible battles of the Somme took place. My cinefilm is of the fighting at Ypres, but I have not had time to do editing or captions yet.'

'Monsieur Bandmann says the moving pictures will put him out of business.'

I chuckled at this. 'Pictures without music would be poor entertainment, I think. They can't compare to musicals and operas. The stage shows in London always cheered me up, even amid the worst doom and gloom.'

Antoinette told me of her family but I struggled to follow it all.

'My father was in French *militaire* and all the time we travel. I was born in Calcutta. I am the only children. Then, you see, we move to Casablanca, and now my father, he lives in Alexandria. My mother she is not alive. In Alexandria, after school, I am auditioning and Monsieur Bandmann he likes my voice and asks I join his company. So now I stay in Cairo.'

We arranged to meet a few days later so Toni could show me her favourite parts of the city. In the meantime, Gullett and I pored over negatives and made our selection for the Light Horse section of the exhibition.

By the end of that week, however, the stalemate in Europe had turned into a catastrophe. German reinforcements broke through in France and Flanders and recaptured all the Allied gains of the last two years of fighting. The Germans advanced through the Somme and occupied Pozières. Ypres and Passchendaele were back in German hands. I had persuaded myself that those killed at Ypres died for a purpose, but now it all seemed utterly senseless. What was the point of my photographs of the 1917 campaign when those gains were now lost, when the men in those photographs were likely wounded or dead? Who could bear to look at reminders of such wanton sacrifice? There was nothing to celebrate. Every image was mournful to me. The AIF London exhibition would surely be cancelled. It now seemed inevitable the war would run a few more years and I had no enthusiasm to return to the shellfire in France.

I attended all Antoinette's performances, and delivered flowers backstage both to see her and to discourage any rivals. Attendance to my photographic work suffered and Gullett lost patience after I failed to turn up on several occasions. He was more than a little rude I thought when Toni visited me at headquarters.

I was so besotted, I found myself scheming opportunities of being together. Nothing else seemed important. The war filled me with dismay. Gullett and I were at odds editing my work. The London exhibition seemed a lost cause. I concluded that I was also very homesick, just as I was at the end of the Mawson expedition when I was asked to stay another winter.

The feelings evoked those several days after my first meeting with Toni came from a part of me I scarce knew existed. I was aware I had been too long in the company of men. My experience of women was limited. In fact, I realised, I had spent several years not just without women friends but without any female society. Female conversation and lingering over a fancy hotel dinner were new experiences. But of what interest was I to Toni? It dawned on me to consider how others might see me. What did Toni think of me? For someone who had always cared little about the views of others, it was suddenly important that Toni should return my affection.

Toni suggested we have morning tea at Groppi, a cafe off one of the main squares and a popular meeting place for the expatriate European community and well-to-do Egyptian society. I sensed all eyes were on us as Antoinette took my arm and the maître d' led us to our table. Antoinette looked stunningly beautiful. I had just my one decent army suit, but Antoinette's clothing was always new and always immaculate.

'You have visited my theatre many times.' Toni leaned forwards across the cafe table. 'You should let me see you at your work.'

Toni understood that I was almost always at work, in the field or in the developing lab.

'I'm afraid you would be quickly bored. My work is quite solitary.'

'So you are married to your camera.'

'Only when I am at work. But I will take a day off if you will be my guide at the pyramids.'

Toni nodded and smiled. Despite the occasion I lacked the courage to take her hand.

•

A day or so later we catch an early-morning tram to the pyramids at Giza. We leave the tram stop and, escaping all the pedlars and camel owners, we walk quickly away until it is just ourselves wandering across the dry plain under an enormous blue sky. There is a cold wind blowing strongly enough to swirl the white sand ahead of us.

Today I am a sightseer, not a photographer, although like a tourist I have a vest-pocket Kodak. I am a free man, unencumbered by my usual paraphernalia.

'But I wanted to be your assistant with the cine camera,' protests Toni. 'Have you taken enough film of Cairo?'

'I have very little film left and no more time for developing. All my time is spent preparing for the exhibition and I've only a week to have my equipment on board.'

'There is a boat? You are leaving Cairo?'

'Well, yes, I have to be in London by May. I've received an embarkation notice.'

'Frank, you didn't mention this.'

'The dates are not confirmed; with the U-boats no one ever knows the real departure time.'

'I see. Thank you for telling me.'

Silence descends and I wonder how I have brought this about and how to respond. Surely she knew I have been waiting to return to England.

We keep walking, heading nowhere in particular but all the time overshadowed by Giza's four-thousand-year-old stone monuments, the tombs of ancient kings. Our conversation has stopped without any accord as to where we are heading. Toni is not dressed for a lengthy expedition. Her silk dress billows under a coat and thick fur stole to keep out the chill desert air. A felt hat with flowers on the brim and a veil combine to prevent me seeing her expression. On the uneven stony ground she refuses my arm, despite the inadequacy of her petite shoes. My mind whirls for something to say but my imagination is defeated.

Looking up, I can see we have passed the third, smaller pyramid of Menkaure. 'We should turn around, Toni—I am not sure it is safe past here.'

'Are you worried you won't reach home safely? There are no Turk soldiers here.'

'You know I meant safe for you.'

'How could I know that!'

I have wit enough to know there is no answer to this. We turn and continue our silent walk back the way we have come.

We are soon back alongside the Great Pyramid, which towers several hundred feet above us. Toni is heading straight to the tram stop. Such a small distance and each step irreversible. A sense of urgency overwhelms me.

'Please, Toni. At least let us sit awhile here so we can talk.'

She turns towards the base of the Great Pyramid and I follow.

The conversation does not go as I would have planned. But my own inchoate intentions have been developing slowly day by day. I want to return to England and I want the exhibition to proceed. With the Shackleton film stalled, it is essential the London exhibition be a success. And then I want to go home, hopefully with something to show for myself. I can't go back to Australia with nothing more than when I left.

I know I am incomplete and inadequate. I should be an equal of a Mawson or a Shackleton. I have a reputation but not an income. I have no business once the war ends and I have no supporters to help me, I wouldn't ask nor expect any favours of Mawson, Shackleton or Bean. I have no wife or close family and receive only the occasional letter from my mother. I am the black sheep. I am the rolling stone that gathers no moss. I have never stayed still long enough. Other than my mother my life is devoid of family. There is never correspondence from my siblings and I send them none. I am lucky to be alive considering all I have done and I am not looking forward to taking my chances on a steamer back to England. I feel embarrassed about my age, my once-thick wiry hair is thinning and I am about to turn thirty-three, the age of Christ when he died. And now, once again, my chance to be married, to be together with someone, with Toni, is already falling apart.

Toni is staring into the distance. The icy wind is creating little whirlies in the sand. Overwhelmed by my own anxieties, I have no insight into what she is thinking or how she feels about me. If I cannot change my departure what can I say.

'Will you marry me?'

This startles her. 'Don't be silly, Frank. You are about to leave.'

'We could be married before I leave. I could speak to your father.'

'Don't say things you don't mean.'

'Toni, I have to return to England. You could come with me.'

'Frank, I cannot just walk out on the cast and Monsieur Bandmann. You haven't thought about this.'

'I am not good at thinking about these things. How could I be, if I don't know your answer? What do you say, Toni: will you marry me?'

'And where would we live? Tell me that.'

'Australia, of course.'

'But your family have never even seen me.'

'Toni, my ma would be over the moon if I was married.'

'You don't know that. I am a foreigner.'

'My mother's parents were French. But would you leave Cairo?'

'There is nothing for me in Cairo except the company. I could leave Cairo, but . . . I don't know.'

Toni is avoiding my gaze and staring shyly at the ground. I am so impatient I leap to my feet and, reaching down, I seize Toni around the waist and lift her high up onto one of the stones of the Great Pyramid so her feet dangle helplessly.

'I am not letting you down until you give your answer!'

'Frank, put me down!'

'I have to have an answer, Toni.'

'Are you sure? Do you mean what you are saying?'

'I could not be more certain. You would make me the happiest man in the world.'

'Then I will marry you.'

I lift her down and we kiss and hold each other for what seems a long time. It must be the desert sand, for we both have tears in our eyes. Toni produces a handkerchief and dabs her cheeks and mine. After a few minutes my awkwardness returns. We sit down beside each other, looking out across the sands. Now I really have no idea what to say. Toni cries into her handkerchief and I hold her hands in mine.

16

London, May 1918

Arrangements were quickly put in place and on 11 April Toni and I were married by the Catholic chaplain at the AIF barracks in Cairo. I wore my Light Horse uniform. Toni floated before my eyes in a dark satin dress. We had a few days' honeymoon aboard a boat on the Nile before racing back to Cairo and then, after a short, distressing farewell at Port Said, I joined a convoy to England, leaving my new bride to await my return.

Once on board, I wrote letters to Toni and Ma, tried to catch up on sleep and started thinking about how I could earn a living to support a wife and family. I had no interest in running photographic studios. Cinefilm production seemed the most likely prospect, but would not produce any immediate income. I needed to exhibit my existing work. I needed to meet with Perris and find out the latest with the Shackleton film and whether I could secure the Australian rights, and perhaps also to the Ponting film. The subject that remained foremost in the public imagination was the war, ahead of all else, including Antarctica. Providing the forthcoming exhibition of AIF photographs was a success, my reputation back home should have a solid base. The exhibition was in the centre of London and surely would draw in the crowds. Due to constant travelling, I had never before been able to arrange a major showing of my work. All I then needed was the rights to run an Australian tour of the exhibition. This would be the only collection of photographs by the Australian official war photographer and would be in demand in each state capital. Not only that, but I was the obvious person to show the pictures in Australia and to provide commentary. For as long as the war dragged on and for some time afterwards there would be an appetite for film and photographs of the conflict. The most immediate threat to my plans was the constant U-boat menace.

It may in part have been the bliss of being a newlywed, but I had cause to be excited. If my luck held in running the gauntlet with U-boats, then the commercial success in Australia of my AIF photographs seemed assured. The Mawson and Shackleton expeditions had made my reputation as a photographer, and I was now on my way to an international exhibition of my latest work. I would be famous in my own right, whatever Shackleton did with his film. And what's more, I had a beautiful wife waiting for me.

My success was hard earned. I had taken risks to see things that few others would ever see. However, what I failed to see was that it was not just German U-boats that could thwart my plans, but people on my own side of this conflict.

It was an uncomfortable, nerve-racking voyage to England. One of the passengers ran a book on how many ships the convoy would lose on the way out of the Mediterranean, how many before the Irish Coast. I did not relax from the U-boat threat until we entered the Thames. By the time I disembarked and reached my room at the Imperial Hotel, I had a severe head cold and fever and went to bed with the shakes. The next day my voice had gone and I was completely disabled for the meeting I had planned with Perris.

London remained full of uniforms. The U-boat campaign meant ongoing shortages. Coupons and rationing were an accepted part of life. Nocturnal air raids continued. In the lengthening evenings, crowds congregated outside the tube stations waiting for the sirens: the old and the young, mothers with babes in arms and children clinging to their skirts. At my hotel there was a letter waiting from Leslie Blake. As usual it gave no clue as to which sector of the front he was writing from. 'This conflict will continue through yet another Christmas,' he wrote. 'I am not sure I can last that long.'

I had been told to report to the High Commission staff at the newly built, but as yet officially unopened, Australia House on the Strand in London. It was a most grand and undoubtedly expensive building, considering we were in the middle of a terrible war. Each of the Australian states had their own floor full of bureaucrats. It was a Buckingham Palace for colonials. Humiliatingly, I had to introduce my mute self by writing notes to the various clerks and was eventually collected by a Captain Smart, who was in charge of preparations for the exhibition, which would open on 25 May. He escorted me to Grafton Galleries for an inspection of the wall space, and then to Raines and Co., where I was ecstatic to see the enlargements of my prints, some of them more than twenty feet long. However we had little more than two weeks in which to finalise picture selection, printing, framing, placement, signage and labelling. There were also projectors to be installed for lantern slides as well as the printing of guidebooks for the exhibition. I had thought from my cables with Bean that the work was more advanced.

Smart allocated me a room at Australia House and I reviewed the prints which had been made. Despite my written instructions, the photographic plates I had identified had not been printed, and locating them proved nigh impossible. Instead, I found images printed from plates I had not selected and which I regarded as inferior versions. Print sizes were completely messed up, which necessitated compromise or reprinting. As a result, and despite my laryngitis and feeling I had one foot in the grave, I had no alternative but to work day and night to save the exhibition. I was not prepared to have the bureaucracy ruin a year's work.

One week before the opening I received the colour reproductions of my Palestine photographs from the Paget Plate Company. These were most gratifying. They captured the very colours and light of the Middle East. Nowhere had I seen realistic colour reproduction as accurate and engaging.

The Sunday before the opening I had managed to get to bed before midnight only to be awakened by the clamour of air-raid sirens, followed closely by the booming of anti-aircraft guns. I listened to voices in the corridor as the top-floor guests evacuated. I stayed in my sickbed. Through cracks in the curtains I could see searchlights combing the night sky. Bombs began to fall, closer than I expected, but it was by then too late to move.

Blasts from nearby explosions rocked the hotel and I heard the shattering of glass downstairs. After two hours the guns and bombing finally stopped and I slept.

Three days out from the exhibition opening and still not a single picture was hung. With my voice recovered, I tore strips off Captain Not-Very-Smart. I insisted on changes which meant hanging a number of temporary substitute pictures until new reproductions arrived. I doubted the exhibition would be finished to my satisfaction for a further week. Others who were less fastidious may well have accepted the selections made by the High Commission staff. Captain Smart insisted they had done their best with the instructions they had. However, when I thought of the risks Wilkins and I had taken to get the perfect shot, and the sacrifices of the soldiers themselves, I could not live with myself knowing the prints were not as they should be. Nor did I want to be associated with the exhibition in its state of unreadiness. Smart looked distraught when I told him, 'Near enough is not good enough. I'm afraid the High Commission will have to conduct the official opening without me.' I had not been invited to speak and, in any case, was unwilling to give my blessing to the chaotic and incomplete arrangements presided over by Captain Not-Very-Smart and the High Commission rabble.

I kept working feverishly to finish the pictures. It was a great relief to hear that the opening was well attended by numerous dignitaries and politicians. An AIF military band played. As I expected, the large composite battle scenes received the greatest accolades among the one hundred and thirty or so photographs. As insisted on by Bean, the exhibition notes explained that *The Raid: An episode during the Battle of Zonnebeke* combined twelve negatives in its depiction of two waves of infantry going 'over the top' amid Bosche shelling and with aircraft bombing the German lines.

The newspaper reviews were very favourable and confirmed the exhibition was in the vanguard of modern photographic technique. Numbers increased from several hundred a day to over a thousand. Each half-hourly showing of the colour lantern slides received applause. However, some of the AIF lecturers for the slides were woeful amateurs who knew nothing of photography and either could not be heard or made up their own inane commentary.

My work on the photographs was not long finished when,

in early June, who should come through the gallery door but George Wilkins.

'Congratulations, old boy,' he cried, shaking my hand warmly. 'So Palestine had its compensations after all. When do we get to meet the lucky lady?'

'Soon enough. I thought you'd never make it here.'

'Left Boulogne this morning. Bean's gone to GHQ—he'll be here tomorrow, though.'

My eye caught sight of a newly minted medallion on Wilkins' tunic. 'What's this then, new silverware? Military Cross . . . you're the one to be congratulated. Well done!'

'Thanks, Frank; not sure I deserve it compared to the things we did together. Bean put me up for it. Actually, he told me he put both our names up.'

'Really? Well, Charlie probably wants to tell me personally. Last I heard you were injured again, George. No good having medals unless you're alive to wear them. How is France?'

'Pretty grim,' he said, shaking his head. 'The Germans control the Paris–Amiens railway line. They could take Paris if they wanted. I don't think anyone knows what will happen.' He grabbed my arm. 'Show me around. Are any of these photographs of your wedding?'

Wilkins was his usual unassuming self and well deserved the MC. But his citation was for the time we worked side by side in Flanders. We had both risked our lives to obtain pictures under heavy shellfire. The bias and string-pulling that went on in the army was despicable.

The following afternoon, Bean came to find me in my room at Australia House. He wore a permanent frown and looked an old man. I was non-committal when he asked about my plans now I was married.

'Well, you should be pleased with the exhibition, Hurley. It has had good numbers through. The press like it.' I knew he would never admit that almost all the talk was about my composite enlargements. They were the pictures that excited public interest; no one had seen anything like them. They dominated the rooms where they hung.

'They said it's superior to the British and Canadian exhibitions,' I told him.

'Quite so. Look, Captain Smart told me about the opening. He was genuinely bewildered by your concerns, you know.'

'I can believe that. Anyhow, I fixed it.'

'You certainly did. The trouble is, Hurley, the exhibition is for the AIF. It wasn't meant to be the Frank Hurley show.'

'That's a ridiculous thing to say.'

'Is it? Well, it looks like a bloody advertisement. The AIF recruited two official photographers, but it's your name on just about every picture.'

'Well that's hardly surprising; I was the senior photographer. George would be the first to admit he doesn't have my skill.'

'But if it's his photograph, it should have his name on it.'

'That's something your Captain Smart was handling.'

'I would have thought you might notice your name on a photograph that wasn't yours.'

'Look here, Bean, I don't need to steal photographs taken by George. And I certainly do not want my name associated with someone else's photograph.'

The next day I raised with Bean what the plans were for showing the pictures to the Australian public.

He was enthusiastic. 'They are entitled see their diggers in action as soon as can be arranged. I need to see how best to do it. You know, Hurley, I am working to establish a permanent memorial.'

I seized my opportunity. 'I would like to offer to tour the exhibition in the capital cities. You need someone who knows how to look after the prints and I can help with lecturing. The prints would ultimately be part of your memorial.'

'What, you want to run the thing in Australia? You mean quit the AIF before the war's over?'

'I'm the best person to do it,' I insisted.

'For a fee, I suppose?'

'Well, some arrangement.'

'I see. Well, that's a matter for the High Commission to approve.'

'So who should I approach?'

'Who should you approach? Well, let me see . . . I suppose the AIF attaché to the High Commission.'

'Who is that?'

'That would be a fellow you already know. I believe you address him as Captain Not-Very-Smart.'

That, I thought, was most unfortunate.

The Sunday crowds at the gallery were the largest. I spent time mixing with the visitors, especially the diggers on furlough, listening to their conversations.

'This one's called *Death the Reaper*. Poor bastard's probably been lying in that ditch for well over a week, I'd say. And look—you can make out the grim reaper in the smoke of the shell burst!'

'Here's *An Incident in the Battle of Zonnebeke*.'

'That ain't Zonnebeke. At least, when I was there it was all mud.'

A week of making appointments with High Commission staff, interminable meetings and having a word here and there with my 'contacts' achieved precisely nothing. It was made clear to me that I would not receive approval to exhibit the pictures in Australia. Finally I tracked Bean down at AIF GHQ.

'Blackall and Brighton!' I exclaimed, unable to suppress my frustration. 'Smart has thoughtfully organised a tour of the exhibition photographs of the Australian Imperial Forces to be shown in Blackall and Brighton and such other provincial English towns as have a civic hall and an abiding interest in Australian soldiery!'

'Really, Hurley, you should be pleased with the exhibition's success.'

'I offered to arrange duplicate prints, so one set could go to Australia . . . but no, this would be unnecessary expense, I was told. Damn it, Bean! I risked my life to take these photographs—surely I should be allowed to use the negatives.'

'There are many who gave their lives with no expectation of gain. The negatives belong to the AIF, not to you. And you haven't exactly helped your own cause, Hurley, by boycotting the official opening. And you may have heard I have to respond to a complaint that you bypassed army censors. I can't say I'm surprised.'

I shook my head in disgust. He stared at me through his horn-rimmed glasses. 'By the way, Hurley, some congratulations are due; you've received a Mention in Despatches. I put your name up some time ago. Took a while to come through.'

A Mention in Despatches for me and a Military Cross for Wilkins! We performed the same duties and I had served across two war fronts. It was all so blatant and tawdry. But to deliberately spite me by denying the Australian public the right to see pictures of their soldiers was pure bastardry.

I stormed back to the Imperial Hotel. I was so aggravated and distracted I was lucky not to be run over by a bus. By dinnertime I was incensed and after what little dinner I had I was fuming. The injustice of it was overwhelming. What was so wrong with trying to make my living away from this immoral war? Bean and I were on the same side serving the same country, yet he carried on as if he was the great friend of the digger. What sort of crusade was he on that I must needs feel ashamed to want to go home and work to support my wife?

After a fretful night I awoke still aggrieved and with a tightness in my chest. I wondered if this was an early sign of angina, and I vowed to never again agree to any deal that left me with no say in my own work. Attending the gallery was now pointless. I removed my things from Australia House and decided to have nothing further to do with the exhibition and the High Commission. Having also had enough of the red tabs, I took the steps needed to have myself posted to the Reserve List. Before I knew it my salary was stopped and I really did need to find a way of making a living. I wondered how my fortunes had declined so quickly. I knew I could have handled things better, but this did not diminish my anger and sense of hurt. These days, instead of taking things in my stride, I found an all-consuming anger was my first reaction to grievances. I blamed this on being very rundown. My cold was back and I often had sleepless nights. There was an epidemic of Spanish influenza in London and I was anxious to leave, but not before I could secure my future. Thwarted by Bean, I could not now rely on my work with the AIF to earn an income.

This made the rights to my Antarctic work even more important. I desperately needed to be free of the Beans, Shackletons and Mawsons of this world. I could see nothing but endless struggle trying to live within the scope of someone else's imagination or subject to their greed. In my experience, the world was fuelled by conflict, from the trivial to the obscene. I could no longer throw in my lot with those around me. There was no one I could fall back on. I determined I had to seize control of my own fate. This war must one day finish. There were still places on earth unseen where I could apply my craft better than anyone, places where I could lead my own expedition, where I could take my own risks. On *Aurora* I had read stories of the Pacific and the New Guinea isles and I knew the very heart of Australia was a nascent beauty waiting to be depicted in theatres to city dwellers everywhere.

Perris was my next port of call. He no doubt saw me coming. He said the Australasian rights for the *Endurance* film were available and that British and European rights had been sold for ten thousand pounds. After weeks of stonewalling and haggling, he eventually agreed to sell me the Australasian rights to the *Endurance* film, but not until I had agreed to give up my twenty percent share in the worldwide rights.

I knew once the war was over the biggest threats would be the Mawson and Ponting films. Although it meant further delaying my return to Toni, I pursued negotiations with Mawson and Ponting throughout July, until I had deals on the Australasian rights to all three Antarctic films. Only then did I feel confident I had a means of supporting my new wife and myself.

Perris mentioned he had been impressed by the AIF exhibition, especially the colour slides. He complained of the difficulty of running a newspaper after losing so many staff to the war.

'I often think,' he said, 'of how Shackleton struggled against the odds to bring back all his men alive—and for what? So they could join up and be killed or maimed in this godforsaken war? McCarthy and Cheetham were both killed not long ago. You knew Wordie was badly wounded and McIlroy at Ypres. And you remember that odd bod Orde-Lees?'

'Yes, of course.'

'He jumped off the Tower Bridge.'

'He killed himself?!'

'Good lord, no. He's very much alive. He wore one of those parachute things to show the Royal Air Force it could save lives, if they would just allow pilots to wear them. Quite an amazing feat, parachuting from the Tower Bridge . . . you'd have to see it to believe it.'

'Oh with Orde-Lees, I believe it.'

At last there was good news from France. The German spring offensive had collapsed and the German forces had fallen back. In the meantime, I was kept busy with the work involved in gathering film and prints to take to Australia.

It was not until the first week of August that I left London for Port Said. By then I had been away from my bride for almost four months. Even before we reached Plymouth there was a loud boom and the ship in front of us was rocked by a torpedo. We did not falter, but steamed past at an increased rate of knots as the crew of the sinking vessel took to their lifeboats. This was not a war for good Samaritans. We were then stuck in Plymouth for a week waiting for a convoy. Just before departure, a letter arrived from Mawson: Leslie Blake had been killed in France. There were no details. I felt quite numb. There was no one on board I could talk about it with—not that I would have—and I was not a drinker. I just kept to myself. The sooner I was home the better.

17

Sydney, 1918–19

We arrived in Sydney Harbour two days after the Armistice was declared on 11 November. In my luggage I had the cinefilm and photographs which I was confident would get me started in Australia. Between Antoinette's extensive collection of dresses and hats and my film equipment, we were a lot more overloaded than the disembarking soldiers. I made sure customs didn't see the film spools and charge import duty. The streets of Sydney were crowded with large numbers from the armed services and others in uniform, along with throngs of well-wishers and many who were just drunk.

Toni was three months pregnant and having been terribly unwell on the sea voyage came off the boat on a stretcher. It was a great surprise to me that Toni was expecting. We had not been together very long. My knowledge of such matters was confined to what I had read in Shackleton's *Encylopaedia Britannica* while stuck on the icecap.

My older sister Nancy offered her house for a small wedding reception because, she said, at Ma's place there was not enough room to swing a cat. Nancy and her husband had escaped the crowded rows of small terrace houses and laneways of Glebe and bought a home in a new housing estate in Haberfield, a few miles to the west. I was, of course, excited for Ma to meet Toni, though strangely a little embarrassed Toni was pregnant. The wedding reception had been my sisters' idea and Ma had reluctantly agreed. Not surprisingly, Toni was quite nervous about her first meeting with my family. She insisted on high heels despite her condition.

I was a little taken aback to find Ma had invited Elsa to the party. After the war started, she became engaged to a corporal who was later reported as missing in action. She had kept in touch with Ma all these years and Ma had insisted she come along. Elsa was most attentive to my wife; she became one of Toni's first friends and, eventually, a nanny to our children.

As things turned out the reception at Nancy's was the one and only time Toni and I got together with Ma and my siblings. Both Toni and I felt uncomfortable with them all and I had never enjoyed small talk.

'Toni, would you like to join us ladies in the kitchen?' said Nancy.

'She'll do no such thing, Nancy,' interrupted Ma. 'Antoinette is not used to being in a kitchen. She's more comfortable sitting on a lounge on the verandah.' Ever since Ma discovered that Toni had never learned to cook, she constantly played on this and steered the conversation towards recipes and her children's favourite dishes.

My sisters and their husbands had little idea where I'd been since the Shackleton expedition. Over supper I was asked what it was like in the Holy Land, but in a very short while the conversation drifted back to cricket, the Spanish flu and prices in the shops. I almost had not recognised my siblings. My brothers drank as if they were in the fo'c'sle of *Endurance*. Nancy had somehow expanded to enormous proportions. I couldn't understand how she or her husband had let it happen. My sisters, I decided, would not be a good influence on Toni. In any case, we would soon have our own family and in the next several months I would be flat out with work.

Toni said very little, and whatever she did say, Ma asked her to repeat. We had been invited to stay the night and Toni retired early to bed.

Ma insisted on sleeping on the verandah lounge. At the end of the evening she sat outside by herself, sipping away on a glass of sherry.

'Poor Jamie,' she said to me. 'You're a photographer and you can't see what everyone else can see.'

'What can't I see?'

'Why, that you've gone away and married a nigger!'

I was stunned. 'But—but you have French parents.'

'She may speak French, but, Jamie, she is a gypsy!'

•

As I had expected, the theatres in Australia are anxious for anything to do with the war. Fortunately I have brought back with me cinefilm from Palestine, not part of the London exhibition, which I am able to cobble together into a reasonable feature, especially when I include the Light Horse in Jerusalem and views from an aeroplane. It looks promising. I spend my days catching the tram in and out of the city to meetings with Kodak and Gaumont and theatre owners and camera clubs. Toni by now is quite uncomfortable and housebound. She is used to me ranting about the buffoons and idiots I have to deal with, but is dismayed when I report my latest adversity.

'Australasian Films had agreed to give the film a run at the New Lyceum, but now it's all off. All theatres are closed because of the influenza outbreak. No one knows how long it will last.'

'Then how can I go to the hospital, Frank? I could get sick there.'

'I don't know about the hospitals, but even the people on the tram are wearing face masks. They won't go near a crowded theatre or exhibition hall.'

'Frank, for once stop thinking about your film. Think about where I will have this baby!'

Of course what Toni does not appreciate is that it is the very thought of her having a baby and me not having regular work that makes me agitated.

Finally, after some months, theatres reopen and my film *With the Australians in Palestine* runs to full houses at the New Lyceum in Sydney. The theatre then agrees to run my Shackleton film, *In the Grip of the Polar Ice Pack*. Australasian Films proposes two weeks in Sydney then two months touring the other states. The theatre's advertising describes me as Captain Hurley. I am told that if we want the public to come along, they have to know I am a returned soldier. Though I have had enough of the AIF, and my honorary commission has been terminated, there is no doubt the title adds to the authenticity and heroic quality of the story I want to tell. It is compensation for the injustice meted out to me by the AIF. And, after all, from now on I have decided to be the captain of my own adventures, the captain of my soul.

Then, to my surprise, Toni gives birth to twin girls. I had not expected twins. Neither of us had. Suddenly we don't have enough space and I have to look for a bigger house to rent. It is winter and with the twins we become housebound. Most days my cabin fever forces me out on long walks. Toni can't keep up with me and prefers to take the twins in a pram at her own pace. I soon find it is best not to tell too many of my colleagues about the twins as it leads to the worst sort of time-wasting conversations.

The touring of the Shackleton film means my first Christmas as a father is to be spent away from home, which I am quite used to but Toni is not.

'Frank, I will have no family with me. Your family don't visit.'

'Toni, it is not my choice. It is the season when the theatres are full. It is the best time for making a good return. I wish you could come, but you can't expect to travel with children.'

'But why so long and why not come home for Christmas? There are others who can read your script.'

'The audience expect to hear from me: Captain Hurley.'

'But you don't do the matinees.'

'Toni, I have spent eight years of hard toil. I can't walk away from this opportunity. Besides, the twins won't notice I've gone.'

'Well, Frank, that is true. But I will. I'll be stuck here by myself.'

'Look, I am no different to the thousands of men who have been serving overseas away from their families for years now.'

'Oh Frank, you are different, very different.'

'What's that supposed to mean?'

'You won't miss us. You do what you want to do. You play with your cameras more than your children. You don't give them hugs and kisses, or me for that matter!'

'That's nonsense. I adore you and the twins.'

'I hope so, Frank, but you don't show it.'

18

Melbourne, January 1920

Successful openings in November at the Lyceum and New Olympia theatres in Sydney softened Antoinette's resistance to my going away. Evening performances were often standing room only and the crowds queued along footpaths to get in. There was no question I had to seize the opportunity.

In the first week of December I bade a fond farewell to Toni and the twins amid the noise and bustle of Central Railway Station. Brisbane was my first stop, then a long train journey back via Wagga Wagga and on to Adelaide for Christmas. I was close to a state of exhaustion by January when the train rolled into Melbourne, where I was to meet my greatest challenge at the Palais de Danse in the beachside suburb of St Kilda.

•

Wearing a jazzy new sports coat and cap, I push through the Sunday crowds outside Luna Park on my way to the Palais de Danse, listening as I go to the murmurs as I am recognised. The Palais has three thousand well-worn seats earning a shilling for each show. I have begun to relish my new-found 'hero' status:

Captain Frank Hurley, polar explorer and official war photographer. My autograph is highly prized and everyone these days seems to carry autograph books in their back pocket.

That spell, however, is rudely broken when I am confronted by an oaf of a spruiker at the Palais entrance. In the summer heatwave his grimy red face drips with sweat. With scant regard for accuracy he is wearing what I take to be a polar bear suit and is accosting the crowd: 'Roll up, roll up! Come 'n' see da captain. Come 'n' see da bloke wot's been ter de South Pole!'

In truth, of course, I have never been to the South Pole, there are no polar bears there, and some will tell you I am not a captain. But the spruiker is not interested in facts.

The real heroes, of course, are here: the now not-so-young-looking men with strained expressions, limping to their seats or with pinned shirt sleeves. I had wanted to show my photographs and motion pictures of them at Ypres so their countrymen might understand what had gone on so far from home. But Charlie Bloody Bean and his stuffy civil service bureaucrats with all their red tape put paid to that idea. No way would they let me charge a brass farthing to exhibit the photographs I risked my life to take.

Despite an opulent façade, the Palais de Danse consists of little more than a huge rectangular corrugated-iron roof perched on brick pillars, with flapping canvas walls giving blessed ventilation in the January heat. As soon as the audience's peanut shelling has died down to a steady crackle and the last squawking infant is removed, I commence my oration with coloured glass lantern slides of Shackleton, our expedition vessel *Endurance* and yours truly. My projectionist, O'Shea, assures me he has not touched a drop today. He takes my cue to commence the motion pictures which have been synchronised to the narration in my script.

My sonorous patter is well honed, but I have not allowed for the rattle and hum of electric tram lines just outside the Palais. Nor was I expecting the accompaniment of raucous shrieking from the Big Dipper switchback railway at Luna Park next door, the noise of which erupts unpredictably throughout my lecture. So when *Endurance* charges into the icepack, splitting the floes left and right as she moves directly towards the cine camera, I hear in the background the ominous clickety-click of carriages mounting the highest point of the Big Dipper track. Then, just as *Endurance* bursts forwards, virtually off the screen and into the audience, there are ear-piercing screams as the Big Dipper plummets. Patrons in the front rows of the theatre duck for cover and I raise my voice in a fight to be heard. Indeed the whole show is a fight to be heard.

Epilogue

I sailed with *Endurance* only the once, but have now performed my synchronised lecture almost a hundred times. It is not all beer and skittles. I have lectured in grand town halls to crowds who were moved to tears and I have endured flea-bitten, rat-infested halls faced with utterly unmoved, unwashed, uneducated mobs.

Shackleton, desperate to clear expedition debts, has lectured in Britain and America three times more than this. He screwed a hard bargain on these Australian rights—especially considering the films are my own work! But it looks like paying off. The release of Shackleton's book on the expedition did no harm in awakening interest after five long years of war. To think my film and photographs paid for the expedition, but he was so spiteful as to leave me out of the tributes in the book's final chapter. Douglas Mawson may be threatening to sue me for not exhibiting his Australian expedition film, but he would not be so ungrateful as to cut me from his book.

The voyage with Shackleton in 1914 is the most famous trip I made. The voyage was a failure but people say it was a glorious failure, a part of the heroic age of exploration. I was still in my twenties then. It was that extraordinary time before the horror of the trenches on the Western Front. Those images won't go away.

The things I have seen haunt me sometimes: young men's corpses in the mud of no-man's-land; shooting our sledge dogs on the icecap; slaughtering unsuspecting gentoo penguins while marooned on Elephant Island. These scenes are imprinted in my head. There was much I could not or would not photograph; I had such high ideals then. But the world lost interest in ideals and I needed an income. Or did I just grow old? No, I am neither old nor bitter; hardened, that is all, and a realist. I alone know what I have seen. It is for me alone to tell. My sense is it must always be this way.

This has been my story. Shackleton's book is really no more than a sailor's yarn in which I rate barely a footnote. I doubt they are even his words. There's no mention of the fact he knowingly sailed *Endurance* to her doom. Perhaps nothing can be the whole truth. My diaries have been my closest companions all these years but they only know what I chose to write. The photographs are out there, of course, in books, libraries and galleries. You might think they'd be enough. But every photograph reveals and conceals. And one thing I have learned, even with photographs, is that people still see only what they believe. A photographer with all the skill in the world can only do so much. It is an art getting the perfect photograph and I worked hard at it, some say too hard, though I never called myself an artist. I was just persistent, single-minded even. Waiting alone for days to get the right light, followed by more days alone in the darkroom. This was of my choosing. And, yes, there were sacrifices.

As for my mother's remarks, I kept them to myself. She stayed away. She rarely showed interest in the twins. I was now a family man, or at least I had a family to support. I found us a house overlooking the Harbour. The rent was high but I could not see myself being content looking into the backyards of others.

Work could not stop now I had mouths to feed. I was happiest working by myself and especially travelling. Inspired by Robert Service, my thoughts of travel and adventure moved from 'the Pole unto the Tropics'. I liked the idea of having my own expedition and being the boss. New Guinea seemed the obvious destination. Only missionaries and gold prospectors went there. But for the time being it would have to wait.

My working life is virtually all I remember. Childhood is a faded memory of that very short crowded existence in Glebe with Ma and Pa before I ran away. Most of my time since then I have been a photographer. Photography was my opportunity to achieve something close to perfection from the mess of life. I grabbed that opportunity and the rest just happened. I learned the only person I could trust was myself. That's why my images are more perfect than the real world, especially where man is involved. Certainly I have lived through catastrophes enough from the killing grounds of Grytviken to Ypres.

And people, even my own ma, will continue to see what they believe. That is why every photograph, just like every story, is a composition. Shackleton and Perris knew this. I wanted people, wives and sweethearts, whoever, and whatever they believed, to see what they would otherwise never see, to have an idea of what the world contained and I wanted to be the one to create that vivid picture. Bean refused to accept. He was stuck in his own vision. 'An Incident in the Battle at Zonnebeke' was an image of courage. Yes, it was taken from negatives of a training exercise in Flanders with Middle Eastern skies but it captured the imagination of everyone who saw it. The image endures beyond the events we witness and the lives of all witnesses. It is fame itself.

And I have become very used to being opposed. After all, life is one long call to conflict.

Author's note

Although this novel is based on the life of the Australian photographer Frank Hurley and there is substantial accuracy both in the story and the historical context, it is a work of fiction. Most conversations are entirely imagined. The letters between Hurley and Elsa and from Hurley to General Birdwood are as imagined. Characters bear the names of real persons, but the characters have occasionally needed to be enlarged and some roles consolidated. The cogitations of Frank Hurley written in first person are those of the writer, albeit with the benefit of having read Hurley's diaries and books and studied his photographs.

With the objective of authenticity, the novel contains quotations from and references to original sources, most of which are apparent from the text, especially the poetry and lyrics from the period. Extracts from the Hurley diaries on pages 100, 269 and 280 and the last sentence on page 354, which is from Hurley's book *Argonauts of the South*, are reproduced with the kind permission of the Hurley estate.

There are other occasions where I have drawn upon anecdotes and expressions found in the various diaries and original sources. I set out a number of instances below.

The remark 'Hurley to bed, Hurley to rise,' (page 62) was originally made by Mawson. The argument with Whetter (page 72) is referred to in several diary accounts. The menu on pages 95–6 is described in Hurley's diary.

The newspaper excerpt on page 133 is from the *Daily Mail*, quoted in Shackleton's expedition prospectus. The initial conversation with the stowaway Blackborow (page 139) is referred to in several accounts. The remarks '*Endurance* cannot live in this,' (page 165) and 'What the ice gets, the ice keeps,' (page 179) were famously said by Shackleton. Orde-Lees' description of smoking (page 222) is from his diary of 28 July 1916, published in *Elephant Island and Beyond: The life and diaries of Thomas Orde-Lees* by John Thomson (Erskine Press, Norwich, 2003). Shackleton's statement, 'Don't we look alright now that we have washed?' (page 228) is recorded in Orde-Lees' diary of 30 August 1916.

Pages 299–300 quote from a recruitment speech Shackleton gave while in Australia in 1917. The sermon on page 301 is inspired by the sermons in the book *Christ and the World at War: Sermons preached in war-time* edited by Basil Mathews (James Clarke and Co., London, 1917). The description of Antoinette as 'raven-haired' on page 323 is from *Once More on My Adventure* by Frank Legg and Toni Hurley (Ure Smith, Sydney, 1966).

The spruiker's words on page 350 are based on an anecdote told by Hurley in a 1919 article called 'Adventure films and the psychology of the audience'. On page 313 the lines of poetry are of course from John McCrae's 'In Flanders Fields'; on the same page, 'George' is the subject of a Hurley photograph, thought to be Trooper George Redding, who was well over the maximum enlistment age.

There are a number of people to thank: helpful librarians, especially at the Mitchell Library and State Library of New South Wales; Alasdair McGregor for his comprehensive biography *Frank Hurley: A photographer's life* (Viking, Camberwell, Victoria, 2004) and for his encouragement; Bob and Irene Goard of Photoantiques, Bowral, for showing me the cameras; Dr Tony Mastroianni for his insights on psychiatry; Jane Palfreyman for her expert guidance; and my agent Margaret Connolly. I acknowledge the influence of Errol Morris's book *Believing is Seeing: Observations on the mysteries of photography* (Penguin Press, New York, 2011).

A very large thank you also to my family for their patience, feedback, love and support.

About the author

Tim Griffiths was living in Papua New Guinea when he first came across Frank Hurley's photographs of that country, leading to a long-term interest in the Hurley story. He has had no experiences on the scale of Hurley's adventures and is yet to have an opportunity to visit Antarctica, but has travelled through Europe, Asia and America. He enjoys bush-walking, cross-country skiing, sailing, kayaking, surfing, diving and cycling.

Tim lives in Sydney with his wife and four children. He works as a lawyer and arbitrator, and has a keen interest in Australian history. This is his first novel.

